THE SECRET
GARDEN ROOM

THE SECRET GARDEN ROOM

Georgette de la Tour

NEXUS BOOKS

A Nexus Book
Published in 1990
by the Paperback Division of
W H Allen & Co Plc
338 Ladbroke Grove
London W10 5AH

Printed and bound in Great Britain by
Cox & Wyman Ltd, Reading, Berkshire

ISBN 0 352 32607 7

FOREWORD

by

The Author

A few years ago I spent, by way of a welcome sabbatical, a long delightful summer in the South of France. I had been commissioned by my family to look up certain old friends and the locations in which many happily remembered holidays and events had taken place. The person I was most anxious to find was an old friend of my father's, now an elderly lady of uncertain age.

I discoverd that she was living in a modest hotel in Monte Carlo. Most of her possessions had been sold off and her grand villa had been demolished to make space for a hideous new development. However she maintained an adequate life-style on account of the wise investments she had made in her earlier well-provisioned life. I found that this remarkable woman had retained the vivacity and charm of which my family had always spoken, and I was amazed at the tenacity and humour which she displayed on recounting how she survived two major world wars, numerous marriages and a string of bankruptcies. Charmed by her wit and energy, I spent many days in the company of this lady who still represented the style of a bygone era. I was amused by the intriguing stories she related concerning the decade immediately after the First World War during which Europe tried to exorcise the horrors of the conflict and threw itself gaily into the abandonments of the Jazz Age. The rich and the famous crowded together into the resorts of the Haute Savoie, Le Touquet and Deauville; fashionable watering places such as Vichy and Wiesbaden; and most importantly of all, the Riviera of southern France.

Nice, Cannes, Le Lavandou, Villefranche, Cassis, Cap Ferrat, Cap d'Antibes, Menton, Juan les Pins, etc, the names are evocative of a lively age when a great number of luxurious villas were built along the golden coast, and grand hotels, bursting to the seams with eager holiday makers, provided an endless round of gaiety. In the many casinos the rich were provided with every opportunity to throw their money away, and in the heady atmosphere a great number of fortunes were lost and made.

Madame X, my elderly friend, a leading light of that world, had already outlived most of her contemporaries, but in her old age she could still recount many a racy and illuminating story. Her tales were of the delights and dangers of the liaisons of this daring age, its reckless gaiety, and the incessant search for happiness by the bright young things, the *jeunesse doré* of the Cote d'Azur.

She gave me various documents, her diaries, and a pile of manuscripts of her own composition. These proved to be a rich store house of the period, documenting in fascinating detail the manners and mores of her younger self and her contemporaries as they strode fearlessly through the Jazz Age. Years before Madame X had considered publishing this material, but the collection of anecdotal and autobiographical fragments proved to be too fragile a mixture for one of no literary pretension to edit into a form that a serious publisher would consider. Since I considered that the papers contained much valuable information I sought her permission to edit them severely and concentrate on a central semifictitious character who would lead the narrative forward. By changing names and locations I hoped to provide an interesting narrative that would not embarrass surviving characters.

The reader may find some amusement in discovering which roles represent Madame X. The guessing game will be an intrigue, I hope, but the ultimate truth is contained only in the fragrant bundle of papers which is locked away securely in my safe.

Chapter One

What a glorious morning, what a marvellous life, what a lucky woman, Bernadette thought. She smiled broadly at her reflection in the Art Deco mirror angled high on the wall opposite the *chaise longue* on which she luxuriated with her foaming cup of chocolate and her favourite brand of Turkish cigarettes.

It was indeed a charmed life, an enviable existence. Here she was cocooned in the refined atmosphere of the elegant mansion which she had inherited some years ago on the sad demise of her husband—the much lamented vicomte—the popular, handsome, virile and generous darling of the Riviera who for so long had been her constant and loving, if often unfaithful companion.

Bernadette sighed blissfully, loosening the neck-tie of her *peignoir* so that its lacy folds fell away from her limbs. She turned towards the photograph of the vicomte which stood imposingly in its exquisitely enamelled frame on a marquetry bureau nearby.

'Darling Henri,' she mouthed noiselessly, 'what a wonderful lover you were,' and she pouted a tender kiss in the direction of the picture.

This room, she thought, let alone the house, the servants and the amassed remaining fortunes of the ancient lineage of her husband, would have been enough for her continued contentment and comfort. What a genius Henri had been, not only to have restored the chateau-sized dwelling to its former glories, but also to have invented such artistic and harmonious ingenuities as this—his very own secret garden room—a private and secluded cloister completely hidden from the view of even the most pespicacious guest or servant.

The room was approached only from a secret panel in a small salon on the ground floor. It had no windows and instead was illuminated by a curved ceiling of the most delicate blue glass over which stretched fronds of jasmine and passion flower causing a dappled effect of light and shade. The room was most charming, reminding one of the filtered atmosphere of an exotic winter garden, or tropical plant house, such as might be seen in the promenades of an exclusive spa resort.

A casual observer strolling in the grounds of the mansion would notice the fine balconies, the olive green painted shutters and the vines and hanging baskets of vivid mediterranean flowers. He would see a series of fluted pillars and be beguiled by the beautifully correct classical proportions into thinking that the interior of the house was of a similar symmetry.

He would have been fooled, since the vicomte, during the extensive refurbishment of the mansion, had managed to conceal an L-shaped apartment within the south wing of the house. In the angle of this private domain was a large room with its own *salle de bain* and small cuisine, and an entrance from a side terrace.

Henri and Bernadette had been charmed over the years to offer their hospitality to a large number of guests. Friends of their own style and age were naturally accommodated in the principal part of the house, but the young and impecunious nephews, cousins and friends of friends were often lodged conveniently in the corner flat. They were made to feel happy to come and go as they pleased, since their late risings and after midnight jollities would not interfere with the domestic arrangements of the main house. Many a blissful summer holiday had been enjoyed by these specimens of the *jeunesse doré*, lodged happily in the extravagantly furnished art deco apartment. However, they were completely unaware that the minutely pierced Indian screen of ivory and sandalwood which had been set into one wall and the very large two-way mirror hanging on another, both provided an excellent view from the secret garden room into the apartment for a discreet voyeur.

The vicomte had spent many happy hours as an uninvited but delighted companion to some of the prettiest visitors to this part of the Riviera, and how considerate he had been finally to reveal his secret to his wife just a few weeks before his untimely death.

Bernadette reflected that without this act of generosity she could have gone on living quite happily in the bequeathed mansion without ever discovering the secret panel in the small salon which, when opened by a hidden spring, slid open to reveal the sybaritic comforts of the garden room with its enchanting views of the innocent occupants of the apart-ment beyond. Never a person to complain of her lot—and certainly not one of those females who indulge themselves in unnecessary sorrowings and beating of the breasts— Bernadette had entered her forties contented and fortified by the memories of the passionate and gay affair that had consti-tuted her marriage to Henri. The sad accident in the Bugatti along the Corniche had brought all this to an end, but, being an extrovert and optimist, she was determined to honour the memory of her beloved Henri by carrying on her life in the

11

same vibrant and fulfilling way that had enchanted him.

Jealousy was an emotion that had never stirred in Henri's heart. Whenever his wife had recounted some amusing detail of an affair, whether of a temporarily overwhelming and romantic nature, or of the more abandoned purely physical kind, he had told her how pleased and flattered he was that other men should find her so compellingly attractive, seductive and inspiring.

'How could I hope, my darling, to keep such a woman to myself?' he would murmur fondly, stroking her raven hair and gazing lovingly into her dark green eyes. 'You are still young and have an appetite for others which I can completely understand. I know you love me, and we have a wondrous relationship which would be destroyed if I allowed you no freedom.'

Bernadette was a wise woman. She knew that many other women would cry out at this and complain that this generous attitude implied a lack of love, an absence of concern, and even a degree of that kind of vicarious interest which some men have in their wives' infidelities. But nevertheless she was grateful, and indulged her whims without suffering any guilty feelings. She was sure Henri did likewise, secure in his love and in the wonderful life they led together.

Now that she had the secret garden room the spritely and adorable *invitées* of Henri had been replaced by a succesion of interesting, sometimes ravishing, young men.

Such a young pair were in residence now. Two young Englishmen, both from well connected, if not noble, families, were delighted at this opportunity to savour the delights of the Cote d'Azur, Charles, tall, thick-set and rather florid, was a rugby-playing athlete from one of the more important public schools. He had distinguished himself by getting the gardener's daughter pregnant and had been quickly despatched to the South of France by an irate *père* to work in his uncle's yacht business. What a boon this punishment had proved to be. For every one of the rich young men with enough cash to engage in this dashing sport, there were three or four extremely chic and decorative female playthings. Charles got jauntier as the weeks of the summer went by and, being an attractive and dangerous looking animal, he assuaged his guilt by charming more than a few of these delightful girls.

His companion Arthur was generally a more fastidious character. Born and reared in a family with a long established connection with the British Army, Arthur was a serious and upright young man with very proper ideas about his responsibilities in life, his devotion to the Crown, to God, his mother, and many of the other afflications of the British.

Slighter than his half-cousin Charles, he had an impressive bearing, with the upright back of his calling, a stiff bristle of a moustache, and the impeccable manners of his class. The rigours of his upbringing had, however, left Arthur with certain difficulties in the realms of his relationships with the other sex. In a word, he was painfully shy of women. He naturally adored them, but when it came to the point of declaring his feelings to a pretty girl, he was mute, as incommunicado as he would have been on parade. But a charming boy, nevertheless, with a very defined attraction for the ladies.

Both men were having a fine summer holiday, though going in their separate ways. Charles's principal conquest was a salesgirl in a chocolate shop in the Rue Garnier who had a small but convenient room above a nearby patissier's establishment.

Arthur was engaged in the silent adoration of Annabelle, the sister of a brother officer who was holidaying on one of Charles's yachts moored near Cap d'Antibes. He exhausted himself daily swimming in the bay in order to be near her, but could not summon up the courage to hail her cheerily and climb aboard and join in the fun and games with his beloved and her happy companions.

It was around ten o'clock in the morning. Bernadette placed her empty chocolate cup on the side table with infinite care and stubbed out her last cigarette. There was suddenly a sharp burst of ringing from a small leather travelling clock which stood on a bookcase near Charles's bed. A hand stretched out, waving in the air rather aimlessly until it found the clock and could press the 'off' button. Placed behind the special mirror Bernadette could see both of the divans the boys occupied, the dressing table strewn with various objects, and piles of untidily discarded clothing. It would seem that her guests had come home yet again a little worse for the drink.

Charles flung back the sheets, and throwing his legs into the air with some determination, lurched out of bed to stand arms akimbo, head jerked back, and yawn profoundly. Bernadette saw with amusement that Charles, as usual, was massively erect—'piss-proud' as she had one morning heard Charles describe himself ruefully to his room-mate.

The vision sent a shudder through Bernadette's frame and her hand went automatically to embrace her private part. Charles's prize possession, as he called it, was without doubt one of the finest specimens of the male organ that Bernadette, in all of her considerable experience, had encountered. It stood almost vertically to his flat athlete's stomach, rising far out of the black bush of pubic hair, so gorged and extended that the enormous pink glans was completely exposed. She quivered as Charles swayed slightly, stretching his arms high and then, with his hands behind his neck, pressed back his elbows as he arched his back in an awakening gesture.

How utterly manly, she thought. The pose reminded her of some of the ancient Greek sculpture which had captivated her in Athens, Ephesus and Heraklion. Charles was even more imposing, she thought, than the bull-warriors of Knossos. And how very charming that, perhaps like the early Greek athletes, this young man could be so uninhibited and so unashamed of his handsome body, even in this priapic-looking condition, in front of his friend.

Arthur had rolled the sheets away from his head and was sitting up in bed exchanging good-morning greetings with Charles. His knees were drawn up to his chest and he scratched his head thoughtfully as he spoke.

'What a dreadful smell there still is from those terrible Turkish cigarettes of yours, old boy,' he admonished.

'My god, there is. They do linger, I must admit. Sorry old sport. I'll open a window or two,' Charles replied. Bernadette of course was relieved that he smoked the same brand and considered that it might still be possible for her to enjoy an occasional cigarette, hidden away in her L-shaped pleasure dome.

Charles walked slowly towards the windows, threw open the curtains and lifted the sashes, then turned and came towards the mirror, behind which Bernadette lay entranced on the divan. As he walked the still-erect penis swayed majestically from side to side and then came to rest when he stood, feet apart, in front of the glass, contemplating his stubble. Bernadette's face was only half a metre away from the beautiful shining object that so aroused her. Charles's organ was so distended that the frenum seemed stretched to bursting point.

How cruel. she thought, *in some men it can be so painful. How I would like to cover it with kisses and smooth away the poor man's distress with my wet lips*. Her tongue rolled over her painted mouth and then flicked in and out in a playful simulation of the relief she would adore to be able to offer. Then, fascinated, and narrowing her eyes, she traced down the glass the line of a thick vein which ran down the underside of Charles's still-upright member. She could detect a thrilling little pulsating movement in the blood coursing through this principal channel, a regular beat which must correspond to the man's heart-beat. Then, matched by a similar movement in her now moist and throbbing centre, she was ravished to note a muscular spasm which started at the base of Charles's penis and moved upwards along its length and came to a climax in a defined pulse in its head. She waited, breathlessly, watching. It happened again, and again, and by counting in her head she ascertained that this auto-erotic coursing of the blood in the main muscle happened every six seconds.

It seemed an eternity but in fact Charles had only spent a couple of moments in front of the mirror, rubbing a hand over his morning's beard and inspecting his tongue a trifle distastefully as he remembered the extent of his liquid consumption the previous evening. Then suddenly Charles turned on his heel and made for the bathroom. His firmly shaped buttocks and well muscled thighs, bronzed to perfection by the southern sun, passed out of Bernadette's view.

From past experience she knew that Arthur would stay firmly in bed until his friend had completed his ablutions, perhaps reading or composing yet another love-letter which would never be despatched to his darling Annabelle. To Bernadette's disappointment this always gave enough time for Arthur's morning erection (for she knew that all healthy males suffer this mild inconvenience) to dissipate itself. Not that she found anything wrong with the normal flaccid organ which had so often absorbed her attention—on the contrary. The appendage of the officer excited Bernadette to a much greater degree than the object which Charles displayed in such a wanton, teasing fashion every morning. This was because, even in its limp state, it was an enormously large object, and held the intrinsic possibility of being, on arousal, the most perfect male adornment that she would ever encounter.

Leaving aside such an engaging consideration Bernadette rose from the *chaise longue*, her thighs and knees trembling a little after the near orgasm she had only just avoided. With her cream lace négligé trailing behind her she proceeded to the other angle of the garden room and stationed herself on a banquette which was on the other side of the wall which held the delicate Indian screen in the guests' room.

On Bernadette's side the wall was decorated with a most agreeable mural, worked in onyx and porphyry and inlaid with lapis lazuli, depicting life-sized naked satyrs and barely clad nymphs in the art nouveau manner. In the centre of the highly erotic landscape, standing on a rock and surrounded by swooning maidens, a satyr stood on his hind legs, towering over a naked and submissive nymph who lay with her legs spread invitingly below him. His massively exaggerated genitalia were worked in bas relief as were other aspects of the whole scene—particularly the sexual organs of other male figures and the breasts and nipples of the females. The satyr's commanding penis was cunningly sited in such a way that it could be grasped with one hand by an inquisitive

17

person using the peephole which was situated a little above the head of the beast. This eye-piece was an ingeniously contrived glass lens, set into the middle of a sunburst whose rays illuminated the scene, inlaid with amber and coral and invoking the sunset which glowed about the archaic characters.

To Bernadette's delight Charles had just finished relieving his bladder in the cabinet. This had been placed out of sight of all the peepholes in the screen by its considerate designer who, being an artist and a gentleman, was naturally disinterested in the more basic bodily functions. The young man was strolling towards the bath, which even with the door fully open as would be normal with two young people as unconcerned with the proprieties as these, was in the direct line of sight of the glass lens.

His tumescence was somewhat declined now the pressure on the muscles governing his urinary tract had been relieved. As he stepped into the large marble bath and turned on the shower he turned and faced towards the partition behind which Bernadette sat transfixed. The magnifying effect of the lens threw the minute hole at the tip of his organ into sharp focus. It seemed to her that she was gazing into the mouth of a cavern whose secrets she must discover. Her right hand grasped the equivalent part of the rampant satyr and with the tip of her moistened forefinger she discovered its corresponding opening.

Charles was singing as the first icy waters gushed over his body. It was not an unmelodious voice. She smiled at the pleasing way in which he ran his fingers through his dark shock of hair and let the water run over his chest. To her surprise the cold water did nothing to further decrease the troublesome outstanding penis. Her other hand roved to her breasts under the half-open négligé. Her nipples were hard

18

and protruding, inviting a caress, as was the stiffening bud of her clitoris which swelled against the flimsy fabric of her knickers.

Charles reached for the soap, bending down and revealing, for a moment, the dark pink aureole between his fine buttocks. Bernadette drew in a short breath and shook a little as she fingered her secret place, marvelling as always at the magic lubricity of the juices which flowed from within her. She passed some of this benign liquid to each of her nipples and circled each in turn, at first lazily and then with more urgency, until she felt obliged to gently pinch and squeeze them. The whole effect left her feeling that the first smouldering between the very tops of her thighs must burst into flames.

Charles, as he soaped his body, was tormented in a similar way. Although the fierce throbbing of his prize piece had eased, as his soapy hands left his upper body and advanced down his hairy abdomen towards his nether region, the detumescent article, with a will of its own, quickly sprang back in all its vigour to its full shape and grandeur. Bernadette grasped the satyr's brandished organ with renewed force as Charles carefully began to soap the distended prop which was vertical again. He sang loudly as if to vanquish it, as the British Tommies had sung marching towards the enemy in the war of the previous decade. But as he carefully washed the almost purple tulip-shaped end of his instrument—peeling back the foreskin delicately and letting the water, which was now running warmly, fall over its creases—a strong tremor in the shaft produced a glistening drop of his lubricating fluid, the threatening juice that signals the imminence of a craving for orgasm in the healthy male.

But such animal pleasure was resisted at this moment by Charles. He took the shower head from its hook on the wall and applied it ferociously to his parts. After all, he wanted to save himself for the time, a couple of hours later, when he would stroll nonchalantly up the stairs to conjugate lustily with Angelique, the gamine treasure of the chocolate shop. There was no such resistance on the part of the almost delirious Bernadette. The foaming soapsuds and splashing waters had brought her to an extremely wettened state. Her mouth found the tip of the raging beast's member and her fingers were pressed deeply into the well-oiled interior of her seat of pleasure until, fearful of the cry that might betray her presence, she withdrew them and pressed herself against the erotic tableau. She then enjoyed the most thrilling series of orgasms; a succession of climaxes which ran into each other in a flow of such magnificence that she leant forward breathless, open-mouthed and exhausted, her cheek close to the hairy rump of the central satyr. In this dazed condition she thought of her husband and of the ecstasies he must have undergone savouring his female guests in exactly the same location, shivering at the thought that even after such extremes of passion he would have come to her boudoir to express his love for her in further physical terms.

When she opened her eyes she discovered that Charles had shut the bathroom door. It was a relief to her since she opined that the possible sight of Charles's self induction of an orgasm might prove too much for her: *Poor boy*, she sympathised, *so athletic and so tormented by the over active impulses of the young*. Presuming that he would soon be able to rejoin his companion in a defused state she arranged her robe neatly around her still tingling body and returned to the other half of the room where the *chaise longue* beckoned invitingly. Through the glass she saw Arthur rummaging in the drawers of the clothes chest. He turned, shouting to Charles who was cooling his fire in the privacy of the bathroom.

'I say, old sport, are you going to be there all day? I haven't had a leak yet.'

A gleaming but detumesced Charles from the bathroom wrapped in a large white towel. He beamed at his friend. 'Sorry old bean, it took a lot of water to bring me round this morning.'

Arthur turned to face him. His thick and heavy looking pendulous penis and generous scrotum seemed disproportionate against his trim lithe body. 'Getting yourself ready for another onslaught,' he queried.

'Oh, I expect this Englishman will do his duty,' Charles smiled. 'Now when I see you tonight I'll want you to tell me that *you've* cracked it, old chum,' he added, swiping Arthur across the buttocks with his hairbrush. The two bantered together while Charles got dressed and Arthur retired to the bathroom.

Bernadette closed her eyes and dozed lightly for a while. She awoke when Charles shouted a cheerful farewell and watched idly as Arthur returned to the room. He went again to the chest and, opening a drawer, he pulled out a curious garment which he proceeded to put on. It was a jockstrap consisting of a wide elastic waistband attached to a stiff cotton pouch joined to the rear of the waistband by a thin strap which passed between the legs and up the crease of the buttocks. Bernadette had never seen such an article before. Arthur was having some difficulty fitting his very large parts into this constricting garment. He pushed and prodded and squeezed himself until his organ and the two attendant rotundities were squashed well and truly into the pouch. To Bernadette's amazement he then pulled over it a pair of the latest style bathing trunks, standing back to view the effect in the dressing table mirror. The large bulge in his centre was, to say the least, very noticeable.

Bernadette stirred on her couch, the visible evidence of Arthur's maleness disturbing her composure. She began to understand. '*Pauvre garçon*,' she breathed, 'demented by the lovely Annabelle he is afraid that his day-long erection will be a gross embarrassment and so, *mon dieu*, he puts on this excruciating corset of the private parts in order to disguise it.' She pondered for a while about the object of Arthur's affections. What would Annabelle think if she knew that the boys parts were so inflamed they had to be held all day in this dreadful bondage?

Arthur had soon finished his *toilette*. He took up the unmistakable props of the lonely—a book, an old newspaper, sunglasses and a pocket chess set—and departed on his undeclared and so, alas, unrequited way. The lady of the house retired to the small salon and ordered breakfast, determined that soon the poor Arthur would take off his jockstrap for her.

Later in the day, after a delicious lunch in the company of two of her contemporaries—one a widow like herself, the other a princess from the family of the deposed Czar—the vicomtesse ordered her car and took a leisurely drive towards Nice and her favourite dressmaker.

Jean-Paul, the chauffeur, an attractive young man, naturally, being in the employ of such a discriminating person, hailed from the higher regions of Provence. He was of a family whose roots were established in that southern terrain as securely as the roots of the olive trees in their groves. With his slicked hair, his dapper uniform, and his glamorous mediterranean looks, Jean-Paul was the envy of several of Bernadette's friends. They were convinced that an affair of convenience was taking place between the beautiful soignée widow, who was still young enough to have considerable sexual appetites, and the young man who resembled some of the fashionable film stars of the day. He undoubtedly modelled himself on Rudolph Valentino, the Latin lover of the silver screen, and had developed a very charming habit of bowing low, kissing hands, and lowering his eyelids etc. But in fact his sexual preferences, known to his mistress because she had discovered him one day in a compromising situation, were for much older women. Bernadette found the subject very amusing. 'My goodness, my dear Jean-Paul,' she would say, flirtatiously, stepping into the highly polished open tourer, 'what a perfect day it is, and how fortunate I am to have such a gorgeous young man to escort me. What a pity I'm too young for you.'

On this particular afternoon, with the sun blazing down from the cerulean sky, Bernadette was particularly skittish, having been stimulated so profoundly by the events of the morning and the secret confidence that soon she would be obliged to press her charms on to both of her new house guests. 'Tell me, Jean-Paul, you must be in love. I declare that in high summer, with the scent of the pines and the perfume of jasmine, all these intoxicating distractions . . . you must be in love. Oh do tell. Amuse me. It's a long boring drive to Nice!'

'*Vraiment*, Madame,' he began, 'there is no-one. I know that you will be kind enough to forget my indiscretion with the lady from Toulouse who was your guest. It was unpardonable, but I was a little drunk and forgot my station. Please forgive me.'

'Nonsense dear boy,' cried the liberated lady. 'It was the best thing that ever happened to her. Lucky thing.'

The conversation bowled along between the boy and his unusual employer in this manner for a while until suddenly Bernadette shouted, 'Stop the car, stop the car, Jean-Paul. I must get out.' The tourer lurched to a halt and the chauffeur raced round to open the door for her. 'Wait here,' she commanded.

Within a second she had stepped carefully over some rocks and, in the shade of an oleander, settled down to inspect closer the figure she had recognised way down on the beach below. On a totally secluded stretch of sand bordered by rocks and palm trees there was the unmistakable figure of the English officer, Arthur, accompanied by a curvaceous beauty of clearly Saxon origin. There was no doubt about it. She must be the adored Annabelle.

After looking backwards across the road and ensuring that Jean-Paul was nicely relaxed in the driving seat, a cigarette dangling from his lips, Bernadette concentrated on the two figures below. The girl embraced the man who swung her round and toppled her into the sand. Arthur, for it undoubtedly was he, fell on the girl like a locust falls on a juicy leaf, devouring her neck, her cleavage, and the bare thighs that were exposed in the hiliarious romping fall to the sand. Bernadette could hear their joyous laughter from high on the cliff where she lay. '*Merveilleux!*' Bernadette exlaimed. How charming that somehow the young officer had 'clicked' with the girl. She knew from Charles's gossiping how long the poor love-sick boy had been panting for the raving debutante, and supposed that finally he had been manly enough to overcome his inhibitions and press his attentions on the girl.

Precisely the opposite had, in fact, occurred. Annabelle had taken pity on the exhausted swimmer who constantly circled the yacht wherever it was moored and invited him aboard for a cocktail. The company were charming, of course—the British upper class on its best holiday behaviour determined to show the raffish Californians moored alongside how the obligations of society must be met. White-jacketed stewards had served delicious iced drinks, deck-chairs were produced and a gramophone with the latest records; in fact Arthur's arrival had precipitated an impromptu party.

The bright young things threw quoits and large rubber balls at each other, the girls leaping and bounding in the manner of Isadora Duncan, and the boys striking effective poses in their swimming combinations and their dashing naval caps. Annabelle was not the only one to notice the alarming bulge in Arthur's trunks. Normally, a well-bred young English lady would avert her gaze from a gentleman's crotch, but this extraordinary swelling under Arthur's striped costume drew the eye automatically and caused a few flutters in female breasts. Arthur was delighted with the attentions of the company. He quickly discovered mutual friends, cousins, old school chums and the like, and settled down immediately to enjoy the unexpected invitation—especially the attentions of the vibrant Annabelle whom he had dogged for weeks. The hot Midi sun beat down on the deck, forcing the party under awnings, or back into the sparkling water for more swimming, where Arthur was relieved of his priapic condition to a small degree. He only wished the sea was as cold as it is on England's shores, and offered silent thanks to his restricting undergarment.

After lunch—a jolly affair with a great deal of chilled *rosé* wine, *langoustines*, *salade niçoise*, coffee and old brandies—the newly aroused and curious Annabelle had suggested a little excursion in the boat's painter across the bay to a secluded cove she knew. It was here, a few kilometres from Villefranche, that Bernadette had seen them gambolling on the beach.

Stretched out on the grass on the cliff top, propped on her

elbows, with her chin on her hands the vicomtesse laughed delightedly in sympathy with the gaiety of the scene below. '*Bravo, Artur*,' she cried as the officer ran his hand up the inside of the girl's exposed thigh. There was a polite cough from behind. Jean-Paul bowed slightly.

'Are you alright, Madame?' he enquired.

'Oh yes. I've just seen an old friend,' she grinned. 'Please be so good and fetch a rug from the car.'

The chauffeur returned with a tartan travelling blanket and a pair of binoculars. He laid the rug down for his mistress's greater comfort and then stood at the cliff edge looking through the glasses at the little boats and yachts bobbing about the bay. There were sails of ochre, red and brilliant white, dotted around the surf-flecked waters and the afternoon sun picked out the golden bodies of the holidaymakers in a most pleasant and artistic way. M. Monet would have approved.

'Lend me your glasses, dear boy,' said Bernadette. Jean-Paul watched as she focused on the new lovers below.

'Isn't that the young Monsieur Arthur who is staying in the small apartment, Madame?' Jean-Paul enquired.

'It is. Take a look,' she replied, handing him the binoculars. The chauffeur tracked along as if he were a cinema camera-man, and saw Annabelle leading Arthur towards the shade of a tamarisk tree close to the base of the cliff. He watched impassively as she pulled over her head the short handkerchief-pointed dress she was wearing and removed the silk underslip, bust-band, and camiknickers, before lying down with a voluptuous gesture of abandonment.

Bernadette had risen and was leaning slightly on the chauffeur's uniformed back. She reached over his shoulder and took the binoculars from his hands.

*   *   *

In the shade of the tamarisk, feeling absolutely secure in its privacy on the otherwise deserted beach, Arthur removed his bathing costume and the athletic support in one nimble movement and threw them together on to a nearby rock. The already-mentioned large member, released from its captivity, sprang in half a second to military attention, pointing upwards past the officer's navel. From Annabelle's point of view the enormous organ seemed even more impressive, even though the sunlight was bright in her eyes and the flickering luminosity of the sparkle from the seashore dazzled and confused her vision.

She was no virgin, having suffered the tipsy aftermath of several Hunt Balls in the Shires with drunken public school boys and having been the subject of the attentions of a certain bohemian distant cousin, an amateur artist for whom she had posed for a series of erotic studies of the nude figure. But her previous experiences had not prepared her for the vision which now towered above her. 'Oh Arthur,' she gasped, in a deep growl whose hoarseness surprised her, 'come and take me.'

Arthur gazed unbelievingly at the gorgeous creature who lay so wildly provocatively between his feet. A throbbing which had been gnawing at his loins for weeks accelerated in the next few seconds into a pounding which shook him upwards from his knees, through his thighs and into his groin. An explosion began in the tight sac of his scrotum and seemed to pass up into his chest as a similar phenomenon gripped the muscles of his buttocks and went roaring up his spine, causing his head to jerk backwards as his semen burst out in involuntary streams in a wide arching trajectory, falling in waves across the girl's abdomen, breasts and face. Still the vast penis, gorged every half second by a violent muscular spasm, discharged more of the ivory coloured fluid as his hands, now clamped firmly around his steel-stiff penis, eased the remainder of his orgasm away to fall in a viscous flow on to the bush of her pubic hair.

A primeval groan escaped from the lips of Arthur's amour. In a trance-like state she struggled to her knees and pressed her wet lips to the tip of his organ, sucking and drawing out the last dregs of his offering. As he had worshipped the spectacle of her sublime body, now she drank at the fount of his manhood, greedy for every drop of his remaining juices. Their first consummation had not been complete but there had been the sensation of drawing on the pagan forces of the ancients and their bodies were now committed to an age old, compelling ritual, the earth-shattering fusion of two bodies into one.

Bernadette swooned to the ground carefully managing, by a deft movement of one hand, to draw up her silk skirt enough to ensure that Jean-Paul had a view of her finely embroidered black crêpe de Chine knickers. The binoculars were pressed across her bosom by her free hand as she sighed, rolling her head from side to side, her half closed eyes and puckered lips signalling a delicious state of arousal. 'My goodness, *mon garçon*, was that not a most entertaining spectacle? What a sublime diversion.'

Jean-Paul noticed the smooth texture of her lightly tanned thigh and the lovely swoop of shin and calf which led to her trim ankle. '*Eh bien*, Madame,' he said over his shoulder as he stole a hand into a trouser pocket to rearrange the erection which troubled the elegant line of his immaculate grey suit. 'But you were in possession of the glasses. I had no chance to see the detail of the scene,' he said with some petulance but also teasingly.

'Come now, Jean-Paul, you must admit it was the most

exciting thing,' the vicomtesse half-whispered, the image of that intimate libation of love juice burning in her brain. 'You know precisely what I mean. Oh God, wasn't it thrilling?'

'Two idiots romping on the beach is nothing out of the ordinary,' he countered, but a knowing smile creased his mouth. 'Please give me back the binoculars. Perhaps there is something I missed.'

The perfect focus and magnifying effect of the apparatus brought him an enthralling view of the pair as Arthur poised himself over the girl, his knees between her wide splayed legs. His hands played over her abdomen, her breasts, and the inside of her thighs. Then, bending lower, he placed his hands under her pelvis and reached to grasp beneath her buttocks. When he raised her upwards to his searching mouth her legs fell backwards so that her feet almost touched the sand where her hair lay in disarray. Arthur's mouth was now exploring the pale tuft of hair which partly covered her precious opening. Watching the up and down movement of the officer's head, Jean-Paul presumed that his tongue was now urgently trying to enter the innermost sanctum.

Being of healthy body, and always having found the greatest pleasure in indulging himself in a similar way, Jean-Paul's blood was set on fire. Holding the binoculars, which were rather heavy, in one hand was proving somewhat awkward, but the other, free, hand could cause a very satisfying sensation through the thin material of his voluminous pocket. He was aware of a certain dampness which resulted from his dextrous manipulation of his throbbing organ.

'What's happening now?' Bernadette breathed, well aware of the subtle movement in Jean-Paul's trousers. 'Don't keep me in suspense, it's so mean of you.'

Jean-Paul said nothing, riveted as he was by the next phase of the lyrical coupling under the tamarisk.

Arthur had placed himself in such a way on his knees that his head faced the other way to hers, allowing him a deeper oral penetration of the opening he so fervently worshipped. With his back arched and his buttocks swaying side to side, he devoured the girl's juices which now flowed freely. The swaying movement of his hips caused his great organ and his full scrotum to caress Annabelle's breasts. Over and over they went as a sailing boat in the sea rolls with the waves. Annabelle clutched his thighs and clawed at his back with her elegantly painted nails.

'You're killing me darling,' she cried, heaving her pelvis still further upwards towards her lover's open, foraging mouth. 'I shall scream if you don't take me. Now, now, come on now.'

With such an urgent command the officer obliged, whirling around with great agility to place himself in the truly favourite position of lovers everywhere, and of all times.

Bernadette had risen, tormented that her knowledge of the display below the cliff was out of date. Her experience of tempestuous carnal love was such that she quite rightly imagined these two newly released lovers would play in ecstasy the whole afternoon, indeed well into the evening when unfortunately, if one were still inclined to be a spectator, the fading light would gradually erase the scene. Prudently she left the binoculars in Jean-Paul's possession. Her own good eyesight was sufficient for her to follow the scenario of the pair's overwhelmingly passionate coupling. She stole a glance at the chauffeur as he trained the glasses on Arthur's rampant strokes.

He licked his lips lasciviously as the officer's hips drove with such rhythmic intensity at the girl who lay beneath him. The pounding and slapping of their bellies became louder,

30

and the noise travelled up the face of the cliff to the ears of the silent observers.

Bernadette's feet were rooted to the spot. They wanted to move her closer to her handsome employee, and her hands wanted to steal round his trim waist. Much more besides, she thought longingly, but the etiquette of their situation forbade such tenuous moves. As Arthur rode impressively towards his own and the girl's climax, Jean-Paul stole a look in turn at his employer.

Her breaths were coming in short gasps and her hands were clutched tightly around her body, one at her breast, the other over her heavily moistened private part.

Instinctively they both gauged the pair below had very little time left before they exploded. It was a correct supposition. When it happened the girl screamed out in the vortex of her pleasure, the culmination of Arthur's worshipping adoration. He, further arching his muscular back, pumped his juices into her in an amazing series of dynamic thrusts.

The vicomtesse's preoccupation with the station of her companion was abandoned as she flung her arms around him, pressing her body against his solid thigh. Her right hand sought the hard bulge in his gabardine uniform trousers and she gazed imploringly up at his face. Squeezing his organ in the imprisoning cloth and moving her hand up and down in some agitation, she murmured hoarsely, 'Oh, how divine, how absolutely beautiful it was. Oh so. Forgive me Jean-Paul, I am overcome, so stimulating.' She removed her hand from the trouser fly that she so desperately wished to tear open, and stood with her chin lowered in a demure posture that she hoped would arouse forgiveness in her possibly outraged chauffeur.

On the contrary. Her submissive attitude encouraged in the young man the feeling that perhaps his employer had

31

wisely succumbed to the notion that it should be the male of the species who should be the first to make a move in the wars of love. Many times he had been bitten by her elegant appearance, her sensuous way of walking, her seductive musky perfumes, and her gay laughter. Yes, she was not such a bad thing, he thought, a creature he was fond of in a way, but her ongoing flirtations so far had unnerved, rather than stimulated, him. A man of the south, proud of his machismo bearing, he granted sexual favours to those ladies who sought gratification through shy smiles, little indulgences such as expensive presents, and advances less obvious than those of the vicomtesse. Such women were usually more elderly ladies, the rich widows of the Cote d'Azur who, like Bernadette, had time on their hands and the money to indulge in a comfortable and harmonious existence.

To the chauffeur's eyes, Bernadette was not only still a little young for his usual taste, but she struck him as being perhaps a little shallow in her interminable gaiety. While she flirted so extensively with him, he wondered often if, behind the teasing, there lay a patronising attitude, a rich lady's contempt for an employee. He did not wish to be a lap dog, a gigolo, to be taken up and then dropped at the slightest whim. Besides, a woman like Bernadette who was clearly experienced in the art of love, and who seemed to be in receipt of the attentions of a fair number of admirers still, would be able to compare his sexual performance with that of a lot of other men—let alone the actual size of his organ. For Jean-Paul, to his chagrin, was the possessor of a penis of a size that would normally grace a young boy. For years he had longed for its continued growth. Indeed he had consulted physicians at great expense, only to be reassured by them that there was no way, not even his continued manipulation of the under-sized organ, in which it could be increased in size.

Hélas, that was the sad situation. But Jean-Paul had accepted the constraint on his physique and had concentrated on those ladies who, in spite of the smallness of his piece, would be grateful enough not to complain. Furthermore, he had developed certain techniques in his lovemaking that endeared him to his partners. They were clever and stimulating attentions to which a better endowed male might not have to resort but which, in all the cases in his experience, had reduced the ladies to a satisfying state of sexual slavery.

Reading Bernadette's imploring eyes, he thought there might be yet another opportunity to exercise his talents in these stimulating ways. But he strode towards the rug, and, gathering it up in his strong arms, addressed his mistress firmly. 'Madame,' he said authoritively, 'we must leave immediately if you wish to arrive at your couturier before closing time.'

Bernadette was loath to leave such an entertaining and thrilling cabaret as the one which would, undoubtedly, continue on the sun-soaked beach below. Aching for the loins of the darkly handsome driver to cool the lust in her body, which had been raging ever since her early morning observations from the garden room, she mouthed a silent complaint but dutifully followed Jean-Paul through the cliff top thicket and over the dusty road to the car.

During the journey to Nice the chauffeur smiled to himself. He was proud of his circumspection in the affair. To have thrown himself at the vicomtesse would certainly have been gratifying to them both, stimulated as they were, but after the immediate urgency had been satisfied, his mistress would have been able, at leisure, to inspect the organ whose lack of interesting size preoccupied him. The instant comparison with the massive weaponry he had just seen in action on the beach, to wit the outsize prick of the

Englishman, would no doubt have led to some disappointment in the vicomtesse, if not some frivolous comment of comparison. As he settled back to enjoy the drive he reflected with some pride that only one such as he, a strong, virile and determined personality, could have resisted the moment's temptation. The small organ, nevertheless, dilated and throbbed all the way along the Corniche, glowing with pleasure at the satisfaction it would get when its master finally decided it would be a good time to strike.

An hour later Bernadette had finished the purchase of some new underwear, necessary on account of the disturbed state of her original garments, and had changed into them in the powder room of the Negresco. Her still-fevered brain imagined the lovers back along the coast road rushing to splash and refresh themselves in the sea before plunging again into another amorous affray. She recalled a similar experience she had enjoyed with a Hungarian gentleman, a celebrated classical violinist, whom she had met by chance in a restaurant at Beaulieu Sur Mer. Over coffee and spirits they had both declared their carnal intentions for each other and had spent the rest of the day in pursuit of the endless satisfaction of their bodies in various locations on a beach nearby, including an abandoned fisherman's boat; on the rocks, in still warm pools inhabited by little fish; and standing up in the sea with the waves washing round their exhausted but glowing bodies. Afterwards the compelling musician had, naked, serenaded her in his hotel bedroom with the windows wide open, letting in streams of moonlight. Like Arthur, his proud instrument, not the musical one, had been of tormenting, delirium-inducing proportions. Between bouts of fierce lovemaking she had massaged this appendage back into life for further assaults on her frame while he played cadenzas for some of the famous concertos in his repertoire. Finally, unable to play any more games, either musical or carnal, the violinist had slumped on the dishevelled bed and Bernadette had crept away into the night exhausted, but determined to buy a season ticket for the concert season.

She had ordered a new gown, something special for the first night of the Ballet Russes whose vivid designs and choreographies were the rage of Monte Carlo. So after changing her underwear she ordered Jean-Paul to proceed towards the salon of the dressmaker.

Throughout the fitting she daydreamed about Charles under the shower that morning; Arthur's adventure on the beach; the talented violinist, and many more arousing visions. The hands of the couturier, who unlike many of his calling was a truly normal man who adored the ladies, brought about yet more frissons as they darted about her body fixing little pins and tucks while he sculpted the new gown into alluring curves which flattered the vicomtesse's figure to perfection. As he smoothed the silk over her bottom and then over her hips, draping the rich material into minute folds and pleats, she trembled slightly, her face flushing into a rosy pink. Lightly she touched his greying head and stroked his cheek. 'How I adore you, Marcel,' she murmured. 'So clever, so imaginative, so original.'

'It is always a pleasure, *cherie*, to make something for you,' he replied. 'You have a perfect body, as well proportioned as the racehorses at Longchamp. Yours is the ideal frame on which to display my creations.' He excused himself with a little cough and a *pardon* as his hand slid underneath the silk to re-arrange the hang of the underslip. Accidentally, or maybe not, the hairy back of his hand brushed against her mound of Venus which was lightly covered by her new camiknickers, and passed on up her soft belly to tug at the offending waistband.

The natural and instinctive movement she made at this small intervention was to arch her pelvis slightly away from Marcel's hand, but a couple of moments later she reversed the tilt of her hips and pressed at first so lightly and then with greater insistence on to the fingers that were grappling with the tiresome undergarment. Marcel was neither surprised nor offended. His fittings, always conducted privately in the comfortable parlour at the rear of his premises far from the inquisitive eyes of the *vendeuses*, had often produced some erotic response in his clients. Indeed, many of them had been willing partners in dalliance of a very pleasurable kind in these cramped and intimate quarters.

'I'm feeling just a little fatigued, slightly faint,' the vicomtesse murmured, and smiled gratefully as the couturier led her gently towards the small divan which was placed behind a gilt screen at the rear of the room.

'Let me take away the pins before you lie down,' he said in as solicitous manner as he could muster, a slight stiffening in his groin anticipating the delicious curves of her body which were revealed as the pieces of flimsy silk fell to the floor. 'What ravishing drawers,' he intoned with the manner of a person who appreciates fine quality in a garment.

As Bernadette reclined against the divan, Marcel ran his smooth palm across her burning forehead and down her naked arms causing minute goosepimples to break out. It was a signal he recognised. With speed he crossed the room to close the door that led into the main salon, locking it deftly and quietly. Returning to the recumbent lady he bent in front of her, clasping her very nicely rounded knees.

'You are adorable,' he said urgently. 'I have wanted to be

your lover for years. You cannot understand the feelings I have when you bring your lovely body to my salon, the desire that wells up in me when I touch you. Oh, my darling.'

'What a pretty speech, Marcel. I'm very flattered,' the vicomtesse replied. 'Why have you not told me these things before?' She took his head in her hands and brought it to rest on her breasts and played lightly with the curls which spilled over his collar.

'All of those years when your husband and I were close friends and played tennis altogether . . . fishing . . . golf . . . I could not abuse my friendship and declare myself.'

'*Mon cher* Marcel, I can't think why not. Many others of the vicomte's friends did,' she giggled, reaching round behind to undo the clasp of her brassiere. Marcel slid the new peach coloured camiknickers down her thighs and pressed kisses on her enflamed orifice, then without further ado threw open his flies and mounted her in a determined and experienced fashion, while Bernadette struggled to kick the knickers from her ankles.

The orgasm, which had been burgeoning for hours, shook her body. Marcel was surprised to have pleasured the lady so speedily. He was so flattered that she took such instant delight the moment he penetrated her that he incurred his own ejaculation much sooner than he expected. He was delighted. He felt like a young boy again and the thought aroused further lust in him. He withdrew quickly, causing her to moan in disappointment, but she grinned delightedly, as he seized her and turned her to squat on her hands and knees with her pretty rump towards him. He bit her there of course a few times, causing groans of pleasure in her, and then parted her lips with tender care, murmuring about their lovely shape and exquisite silky texture, before he plunged himself deep into her interior.

Bernadette squealed with delight, hoping the sound would not travel into the shop, feeling the penetrating organ sink further into her abyss of infinite sensation. Holding her shoulders he pushed until he had reached his final limit, and then stayed motionless, the throbbing muscles of his organ sending her involuntary waves of urgency. Deciding that a second orgasm need not necessarily be produced so quickly as his overexcited first, the well-practised lover let the principal sensations in his body die down a little, though he held his penis in a perfect erection, and directed his attentions to those parts of Bernadette's body that he knew would give her the greatest thrills. He massaged her pendulous breasts and then her belly, the soft down underneath and the hard swollen stem at the gate of her temple. Bernadette moaned and squirmed backwards against the hard intrusion, but he slapped her gently on the backside and bade her be still, urging her to let him take his time for the greater benefit of them both.

'Ah, Marcel, you are a master, and not just of the couture,' she whimpered. 'But I implore you—continue—I am in a limbo. I will die if you do not ravish me and put me out of the torment I am in.'

Inspired by her impatience, and by her continued writhing against his pelvic bone which set up the most agreeable sensations, Marcel set to work again. First he moved slowly, sliding his erect masterpiece in and out of her orifice with a majestic proud gait that enthalled her, causing her to almost sob in her passion. On occasion he slipped completely out and rubbed the outer lips of her parts with the tip of his penis before slowly but forcibly re-introducing it. Then with quickening speed he slapped his body against her buttocks, thrusting deeply inside her, pulling her hips towards him. For a variation he circled his hips and hers together, at the same time running his nails down her spine, while she clenched her hands into the little pillow, anxious not to scream out. His momentum gathered speed. She was now thrust backwards and forwards like a rocking horse as he, with his head thrown back got nearer to the inevitable conclusion.

The chief *vendeuse* in the salon coughed loudly, and noisily dropped the cash box on the marble floor in a loyal attempt to deflect the attention of a customer who could certainly hear, and could understand the significance of the climactic squeals and groans of the pair as they flooded their juices into and over each other, murmuring words of true love that of course neither believed but, in the circumstances, seemed appropriate.

Jean-Paul, seated in the car outside the premises, lit another cigarette and wondered why Madame was taking such a long time at the fitting. For sure it must be a very special dress.

Chapter Two

Charles, strolling along the promenade, congratulated himself on the success of the day so far. The morning had been particularly good for business. Three groups of friends had wanted to hire yachts for the season and he had received a large sum of money from a notoriously bad payer whom he had threatened to evict from his vessel if cash was not forthcoming. A charming little lunch with a couple of cronies and their girl friends had produced the promise of a party the next weekend complete with dancing, nude swimming, a demonstration tango by a pair of itinerant Argentinians and fireworks over the bay at midnight. He swung his Malacca cane jauntily as he strolled gaily past the gaudy display of beach toys for sale, the flower sellers and the man with the monkey who took photographs of willing holidaymakers.

He was dressed in the manner of an American actor in a film he had recently seen—a check-suited villain who had abducted Fay Wray and seduced her in a seedy hotel. He thought how wonderful it was to be so relaxed and happy here in the South of France, rather than to be stuck earning a hard penny in the treadmills of the City of London; or to be in the armed services like his friend Arthur; or even worse, despatched by his disagreeable family to some disgusting British colony populated only by black sheep similar to himself, the rejects of society who were no longer welcome on British soil. Where on earth he wondered, apart from the Riviera, would he find a girl as compliant to his needs as the elfin, doe-eyed, skinny little Angelique, the sales assistant in his favourite chocolate shop.

He blessed their meeting over his deliberations between the pralines and the *cafés crèmes*. How kind she had been to press a few samples on him, indeed popping them personally into his mouth. A wink, a nod, a little squeeze over the counter, and the sparrow of a girl had been his, a summer toy to use whenever he wanted, and one which he could throw away without a single regret when it suited him. Lord, how she revelled in it—even more than the gardener's daughter whom he had disgraced last summer in the orchard of the family mansion. She suffered a sort of nymphomania that both attracted and repelled him, often going into such raptures that he feared for her health, if not her sanity. But such a girl was exactly what Charles needed for that particular enforced sojourn in the South in order to boost his morale. She had certainly done a good job on him. He reminded himself to buy her a present, perhaps a little blouse or a bit of cheap jewellery.

His mind played on the afternoon siesta today. He smiled to himself, remembering the couple of hours when the chocolate shop, like all the other establishments, closed for the essential lunch and lovemaking favoured by the French. The heady Provençale wine he had consumed with his friends had helped to arouse in him a half drowsy lustful feeling that had propelled him towards the side street where Angelique resided in an attic of great charm, complete with a canary in a cage, trailing geraniums at the windows, and an over-large creaking brass bedstead. He found her half asleep, the sunlight filtering through the shutters illuminating her pale skin as she lay naked on the lace cover. He lifted her up bodily, not a difficult task for a burly man confronted with such a delicately shaped girl, and threw her over his shoulder, whirling her round before coming to rest on a chair, his free hand opening his flies and pulling out his already tumescent sexual organ. The sleepy girl smiled and caressed his face as he parted her legs and straddled them over his lap, until her moist opening sunk over and engulfed it. She faced him and rained kisses all over his face, and then sank her probing tongue into his open mouth. Charles leant back somewhat, holding Angelique a short way away from him by the shoulders and smiled gleefully as she squirmed her bottom around in order to gain total captivity of his organ. She was, although small and thin, of perfect proportions. Her high cheek bones and dark glossy hair the stuff that painters lust for, and the bright light in her chestnut coloured eyes now showed the fire that had started below.

Not a word was spoken as Charles, lifting her from underneath her bottom, eased her up and down his member, the movement causing a slight sucking sound. She whimpered softly in his ear, biting his lobe as she did so with her fingers locked in his hair. Though he was strong he soon tired of this effort, after which Angelique continued the rising and falling action by herself, pushing with her feet on the side staves of the old chair. A small clock on a dresser chimed the quarter. Alerted to its presence, she began to time her movements in rhythmic accord with its ticking, perhaps it was one stroke up and then one down with each passing second.

Charles's eyes were closed, both on account of this prolonged and engulfing activation of his member and the effect of the strong hot sunshine leaking through the shutters. The lunchtime wine had deadened his senses enough for him to be able to accept this treatment lazily. Without moving a muscle he sat, or rather sprawled there, indolently glorying in the friction of her private passage over his frenum and then down to the base of his masculinity. A sigh of the deepest gratification passed his lips. This encouraged the little shop assistant to move double time to the clock, a manoeuvre which soon brought her to a gigantic climax in which her love juices flowed from her vertically down the shaft of her lover's inserted penis, drenching his engorged scrotum underneath. When her tremors had subsided she gently tapped and plucked at Charles's face.

'Are you asleep, *cheri*,' she enquired, 'or am I boring you?'

'Certainly not, my little pigeon,' Charles answered as he rose to his feet, still clutching the curled-up form of Angelique. Now her feet were crossed over the small of his back and his arms were crossed in a similar way around her waist. He began a curious swaying motion, first relaxing his knees and bending inwards to a half crouch and then straightening up in an arching movement. The tip and then the whole of his member sank in and then pulled out of her well moistened tunnel of love, a procedure which was so pleasurable that the physical effort involved, which anyway was slight on account of the girl's thin frame, was negligible.

Knowing he was nearing that unavoidable point of departure which is heralded by a sudden devastating effulgence of sperm determined to leave the loins, Charles stood completely upright, and by bouncing Angelique up and down on his member brought the affair to a rapid conclusion, the muscles of his legs and spine shuddering as he ejaculated in waves of awesome force. He lifted her up and away from his body and kissed her lightly on the mouth before slumping on to the bed in an exhausted heap. The canary sang him a lullaby as he drifted off to satisfied sleep, and Angelique began her *toilette* in order to return to her duties at the chocolate shop.

Bernadette had slept late that morning. When the maid brought her coffee and the newspaper, the sun was already high in a sky of heavenly blue, and when the windows and shutters were opened wide the heavy scents of roses, jasmine and gardenias came flooding into the comfortable large bedroom she occupied on the first floor of the mansion. She dismissed the servants for the day and lay back in the damask sheets, curling her limbs, which were clad in a white négligé of the finest chiffon, into a ball of satisfied and lethargic tiredness.

The room was lavish in the extreme, decorated principally with paintings of the *Belle Époque*, a style of which the late vicomte had been especially fond. He had spent fortunes in the salerooms of Paris, London and New York acquiring a notable collection. Ladies of a refined appearance, complete with *robes decolletées*, holding fans, with plumes in their hair, gazed down from their gilded frames, smiling enigmatically at the occupants of the room. There were large canvases of groups of bohemians, painters and their models and the like, disporting themselves by the waters of the Seine on sunny afternoons, brazen in their wilful abandonment of their bodies to the intoxicating heat of the day. Another favourite painting of the vicomtesse showed a well formed woman of middle age stepping out of a small bath, her breasts still wet and her pubic hair barely hidden by the small towel she held modestly in front of her body.

The alcoves contained certain Etruscan sculptures of great value which the vicomte had purchased in circumstances which would have caused concern in the art world, during his and Bernadette's foraging tours. His particular tastes and propensities had been well known to a few dealers on the fringe of the questionable cartel who are involved in the international art trade. Henri, being able to pay extravagant sums for stolen goods without regard for their provenance, had acquired a remarkable set of erotic figures and groups which, if purchased by major museums, would have been consigned to private rooms for study by a few privileged scholars. There were also fine reproductions of some of the discoveries in the ruins of Minoan temples in Crete. The famous bull-warriors and priapic gods of war from that ancient civilisation stood erect in a permanent display which evoked a sense of pervading strength and sexuality.

Also represented was a small group of impressive artefacts and figurines from the excavations of Pompeii and a serpentine, convoluted piece of erotic carving from the Indian sub-continent executed in a rich dark wood inlaid with ivory and precious stones. Bernadette now often smiled to herself when she fondly remembered the many occasions when she and her adored husband attempted to reproduce, on their own bed, the spectacularly athletic couplings which were represented in the carving. The grouping, in the Hindu manner, contained many figures, and the effort of copying each segment of the frieze had naturally often led to complete exhaustion.

The bookcases and shelves held a vast collection of manuscripts, texts, prints and coloured engravings which also testified to the vicomte's love of erotic, if not pornographic art. The common thread of the collection was the vision, which many great artists have shared, of the perfection which is manifested in the total fusion of the male and female of the human species in harmonious conjugation. This elevating process was so well reflected on the walls of this remarkable room that Bernadette considered herself a fortunate woman. She had been privy to the mysterious process which, by the intervention of God-given genius, translates life into Art.

She slumbered happily through the morning, oblivious to the sounds of the doves in the gardens outside. A casual observer would have noted a woman in her prime. At the age of forty-two she still had the figure of a young woman. Her skin was pampered, oiled and massaged, and always had an aura of the most expensive rich perfumes. Though fond of good food and drink she was abstemious enough to have avoided the tell-tale coarse veins and reddened eyes which disfigure greedier ladies. Tennis, swimming and dancing kept her muscles in good shape, and the best couturiers, as we have already discovered, made painstaking efforts to clothe her in the manner of the *beau monde*.

A continuing distraction was that no man could ever replace her darling Henri as her permanent lover. What woman who had been so adored could be base enough to seek a replacement? The answer must lie, for a woman still in the prime of her life and with the normal desires of a healthy female, in taking suitable partners when the opportunities presented themselves and the sexual vibrations promised correctly.

As she bathed, later, anointing herself with sweet smelling unguents in her sybaritic bathroom, she considered these matters. Sophie, her half cousin from Bordeaux, was expected shortly. Like herself, her relative was a woman of the world, a person of humble birth who had achieved a place in the world through good fortune, good looks and that kind of tenacity and humour that is required of a survivor. Bernadette was looking forward immensely to her cousin's visit. Of all her close circle, Sophie was her only real confidante.

46

Charles and Arthur also rose late. Charles had spent the evening at a tango dance at which the new Charleston had been demonstrated by a group of wild flappers and their boyfriends from Chicago. Enervated by his excesses with Angelique, he had at first been listless, but had later been captivated and inspired to new energy by the hot rhythms of the accompanying jazz band and the wide range of fashionable cocktails which were provided by the considerate and wealthy host—an American novelist who was enjoying a successful, if drunken, vogue on the Riviera that year.

Arthur slept fitfully. The romantic aspects of the holiday were troublesome enough. His heart was full of his new love, the nubile creature whom he had worshipped from afar for so long before the mutual seduction which happened so fortuitously on the secluded beach with such complete and fulfilling gratification to them both. A more serious distraction was the *maladie d'amour* that he was now suffering. Well known to the rampant sexual athlete is the gnawing pain that can surge through the loins, belly and back of a lover who has over-indulged himself in carnal delights. These painful reminders of profligacy are well recognised by a practised lover, but to one like Arthur, a gentleman whose sexual exploits so far were of a very limited variety, the symptoms did not arouse the fond memory of his abandonments. They suggested that maybe he had done himself some irreversible damage. As he staggered to the bathroom his testes weighed on him heavily and the soreness of his unpractised glans and frenum filled him with foreboding. To his relief, after a long soak in the tub and a lot of splashing with *eau de cologne*, Arthur's appendages felt much better, and like all committed lovers, he began to lust again after the object of his desires.

Charles, like a bull in a pen, was avid for further conquest. Though he had delighted in his association with the little chocolate seller and was determined to play the field in her direction when it suited him, he was now anxious to gain the favour of Edith. She was one of the flapper team who had danced so expertly on the terrace last night, dazzling the British with their transatlantic franzy. It was Edith who had later torn off her fringed knee-length dress and dived into the pool with a bottle of champagne, daring the best of the boys to join her for a drink. Needless to say it was one of the despised American youths, a slicker with greased hair and severe acne, who had accepted the invitation with the most readiness.

Charles slapped Arthur's behind with a wet towel in his usual fashion. 'Hello, old sport, been up to any tricks I should know about?' he blustered. 'Got the old ramrod up anywhere yet?'

Arthur pulled up his pants around his recovering genitals. He had the natural braggart desire of the successful male to elaborate the delightful nature of his encounter with Annabelle, especially since his companion had so often teased him about his seeming lack of success with the members of the fairer sex, but he decided that it would be prudent to refrain from such a narrative. Charles would only be curious and envious, a possible threat to his continued association with the highly desirable debutante. With this in mind the officer got on with his *toilette* in a businesslike manner and assured his companion that his affair was purely platonic, after which Charles gave him a blow by blow account of his afternoon with Angelique in the attic over the patisserie.

Arthur listened agog, as his knowledge to date of variations in sexual technique was confined to his own naturally

48

inspired inventions on the beach the previous afternoon. He determined to try a few of the novel modes of lovemaking the resourceful Charles so graphically described the next time he conjugated with his beloved.

Sophie arrived at the mansion a few days later in a large open tourer which had been the gift of an elderly nabob, her most recent admirer. The expensive Vuiton luggage was despatched to her quarters by her maid and Jean-Paul, whose general appearance and polite demeanour naturally appealed to Sophie as much as they did to her half cousin.

The two ladies spent a couple of hours in the gazebo deep in the recesses of the vast garden in animated discussion. Both were anxious for the latest gossip and details of their amorous adventures, not a surprise since it had been a year since they met in a situation where they could reveal to each other their worst indiscretions. How they loved each other, they cried. Both girls had come from a similar background of genteel poverty and had worked their way through the ranks of French society to achieve the enviable positions they now held.

Sophie had worked as a stenographer in the provinces for business men, an architect and a package steamer company before marrying a wealthy merchant from Nantes who made a fortune in the import of North African dates and died a millionaire.

Bernadette had been brought up in the pre-war world of Paris and followed all the usual trades available to young girls, including working as a milliner's assistant, a laundry girl, cabaret singer, dancer and artist's model before she became the mistress of a painter who achieved world wide success but died from the effects of the vast quantities of absinthe he consumed. She was found by Henri in Marseille where she was on tour with a small variety show in which she performed artistic dancing in the manner of Loie Fuller, draped with diaphanous chiffons and gauzes which she manipulated to hypnotic effect. The enchanted vicomte had taken her on a whirlwind tour of Europe, Asia and India, widening her education and culture in order to introduce her to the society to which he belonged, which flourished in Paris and Rome in the winter and the Riviera in summer. The new vicomtesse was readily accepted by his friends. They all came from a world in which a *midinette* or a courtesan could succeed if she had the charm and originality to grace a society which valued style above all else, and had none of the snobbery of a more provincial élite.

It would be fair to say that without their bounteous physical charms and amorous natures, neither of the two cousins would have succeeded in this social transmogrification. Everywhere they appeared gentlemen and lechers of all kinds lusted after them. After going their separate ways, they came together again as wealthy widows who could congratulate themselves on the fortunate outcome of their careers, both having a store of vivid memories of good times, good lovers and the blessing that, still seductively attractive, they could look forward to an engaging future.

After an agreeable gossip in the gazebo, the two ladies were ensconced in the small salon which, if a hidden button was pressed, led into the secret garden room devised by the vicomte. Both had removed several layers of clothing on account of the fierce heat of the day and the distracting nature of their mutual revelations.

'Tell me,' said Sophie, 'you mentioned those two English visitors who are staying in the guest wing.' She smiled, assuming an air of innocent enquiry. 'Are they interesting?'

'You shall meet them soon,' replied Bernadette, pressing

50

the little button which was hidden in the rosewood chiffonier. Her face held an enigmatic expression as, to Sophie's total amazement, the secret panel beside the ornately carved fireplace slid silently away into the wainscotting, revealing the beautiful and alluring aspect of the domed garden room, As if it were the most normal occurrence, she continued in a matter of fact voice, 'They are normally out all day, in the pursuit of either business or love.'

Sophie moved forward like one in a trance. She was stupified by the beauty of the room – its furnishings, rich hangings, chandeliers of Venetian glass, precious antique *objets d'art* and rare paintings—bathed in a luminous glow by the sunlight and flickering shadows which filtered through the azure glass of the curved ceiling and its partial cover of flowering ramblers. She cried out in delight, 'But this is ravishing, my darling, it is the prettiest room I have ever seen. It's a miracle.'

Bernadette wore a bemused expression as she watched her cousin run hither and thither in the room, touching various objects, running her hands appreciatively over their surfaces and feeling the luxurious textures of the hangings and drapes. She was thinking ahead to the greater surprise that she had in store for her delighted cousin when the boys returned to their lodgings, anticipating that this would take place after the cocktail hour when they were sure to come back in order to change for their dinner engagements.

Sophie turned to Bernadette with a look of mock indignation 'How can you have withheld this cunning secret from me?' she demanded. 'How long has this room been here, like this? I don't understand where we are. Are there no windows? Is this room squeezed between the library and the dining room?' She puzzled much more in this vain, desperate to understand the geography of the floor plan; all of which

51

brought much satisfaction to Bernadette since it proved that Sophie, in spite of having been a frequent visitor to the house, had never suspected the garden room's existence.

She placed her cousin on the divan and swore her to secrecy. As little girls they had made many such pacts and she knew Sophie would honour her pledge. Afterwards she explained how the vicomte had designed and executed the hidden sybaritic room while she was on an extended holiday and had confided its secrets to her as a wonderful surprise. 'I am doing the same for you now, my darling. You are my closest friend and I am giving you, alone, the knowledge of this special sanctuary.'

Sophie was overcome with gratitude and affection for her cousin. She revelled in the peace and tranquillity of this remarkable apartment, sipping a cup of the delicious tea which Bernadette prepared in an ornate silver Russian samovar which had been the gift of the deposed Czar. The vicomtesse handed her *petit fours* which were arranged daintily on a Meissen plate of great rarity and value, painted with birds of paradise and exotic flowers in brilliant colours.

'There is something else concerning this room,' she said in a tantalising fashion, 'which you shall learn later. But for now, you will have to wait.'

They relaxed over their tea and began again to amuse each other with their anecdotes; two women of the world who had led extraordinarily lives and were grateful for that precious asset of human relationships—the ability to confide the most intimate details of life and love to a close and loving companion.

Sophie recounted at length the *histoire* of a long sojourn she had spent with the nabob cruising in the most incredible luxury through the Far East in his extravagantly equipped liner. The journey had started in Hong Kong and taken in the

South China Sea, and after visits to the great temples of Bangkok and the hinterland of Thailand, had continued through the maze of the islands of Indonesia and thence to Papua New Guinea. The thoughtful nabob, whose advanced age precluded him from any amorous activity of a physical kind, had provided Sophie with a host of unattached male companions; the ship's company included a fair number of distinguished Swedish, German and British scientists who had gratefully accepted the invitation since it provided a once in a lifetime opportunity to study the flora and fauna of the barely charted and rarely visited regions.

In the company of such men (who were, after all, to a man jack, severely affected by the hot tropical nights and the inevitable *longueur* of the balmy days at sea) Sophie found plenty of opportunities to slake her physical needs. She related a few of the most outstanding episodes to her amused cousin who begun to feel it would have been solicitous of Sophie to have taken her along on the trip, such enviable lustful impromptus having been the order of the day. The returned voyager's *pièce de resistance* concerned an amazing event on a remote island, the precise location of which Sophie, whose knowledge of geography was a little sparse, could not reveal. The liner's arrival had coincided with the discovery of a hitherto unsuspected tribe of Stone Age primitives whose existence provoked the most profound interest among the scholars. The art work, tools and hunting techniques of the tribe provided valuable study fodder for the scientists and the social structures and sexual mores of the indigents were a rich hunting ground for the excited anthropologists.

The culmination of the exploration was a huge ceremony which lasted several days of the spring equinox. The gathered tribes drank large quantities of potent liquids distilled from the roots and barks of trees, fermented by their own saliva and the juices of berries. They also smoked aromatic and noxious smelling substances through bamboo pipes. Wild intoxication followed the consumption of these raw alcohols and narcotics. The music of gourds, conch shells and drums rose to a frenzied pitch as the young girls of the tribe danced in circular fashion on the trampled earth.

They swayed and undulated their hips in front of a phalanx of pubescent males who were to be initiated. The sight of so much naked flesh was at once moving in its primitive simplicity and provocative in its unadorned glory. Then, massed in the centre of the ring, in a grouping of savage splendour the young girls came to rest in unison. Their feet ceased pounding the earth and their breasts took over the relentless throbbing beat of the drumming. At intervals the action moved to their navels which shook and quivered together in a strange ritualistic evocation of female sexual power, and then to their hips which trembled violently. Turning their backs on the youths at a sudden change in the rhythm, they shook their posteriors in an amazing fashion. The implied invitation to the assembled boys proved too much for the elderly nabob who suffered for the first time in years an involuntary ejaculation. A blast on a horn fashioned from the antlers of a jungle beast signalled the girls to take their places in a ring as the boys took up the central position.

They were decorated with intricate tattoos only. Their bodies gleamed in the firelight as they stamped ferociously, waving the plumes of the feathers which sprouted from their heads. The enticement shown so seductively by the young females had aroused them all to full tumescence. As they switched their hips from side to side their erect penises slapped their groins. At a signal from the headman the drumming stopped and all the spectators could hear was the concerted slapping of these swollen organs by their owners, beating a rhythm on their own flesh. By some predetermined arrangement or perhaps by a hypnotically induced moment of mass hysteria produced by the drugs and the primeval dance, the ensemble changed the direction of the movement of their penises which now, caused by thrusting jabs of their pelvises in a simulation of the principal male sexual action, beat on their bellies. The sound of this collective percussive manipulation of their organs rang out through the tropical night with awesome effect, galvanising the girls to come forward, mesmerically attracted to the phalluses whose dance represented the continuation of their tribal life. Each chose a partner and led him towards the shade of the straw awnings which surrounded the site. It was a mass coupling of paroxysmic intensity, encouraged by the shrieking of the elder women and the baying of the warriors of the tribe.

Sophie paused for breath, clearly distracted by her story-telling, as was Bernadette. Each woman had a hand at her crotch and the other at her breast and trembled in delight at the vision of this apotheosis of the nabob's odyssey in search of the unspoilt world. The vicomtesse, hearing voices in the distance, placed one imperious forefinger on her closed lips and gestured with the other hand, palm upstretched, in the universal sign of conspiracy in silence. Sophie immediately ceased her babbling and Bernadette stealthily crossed the room to draw aside the embroidered hanging which had so far concealed the two-way mirror.

Her cousin was stunned into silence by the aspect revealed. A handsome man strode into the room beyond, guiding in a beautiful curvaceous girl. The pair kissed passionately and fell on a bed laughing. The man took off her shoes and kissed her feet through their silk-stocking coverings. The girl unbuttoned her blouse and threw it over her head and then removed her bust bodice. She had large pink aureoles and darker but exquisitely shaped small nipples which the watching pair could see increase in size as the man reached for her garters and, now kissing her rounded knees, pulled them and her stockings down to her ankles. He lifted her skirt and with great care laid it out like a fan over her belly. Her skin looked soft and golden, tinted by the summer sun. The man buried his face in the shining *eau de nil* of her knickers, reaching for her swelling breasts. The girl tossed her head with its auburn close-cropped hair from side to side in her obvious pleasure.

Bernadette and Sophie looked at each other. The events since the vicomtesse's revelation had happened so quickly neither had had time, till now, too see each others reaction. Sophie was wide eyed in amazement and Bernadette, hugging herself, looked like the cat with the cream, delighted as she was to have stage-managed the surprise so well. The sparkle in her eyes led Sophie to grin. She shook with silent laughter at her cousin's impudence. It was typical of Bernadette's behaviour, she thought, relishing the way she had been lulled into the cosy atmosphere of the small salon only to be given this scandalous and riveting shock.

Bernadette, turning once again towards the amorous pair, felt mildly annoyed by Arthur's behaviour, bringing the ravishing Annabelle to the apartment. Was it quite right for the officer to abuse her hospitality in this way, she wondered. Good sense prevailed after a moment's consideration. Their tempestuous affair could not continue with any propriety in the *al fresco* situation in which it had been initiated, and it would be fairly unsuitable for him to take the girl to an hotel bedroom. That sort of thing was for more experienced men of the world and their casual pick-ups, not attractive *jeunes gens* like these.

Arthur, still fully clad in his striped blazer and flannels, now devoured her throat, kissing it a thousand times and nibbling her ears. The girl's laughter rang out infectiously.

'Stop, stop,' she implored, giggling like a tickled schoolgirl, trying to push him away.

'I can't,' he cried, 'you're like a delicious pastry, a box of chocolates. I can't get enough, you're so sweet.'

With an enormous effort she pushed him away from his meal and he went dancing round the room, leaping over chairs and pirouetting in his joy. Annabelle sat up on the bed. 'You silly boy, I adore you. What a lovely idiot you are.'

'I love you, worship you,' the crazed boy cried, throwing himself at her feet.

To her astonishment Bernadette saw tears welling in his eyes. He smiled bravely through his torment and Annabelle, her breasts heaving with emotion, clasped him to her bosom. They both cried heartily in their new found love. The cousins gazed at this tender scene, with compassionate feelings stirring in their breasts, then after looking for a moment at each other and, nodding sagely, they stole away from the salon, leaving the innocent pair to continue their devotions unobserved.

Arthur had no need to take inspiration from the few mildly erotic pictures he had been shown by comrades in the officers mess. Nature led him irrevocably and dexterously through a maze of little attentions and courtesies, embraces, sighs and kisses, towards the surrender of the already aroused young lady. Memories of the previous afternoon led him towards the baring of her furry crotch and the moistened outer and inner lips that were contained there. He took her knickers by the waistband and drew them lightly down her thighs. She sighed deeply as he brushed his moustache in the light brown hair of her pubis and just resisted an urge she had to finger her own clitoris.

57

His tongue took over the task instead, bringing her the most satisfying sensations, with his hands rubbing firmly from the slight indentations above her pelvis down the outside of her thighs. Like all men he wished also to explore the erogenous zone in the soft parts behind the knees of his lover, the insides of her elbows and her solar plexus. Not a part of her was left out of this investigation with his mouth and his hands. He marvelled that he could play in this fashion so long without automatically mounting her, but her rapture in these things was so great that he could resist the awesome temptation. Soon she longed for his naked body. She wanted to run her hands over his hard muscular frame by return. Rolling from the bed she took off what remained of her clothing and taking his hand, pulled him to his feet.

She had never undressed a man before. Apart from the erotic implications, it was odd dealing with his tie, cufflinks and shirt buttons as he stood in front of her a little sheepishly. She quivered as she undid his fly buttons and let his trousers fall to his ankles. He bent as if to take them off but she straightened him up and knelt herself to ease his feet from them. Then with a deft movement she pulled off his blazer and hoisted his shirt over his head. It seemed, from the position where she knelt in front of Arthur a moment later, that his brazenly protruding member would burst from his combinations, but placing her hand gently through the fly, she found the thick pulsating article and led it through the gap. His jissom was flowing freely and as her thumb and forefinger passed from the base to the tip, large oozing drops emerged and, in one continuous viscous flow, fell in a slow steady stream to the floor. She marvelled at this liquid, drawn from the depths of his body, clear and lubricous, and with a finger ran it round the tip of his glans and then down the surface of his stem.

Arthur was anxious not to let his first blissful emission lose itself in the air today, therefore he took hold of her by the waist and lifted her off her feet. Nature bade Annabelle open her legs to forty-five degrees in order that when he lowered her, her grateful vagina slid over his taut and throbbing organ until that whole wonderful instrument was engulfed completely. Arthur pressed his lips to hers and then with his eyes closed explored her mouth with his tongue. With their arms tight around each other they swam together into the most perfect sensation as their juices pulsated into each other without a single thrust. They stood in this way, swaying gently together, until Arthur lifted her off his waning organ and led her back to the bed where they drifted into a deep sleep wrapped in each others arms.

Sophie, upstairs, bathing and dressing for dinner, relished the prospect of further visits to the garden room. Bernadette had told her of her surprise at the turn of events, and assured her that next time the cabaret would be an all-male event.

'*N'import'quoi*,' she laughed. To a student of the human condition and all the foibles, vanities, weaknesses and splendours involved, life and love of any kind were of paramount and consuming interest.

Chapter Three

Some days later Marcel, the grand couturier, arrived at the mansion in a Mercedes-Benz, with an assistant, bearing the new gown which the vicomtesse proposed to wear for the gala opening of the Ballet Russe's season in Monte Carlo. It truly was a magnificent affair, a *grande creation* highly suitable for the occasion, which promised to be the most glittering evening on the Cote d'Azur that year, attended by anyone of any importance in the social milieu; diplomats, international balletomanes and a veritable crop of crowned heads.

Bernadette had already surrendered a turquoise necklace, with matching earrings and bracelet, to the *régisseur* of the company; Sophie had generously parted with an emerald the size of a quail's egg but, in fact, had placed it in the hands of Dhokouminsky, a principal dancer of the troupe, whom she believed held a strong passion for her that would come to fruition that summer in the holiday after the season. These bijouteries were to be sold by auction, with other valuables donated by the patrons of the ballet, at the ball which would succeed the opening performance—a necessary contribution to the coffers of the financially pressed, but prestigious company.

'My dears,' said Marcel, regarding these generous gifts. 'I admire your dedication to Art, and your support of those dedicated artistes. However, you do realise, don't you, that a large percentage of the proceeds will end up in the bank account of that dreadful old lecher Borzdoff, the manager of the company, who has swindled his way across Europe more times than we have had hot croissants.' The ladies agreed that it was unfortunate that such a money grabber could be so low as to make a personal profit but, their station in society made a contribution *de rigeur*, and anyway they had so many jewels they would hardly notice their loss. '*Eh bien*,' said Marcel stepping back to admire his work of art. 'My own contribution will be a picnic for the *petits rats* of the *corps de ballet* who are half-starved and emaciated, living on the pittance Borzdoff pays.'

'Bravo,' said Bernadette, 'and I suppose that afterwards you will be rewarded. A splendid arrangement.'

She swept him down to the dining room where they were joined by Sophie and the fourth guest, a Monsieur Rognon, an art dealer of the region who had been of great importance in the establishment of the vicomte's considerable collection. The conversation between these four sophisticates was bright and brittle, ranging from the doings of their neighbours and friends to the idiocies of world politics. The meal, prepared in Bernadette's kitchen by the profoundly committed gastronome in her employ, was a delight of four courses, served with intervening sorbets and wines of the finest quality.

Over the opening course, a fragrant conconction of *soupe de poissons*, Bernadette set the tone of the gay evening by recounting an amusing incident that had happened long ago when she was a professional dancer in a touring revue. It happened, she explained, that a certain Monsieur B., a mayor of a town in the northern regions of France, was her lover at the time. Like many Frenchmen he was of enormous girth, being addicted to food and drink as these noted epicureans are. The charming mayor had many good attributes, notably good humour and generosity, and a rare sense of humour endeared him to Bernadette. He had a passion for chocolate in which she indulged him, buying from the specialist shops all kinds of sweetmeats and bonbons, truffles and pralines. His very favourite passion was for liqueur-filled chocolates which he devoured in large quantities. After a good meal and a couple of bottles of good wine and a few brandies, the good mayor liked nothing better than to lie in a comfortable armchair and watch as Bernadette danced to the record player while he tucked into his selection.

One evening, on an impulse, while he was fondling his beloved, he tucked a strawberry cream filled chocolate into her private part and then proceeded to retrieve it with his tongue. The game was delicious, naturally, for them both, especially when he soon had the idea that she should blindfold him in order to make both the search for, and the identification of, each variety a more intriguing situation. They laughed continuously as he not only indulged his passion for chocolate but pleasured her as well, besides correctly guessing all the flavours.

'What a novel idea,' cried Marcel. 'I must try it one day.'

Tears were rolling down Monsieur Rognon's face for, of course, without admitting it, he had often played the same game. But the best laughter was saved for the denouement when Bernadette continued that after properly identifying chartreuse, crème de cacao, crème de banane and kirsch, the mayor had pleaded for the cherry brandy to be placed in the inner sanctum. 'Impossible,' the lady cried. 'I have eaten it already myself.'

The next course was a simple dish of fat asparagus served with melted butter. The phallic shaped vegetables were strewn across an oval platter, glistening in their juices and slightly steaming. Sophie managed with great delicacy to convey to her hostess an erotic joke as she dipped her serving into the golden butter and bit the heads off one by one.

A count of the crayfish tails of the first course had decided that Monsieur Rognon had to tell the next story, he having been found to have consumed the most.

A client of his, a sculptor and painter, had been commissioned by a municipal council to create a work of art. The subject, a male nude, was the figure of an athlete, and it was to decorate the entrance hall of the *Mairie*. After a long search the artist found a suitable model, a Corsican youth of great beauty, and set to work.

He was working in wax on the life-sized figure (Monsieur R. explained it was a difficult medium), built up on a large metal armature, and the work was going well. The committee came several times to the studio and were agreeably enthusiastic. One day a lady with whom the artist had an appointment—he was to sculpt a head of her for her husband—came to the studio a little earlier than had been arranged.

'*Bon jour*, Madame,' he said. I am afraid I am not ready to see you yet. I am still working with another model.'

'Oh, I am so sorry,' she replied. 'Do you wish me to go away?'

'*Mais non*,' he answered, being a proper gentleman. 'But, er . . .'

'I should find it fascinating to see you at work, *cher maitre*, she proferred, 'that is, if I wouldn't be disturbing you.'

The artist of course showed the interested lady into the studio. He himself suffered no embarrassment at the sight of the nude figure, after all, and being a simple man could not envisage the possibility of it happening to others. The young man was taking a short break, sipping a glass of cassis when the lady entered. The formal introductions having been made, the boy slipped off his robe and lithely mounted the rostrum once more. The artist had only another hour or so still to do on the piece. He happened to have left the genitalia till last.

The lady watched, fascinated as he shaped wax in a rough approximate of the Corsican's appendages and placed it on the model. As the artist worked he explained the processes of working in wax and how preparations were made to cast the piece in bronze, firing and destroying the original. The lady listened politely but her main attention was on the beauteous youth.

His slender torso was well muscled and oiled to reveal its shape more clearly to the artist. He had strong fine thighs and lean buttocks, a handsome head of black curly hair and a profile reminiscent of Apollo. The pose in which he was arranged was both strong and tender, the lyrical juxtaposed to the forceful, the contemplative against the aggressive.

The lady turned to the wax model, then again to the boy, marvelling not just at the likeness, but at the way in which the artist had captured the spiritual quality of the boy. She could not quite believe it, but she was convinced that since the model had first mounted the podium, his penis had grown in size. Looking back to the wax, she saw, true enough, a reproduction of what she had first noticed, a small neat member, perfectly nestled under a black bush of pubic hair, nothing at all out of the ordinary.

The boy was perspiring a little. A bead of sweat ran down from his forehead over his cheek, but he did not flinch from his pose. The lady looked again at his penis and detected the slightest twitch in the short stem. Then a considerable lengthening and swelling until the article was no longer in a perpendicular state but stood away at a slight angle. The artist, engrossed in his work, attacked the sculpture's genitals with more wax, occasionally walking across to hold a pencil near the young man's parts to measure their relative size, and the lady fascinated by the tumescence she was witnessing, fixed her gaze on the young man's crotch.

The poor boy gallantly soldiered on without complaint. Without flickering an eyelid or blushing he maintained the beautiful pose, hoping the lady had not noticed his embarrassing protuberance. He had no need to look down to know what a state his penis was now in. The reflexes coming from it were so strong he thought that the artist must soon complain. But the sculptor, deep in the act of creation, faithfully mirrored what he saw in the little dabs of wax which he continually applied to the region of the sculpture that remained to be finished.

By thinking of his dear mother, the Blessed Virgin, his deceased father, his confirmation and much else, the boy managed to stop the further enlargement of his part and, finally, was allowed to dismount from the rostrum and don his dressing gown.

The lady, much amused by this episode, found the artist in an enraged state when she came to his studio for a sitting some time later.

'Do you know,' he yelled, 'the committee has rejected my work, the nude bronze has been turned down.'

'Why on earth?' she sympathised. 'It was wonderful.'

'They say, of all things, that it is pornographic, that the lad is over-endowed, out of all proportion, impossibly large in the genital area. What philistines.' He cried into his spotted handkerchief and the lady poured him a large *fine*.

'I'm so pleased,' she said. 'I shall buy it myself if you will permit me the honour, for not only is it a great work of art, it is genuine representation of glorious manhood.'

Sophie's contribution to the naughty compilation of *histoires* began after the butler had served an aromatic and spicy saddle of venison. Marinaded in the good red wine of Provençe, and seasoned with fragrant herbs, the juicy meat was embellished by a sauce made from red currants and apricots simmered in cognac. As the lid came off the dish the guests inhaled the subtle aromas and applauded as true gourmets should on such an occasion. Bernadette was pleased with the chef's efforts, an epicurean triumph, and made a mental note to give him a rise in salary. The perfect accompaniments to the venison included *pommes vapeur* of the creamiest texture, *haricots verts* and *épinards*. The feast caused a stir in Sophie's memories concerning an event that took place on the Orient Express somewhere on the stretch after Venice.

Sophie recalled that after eating in the dining car she went to bed early, leaving her current paramour drinking in the bar, but taking with her the remainder of the vintage champagne they had been drinking. She described how she lay in the berth of her cabin, sipping the champagne and wishing that her lover would come to her. She felt annoyed as the trip had been arranged in celebration of the anniversary of their first meeting and she considered that her beau should have felt as romantic as she did in the exciting circumstances of such a journey. As he failed to show up, she fell into a drowsy sleep, lulled by the monotonous clicking and rumbling of the wheels and the swaying movement of the carriage.

Sophie slowly awoke in the dark, with the pleasurable sensations warming her loins. In the gloom of the sleeping car she saw her man standing with his head underneath the blanket. The soft caresses and kisses he was pressing on her mound of Venus provided the most charming arousal. She felt his tongue delicately part her lips and investigate the inner parts, as his hands gently stroked her belly. This adoring attention lasted a long while as the train rocketed through tunnels and charged over viaducts.

Sophie was deliriously happy now that her lover was presenting her with the anniversary present she desired, or at least the promise of it. She tried not to moan or to cry out, as the intimate spaces of sleeping cars, even on such a luxurious train as the Orient Express, are so close that sometimes even decorous conversations can be heard through the panelled walls. The kisses spread down her legs as he parted her thighs and tenderly implanted his love bites. Her toes were given a similar treatment, as were her calves and her ankles before he returned to the main source of both his, and of course her, pleasure.

By this time she was in a fever for him to possess her completely. Sophie recalled that she was husky of voice in her excitement. 'Come, cheri, take me now, or I die,' she murmured. At the command the lover climbed the little ladder to her berth and made preparations to mount her. She took hold of him by the shoulders and ran her hands down his back.

Oh horror, this man had a hairy back, and her lover was smooth skinned. His chest, also, was a tangled mat of curly bristles which were quite unrecognisable to her. She lay terrified in the dark wondering what to do, when suddenly the man said, seizing her breasts with some passion, 'My goodness how you've grown, darling, what on earth's been happening?'

Sophie switched on the lamp which stood beside the sleeping berth. There, to her amazement, was a gentleman who had been dining a few tables away from her fiancé and herself in the salon.

'*Monsieur*', she said with some aplomb, 'my breasts have been the same size all my adult life. I think you are paying homage to the wrong pair.'

The man gallantly slipped off the bunk, quickly adjusting his clothing '*Milles pardones*, madame,' he bowed. 'An unfortunate, but pleasurable mistake. I will return to my cabin at once. If I find your husband there in similar circumstances, I shall return him at once to you.' As he opened the cabin door, he made a discreet cough and asked in the politest way, 'May I asked madame how she discovered that I was the wrong gentleman?'

Sophie replied, 'Monsieur, my fiancé is smooth skinned.'

Through the crack of the door the intruder whispered, 'Madame, goodnight. I am returning to my own cabin, where I shall shave. *A bientot.*'

A few moments later her fiancé, rather the worse for drink, reeled into the cabin and began to undress. 'You know darling, the funniest thing happened. It was dark in the corridor and I seized hold of a woman passing by. I truly thought it was you, my darling. She wore the same perfume but, thank heavens, I soon found out I was deceived. Do you know she had the smallest breasts in the world. Not a patch on yours, sweetheart.'

The four diners were now, naturally, considerably warmed by the delicious food and the fine wines, let alone the *risqué* conversation. Marcel, sitting opposite Bernadette, had removed an elegant shoe and was pressing a toe, clad in a fine silk sock, at the sensitive area between her thighs. Sophie had

68

similarly relinquished her satin pumps and placed her tiny feet on Monsieur Rognon's knees. Inevitably he had caressed them and stroked them as if they were fine artworks and gradually drawn them towards his crotch where he and Sophie, meanwhile playing a wonderful game of eyeball to eyeball confrontation, managed in a subtle way to stimulate his nether regions to near bursting point. Above table all was civilised but beneath it was a case of indulgence and exposure.

The evening continued with the next course to arrive at table. Bernadette's resourceful chef had concocted a dessert of extreme elegance and beauty. Served on a glass cake stand was a grand pyramid of layers of meringues alternating with an amazingly diverse selection of local and imported fruits. The kirsch and maraschino he had poured voluptuously over the whole had soaked beguilingly into the sugar confectionary and into the figs, strawberries, mangoes, passion fruits, pineapples and so on, turning the handsome pile into both a tasteful and alcoholic sweet. As the other three tucked into the appealing dessert, Marcel felt obliged to begin his story.

He revealed he had been orphaned as a child, reared by a kindly couple in the Dordogne, and placed as a trainee gardener in the employ of the Duc de— His estate at Montpelier contained elaborate and ingenious gardens and was famous to the extent that there was a continuous stream of visitors who came to admire its beauty.

Marcel described the parterres and mazes, the pleached limes and colonnades of laburnum, the water gardens, rockeries, fountains, orangeries and arboretums with such entertaining and graphic evocation that the company decided there and then to pay a visit to the incomparable place as soon as possible.

'What picnics, bathing, excursions, we shall have,' they cried. Bernadette resolved immediately to reserve hotel rooms and alert Jean-Paul to their plans.

The famous couturier related to them how, in those days, he was an uncultivated country boy. He had no shame in admitting his low class antecedents. After all, were they not all of humble origin, self-made individuals who had triumphed over their unpromising beginnings?

It so happened that when he was about sixteen, he was secretly observed by a niece of the Duc de—who was staying at the chateau during the holidays, as he pleasured himself over a collection of erotic photographs which had been given to him as a present by the head gardener. Ghislaine, an amateur photographer, had been wandering through the immaculately kept grounds, taking snapshots of the flora and fauna. Which existed in such abundance there and had chanced upon him, unobserved, as he pored over the highly indecent pictures which had originated in Morocco. Peering through the overhanging branches of a magnolia tree she found the drowsy youth contemplating his collection of over-weight females from a kasbah. The afternoon was hot and sultry; crickets and cicadas chirped in counterpoint with the frogs in a nearby pond and the sirocco stirred the leaves of the trees causing them to flutter and rattle against each other.

Marcel recalled how the odalisques he saw draped on their tasselled beds and reclining on their silken cushions had caused an involuntary travel of his right hand towards the flies of his trousers.

'Quite right,' interposed Sophie. 'A young boy should be interested in those things.'

He thought he heard a crack or a snap of a twig, but carried on in his harmless and, he thought, unseen fantasy and, as he discovered later, his ensuing boyish orgasm was recorded on film by the resourceful Ghislaine, Marcel continued.

'Hello,' she said a few days later, 'what's your name? I haven't seen you around here before,' she said slyly.

'Marcel,' he replied, blushing before the high breasted girl who stood swaying before him in the copse of young walnuts, her long dark hair hanging down underneath her battered straw hat.

'My goodness, you're very brown. I suppose it's all this country living,' she said, appreciating his tanned chest and youthful good looks. 'You can walk along with me if you like. I'm looking for a particular sort of spotted woodpecker.'

They ambled through the alleys of azaleas and rhododendrons before coming to rest by a low wall which bordered a pond filled with water lilies. Sitting down, she rested her dark eyes on his and said mischievously, 'Are you interested in girls, Marcel?'

'Not particularly,' he replied. 'I don't get much time with my work, you know, and there aren't too many pretty ones around here—apart from yourself, I mean, miss,' he hurriedly added.

'Very well said,' she said smiling, 'but I'm afraid I don't believe a word of it.' From a folder she was carrying she took a photograph which she placed in his lap. 'Here is evidence to the contrary.'

The blushing boy wished the ground would open up and swallow him in one piece. There he was, unmistakably revealed in black and white, his figure sprawled in the grass in the dappled shade of a small clearing, his flies undone and his hand clasped firmly round his erect penis. There was also a small blur of white a few inches away from its swollen head. It could only be the first spurt of the orgasmic pleasure that he had induced. The evidence was incontrovertible. Hanging his head in shame he said, 'What are you talking about? That's not me you know. It's someone who looks like me, that's all.'

'Rubbish,' she cried gaily. 'I saw you the other day. You were so engrossed in having a good time with your filthy pictures you didn't even hear me when I snapped you.'

'"It's a lie," I cried,' said Marcel.

'Poor boy, you must have been so ashamed,' murmured Bernadette. 'Everyone knows boys are up to all kinds of tricks, but to be found out . . .'

'Oh do carry on,' Sophie implored.

'She was so pretty,' Marcel shrugged. 'Even without her revelation I would have been profoundly embarrassed by what happened next.'

He told how the girl had pushed a hand into his shirt and brought out the packet of photographs which had been the source of his undoing.

'What a dreadful boy,' Ghislaine rebuked, pouting. 'They're not even pretty. How can you get so worked up about such dreadfully flabby females?' And after a pause, 'Would you not say I'm much prettier?'

'It's not my place, miss,' said the chastened Marcel. 'We're not supposed even to talk to the grand folk from the big house.'

'Well, you can talk to me,' she answered. 'And you can walk with me to the studio. I've a few things I want to say to you, young man.'

Marcel interrupted his story as he reached for another glass of the Chateau d'Ychem which so satisfactorily had accompanied the dessert. 'What a *problème*', he mused. 'The young guest of the duc was far above my station but she used this dreadful evidence to lure me into an unbelievable situation. A summer house had been transformed into a darkroom and photographic studio by the duc, who was himself a keen amateur. It was at a distance from the chateau, and anyway he was abroad at the time so the wretched

72

Ghislaine—no—the charming, clever, little Ghislaine, had the place all to herself.'

He told how the girl, having pored over his miserable collection of erotica, had decided she could do much better. He had been despatched to the gardens to fetch armfuls of leaves and vines which she had arranged into leafy arbours in the studio. Lying in tantalisingly provocative poses she had, after fixing the lights, shutters and exposures of her cameras, instructed him when to squeeze the bulb that would immortalize her in the nude, on film.

The resultant photographs had been superb. He could remember now the exquisite symmetry of her limbs and the careless charm of her poses; her petulant expression as she teased him with the delicate hand she placed over her private part; the terrible hardness in his trousers which he had to suffer without the promise of release.

Ghislaine despatched him to Nice with the photographs and an appointment to see a gentleman who traded in the kind of photographs Marcel had received from the head gardener. He was profoundly moved by them and also by his expectations of the profit he expected they would make for him, and paid a large number of francs for their negatives.

'How reckless,' M. Rognon fumed. 'If such a photograph had come into the possession of the duc she would have been disowned, disinherited, thrown out!'

'Nonsense,' chortled Sophie, 'I think she showed admirable resourcefulness. I don't suppose her pin money was all that great.'

'It didn't stop there', said Marcel. 'She got greedy. When the Algerian gentleman asked for double poses she arranged an extension of the shutter-press cable so that we could lie together and press the button from a distance.'

'What invention,' mused Bernadette. 'And what an

73

opportunity for such a young boy,' she said, rubbing her most sensitive area against Marcel's silk clad foot which still pressed urgently on her.

'Of course, it was a remarkable experience,' Marcel grinned, 'but not without its dangers. Once I was obliged to dive naked through a window when a delivery man arrived with some fresh photographic equipment. I landed in a bramble bush.'

'I suppose *your* equipment survived the fall?' Sophie enquired in the mildest tone.

'*Mais non*, madame. I was, unfortunately, lacerated quite badly in the area Ghislaine most wanted to feature in her photographs. She complained much about having to postpone our sessions until I had recovered.'

'At least it stopped you from further abusing yourself,' M. Rognon roared.

'She was appalling,' the couturier continued. 'At first I was so shy when I undressed as she commanded me, that I was unable to offer her the erection she required for her exposures. She resorted to all sorts of tricks, for example, tickling my parts with a feather duster or even with her own long hair.'

'I imagine you made a quick recovery,' Bernadette nodded wisely.

'*Bien sûr*,' Marcel agreed. 'Oh, but what torture to be so aroused so often, and for so long. Imagine how I felt when she placed some coffee *glacé* on the stem and the tip of my boyish organ and then slowly, but so slowly, licked it off.' His voice trailed away at the memory of this indelicate but tasty moment.

'It sounds as though you had a lot of fun with the little minx,' M. Rognon proffered, considering that this particular diversion should be added to the catalogue of his indoor pursuits.

'Well,' Marcel continued, 'the perverse little madamemoiselle certainly knew her stuff. She would arrange us in the most intimate poses, placing my wretched object a centimetre from her lips or from those . . . er . . . lower lips, contort herself into the most inviting, lascivious shapes, and then require me to hold myself stiff,' (the company laughed out loud at his unintentioned joke) 'while she groped for the remote control button of the camera. There I perhaps stayed for minutes at a stretch, with her spreadeagled underneath me on a rug, or hanging upside down from a trapeze, even, while I struggled to contain myself and not let my bursting member thrust itself into the proferred opening. She took dozens and dozens of these photographs. I can tell you that it was highly frustrating,' moaned Marcel. 'I have heard since that her work is thought of very well by connoisseurs of erotica; it is still popular, and now seems to attract huge prices. Thank goodness I have changed enough to be unrecognisable. I happen to have a few examples on my person should you be interested,' he added rather shyly.

He pulled a wallet from a pocket and passed several faded and crumpled photographs round the table. They were certainly good of their kind, possessing, in their naiveté and insouciance, an affecting quality that bordered innocence. Both figures were perfectly proportioned, lithe and youthful. There was a pastoral quality in the beautifully lit compositions; it was as if an Echo and Narcissus, or an archaic shepherd and a nymph had come together in these sculptural arrangements. In one, the youth cradled the prostrate girl's head with his knees whilst bending forward to caress her mouth with his stiff rod. In another they lay in a bed of roses, his mouth to her pelvic centre and her parted lips poised to enclose the head of the boy's handsomely engorged member.

'They were quite ravishing,' said the vicomtesse

appreciatively, squeezing Marcel's foot and moving it over her well aroused private parts. 'I think my favourite is this one.' She passed another picture around.

The young lovers were depicted in a pose of some beauty. Inside an arbour of vines and flowers the young Marcel was positioned in an arc, his buttocks resting in the opening of an antique Grecian urn. His legs were splayed wide and his shoulders were flung back in such a curve that his curly locks brushed the leaf-strewn floor. Ghislaine was poised over him from her position astride the handles of the jar. Her long thighs were bent in such supple fashion that her mound of Venus almost brushed the tip of Marcel's vertical erection which stood so proudly on account of the upward thrust of his loins. Her dark fronds of hair, curled in a most charming manner, seemed imperceptibly to caress the very tip of the poor frustrated boy's glans, and permanently recorded on the celluloid was a small glistening drop of his jissom.

There was a licentious air to the photograph which recalled the bacchic friezes of the ancient Attic world or those erotic drawings which are sometimes discovered in the cave-dwellings of primitive man.

'Not bad, really,' said Marcel with justifiable pride.

'Oh, I don't know,' Bernadette countered, in the full knowledge that her liaison with the raconteur was well known to her sympathetic cousin and the worldly wise art dealer. 'I would say that while the photographs reveal an artistic imagination I would have thought well beyond the powers of an adolescent provincial, they might have been improved had they not featured the slightly underdeveloped organ of a pubescent boy, but the more interesting flagpole of an older man, something more like the prize you possess today.'

'You are wrong, my dear cousin, and I will tell you why,'

Sophie interjected. 'The very careless charm of our friend here, whom we have been privileged to observe at the crossroads of his growing manhood, is at the heart of the matter. The girl's genius told her that the naughty boy she found in the woods should be her model. A bigger boy would have been coarse and infinitely less amusing.'

'You are right. Youth has its own charm,' said M. Rognon, who had been deeply impressed by the successful way in which the photographs realised their intention to arouse the instincts!

'Ah, beauty is always a distraction,' agreed Sophie. 'Poor Marcel, what a delightful but frustrating enslavement the wretched girl subjected you to. But I suppose that on those hot afternoons in the summer house, when your work was done, she eventually, and with some gratitude, or sense of payment sacrificed her body to you?'

'Oh, no,' Marcel replied, laughing. 'She said that her morals would never let her have anything to do with a committed onanist.'

'So you retreated yet again with the Morrocan ladies into the bushes?' asked M. Rognon wearily, for it was getting long past his bedtime.

'*Naturellement, mon vieux,*' Marcel smiled urbanely, and continued, turning to the ladies, 'and I hope that you will not be offended by the remark, but when no suitable lady companion has been available, I have done so many times since.'

Bernadette took his hand, rising from her chair. '*Pas ce soir, cheri.*'

Chapter Four

Let it not be supposed that, while Bernadette and her entourage whirled in a delirium of wordly pleasures through the season, the household and its management suffered in any way. On the contrary—the discreet, and largely unseen, staff fairly revelled in the absence of their mistress on the occasions when her excursions provided the housekeeper with an opportunity to refurbish and re-organise the residence.

Apart from the secret garden room, the staff had complete access to the principal apartments. Naturally, the young maids tried every phial of costly perfume, nibbled at truffles and chocolates, and tried on and paraded in some of the exquisite couture garments that hung in every closet. It was a pleasure to work in such elegant, gilded surroundings, especially for those young members of the staff who had been recruited from humble backgrounds.

One such was Marietta who had been sent for six months previously. She had left her childhood home in Corte, the ancient stronghold high in the wild mountains of Corsica, and embarked for Nice in the packet boat from Ajaccio. She had had five francs in her pocket, some simple village clothes, and a sepia photograph of her hero and long-time admirer Etienne, who had been obliged to run away and join the

Foreign Legion after an unfortunate fracas between the opposing sides of a local vendetta.

At first Marietta was teased for her patois and her rough and ready table manners, but after submitting to the kindly but insistent guidance of her downstairs superiors she was welcomed into the bosom of the family and cherished for her bright willingness and bubbling charm. Her attractions were not unnoticed by Yves, the boot-boy and doorman. They had both come into close contact several times as Marietta dashed about the house carrying mop and pail, swerving round corners and falling into his arms. Naturally, Yves, a stocky shepherd boy from Megéve, had saved her from falling by embracing her manfully, and had felt the ample swell of her bosom underneath her starched apron.

They had rooms on the same corridor in the attic to which they had retired after a hard day of polishing and cleaning. It was a Sunday morning after a night of blessed sleep. Doves on the tiled roof took over from the exhausted nightingales who had serenaded the night and gently woke the young pair from their dreams. Yves was promised to a game of *pétanque* with a gang of youths in a nearby square, a few beers, and a stroll along the promenade. He washed carefully with a flannel at the basin, shaved, and pommaded his close-cropped hair, eyeing himself with some satisfaction in the mirror over the dressing table. As he whistled to himself he heard a strange murmuring sound coming from the room next door which was occupied by Marietta. He pressed his ear to the wall, listening intently, and smiled, thinking of the well shaped Corsican breasts which could be heaving under the cotton coverlet in the adjacent room. His hand strayed through the tear in his trouser pocket towards his prize piece of flesh and enclosed it firmly as he kissed the fading wallpaper. There was another little moan and then silence.

Lascivious thoughts rampaged through Yves' mind, and a strong tremor invaded his fifteen centimetres of frustrated sinew.

Suddenly the clock in the belfry outside struck the hour and a flock of doves took off in an agitated swarming flight across the gardens towards the lake. Reluctantly Yves released his grasp and waited a few moments for his tumescence to subside. He would be late for his *copins*, the game might start without him.

He left his room quietly and started down the corridor on tiptoe. As he passed Marietta's door he heard a short muffled cry, followed by a lower moaning sound such as had emanated previously. Yves looked nervously along the passage and listened attentively, but there were no other sounds in that part of the house. He pressed himself up to the door with an alert ear and waited. 'Ah, ah aaaaah,' came the sound again, followed by 'Etienne, *que je t'adore.*' Nothing could have prevented the next move by the aroused boy. He knelt and peeped through the keyhole, breathing as quietly as he could manage, jealousy pounding in his chest as he imagined the lovely Marietta enjoined with another member of the household staff, or even worse, an outsider whom she had smuggled into the villa. The interior of the room was somewhat dark as the blind was still drawn, but gradually Yves could make out the figure of the housemaid. She was sprawled indecorously, with her head hanging over the edge of the mattress nearest to the door, and her knees were drawn up and splayed outwards. In one of her hands she held what looked like a small picture frame which she kissed at intervals, and the other waved langorously to and fro with a crumpled hand written letter.

My God, he thought, *she is alone, and occupied with what I would have been doing if my mates were not waiting for me at the*

Cafe des Sports. Crouched as he was, with his eye pressed to the small aperture, he developed a little crick of the neck and cursed inwardly, but the pain naturally dispersed with the inevitable flow of blood to his groin that resulted from his act of voyeurism. His breathing came faster as he watched Marietta rub the little snapshot over her breasts, around each of the aureoles, and then down over her belly. Meanwhile his own right hand had instinctively travelled through the pocket hole, and his left began to caress his scrotum through the crotch of his trousers. *What a waste*, he thought. *Two lusty people, alone and unloved, making do with their own little improvisations, and just this door between us. Dare I enter? Would she scream out? Perhaps she would be ashamed of her actions. She would hardly like to think that I could tell the entire household what I have seen. Maybe she is so frustrated she will want me.* On and on the tormented youth deliberated until sheer lust drove him to rise to his feet. He took another furtive look around, turned the door knob and eased himself into the small, hot room where the dust hung sparkling in the air and the plump Corsican lay writhing on her simple cot.

Marietta heard no sound as Yves approached the bed stealthily. He thought that she must eventually notice the pounding in his chest that was echoing up fit to burst his eardrums, but still she squirmed in her passion, with the picture of her bandit lover now pressed between her legs. Yves's mind and body raced, taking in every small detail of the erotic vision spread before him, the dark hair of her forearms, and the even darker shade of the extravagant curls of her pubic down. Her thighs were well moulded and sinewy, leading towards fleshy knees and strong looking feet—arched in the ecstasy which held her enthralled.

Marietta's head turned savagely side to side as she massaged herself libidinously, the graven image of her lover becoming damp with her freely running juices, and the faded letter crumpled into her mouth to prevent her from calling out, hoarse and animal in her desire. Yves found that, without thinking, he had released his organ from where it was bursting against his button fly, and his two hands were tight around it, struggling to contain the savage movement that pulsated through its length.

The maid arched her back upwards as she approached her self-induced climax, causing her head and neck to slide further over the side of the bed. Now her fingers were inside her raging parts, the photograph thrown aside, and her other hand roved wildly around her breasts and over her throat. Her eyes were closed in her delirium. She did not see Yves, behind her, his feet wide apart, his mouth open in a silent scream. He jerked his hands into action—as one grasped his scrotum, the other raced up and down the length of his swollen growth, turning the fine membrane to fire as it passed rapidly over his bursting glans and produced a great spurt of semen which travelled in an arc and laced across her breasts as she lay breathless from her endeavours. Her hands passed over the viscous liquid. It was unnoticed. She thought it was her own perspiration. Yves stood behind her and squeezed the last few drops of his offering from his stem. Her eyes opened dreamily. 'Etienne,' she murmured, as a glistening pearl fell on her cheek.

'*Mais non, cheri, c'est moi,*' said the thick-set bootboy. '*C'est moi.*'

The few syllables, so quietly expressed, seemed to go winging round the small hot room while all physical action seemed to have been stilled artificially like a freeze-frame in classic cinema photography. The doves on the roof outside had resumed their burblings and cooings, and from far away, near the Corniche, came the sound of the Blue Train from

82

Paris arriving at the Riviera. There was also a faint sound of gravel being raked on the path below as the gardener began his toil.

Such sounds were imprinted in the brain cells of the erotically aroused pair, and locked in their memories, as were other jumbled traces from their past. Fragments of the mosaic of their sensuous lives came teemingly alive in those extraordinary moments of mutual self discovery; excitement, shame, allure and abandon, deliciously, but disturbingly weaving their spell in the small space between the two pairs of staring, fascinated eyes.

Yves remembered, still with an awesome sense of regret, the terrifying episode whn his peasant mother came across him at the climax of a furtive, but highly lascivious, exploration into self-abuse in the woodshed. Whirling round when he was disturbed by her entry, his juices had slashed across her black apron, a stain on his unconscious memory for ever.

Marietta recalled the fury of her lumbering, heavy jowled father when he discovered her locked in conjugation with her reckless Etienne in the loft of the barn, her screams as he beat the pair with the handle of a pitchfork, and the squawking of the hens who flew agitated around the tempestuous scene.

The silence in the room was a microcosm of the brooding quiet of Marietta's household after the discovery, her anguish when Etienne was obliged to run away to enlist, and her fantasies which took her, in her mind, roving across the inhospitable deserts of the Sahara in search of the dust-covered lonely soldier she loved. But this highly charged moment was not destined to revive either a sense of grief or of shame. Both expressions slowly turned to a shy smile, a creased grin, then silent mirth which shook the pair until Yves dropped to his knees, opened his mouth wide and fell on Marietta's lips and neck with a showering rain of burning kisses which exorcised any feeling of degradation or self reproach.

As his tongue burrowed freely into her mouth she stretched her arms across his broad back, digging her nails through the thin fabric of his shirt to the flesh. It was a glorious moment of abandon.

'Why, *cheri*, what a laugh, what fun,' Yves groaned as he fumbled at her chemise. 'It's so much better together, don't you think?'

'Hello, young man, why didn't you come sooner?' Marietta gurgled, half smothered by his fiery kisses.

'The real thing is always best, *n'est-ce pas?*' the boy managed to breathe into her ear as he drew up the garment to reveal the whole of her handsome body. 'What's all this? Doing it with a photo, when there's a lusty young man like me next door?'

'Ah,' she whispered, 'you are so like him, it's wonderful. You kiss me the same way. You are greedy. You boys are all the same.'

'You're right,' he exclaimed as he tore off his shirt, then his trousers and underwear, kicking his boots into a corner. He jumped on the bed, straddling between her thighs, his arms akimbo. 'Not bad, *hien*? And you're a bit of alright yourself, little darling. Isn't this great fun?'

Yves swung his hips from side to side, bending his knees so that his impressive erection came nearer to her belly, then took her breasts in his hairy fists, kneading them like his mother used to knead the bread dough in the old farmhouse at Megeve.

'What a horny boy,' Marietta cried, 'and what a tool. Oh *mon Dieu*, I need one badly. Give it to me.'

'Here you go, then,' Yves grunted as he pushed her knees wide and back, thrusting as he did so at her streaming fount with his thick stem, entering her in one decisive rapacious movement as she was so lubricated from her orgasmic pleasure at the prolonged sight of the powerful Corsican.

The tip of his anguished organ penetrated to the very depths of her willing body, stimulating her to raise her buttocks from the mattress, and to lift even Yves's body with hers in the process. He felt he was floating in air as he pulsated into her, filling her with his foam as she came to a frenetic climax, gasping through clenched teeth.

'Ah, aaah, go on, go on. I can't get enough, more . . . give me more.'

'I will, I will,' he replied enthusiastically, continuing his rhythmic pumping at her pelvis, his hands now tangling fiercely with Marietta's polished raven black hair.

Her legs rose up until her feet touched the back rail of the bed, allowing him greater access and stimulating him to still more powerful thrusts which caused the entire piece of furniture to creak and groan as it moved sympathetically in gear with his strong and relentless action.

It had been a long time since Yves had enjoyed a girl in this manner. Recently there had been a few stolen moments of passion with an attractive little *vendeuse* whom he had met in a public park during her lunch hour. But, exciting as it had been, making love standing up in darkened doorways, or in the bushes of her family's back garden, there was no comparison to this particular wonderful adventure in the total privacy of Marietta's room, centered on a pliant, aggressively sensuous young woman. He could not believe his good fortune, and he worked hard to prove to himself that he deserved it.

At that time of young life some studs are capable of a continuous chain of ejaculations, the one provoking the next, and so on, until the female partner is so besotted and dying of love, or until her private parts are so bruised by the very force of the sexual act she adores, that she is obliged to beg for release from the pleasure that is unfortunately destined to become less of a transport as the discomfort grows. But, as the reader knows, love is a drug, the strongest addiction to inflict itself on the human mind and body. So it was with Yves and Marietta that Sunday morning as crowds poured into Mass and a gang of youths played *petanque* and drank beer, wondering what their friend had got up to.

When the first interval in their lovemaking came, Marietta rolled over on to her belly, exhausted, but tingling with satiation, while her gratified boy lay on his back smoking a cigarette. His free hand strayed over her back and down the crack between her plump buttocks. Her part was wet and heated to the touch, and the curly tendrils of her pubis lay dank and limp.

'Thank you,' he said, profoundly moved by the experience. 'You're a real sport.'

'You're welcome,' Marietta said, in a low, tired voice. 'Anytime.'

Yves was full of a sense of power. Not only had he had the nerve and the courage to enter her room, but he had found the means to overcome their joint shame at the ridiculous situation they were in. His flaccid penis stirred back halfway to life, in a tumescence which filled him with wonder. *What a greedy little beast*, he thought with some detachment, watching it grow. He mused that if he regarded it with the indifference a man would view another's organ, that it might come to rest of its own accord. Consequently, he shut his eyes and tried to blot his surroundings from his mind. He thought of his old school, the village priest who had prepared him for confirmation, his grandparents who still lived off the fruits of their orchard, their vines and olives.

Marietta's deep breathing interrupted his reverie somewhat, so he rose and went towards the window and peered through the small gap between the blind and the frame, relating the view of the gardens below to the beloved landscape of the Alps from whence he came. But to no avail. The previously half-limp protuberance had swollen once again to its full size, and the tulip-shaped tip was fully extended from its sheath of protective skin, and rested proudly on the window ledge. A faint steam came off it. He thought of a railway engine standing in a station, its journey about to recommence. The image provoked yet a further stirring in the object, a tightening in his loins, and the hair on his legs bristled as he contemplated once more entering Marietta with the now fully gorged machine.

He turned towards the bed and called low to the sprawling girl. 'Look here, darling, little Jo Jo wants to play again. Can he come in?'

Marietta rolled over, an indulgent smile on her lips. She thought that if the morning's activities could be related to a play in the theatre, act one and two had passed thrillingly by already, and that perhaps she could just manage, lazily, act three, if the author promised to be gentle. '*Quel garçon*,' she said admiringly. '*Allez doucement*.' With that she gathered the pillows underneath her breasts and belly, curving her body into a ball, with her weight on her elbows and knees. Then she clasped her hands behind her neck and waited, prone for him to approach.

Yves slowly climbed on the bed and gazed at the proffered opening. Her orifice pouted towards him, the fleshy lips a shade of dark pink. As if by its own will, the boy's organ pressed against it and slid to its hilt in one easy gesture. Recumbent in the warm innermost recess it lay throbbing as Yves caressed Marietta's spine with long slow touches or as he felt around her neat belly, lightly tickling and soothing. He began with slow strokes, sliding his penis out completely, then re-inserting it, delicately, breathing in time with the motion of his pelvis.

Marietta's body was completely still, though the muscles of her interior clutched his member in a spasm each time it was introduced to the greatest depth. Her sighs came deeper with each entry. Sometimes Yves held his replete offering still for as long as a minute, savouring the perfect conjugation to the full, feeling the throb of his submerged veins against the muscled walls of her cavity.

'Do not move,' she pleaded, when his rhythm grew faster, 'or I shall die—stay still. I can feel your thing speaking to me.' Then she twitched an urgent message to him, clamping and unclamping in thrilling vibratory fashion, to which he replied in kind.

They played this delicious morse code game in silence until Yves came to the fulcrum of his desire. Arching his back, he thrust to his utmost and in one long worshipping and climactic release ejected waves of his pent-up fluids towards her womb.

She felt his emission strike into her as rollers crash on to the shore, great breakers gradually giving way to lighter undulations and finally the ebb and flow of riplets and eventual stillness. Stranded thus, on a far-flung beach, with her new lover slumped over her body in an attitude of utter drained satisfaction, so she then enraptured him with her last outpouring, gushing her hot juices over his ensnared genitals, but her mouth was pressed to the small photograph deep in the pillows and she and Etienne walked in the sunset towards a gilded oasis.

* * *

Lisette, the little *vendeuse* who had been Yves's favourite until he came across Marietta in such a fortuitous manner, was puzzled that he had made no effort to meet her recently. She knew that his work at Bernadette's residence kept him busy, but he had always managed to sneak away from the house on some pretence; a little shopping for the cook, for instance, or a free evening suddenly awarded if the vicomtesse and her guests went out to dine and the housekeeper happened to be in a good mood. *It's all very well for him*, she pouted, *mixing with the nobs and gentry. No wonder he's lost interest in me.* Once she walked to the residence and daringly rang the bell, but a thickset, attractive Corsican looking girl, wearing a fetching uniform, shooed her away, pretending she could not understand Provençale dialect.

Lisette found the boys of her *quartier* dull and uninspiring. All they wanted to do was to race along the promenade on their bicycles, play *boules, pétanque,* and drink for hours in the dozens of male dominated bars. Then they expected a girl to come running at a wink or a squeeze. This was not for her, she decided. Yves was different. At least he sat with her sometimes over an ice cream or a crème de cassis and amused her with stories about his rich employer and her exotic circle of friends, before going hand in hand with her to some discreet spot to kiss, cuddle and once or twice make furtive love. She needed a small apartment of her own, she thought, a cosy nest where Yves could really show her what he was worth. *Mais, hélas*, that was the situation, she pondered morosely as she sat in the *jardin publique* nibbling a bar of chocolate.

A party of convent school girls walked past, chattering gaily, under the watchful eye of a sister who wore a vast headdress whose starched outrig blew in the breeze like the sails of a galleon. *At least I have won my freedom from school,*

Lisette thought, recalling the long days of study and devotion with the good nuns, and the hot nights when she secreted romantic novels to her bed and learned from the printed page what love was all about.

The first necessity was a handsome man, then an attractive wardrobe of silks and satins, a private allowance, a sports car, an elegant apartment designed by an expert interior decorator, and *voilà*, a girl like her could become as enchanting a seductress as anything she had come across in the forbidden novels.

Such a handsome gigolo was lounging on a park bench, looking at the passing schoolgirls with a lascivious eye, wishing the breeze would make the nun in charge take off like a boat leaving the harbour so that he might inspect the young things closer. But they passed, and his attention was drawn to the slight girl sitting on the next bench. Waif like, but charming, he thought. Not much bust under her skimpy voile dress, but a good skin, with the bloom of childhood still on it, long golden tresses bound up with a blue ribbon, and the slimmest, most dainty pair of ankles he had seen in a long while. Sixteen, seventeen? he wondered. A virgin certainly. A chicken on a perch, waiting to be pushed off into the adult world.

Lisette took a small mouthful of her delicious bar, and he watched her roll her pale tongue over her lips which were devoid of make-up. Occasionally she raised a hand to restrain her locks from moving in the breeze, crossed and uncrossed her silk stockinged legs in a most provoking manner, or threw her head back in an insouciant fashion. She teased the watching gigolo, unwittingly, to such a point that he drew himself to his full height and sauntered along the path and came to rest, almost insolently, and certainly too closely, by her crossed ankles. He doffed his fedora, lightly brushing his waxed moustache, shot his cuffs, displaying a pair of over-large gold links, and addressed her.

'*Bonjour*, mademoiselle, I have been watching you from a distance. I must say I find you absolutely charming. My name is Raoul Sebastian de Villiers, and I am your admirer for life.' He bent low and kissed her hand, searching into her eyes with a vivid intensity which the young girl found strangely disturbing. 'I thought, at first, that I knew you . . . you know, perhaps the daughter or a niece of an acquaintance, but I confess I was wrong. I now know that I have never seen such an exquisite flower.' Lisette blushed to the roots of her golden tresses, but her body posture remained the same, frozen in its attitude as a baby frog might be when fixed menacingly by a snake. 'Are you alone?' he enquired, thinking that a mama or papa could be in the vicinity. 'Or maybe, waiting for a companion?'

'I was hoping to meet a friend,' Lisette replied, 'but I think now it is too late and I should be going home.' She stood up, still flushed, with her eyes downcast, delighted with the stranger's compliments and trembling within from the pleasure they evoked.

'*Mais non*,' Raoul exclaimed. 'You and I are both as free as the wind, it seems. Neither of us has any appointment. Will you be my guest at the little brasserie over there? We could have a glass of tea, or an ice cream, perhaps. I am a stranger in these parts. I come from Paris you know. Come,' he said gaily, taking her arm and leading her to the park gates. 'I feel we are old friends already.'

'But, monsieur,' she remonstrated, 'it is nearly time for dinner, my parents will be expecting me.'

'Surely not on such a fine evening. They must know that young people are disposed to amuse themselves. Come, let us have fun, life is far too short,' the eager gigolo replied, hardly

91

able to believe his luck as he steered Lisette across the boulevard towards the brasserie, dodging between the Bugattis, Fords and Chevrolets full of the *jeunes dorés* who had flocked to the Riviera that summer for fun and romance.

'Waiter,' Raoul called, 'bring your best fruit sundae, with lashings of cream and syrup for this enchanting young creature, and I'll have a whisky soda please.' The pair were seated in a booth at the rear of the premises. The lighting was dim and discreet, emboldening him to reach across the table and take her small hand in his. 'How kind you are to keep me company. I shall not disappoint you,' he proffered, squeezing her slim fingers. Then he proceeded to entertain the young lady in a very amusing way. He spoke of the latest plays and operas, the fashionable magazines, his chateau on the Loire which, by the way, was purely imaginary, and his vast collection of friends, rich internationals who plied their way between London, New York and Venice at will, without thought of expense.

Lisette was dazzled by the raconteur. A gold tooth shone like a beacon through his attractive lips and he exuded an aura of costly perfume which mingled with the odour of his black Russian cigarettes which he smoked in a long ivory holder. She smiled when Raoul edged his chair further round the table to a point where he could place a beringed hand on her knee. He patted her solicitously as he asked whether she was enjoying her dessert, but he allowed it to remain there, applying a delicate though invasive pressure to her flesh.

'*C'est bon, merci,*' she replied, her lashes lowered.

Raoul bent forward. He could see through the thin fabric of her voile summer dress that underneath she wore a camisole of the sheerest silk which did not entirely obscure the presence of her small nipples. He noted also the delicate structure of her collar bones and the faint child-like down which covered part of her cheeks. Her nose was tiny and uptilted. It reminded him of the beak of a small caged bird, and delighted him when in reply to one of his jokes she wriggled it so prettily. Slowly he stole an arm round her waist as he enlarged on some story, revelling in the elfin girth he found there, and higher up, the enticing structure of her ribs.

None of these attentions were lost on Lisette. She crossed her legs firmly in an effort to reduce the inflammation that began to be aroused in her parts, and hoped the enlargement that she felt in her nipples could not be detected. Of course, the highly experienced Raoul, as susceptible to the nuances of a young female's sexual responses as litmus paper is to certain chemicals, recognised every single shade of Lisette's burgeoning arousal and calculated gratefully that he had found himself an enchanting new little friend of exactly the right calibre for his needs.

He recalled the divine Paulette, a second cousin twice removed, with the face of an angel and a wicked way with a whip. And Bertice who sang in the choir, wrote childish verses and still played with dolls houses, but knew how to handle his requirements. 'How old are you, *cher enfant*,' he suddenly asked.

'Sixteen, monsieur,' Lisette answered firmly. 'It was my birthday last week.'

'In that case, may I buy you a small present? Meet me here tomorrow for lunch at one o'clock, and I shall give it to you.'

They rose to leave. He bent down and offered a cheek for her to kiss. Her light breath and the faint brush of her eyelashes devastated him. '*A toute à l'heure, mon enfant*,' he whispered in her ear as she turned to leave. Raoul watched as the girl went skipping along the street. He trembled a little, wrung his sweating palms, and walked out of the café with his fedora placed over his crotch to disguise the growing bulge.

He slept fitfully that night in his hotel suite. It should be explained that he could afford such luxurious accommodation on account of his principal earnings, which came from the rich, lonely ladies who were his mainstay. Financial necessity aroused his libido sufficiently to pay a select few the proper attentions, though his own personal erotic fantasies were of a different order.

His sleep was interrupted frequently by visions of the birdlike girl, with the consequence that he spent most of the night in an erect state; waking up was painful and full of frustration. None of the visions had been of naked appearance, of course. His proclivities demanded accoutrements belonging to childhood and adolescence. Hence Lisette had come to him in the guise of a scantily clad young peasant, bearing garlands, but armed with a fearsome forked stick, a brazen hoyden of a chit wielding a tennis racquet, and a fearless pubescent horsewoman carrying a riding crop.

As he shaved and bathed, occasionally massaging his private parts in anticipation of the afternoon's events, he pondered over the possibilities of play with the girl.

On leaving the hotel he left strict instructions concerning a couple of bottles of champagne which were to be placed in his room at precisely half past two in the afternoon and made off for a certain department store in the main shopping street. After much pondering he purchased a navy blue gym slip, a white blouse, some thick woollen stockings, a straw boater and a hockey stick, requiring that they be sent round immediately to his hotel. From thence he proceeded to the brasserie, stopping off after an inspired and inventive consideration, at a sweet shop where he bought a large red lollipop and a stick of liquorice.

Lisette was waiting for him in the cafe. She wore a becoming blouse of broderie anglaise with a neat cameo at her throat, a short skirt of swishing taffeta, and a pair of bright orange pumps. The whole effect was one of wholesome and innocent youth. Raoul was, naturally, delighted.

'*Bonjour, cherie*', he murmured. 'Your present has unfortunately been despatched to my hotel, but no matter, we shall retrieve it later.'

Their lunch was gay and relaxing. Lisette blossomed under the attentions of her host. They sat at a table outside, Raoul waving to his many acquaintances. Lisette felt very much part of his expensive world and not unable to order some quite expensive dishes. The wine and conversation flowed easily. A casual onlooker might have thought that a generous uncle was treating his niece to a last jolly meal before she went back to boarding school, or something equally tedious.

Scampi, frites, salads, fruits, cheeses and puddings came in succession to the table. The elegant ruffian watched as Lisette demolished every plateful. *She will have fire in her belly*, he thought, *or at least she will be beholden to me after I've paid such an enormous bill*. There was a small distraction as another *jeune fille*, of similar age to his companion, strolled into view on the arm of a lady who must have been her grandmother. The elderly lady carried a lorgnette and a parasol. She looked forbidding enough for Raoul to concentrate his attentions on Lisette who, after all, was being properly primed.

Lunch over, they strolled along the promenade arm in arm. The girl could not think she had ever been happier. Here she was in the company of a rich, handsome man, so like the characters in her favoured novels. *Never mind his age*, she thought, *he adores me, and soon I shall be leaving childhood behind*. Arriving at the hotel, he bought a single rose from the girl at the florist, rang for the lift and courteously bowed his companion into it when it came.

Lisette was much impressed with the suite of rooms. She

ran about excitedly, looking out of the windows admiring the extensive views, playing with the ornate bath taps and so on, much to Raoul's pleasure, as he opened the champagne which had been left on ice by the considerate management.

'Where is my present,' she demanded eagerly, 'I must have it, oh do get it, I can't wait.'

Raoul opened a closet and threw a large box on to the bed and then went to stretch out on a *chaise longue*. 'Go on. open it,' he ordered. Lisette's face was a picture of misery when she saw what the richly wrapped box contained.

'But, monsieur, I have left school,' she whimpered, 'what do I need these clothes for?'

'My child, put them on. Your youth will never leave you. May you always look as you do today. The charm and innocence that you exude moves me greatly. I cry to see the childlike sincerity that inhabits you. Please, oh please, put on the clothes. I need an image in my mind to remind me of the lovely times we have spent together.'

Tears ran down the girl's face. It was ridiculous of him to think of her in these terms when she had been prepared to throw off her clothes and dive into his bed, satisfying him in any way he wished.

'Besides, if you will do me this small favour, there is more to come,' he said, opening a little leather box in which she could see reposed an antique pendant of considerable worth, studded as it was with rubies and diamonds.

So the pantomime began. Elegantly disposed on the sofa, Raoul watched as Lisette disrobed.

'No, darling, please take everything off before you put on anything new,' he interjected.

There was for him a glorious moment when the child, backed by the light from the window, stood in all her natural glory, bony and underdeveloped. She was awkward and gauche, rather like a fledgling sparrow, certainly not the promising sophisticate she imagined herself to be.

'Have some champagne,' he urged, and she drank gratefully.

If I must earn this pendant, she thought, *so I will*. She drew on the thick woollen stockings first, and posed with a foot on the divan; then the pumps, and the gym slip, giggling from the effect of the wine.

'Bravo,' he cried. 'What a comedienne you are. Have another glass.' She bent down to tie her new shoe laces and one of her thin breasts fell out of the top of the slip. 'Hurrah,' he yelled.

Lisette had begun to get his measure. She poured herself another hefty glass and posed dramatically with the straw hat askew on her head. 'Hello, old boy,' she yelled, 'fancy a game of hockey?'

Raoul fell off the *chaise longue* in his delirium of excitement. 'Perfect, what an actress. Get the stick. Wave it about. Like a tomboy. Oh you little treasure, I adore you.'

Lisette knocked back the wine. It was going to her head. 'How mean you were, getting all this stuff.'

'Yes, wasn't I mean. I'm a naughty old uncle aren't I? Stupid and silly. I deserve a good beating, don't I?' With that he tore his trousers down to his knees and bent over the back of a chair, meantime handing her the lollipop. 'Go on, give me what I deserve, and don't spare me.'

Lisette took her cue and landed a neat blow to his backside with the stick. 'Yes, you're right. You're a mean old so and so. Fancy giving me this rubbish.' And she hit him again, but this time much harder.

'Oh, oh,' he cried, watching as his erection grew and passed through the staves of the back of the chair. Drops of seminal fluid appeared at the tip of his organ, oozing out each time she landed a blow. She gazed at this, sucking on the lolly.

'Harder, harder, I truly am sorry, punish me as you wish,' he shouted.

Lisette ran for the hair brush on his dressing table. 'Do you want the flat side or the bristles?' she squealed.

'As you wish, but get on with it,' he urged, passing her the stick of liquorice.

Lisette had not failed to notice the agitated state of his throbbing member and the glistening drops which emerged from it, and if one instinct told her that she wanted close contact with it, in the normal intimate way that happens between the sexes, then another announced that perhaps the occasion was inappropriate.

Her spanking with the brush resulted in the desired effect. With a great deal of groaning and moaning the victim of her punishment heaved, suddenly, into an awesome orgasmic eruption, shedding a large amount of his liquids over the dainty *petit point* of the embroidered chair cover. She was spellbound by its opaque pearly colour, never having seen the male sperm by daylight before. If the reader cares to remember. Young Yves had done most of his courting by night in the dark of shop doorways.

'I adore you,' Raoul said. 'Take that leather case. The pendant is an heirloom of my ancient family. Never give it away or lose it.'

Lisette thanked him gracefully, changed back into her normal clothes, and after some desultory small talk, left him lying exhausted on the bed, and walked out of the hotel. *Of course I shall sell it*, she thought. *It may buy me the lease of a small flat.*

Raoul staggered to the window and watched her disappear at the end of the boulevard. 'Don't get excited, darling,' he grimaced silently, 'it's paste.'

Chapter Five

The long-awaited opening night of the Ballet was a triumphant, glittering affair whose brilliance surpassed anything that had ever been seen before on the Riviera. Those lucky enough, or rich enough to gain tickets for the prestigious event, began to arrive in their glossy cars or strolled from the nearby grand hotels in the early evening. There took place a promenade of such elegance and an ostentatious display of wealth that outshone any previous social event of the Principality.

Charles strolled through the formal gardens of the Casino in proud possession of Edith, the charleston dancer from Chicago, whom he had ravished that morning in the close confines of a cabin in the sleek yacht her rich father had bought her for a birthday present. How suitable it was, he thought, not only having a girl friend rich enough to bring him a handsome sale, but also one who could provide him with a location in which he could enjoy her body. What a body it had proved to be, he thought with some relish. Raised on wholesome American food and subjected to the rigours of tennis, swimming, and gymnastics, Edith had emerged from High School and College the very image of a modern woman, with a body of such bone crushing strength that even the redoutable Charles had shrunk from the fiercest of the muscular paroxysms that she suffered in the extremes of her passion.

Even now, hours later, as they strolled arm in arm, watching the arrival of the brilliant throng, his knees trembled and his legs shook. He wondered if he was entering the first stage of a nervous eurasthenia induced by Edith's onslaught on his sexual capacities. He found an unoccupied bench and was grateful for the rest it provided. However, Edith squeezed herself so closely to his battered body that he winced. The love bites and scratches that she had implanted with such energy all over his frame were aggravated by this close contact. He closed his eyes and racked his brain trying to work out a good enough excuse to avoid her further attentions that night; while Edith, fondly thinking that his attitude of repose indicated the stirrings of fond love in Charles's breast, happily inspected the passing crowd.

Bernadette and Sophie, escorted by Marcel and a merchant banker, a friend of Sophie's with an unpronouncable Greek name, drew gasps from the onlookers.

Marcel's creation, in its evocation of aspects of the designs of M. Bakst, was especially suitable for wearing to the gala. Swathes of amethyst-coloured silk draped Bernadette's trim body down to a hobbled hem. The whole dress was encrusted with beading and semi-precious stones of darker purple, enlivened by shimmering clusters of pearls. On her head she wore a toque constructed from silver lamé and topped by nodding plumes of peacock feathers. The same feathers covered her shoes entirely and also the small clutch bag she carried.

Her *maquillage* was heavily applied and just as heavily derived from observation of the techniques used to enhance the looks of certain Hollywood stars. The year before,

Bernadette had favoured Mary Pickford, the darling of the silver screen, but this year, both in order to match his creation and also to be more in keeping with her age, Marcel had discreetly suggested something more in the style of the vampish Theda Bara. This was how her lips had come to be painted with a lipstick of dark cerise and her eyelids a glossy magenta. The contrast between these fetching colours and her clown-white face created a stunning effect, as did the langour of the gait which she had been practising for weeks, and the clouds of intense musky perfume which trailed after her.

Sophie was no less of a sensation. Her dress was in the grand manner, designed by a Parisian master whose collection for the season had been inspired by the paintings of Veronese. Making absolutely no concessions to the Jazz Age, the clever couturier had created a dress whose simple grandure made Sophie stand out in the crowd. The folds of the gown started above the bosom, falling in a wide arc, echoed by a long train behind. The plain, but rich taffeta was of a pale gold colour, undecorated save for a corsage of yellow rosebuds. Sophie wore at her throat a band of topaz set in gold, each stone the size of a walnut. They came from the collection of the wealthy nabob and were worth a prince's ransom.

The effect was not lost on the Greek millionaire who towered over Sophie's head, lost in admiration for the sleek chignon which was poised above her slim neck, pinned in placed by a matching topaz of enormous size. Earlier that afternoon he had spent a half hour nibbling the ears that were decorated by minute versions of the same stone, and he was looking forward to the possibility of this dalliance continuing, to better effect, after the performance.

And so, the parade of affluence and envy went on its

inexorable way. The rich, the famous and the notorious, vied pleasantly with each other for the attention of the crowd.

The cocktail bars and brasseries of the *quartier* were filled to the brim with the gay crowd of socialites masquerading as theatregoers. Assignations were made, pleasantries exchanged, and old enemies snubbed, as the monied classes of the Cote d'Azur, le Tout Paris and the visiting worthies assembled for the artistic zenith of the Season.

Angelique, the elfin chocolate salesgirl who so recently had occupied Charles's mind and body was earning a few extra francs as a cloakroom assistant. The work was hard and she was wondering how much money would be left from her pay after she had paid her autobus fares; it all depended on the generosity of the theatregoers in their tipping. She had never seen such luxuriant fabrics, or handled such expensive cloaks and furs. One of the items alone would have cost her a year's earnings at the chocolate shop, but she smiled and bobbed prettily as the ladies bestowed their belongings into her charge, secure in an instinctive feeling that in her own little bombasine frock she cut a better figure than most of them.

Also, the most romantic meeting had occurred the previous day, an event that brought a smile to her face when she recollected her thoughts. Whilst waiting for Charles in a little cafe they used for their rendezvous (of course he did not arrive, he was in the throes of his dalliance with Edith), a slant-eyed Mongolian looking boy, who was in fact a new member of the *corps de ballet* of the Ballets Russes had planted himself at her table, and although he spoke not a word of French, and Angelique's Russian was non-existent, he had managed to make it quite plain that he desired to possess her body and the sooner the better.

The performance by the renowned troupe was a triumph. Ovation after ovation rang out in the gilded theatre as the company took their well-deserved bows. They had completely seduced their audience with a display of bravura and athleticism in the *grand divertissements* where they flew through the air in soaring jumps and whirled on their toes at incredible speed. The finale was a magical evocation of the savage dancing of primitive Tartars set to music from a great Russian opera, with a great body of singers pressed into the wings and every available space, doubling the sound of the large orchestra.

Dhokouminsky, the principal dancer of the company, the gentleman whom Sophie had presented with the over-sized emerald for sale in the fund-raising auction, had played the central role in this final act. What bounds and leaps, what acrobatic feats, the dynamic dancer had achieved; how cruel had been his domination of the tribe of warriors and his ruthless exploitation of the Persian slave girls in their captivity.

Sophie shivered when he cracked the long whip he brandished over his head, galvanising the dancers into frenzied action. She took a peep at the back page of the souvenir brochure, trembling in her excitement. Surely, she thought, at a later programme, there must be a different finishing ballet in which Dhokouminsky, if he danced the leading part, would have a less taxing role. For she imagined that after such feats he would be uninclined to, or incapable of, further achievements in her bedroom.

The house rose and moved in a body to the Cafe de Paris for the resplendent reception provided by Borzdoff in anticipation of the large amounts of cash he hoped to raise at the auction. As the dancers entered the guests cheered and raised their glasses, only to be pushed aside as the artistes made a headlong dash for the buffet. Paying no heed to their social betters, they fell on the food like hungry Siberian wolves, spitting chicken bones and cherry stones on to the rich carpet, devouring in such vast quantities that a paying guest was lucky if he found a celery stalk. Dhokouminsky ate so many pieces of chicken he must have consumed the equivalent of two and a half birds, so great was his hunger after his manic and thrilling performance.

Sophie extricated a waiter from the throng and pressed a large note into his hand. The greasy lackey promptly produced a magnum of champagne for the thirsty warrior who, being of peasant stock, began to drink from the bottle, but Sophie managed, by pouring for him an endless succession of glasses, to keep some sense of decorum. Wiping his mouth on his sleeve and burping with satisfaction, the great dancer gazed at this helpful woman who stared into his eyes so imploringly and with such devotion. Being an experienced artiste he realised that here was a balletomane who was intent on making his season in Monte Carlo not only a profitable one but a pleasurable one as well.

Angelique made for the autocar stop in an elated condition, her purse bulging with francs from the generous ladies of the audience. She also had in her possession a diamond clasp which had fallen from the collar of an unfortunate theatregoer's opera cloak.

Pondering what to buy as a present for Charles with the money she would realise from its sale, with a small stabbing sensation in her little rib-cage she came across him, sprawled at a table outside a restaurant, his hands clasped together in the grip of a well-covered female.

Angelique watched as the thick-set girl immodestly rained kisses on his fingers and made tiny nibbling bites on his wrists. Charles looking up wearily, his bloodshot eyes reflecting none of the lust which was so obviously welling up again in the Charleston expert, and unable to focus enough to recognise the girl who had pleasured him so greatly in the attic over the patisserie. But had Angelique known what was in his heart at that moment she would have been less desolated than she seemed to be.

The exhausted lover, if not exactly pining for the bird-like girl for he had never entertained a real affection for her, was suffering a little nostalgia for the sun drenched afternoons he had spent with her and the canary, longing, perhaps, to satisfy someone over whom he had sexual dominance—a girl less aggressively active than the hefty nymph from Chicago. However, this was lost on Angelique, and as she boarded the bus she thought what fun it would be to spend the money instead on a good meal or two for the hungry looking boy of Mongolian appearance who had riveted her attention in the cafe the day before.

After the opening night party the great ballerina Vera Lidova reclined her elegant limbs on a sofa in the Hotel de Paris where she had repaired with Vossoudossoulos, the Greek millionaire who had been abandoned by Sophie now that the lady was so inspired by Dhokoudovsky.

The renowned dancer had the ability, from much experience, to smell out money the moment she entered a room. Making an imperious entrance, draped in black panne velvet, after the hungry hordes of the *corps de ballet* had

105

devastated the buffet, she had made a direct line towards the affluent banker. Like a pouncing leopard she flashed her eyes over his tall figure in its impeccable London-tailored suit, and rightly guessed that she had found herself a generous provider. She declined his offer of champagne. 'Nothing, thank you,' she said. 'I must to stay thin,' and threw a slim leg into the air, arching her foot in the most incredible manner.

'Perhaps,' Vossoudossoulos murmured, 'we could talk more cosily in the hotel. I am your greatest admirer. Your performance of the Dying Swan was a work of art.'

'That,' she retorted. 'That is old fashioned rubbish. I am much good in the avant-garde works. Come darling, we go.'

The banker was overwhelmed by her vibrant presence. She was incapable of making an ugly move or an inelegant gesture.

To his surprise, now they were in the hotel, she ordered Dom Perignon and oysters, which she devoured with vast quantities of bread and butter. As she ate, she told him amusing anecdotes and scandals, making wickedly accurate impersonations of rival ballerinas, illustrating her stories with graceful arabesques of her bejewelled hands in the air. Next she consumed a large steak tartare and a bowl of mixed salad with another baguette and a bottle of Macon. Several pastries later, she declared herself replete.

'Let us to your suite go, darling,' she ogled. 'I must stretch out my poor tired legs'. On their way to the lift she grabbed a passing waiter with an order for coffee, cognac, *petit fours* and a selection of *glacé* fruits.

Inside the door she kicked off her pumps and threw herself on the divan. Her legs went up in the air vertically, and she wiggled her aching toes in squirming pleasure. The banker needed no encouragement to massage the feet which had been so tortured by her pointe shoes.

The waiter arrived with a trolley as the Greek was removing her silk stockings, her legs still pointing skywards. Without a second glance, for he was well used to the outlandishness of these Russian visitors, he left in haste in order to resume a little game he was intermittently enjoying with a maid in the pantry.

Vera fished in her capacious handbag for a bottle of olive oil, the panacea of her aches and pains, and lying down on a polar bear rug instructed her new friend to apply it to her legs.

To make the task easier he took off first his jacket and then his waistcoat, and to save her dress getting soiled Vera pulled it over her head and threw it carelessly into the fireplace. He will buy me many new ones tomorrow, she determined. As the banker rubbed gently at her ankles, she sighed with satisfaction, her head propped comfortably on that of the polar bear.

'More,' she cried. 'Much hard. My legs are not of glass, you know. They will not break, darling.'

He knelt to the task with renewed energy, applying more oil to her calves and knees. The stimulation of her finely honed muscles began to work its spell on him. She became aware of the swelling that took place in his crotch.

'Marvellous,' she murmured, lowering her long false lashes, 'you are doing a much wonderful job.' He broke off to bring her some refreshments and poured her a large glass of cognac.

She lay on the white fur purring like a cat when he resumed the massage, working with sensitive deliberation on the inside of her thighs, and turned over at his suggestion in order for him to work his way along from behind her knees to her buttocks. She lay most contentedly with her mouth almost in the dish of *glacé* fruits, gulping the brandy at frequent intervals, while he persevered in this manner, revelling in the comfort of the situation. Of course she knew that with her startling good looks and dramatic interpretations the season would automatically bring her many admirers, men who would vie with each other for her attentions, wine and dine her and present her with fabulous jewels. This was the norm, and it was her custom to take all their gifts and attentions and then depart with the man of her choice to her next engagement if he was sufficiently enamoured to trail her across Europe.

She couldn't believe her good luck that the very opening night had produced a handsome rich man completely to her taste, a person who would be a perfect and generous companion. She had been protected in this way by many lovers, but this Greek fascinated her more than most. He was dark and suave, stubbly in an arousing masculine way, and oh, she thought, such strong fingers as he ploughed into the muscles of her slim behind.

He was now breathing quite heavily from his labours, and also from the libidinous thoughts that disturbed his equilibrium. The warm oil and her olive skin together were a provocation he could happily endure and he noticed that Vera's sighs seemed to have gone into a deeper key.

The intimacy of the situation gave him the right to draw her silk knickers over her hips so that he could attend more properly to her posterior. She gasped sharply at the moment when the gusset of the garment parted from her crotch. The denuding of her part by the withdrawal of the wispy piece of lingerie aroused the most intense erotic sensation, as did the novel feeling of her knickers enclosing the top of her thighs.

He applied himself more strongly to the base of her spine, pressing with his thumbs and with the whole of his palms. He then rubbed over the whole area, with his fingertips straying over the crack between her buttocks, or with a hand on each of her cheeks, pushing outwards and then inwards in opposite circles. The parting and contraction of her cheeks affected the organ that was contained between them in a delicious way, bringing a warm diffusion to the parts which led to a release of her lubricant liquid. Vera knew how to bide her time and did not wish to signal her early arousal to the stimulating massage, so she turned over on to her back, having removed her underslip. She bade him to change his position. He knelt, cradling her head on his lap.

As he applied his fingertips to her shoulders and the tops of her arms she could feel, through the tight bun at the nape of her neck, the throbbing hardness of his erectness. In this position she could look up at the attentive masseur. She noticed the strong line of his jaw and the heavy hood-like shape of his eyelids. Such a man will be a satisfying lover, she thought, nuzzling deeper into his crotch with her head.

The Greek said nothing as he explored her breasts with a fresh application of the oil. Cupping his hands underneath them he drew the small but perfectly shaped roundlets upwards and then let them slide from his grasp back to their normal position. He continued this to hypnotic effect, varying it with a subtle movement downwards, his palms sliding over her breasts on to her firm dancer's belly. Feeling the abnormal strength of her muscles was a novel experience for the banker. He ran his fingers over their contours, marvelling at their suppleness and their rigidity when she obliged by contracting them. It had already occurred to him that coupling with the ballerina was going to render him some very new erotic sensations. Normally women's bodies were soft, he mused. They took pride in their curves, had none of the hardness of men. This woman had the figure of an amazon, a sinewy complex of nerve and muscle trained by daily submission at the *barre* into a perfect instrument.

He stole a hand down the length of her abdomen and lingered a finger lightly between the outer lips of her vagina. A strong pulse manifested itself to the pad of his finger, a movement which intensified as he curved his digit downwards to enter first the outer and then the delightfully lubricated inner lips, which yielded their secret at his touch. With his head pressed into her firm belly he worked his finger deeply into her hidden recess until it was completely enclosed. The ballerina let escape a deep sigh. Her performance at the premiere was completely forgotten as she submitted to his gentle exploration. The interior muscles about which he had speculated tightened around his finger like a vice until he felt fully imprisoned.

He lay there moving the tip of his finger fractionally in this enchanting jail while she felt through his trousers at his hardness. He arched his hips away from her to ease her undoing of his fly buttons and then sank back as she grasped his organ with her slim hand. By slowly moving his pelvis he caused his member to slide in and out of its own outer skin as she held her grip, and he timed his movement to coincide with the slight manipulation of his finger in her sanctum.

They stayed in this position for a good quarter of an hour, savouring each other's organs, he by moving forward in order to be able to apply his lips to the soft parts he had been touching, and she by wriggling back down the polar bear skin until she could contain the tip of his thick penis in her painted lips.

When she could contain herself no longer, the long limbed dancer stood to her feet with some impatience. Pausing only to pour herself another cognac which she tossed down her throat, she attacked the task of removing the Greek's trousers with gusto. He lay back on the rug laughing as the diminutive dancer struggled with his garments. When he was finally uncovered she knelt in front of him in homage. The short but enormously thick stem of his trophy stood proud of a massive tangle of hair, with a bulbous scrotum underneath. She weighed the swelling testicles in an appreciative hand and then pour a tiny stream of cognac over his member. He groaned deliriously as she licked it off, paying great attention to his frenum and the outstanding vein that ran along the underside of his penis. The throbbing article wanted only to enter the warm, soft chamber that awaited it, but she stifled his pantings and his groans by pressing deep kisses on his mouth and eased herself over his loins until the moistened lips of her part touched the tip of his bursting organ. He watched unbelievingly as she suddenly lifted her body away from his; he feared the lady could not continue the assignation he had drawn her into and inwardly cursed her for standing up and walking away from him. But she rummaged in her bag and came back with a little packet.

'This is very good, darling. I buy them in Zurich in a wonderful chemist.' She opened the packet, and deftly drew out a bright pink condom which she blew into before stretching it over his outstanding part. 'Stay there darling, just a minute,' she implored like a petulant child, before languidly moving over to the telephone table. '*Allo*, reception. Please to cancel my room from tomorrow. I will moving to be the guest of Monsieur Vossoudossoulos in his suite. Thank you. Good night.'

Pausing on her way over to her lover to pick up the last of the *petit fours*, and singing an old Russian folk tune, Vera lowered herself into the splits over the expectant body of Vossoudossoulos until the moment when the parted lips of her vagina slid over the tip of his bursting member. 'You see, darling, what good practice I am in,' she murmured, sipping the last dregs of cognac.

111

As she lowered herself to the deepest point, enclosing his entire organ in one sweeping downward thrust, he made a mental note that such expertise in acrobatics should not go unrewarded.

Vera did not know it, but her athletic introduction of the Greek millionaire to the delights of the ballet had guaranteed that Borzdoff, her employer, would receive a large cheque the next morning, by way of subsidy, and that each time she rose and fell of his enflamed member, another nought was added to the amount.

A more lowly member of the Ballets Russes, the slant-eyed Mongolian, Vladimir, who danced in the *corps*, unnoticed by the great ballerina, had a rendezvous with Angelique at roughly the moment Vera rose exhausted from her bed the next day.

They met in a small café and drank several coffees, gazing worshipfully into each others eyes. He had brought her a small posy of flowers, stolen from the municipal gardens. *What a romantic gesture*, she smiled, sniffing their perfume in the dimly lit bistro.

He looks so underfed, she worried, grateful for the forethought she had shown in preparing the *blanquette de veau* which was, even now, simmering in her oven.

The skinny boy, so far from home, and surviving on a pittance given to him by the greedy impressario Borzdoff, was desperately hungry. A growing lad, he had left his native land in search of fame and fortune, only to find that the foyers of theatres were not paved with gold. Indeed, the much abused *corps de ballet* were supposed to look after themselves with baskets of picnic food brought in from the mother country. He had no such stock, and had long since given up looking to the others for help.

After she had paid the bill, for he had not a single franc in his pocket, Angelique led him towards her little attic flat. His first thought, like his superior, the grand ballerina Vera Lidova, was that he should immediately economise on his hotel bill. The Hotel de la Poste, cheap as it was, still represented a huge drain on his monthly stipend. He determined, come what may, to move in with the charming girl tomorrow.

The veal stew was delicious, a concoction of some quite nice cuts of meat simmered with carrots and potatoes, flavoured in a simple way with onions, bay leaves and pepper. Easy to eat, and easy to digest, it was the perfect dish to set before the hungry boy who had to dance a few hours later in a punishing programme. He murmured his thanks in a thick Siberian dialect which was incomprehensible, of course, to his hostess, but she was thankful to see a little colour come to his high-boned cheeks and his thin ascetic-looking lips.

She produced a box of reject chocolates which she had filched from the establishment down the street where she worked, and the boy's joy knew no bounds. As she prepared a pot of coffee and turned down the sheets of her bed, she watched him, in the mirror, devour the broken and mis-shapen chocolates as if they were manna from heaven.

Having nothing much more to say, she slipped out of her clothes and slid into bed, a hand extended to the skinny youth. Without a word he quickly undressed and joined her on the thin mattress. Their bony bodies wrapped together in a trice, his head on her small breast. She felt his thin ribs and stroked his face, anxious to communicate her thoughts to the foreign youth, but he was fast asleep on her chest, and groping down underneath the coverlet she found his slightly distended member. Squeezing it gently in her hand she also passed into a deep slumber.

She awoke to him knawing at her breast. He fondled her neck and her cheeks, bestowing kisses as he chose, straying his hands through her long tresses and sucking at the soft indentation at the base of her throat.

His kisses then began to rain down her belly to her knees and he threw off the cotton overlay and turned her over so that he could bite down the length of her spine. She squirmed in pleasure at this onslaught, moving her hips from side to side as he bit into the soft flesh of her lower back and buttocks. She bit into the pillow so as not to cry out through the thin walls and arched her back in order to facilitate the inevitable passage of his kisses towards the crack between the cheeks of her bottom and the softer moist area underneath.

He rolled over on to his knees, and holding her by her hip bones, lifted her up so that her back was arched and he could reach her secret parts with his mouth. Burying his tongue deeply inside her, he squeezed her breasts with passion and fingered her aroused, hardened nipples, causing her to cry out in her pleasure as she foamed her liquids on to his tongue and sank back on to the mattress in a spread-eagled position. He mounted her as she was, thrusting his long, thin member to its extremity into her dampened interior. His hands were underneath her, cupped to her down-covered and palpitating clitoris. His every thrust brought her a new orgasmic outburst, each one lubricating her innermost recesses and allowing him further access until, in a final fusion, they collapsed together in another deep but satisfied sleep.

Chapter Six

The vicomtesse and Sophie, mildly piqued at losing their gems, were pleased nonetheless that they had fetched such good prices at the auction. Firstly, they had been given a huge round of applause by the assembled crowd as a token praise for their generosity, and secondly, the large sums the trinkets had realised reflected the good taste and prudence of their respective husbands.

Early in the morning, as the sun rose over the bay, the throng departed in their various ways. Marcel left for Paris where he had important business and Jean-Paul drove the cousins back to the imposing villa. It was a lovely morning. The dew lay on the grass in the manicured gardens and the mimosa trees wafted an incense-like perfume through the air as Bernadette and Sophie strolled through the grounds. The abnormal earliness of their promenade gave it a special cachet.

'Why, normally we are fast asleep in our beds at this hour,' Sophie beamed as she gathered an armful of lilies, savouring their heady scent. 'It is so glorious we really should get up earlier and enjoy these exquisite *jardins* more often.'

There was an air of unreality in the secluded garden. The tall pines stood perfectly still in the morning air and even the eucalyptus trees were motionless. Arbours of pale roses and honeysuckle provided shady alleys to wander through and dense thickets of bamboo gave shelter to hundreds of twittering birds. A fountain played in the distance, water cascaded down a rocky-face, splashing into little pools stocked with carp and goldfish, and the magnolias raised their enormous white blooms up to the warm rays of the sun.

In a far off part of the grounds was a sunken garden which contained a swimming pool of brilliant artifice. Completely constructed of natural rocks, the pool seemed more like a natural pond in a forest glade. Ingenious steps were carved into the sides to allow the bather easy access and in the middle of the water there was an island large enough for a sunbathing area as well as an overhanging willow tree to give shade. A Chinese-looking bridge led to this from a grotto carved into the rock which contained changing rooms, showers and a bar stocked with all manner of refreshments. In all it was a perfect location for leisure and relaxation, and it was here, as well as the main house, that Bernadette intended to stage a lavish end-of-season party for the artistes of the ballet.

She discussed her plans with Sophie as they discarded the fine garments they had worn to the theatre. 'We can leave everything here,' she said. 'I will send Marthe over to pick them up later.'

Sophie ambled naked into the bar and had a wonderful time fixing drinks. She found fresh oranges and squeezed them into a large jug which she filled with Veuve Cliquot. '*Quel petit dejeuner*,' she enthused, returning to her cousin.

They lay on a pair of swinging sofas enjoying their drinks, the warm sun caressing their limbs, blissfully content with the day, while doves cooed in the trees overhead and the sounds of trickling water lulled them into a peaceful state of repose.

'*Attention, cheri*,' whispered Bernadette who had suddenly

caught sight of what was unmistakably human flesh through the hanging fronds of the willow tree on the island.

Sure enough a nude man had risen from a bathing towel and dived in a perfect arc into the still waters of the pool.

His body stayed submerged long enough for the ladies to become a little agitated, but suddenly it broke to the surface and the swimmer swished through the water in a fast crawl and went out of sight.

'My dear, who was that?' enquired Sophie as she reached automatically for a robe. 'His face was completely covered by the foliage, I couldn't make him out at all.'

'It's Arthur,' said Bernadette. 'I would recognise that piece of equipment anywhere'.

Sure enough, when she thought about it, Sophie did, in her fleeting glimpse of the man, catch sight of an organ whose very size stirred a memory. She recollected the scene in the secret garden room when she had been privileged to witness moments of the burgeoning affair between the young English officer and his debutante girl friend.

Arthur came back into view, this time swimming lazily with a back-stroke. The organ which compelled the interest of the ladies stood out of the water as he cruised in circles, rather like a periscope or the fin of a sea creature, Bernadette thought. Blissfully unaware of the cousins' presence, the officer then went into a series of aquatic flips, turns and somersaults, a repertoire that an experienced and enthusiastic swimmer indulges in by way of his complete satisfaction in a watery environment. Each time his body curved from the now-foaming pool the very considerable ornament flashed through the air, sometimes slapping his belly, and made its very own splash on re-entering the water. It was a display which captivated the seated ladies as they sipped their drinks with amused grins on their faces.

'Come, Sophie,' Bernadette invited, 'we shall take a stroll.' Sophie made to put on her robe, but the vicomtesse gently took it from her hands and laid it back on the sofa. 'Nonsense, darling,' she said. 'This is my house, and my garden. You are my invited guest, and surely in its privacy two ladies can parade, looking as nature intended. Arthur is not an intruder, after all. I gave both him and Charles permission, naturally, to use the pool, and it is he who should have the courtesy to remain dressed. Come.'

With full glasses in their hands they strolled nonchalantly around the pool and over the Chinese bridge, looking anywhere but in Arthur's direction. After a while they began to talk, bright brittle chatter of a kind that amuses women friends, casting furtive looks towards the swimmer.

The splashing sounds ceased. When they looked, a dark ripple in the water revealed the path he was taking towards the other bank and the shade of the trees in order to evade a confrontation.

By moving fast along the path they managed to be at the precise spot where he slithered from the water and ran, in a crouched position, for cover. But, instead, he ran into the two naked ladies, almost making them spill their drinks.

'Good morning, Arthur, what a lovely day. I'm so pleased you have taken up my invitation to use the pool whenever you like,' Bernadette said kindly, speaking as if they were in a normal situation in a drawing room.

Arthur, his hands trying to cover his crotch where they had flown automatically in an instant, blushed furiously and retreated into the stammer which sometimes afflicted him, apologising for his embarrassing appearance.

'N'importe quoi, cher garçon,' Bernadette soothed him, firmly taking an arm, winking at Sophie to do the same.

Any Englishman is obliged from birth to recognise the

respect he must show to a lady. If a lady wishes an arm to lean on, or to link with, a gentleman must provide it. It is a reflex as automatic as that which sends an Englishman to open a door or help a lady into an automobile, so therefore Arthur was constrained to give up the concealment of his genitals and escort the ladies back to their sofas. He walked there stiff-backed as an officer would, his bristled moustache twitching in his confusion. The over-large member, which the cousins were studying under lowered eyelids, swung impressively from side to side as he strode between them.

'Please don't be at all uncomfortable, my dear Arthur,' murmured Bernadette. 'We all bathe naked here. It is so secluded that we can be *au naturel* without any offence. Here is all peace and calm. My goodness I sometimes feel that I am on a deserted tropical island, it is so quiet and absolutely private. Sophie, dearest, please pour our young friend a drink. After his exertions he must be in need of one.'

She motioned the officer to come and sit beside her on the hammock swing. As he did so he tried, by crossing his legs, to hide his parts, but although his large testicles were taken up between the tops of his thighs, much of his penis was still revealed. The pink glans of handsome proportions lay to one side, occupying the fold between the top of his thigh and his groin.

Bernadette patted him on the knee in a friendly way. 'Do feel free to come here when ever you want, my dear. Actually the pool is rarely used. It's a pity, but one is so busy, so much to do. Therefore it is mostly for the use of my guests.'

'Thank you, you're very kind,' said Arthur, noting the generous size of her curving breasts and the nicely rounded shape of her belly. He glanced down at her slim legs and the tuft of silky hair at the centre of her body, noting how it had been trimmed carefully into a perfect triangular shape. The

119

same care had been paid to her toenails which were painted silver to match her fingernails.

He watched as Sophie returned with a large glass of champagne and orange juice which she gave him with an appreciative sweeping look which travelled down his hairy chest to the provocatively placed organ, whose existence Arthur was trying desperately to put out of his mind.

'You didn't tell me, *chère cousine*,' she simpered 'that you had such a handsome guest in the little apartment. I suppose you wanted to keep him all to yourself.' With a tinkling little laugh she planted herself at Arthur's side so that he was now wedged between her and Bernadette, and in a most natural manner placed an arm around his shoulder as if they were both the oldest of friends. One foot was tucked up underneath her posterior. With the other she set the seat in motion, swinging it gently to and fro as she continued the conversation.

'Tell me about your girl friend,' she said. 'Bernadette says that you have the most delightful English girl in tow. What's her name?'

Arthur looked enquiringly at the vicomtesse. He thought he had been discreet in his dealings with Annabelle and was surprised to hear this.

'Really, *cheri*,' Bernadette murmured, 'you can't do anything on the Cote d'Azur without the world knowing. From my car I have often seen you with your charming friend. She looks adorable.' She closed her eyes as if the sun was troubling her, but behind her closed lids she envisaged the scene between Arthur and Annabelle that she had seen played out on the beach beneath the vantage point of the cliff from where she and her chauffeur had espied them.

Sophie was remembering how tenderly the officer had removed the English girl's lingerie during the rendezvous she had witnessed through the two-way mirror; the tearful way in which the sweet boy had thrown himself on to his knees to declare his passion before she and her cousin had stolen away to leave the pair of lovers to nature's embrace. She also remembered the story Bernadette had told her about the athletic support the young man had to wear on account of the priapic condition his passion for Annabelle had engendered. Looking down at Arthur's crotch again, she began to see for herself the necessity of the peculiar constricting garment.

His penis had been brought to a certain degree of tumescence because of the pressing closeness of the two attractive female forms and his damp nakedness. The warmth of the sun had partially dried his body, but a few sparkling drops of water remained in the bush of hair which might have, at least partially, covered some of a smaller organ. A few of these drops ran down to fall on his faintly stirring member. Even this almost imperceptible sensation caused an extra frisson which speeded the gentleman towards an embarassing half-erection. The swelling in the stem reached the pink head of the glans, raising it intermittently from its resting place in small, but now noticeable, movements, his being placed in such close proximity to two creatures of incipiently erotic possibilities.

'It's too hot,' he said, and rising to his feet as fast as he could, he dashed for the water, clutching his parts with both hands.

'The poor darling is tormented,' Bernadette sympathised. 'Let him cool off a little.'

Safely in the water, splashing around behind an outcrop of rocks, Arthur made a big mental effort to reduce the swelling that had led to his rapid immersion. He thought sadly about Annabelle's approaching departure for England and his

121

eventual return to his regiment. Perhaps he could make another dash for his clothes he thought, but no; he saw Sophie in the process of retrieving them from the island for him, an act of kindness no doubt, but one which made his escape less possible. His concentrated efforts brought him no success. Thoughts of Annabelle only served to arouse him further and the two laughing, attractive women waving so gaily to him added to the problem. It was worse when, to his horror, they both suddenly dived in the water and swam quickly towards him.

It was inevitable that a hilarious water game would ensue. Laughing, splashing, thrashing about in the pool like children on holiday led to a breathless gurgling conclusion, the three swimmers in close intimate contact, joking and chiding each other, teasing playfully in their enjoyment of each others company.

One of the ladies managed to brush a breast against one of Arthur's hands, another to kick his backside lightly and then, as it were by accident, bump into him when she swam between his legs. The old formula worked well as always. Soon the trio were in each other's arms. Arthur found his apprehension thrown to the wind, and soon also found a hand enclosing his stem and another reaching from behind to stroke his scrotum.

The large glass of champagne had released some of his inhibitions by now and the rest vanished when Sophie, leaving him for a few moments in Bernadette's pleasant grasp, returned with a tray which she set beside the water's edge.

How pleasant it was to stand in the pool, consuming more of the intoxicating orange and champagne mixture. The officer was delighted to find his mouth at Sophie's breast, and then at Bernadette's. He drank deeply as they massaged his manly shoulders and strayed their hands down his hard body.

How they giggled when they finally dared, both in turn, to take a firm hold on his throbbing protrusion. Of course they laughed happily because, even with two hands, neither of them could hold the entire length of his enormous stem. Three hands were necessary and they naturally obliged.

Arthur began to feel he had never had such a delightful morning. The sun, the wine, the water and these two comfortable but elegant women helped to dispel the consuming interest in his beloved that had tortured him for weeks, and anyway what healthy man could resist such attentions?

'My, what a big boy,' Bernadette whispered in his ear as, with her arms around his neck, she hoisted herself up to wrap her legs round his waist. She lowered them slowly until the tops of her thighs clasped around his massive erection. She felt for his frenum which protruded way past the opening between her buttocks. 'It's like being on a rocking horse,' she laughed.

'Let me try,' Sophie implored. 'You can't have all the fun.'

She played a little deceit on her cousin by starting in the same way, but on the way down carefully arranging her descent so that her parts landed over the tip of his upright organ. Lubricated as she was, as a result of the water sports, even though Arthur's member was of such unusual size, she managed to slide over it until she enclosed it completely. The novel experience of containing this probably record-holding prize possession brought her into an immediate shattering orgasm. Her ecstasy was evident to both Arthur and Bernadette. The latter, being a generous soul, was not miffed. It had to be one of them, she thought, as nature had taken such a sensuous course, and with nothing else to occupy them that lovely morning, it could only be her turn soon. Arthur amazed himself as the morning progressed.

They had retreated to the luxuriously appointed dressing room suite, where the ladies at first lay on separate beds.

He had opened another bottle of Veuve Cliquot, spurting some of the contents in the air, where they had landed on Bernadette's breasts. After nuzzling the drops away, he had entered her, but remained still for a long time, sipping at his fresh drink, while the vicometesse stirred beneath him voluptuously.

During their play Sophie could not resist paying a little attention to her flushed part and the throbbing bud at its centre.

'Fair's fair,' Arthur smiled, moving over to the second bed, where he repeated the same leisurely intrusion.

Bernadette followed and knelt by the bed, lightly stroking his back and his buttocks, marvelling at the muscular strength in his posterior as he thrust deep into her cousin. She slowly slid a hand between his legs, past his scrotum to where she found the base of his organ at the point of entry, but her touch was light. She did not want to disturb his equilibrium, sensing that the charming and considerate officer wished to divide himself fairly between the two of them, and could only achieve this parity by beginning in a calm unhurried way.

Arthur's intentions were all very well, but eventually he was drawn irresistibly from his slow motion perambulations into a more passionate, and later abandonedly frenzied pursuit of their mutual satisfaction. His natural endowments and his aforementioned priapic disposition aided considerably in this gratifying search.

They tried every variation of posture and grouping as Arthur proved his manhood. Courteous and obliging he brought both ladies to an excess of orgasmic satisfaction, surprising himself at his self-control and also the number of times that he reached such overpowering climaxes. Eventually all three lay in a heap of exhaustion together, fondly embracing each other, lost in the wonder of the powerful consummation that had taken place.

After a relaxing and leisurely swim they donned robes and walked arm in arm back to the house, thoroughly taken by the turn of events. Both ladies made assurances that the precious Annabelle would hear nothing of the episode, and Arthur, smiling to himself, began to realise that when his love travelled north on the Paris Express to return home, all would not be lost.

The moment of Arthur's parting from the debutante at the Central Station in Nice was a sorry affair. She had been crying most of the night, cradled in his arms, in a room in a hotel he had gallantly booked in order for them to spend their last few hours together. There had been no embarassment explaining her departure to her friends on the hired yacht. They had presumed only that she was leaving for home a day earlier than had been planned, and anyway, they were all so involved in the pursuit of their own hedonistic pleasures, they scarcely gave a thought to losing her company. Indeed, all were looking forward to some fresh arrivals the next day.

Arthur tried hard but could not match the degree of emotion that Annabelle displayed in the last few harrowing hours. He tried to console her with kisses and promises of further distractions, but her sorrow was so great that she could not respond to his half-hearted attentions. The officer began to entertain a creeping sense of guilt for having lost some of the reckless ardour that had plagued him for so long. He was not yet either old or experienced enough in the affairs of love to know that the deep passion that he had felt for the charming debutante was seated more in a sexual, rather than a spiritual attraction. Like many a heady romantic young man before him he had made the common mistake of idolising the object of his lust, worshipping her for her mind as well as her body, and now he found her tears and sobs distracting. An instinct told him that he had been deceiving himself, that a true lover's emotions would have welled up in a way that evaded him. He wanted the end of their new found romance to be gay, not filled with grief, but he was paying the price of having aroused in Annabelle a more profound devotion than his own, which was, after all, founded in calf love and promoted by the needs of his loins.

'Come on darling', he implored 'let's make our last night fun. Please be jolly.' Wiping away her tears he remembered the occasions when he had agonised on the quay, looking enviously over the sparkling waters of the bay towards the sophisticated parties of holiday-makers, and how this auburn-haired girl had seemed to epitomise that carefree spirit that imbued the summer. *What a different thing now*, he pondered, remembering the contrast of the gaiety of the swimming party in the villa's garden, as Annabelle cried copiously.

'Promise me that you will come home soon, that you will keep yourself for me. We'll find a way of carrying on back home. Daddy would be raving if he knew. It would kill him, and Mummy would be furious too. I could get a job to be near you at the barracks, darling. Promise me it will be alright, oh Arthur . . .' she wailed inconsolably.

Her outbursts, for there were many, caused a heavy depression to settle on Arthur. In such a condition he found that for the very first time he had no desire to make love to Annabelle, and she was so occupied with a frightening concern that her parents would find out about her indiscretions, that they lay together in the vast double bed without a single thought of physical love.

After breakfast they took a taxi to the station and Annabelle boarded the train with a brave stab at the gaiety she had known the last few weeks. 'Goodbye, you bad boy,' she laughed, waving her gloves from the carriage window. 'Send me a postcard.'

Arthur hailed another taxi. He was expected to lunch at the villa at twelve.

Around the same time, Charles, with some of his earlier jauntiness, was striding along the promenade very pleased with himself. He had managed to steer Edith in the direction of a football player from Michigan who had expressed much interest in the lady, and he was on his way to reinstate himself in the affections of Angelique, the salesgirl.

Another balmy day, he thought, whistling an old music hall tune. He noted the little clouds scudding across the horizon and a white-painted steamer chugging towards the anchorage. The beach was filled with brilliantly coloured parasols and deck chairs as far as the eye could see, and people streamed in and out of the fashionable hotels in their bath-robes, carrying all kinds of equipment for games and fun. The ornamental flower beds and hanging baskets of the promenade were rich in their varieties of plants, carpets of exotic brilliance in the partial shade of the palm trees, and the awnings and bright table cloths of the restaurants added to the jollity of the scene.

Sophie and Dhokouminsky were in witty conversation over a glass of cassis outside an elegant brasserie. She waved gaily to Charles as he passed by, having recently been introduced to him by her cousin. Seeing the good-looking fellow stride proudly along the crowded pavement and having him raise his straw boater to her in such a gallant way reinforced her anticipation of the event her cousin had promised would take place soon—observing the morning ritual in Charles's and Arthur's bedroom.

'This is another of your lovers?' Dhokouminsky demanded.

'Jealous boy, it's a nephew of mine,' she lied engagingly.

The long-limbed, muscular dancer, whose sexual proclivities had been often compared to those of a buck rabbit and his performance and staying power to those of a stallion, grinned unbelievingly as he clamped his right hand over her knee, calling to the waiter for more drinks. At a nearby table Vera Lidova sat admiring the sapphire bracelet which imposingly circled her slim wrist. It was a present from M. Vossoudossoulos, the latest in a series he had given her as a token of his gratitude for his initiation into some remarkable sexual variations. The gifts had included the several dresses she had quite rightly anticipated, bought from the establishment of Bernadette's lover, Marcel, a set of Vuiton luggage in ivory-coloured leather, a large phial of expensive perfume, several frivolous hats, a fox fur stole, six pairs of shoes, two handbags fashioned from crocodile skin and a collection of lingerie that would have been sufficient to clothe the chorus of a scene in a Hollywood musical.

Also nearby were Jean-Paul, the chauffeur, and a German matron of some age. The lady was holding his hand under the tablecloth, squeezing it in fervent gratitude for the attentions he had been recently paying her. His wallet, comfortably nestling in the pocket of his blazer, was stuffed with a large number of Marks, her calling card, and the address of an hotel in Zermatt to which he was to be summoned when he took his holiday from the employ of the vicomtesse.

The elderly Frau was fondly recalling, in particular, the pleasant way the young man had in running a bath, filling it with bubbles and scented oils, and lowering her body and his into it. Ah, the perfumed magic of it, she thought, savouring again the memory of how he had sponged her and scrubbed her with a loofah, flannelled her bosom and soaped her bunioned feet. She had wallowed in the huge bath like a porpoise as he had slid his body up and down over hers, or when he sat at the other end of the tub wiggling his big toe in her private part.

His miniscule organ had not been a disappointment at all. She was sick of men and their thrusting brutish members and adored the neat little penis that reminded her of the sort of adornment a choirboy might possess. Yes, she thought, the boy had been positively angelic, and she ordered him another sundae.

Charles rounded the corner and turned into the street where the chocolate shop was situated. There was a convenient florist nearby. He purchased a large bunch of asters and gladioli, and on a last minute impulse, a dozen fragrant carnations. Armed thus, he strode down the narrow street, his heart pounding, and entered the sweet-smelling shop.

'*Helas, monsieur*, she has gone to lunch,' the proprietor informed him. Without further ado he bounded along to the quartier alongside where Angelique resided over the patisserie. He ran up the stairs and knocked loudly on her door. It opened to reveal an emaciated but vigorous looking youth whose slanted eyes burned with the intensity one might observe in a poet or a painter.

'Thank you,' the young man said, seizing the bouquet. Fresh into the *corps de ballet*, Vladimir was enchanted with what he thought was Charles's proferred testimony to his artistry.

129

Charles retreated disconsolately back to the street below, mouthing a silent curse. In his anger he failed to notice his friend Arthur, relieved of the wailing Annabelle, speeding by in a taxi, waving gaily from the window, thrilled with anticipation of his next appointment.

The al fresco luncheon at the mansion, the preparations of which had been supervised by Bernadette in conjunction with her talented chef Jean-Louis, was a decorous affair by the prevailing standards of the Cote d'Azur, though there were some serious undertones of a disturbing nature and some sexual overtones of a more frivolous kind.

It was attended by Sophie and Dhokouminsky, Arthur, M. Rognon, Marcel (newly returned from business in Paris), Vera Lidova, M. Vossoudossoulos, Borzdoff accompanied by his diminutive and rampantly bisexual assistant Leonide, several of the other principals of the company, and various friends of Bernadette who were invited for old time's sake or simply to swell the ranks. Their invitations had been by telephone that very morning.

One such was Carlotta Bomdieri, an Italian grotesque who claimed to be descended from the Medicis but was, in fact, the daughter of a famous Neapolitan courtesan and owned a thriving bordello in Marseilles. This fact was, of course, unknown to her friend Bernadette. Another was Frederick Fanshawe, a drunken American novelist who was researching the bull culture of the Camargue, accompanied by his wife Lady Letitia Whitmore who was famous for her infidelities. The guests were admitted by Marthe and shown to the terrace.

Bernadette made a sumptuous entry wearing a black beaded gown and flanked by her pet dogs, a pair of borzoi hounds, in the manner of Erté, the celebrated theatrical designer. The beasts were quickly despatched to the kennels when one of them made a lunge at the overflowing table and seized a whole delicious cold *roti de boeuf*.

The meal consisted of an array of seafood, placed in the centre of the table, which dazzled the eye in its generous abundance. Lobsters, crabs, crayfish, muscles, baby squid, whole salmon and scallops vied with each other in their scintillating and appetising display.

On either side were dishes holding the chef's speciality. In each case a boned song bird had been placed in a blackbird which in turned had been used to stuff a boned pigeon. This had been used to stuff a chicken which was fitted inside a turkey. The thoroughly boned complexes were already sliced, each piece showing the different colours and textures of the various meats, ready to be served with a sauce of wild herbs and berries cooked in Muscadet.

At the rear of the table stood a dish of *fraises du bois* which had been soaked in the finest champagne, and dishes of *crème chantilly*.

At the front were plates of Beluga caviar decorated with sliced lemon and slices of parma ham wrapped around asparagus. There were also *médaillons* of veal crowned with truffles and quail eggs served in aspic.

In all it was an impressive sight which brought tears to the eyes of Dhokouminsky. He helped himself to large plates of food even though there were uniformed maids to assist, and retreated to a table where Sophie joined him.

He was suddenly thrilled that he did not have to dance that night and could indulge to his heart's content. Earlier he had been extremely surly with Borzdoff who had relegated him to a smaller part in one of the ballets because he had fudged the big pirouette at the end of his solo.

Sophie watched him eating. Though she adored him and

his virile dancing and looked forward to getting him in her bed, she thought he was an animal. Perhaps that was the attraction, she speculated, gazing across to Arthur, another object of her affections.

The officer was engaged in conversation with Vera who had noticed the pronounced bulge in his slacks and was wondering whether it merited causing a diversion from her Greek protector.

Vossoudossoulos was busy assisting Carlotta Bombieri to extract the meat from a lobster claw. The overblown and overperfumed dwarf held no attraction to him, but she had noticed his impeccable manners and good suit and wondered if he might become a paying client at her dockside establishment.

Vera Lidova was making a fair impression of being a lady. She had by now travelled extensively in Europe and had been fêted and dined by many rich admirers, so she had a chic façade of sophistication which was far more effective than her less experienced colleagues.

She was now paying gushing tribute to Marcel, the couturier. How she adored her new dresses and matching turbans, she told him. He was more than a little aroused by the closeness of her slim body and her penetrating and voluptuous stare. Over his shoulder he could see Bernadette monitoring the progress of his rapport with the ballerina and decided to move away from the fascinating lady as soon as an appropriate moment came.

Bernadette could not decide whether to remove Marcel from this dangerous close contact or intervene in a conversation Arthur was having with one of the minor soloists of the ballet. A stud of his calibre would be a welcome lover in that bizarre ballet company, she thought, and that would upset her own plans for the officer.

She was interrupted in her reverie by Frederick Fanshawe, the American novelist who had unfortunately been reduced to writing pornography of the worst kind since publishers were not interested in the boring psychological novels which his life-long study of Gorky, Ibsen, Chekov and Tolstoy had inspired. He was bored with his equally drunken wife, the febrile Letitia, and saw the possibility of a rich *patronne* in his hostess. Letitia had found comfort in the company of M. Rognon who had just escaped the attentions of Borzdoff who was still looking for backers. But the art dealer gazed longingly instead at Sophie who was now sitting on Dhokouminsky's knee, looking a little dishevelled. It seemed only a minute since the jolly dinner for four which he had so enjoyed, with her foot in his crotch.

Arthur, rather tipsy by now, wondered at his luck. From the gruesome celibacy of his army mess he had whirled into a rich pasture. Annabelle's tears were forgotten, and now he was, though still relatively inexperienced in the ways of the world, surrounded by glamorous, rich and available females. He eyed the scene. Sophie, Bernadette, his conquests at the swimming pool; Lidova the exotic star of the Ballets Russes, Galina the young *étoile* and the other equally attractive dancers who smiled so freely, kissed one on the cheek and so on. What a tale he would have to tell.

Vossoudossoulos staggered over to Lidova, who now had her arms around Marcel's neck and pulled her away. She slapped him across the face with some force. Her lover reacted as many men would do and slapped her across the behind. Dhokouminsky roared over and took the Greek by the lapels of his expensive suit and threatened to cut off his testicles if he did not apologise. Bernadette moved in to smooth the ruffled feathers, coaxing and soothing. Everyone laughed and the party took off again.

Several hours later when the guests were strolling in the garden, the borzois escaped from their kennels and devoured the remains of the feast. Carlotta Bombieri was asleep at the table at the time and nearly suffered a fatal heart attack when the great beasts leaped over her lap in their race to the food. She left in some distress without saying goodbye to her hostess. By the time they had all gone away in their various limousines, the following arrangements had been made.

Lidova had given Arthur a box seat for the next evening's performance. Arthur invited Galina to dinner at the Hotel de Paris. M. Rognon gave his card to Letitia and asked her to see his forthcoming exhibition. Borzdoff promised Frederick Fanshawe the company of a *corps de ballet* girl of ample proportions if he gave a thousand dollars towards the new scenery. Leonide, his assistant, arranged a rendezvous with Jean-Louis, Bernadette's chef. Marcel implored Bernadette to visit him once more at the salon. Dhokouminsky threatened to kill Sophie if she was not at the stage door waiting for him at the end of that evening's performance.

They all agreed it had been an enchanting afternoon, all that is, except for Lady Letitia who, yet again, left a social function in tears, reduced to a quivering mass by the loutish behaviour of her drunken husband, the failed American novelist Fanshawe. She left separately and went back to her hotel room where she opened a fresh bottle of gin in the spirit of consolation.

'I will leave him,' she cried into her pillow, 'he doesn't deserve me.' With that decided, she packed her valises, paid the hotel bill, for she knew that Fanshawe was broke, ordered a taxi, and left on the midnight express.

Chapter Seven

Lady Letitia's peregrinations brought her eventually to Florence, in the company of a virile young stud who intended to enrol as a student in one of the many schools of art which are established there. She had found him penniless on the Grand Station in Milano, dishevelled and hungry. His mean good looks had appealed at once to her. Erudite for one of his age, ascetic in appearance and devastatingly slim, the lad who, in her eyes, could have been carved by Donatello in his prime, was sent by destiny to this fortunate encounter with the minor English aristocrat.

Her complexion bloomed and improved on a diet of love and good Italian cooking. Many times, over a bowl of steaming tagliatelle, lavishly oozing with pesto, the aromatic concoction of olive oil, crushed pine nuts and basil leaves of which the Florentines are inordinately fond, she had to pinch herself in order to be convinced that she was not in the middle of a romantic dream inspired by the works of D'Annunzio. Indeed, Letitia exalted in this paragon of male beauty. He was her toy to picked up and played with as she wished.

Paolo played the role to perfection. He would smile dreamily, flickering his long dark lashes with practised dexterity, exposing the flashing teeth which he used to such great effect on her flesh when they were locked in the rented apartment. '*Carissima*,' he would murmur as he passed her a glass of rich red Chianti or served her with another helping of *arrosto di vitello*, thrilling Letitia to the very marrow of her delicately shaped bones, 'I am so happy, so grateful to you. You are an angel, I adore you.'

These lies were music to her ears. She lapped up his sibilant endearments greedily, with a transported sensous look in her eyes when he put his charming tongue to work in this, and other ways. He would be rewarded for his compliments with yet another thick bundle of lire, fished from her copious dorothy bag, and afterwards, as an additional treat, they would go shopping for a few ties, shirts, a silk suit, or a new dressing gown. Letitia was grateful to her protégé. Not only were his manners impeccable, but he possessed a long rapier-thin boyish looking organ and a tightly packed scrotum, and she adored the way he used them.

Paolo was of an age during which the young male can be spectacularly ardent. His carnal instincts in his late teens, not so far removed from the onset of puberty, placed him in a different category to his older brothers. They may, if they are sensitive to the proper needs of a sexual partner, have succeeded in calming some of the wilder ejaculatory impulses of youth, and learned a restraint that is both satisfying and civilised. But ladies of a certain age have occasionally been known to fall desperately for the charms of callow youths whose orgasms are induced so speedily, reflecting in their haste the recklessness of animals such as rabbits and hares at the start of spring.

Pondering all these considerations, Letitia decided her time had come. She would impinge in a little juvenalia. Love in short sharp, but frequent bursts would suit the mood she was in, rather than long, tiring tumultuous couplings of the

136

kind which, in the past, had exhausted her and a certain number of her lovers.

One early evening they lay on the large double bed resting, after such a spirited attack by the boy. His few deep jabs at Letitia's part had inflamed her, but not given her the satisfaction she craved. *All in good time*, she thought. His flaccid organ, lightly spread with love juices, had slipped sideways over his groin under his black bush of pubic curls.

'I adore watching it grow,' Letitia whispered. 'Tell me, *caro*, when is it is going to happen again.' But the boy was snoring from a fatigue that originated both in the copious wine that had been quaffed at lunchtime and his erotic endeavours so far.

Letitia's rock hard nipples afforded her some satisfaction, as did a gentle stroking on the delicate membrane that protruded, sending sensations that were out of all proportion, as she always thought, to the size of that tiny bud. It was amazing that such a small secret place could yield such pleasure. Leaning across his slumbering form, she applied her lips to the very tip of his organ, couching his sac with one of her hands. The other hand played with the soft spongy lifeless object on which her lips and tongue were paying attention.

The processes of nature are relentless and profound. In his sleep Paolo's brain was besieged by erotic messages. It is likely that his cells were not actively concerned with his present whereabouts, but more with the built-in memory of his first sexual encounter, the very gauge which controls most men's carnal instincts.

He was recalling, at that moment, an incident in a flower strewn meadow when a powerfully made shepherdess, employed by his farmer father, showed him where the spring of his erotic life was situated and how it could be made to bring him great joy. First she coached him in milking the ewes, how to squeeze the udders to release the flowing milk, and then, stretching the lad out in the meadow of flowers, by using the sucking action of her mouth on his childishly shaped organ, made his own milk appear for the first time. Such was the baptism that his unconscious mind recalled as Letitia applied the same treatment.

The natural detumescence of his shaft had reduced its size to such an extent that Letitia could draw in its entire length. She nuzzled it thus with her nostrils buried in the bush of his pubis. Occasional flickers of life ran through the member as the first flashes of memory were stirred into action, and the pulse began to beat stronger, in response to the effort Letitia put in to the arousal she wished to bring to her sleeping partner.

Paolo dreamed of the high fleecy clouds that swelled in the sky on that distant day in the mountain meadow. He was the captain of a many-masted schooner, riding the waves on a long voyage in the tropics. The clouds turned into the white of the girl's apron as she bent over amid the flowers and nodding grasses. A voice came sweet and soft to him, as the girl sang an old peasant song, and the sweetness turned to a feeling of great joy as her mouth closed over his small prick. The vision and the delicious, novel sensation transformed itself. He saw the ewe's teat and took it in his hand, squeezing it in the way he had often stimulated his own diminutive appendage. His head was underneath the animal and the flow of milk was delicious as it fell on his lips, as delightful to the taste as the liquid of his first and surprising emission was to the shepherdess.

Now throbbing with enormous energy, swelling with haste into its proper state of erection, Paolo's member grew to its normal length. Letitia rose to her haunches and slipped her moist part over it while the boy still slept. Her slow raptured undulations roused his piece to even more solid rock hardness, and her urgent muscular contractions were echoed by throbs from the slumbering Paolo. Driven to distraction in her parts by this friction, Letitia rode him hard, driving up and down on the engorged shaft as she worked towards her frantic climax.

Paolo jerked awake, flooded with a generous emission and a satiety of delightful childhood memories, and found the shepherdess into the shape of his present benefactress in the full flow of orgasmic pleasure that his youthful ardour had previously denied her.

Perspiring and feeling faint with lust and emotion, Letitia fell across his body, raining him with kisses. 'The growth of the male, the rise of the phallus, is the most exciting thing that a woman can witness,' the enthralled aristocrat moaned. 'Of course, without it, no intercourse between the sexes would be possible.' Paolo agreed with the tenor of her claim, but had little time to ponder as he immediately fell sound asleep again, cradled in her arms.

The germ of an idea had been planted in Letitia's mind, but she did not become aware of it fully until after a visit to the Uffizi Gallery.

Paolo, she, and two American friends were sitting at a pavement cafe.

'I've had a stunning idea,' Letitia said. 'It must be this place. Why, the whole town is stuffed with male nudes, statutes, drawings, paintings, and they're all of men and boys in the, well you know, limp condition. That's fun of a kind, and they're very beautiful, but what about the erect phallus in Art? You only see that in Pompeii, or in those ghastly Indian or Japanese manuals that are all the rage. Why, the process of tumescence is beautiful. I shall publish a great tome about it.' Convinced that she was on to a winner, Letitia made expensive calls to London explaining her emission to an important publisher. A few days later he turned up in Florence, only keen to get away from his boring harridan of a wife and the wet English summer. 'I know it will sell, Maurice,' she argued. 'We need a large format, the most expensive paper and bindings, and exquisitely lit photographs. On one side of the page, the limp penis, and on the facing page, the erect version in all its glory.'

Maurice was shocked, but he began to see commercial prospects in the scheme if he marketed the edition discreetly as expensive pornography, rather than the arty stuff Letitia had in mind.

'We shall have reproductions of the penis in Art, Letitia said, 'in a special corrolary at the back, indexes and so on, with perhaps a foreword by an eminent Art critic.'

'What of these photographs? Where are you going to get them?' Maurice demanded.

'I shall hire a photographer and begin with Paolo,' she said defiantly.

'Come, darling, there's much to do.'

Over the next few weeks there was great activity. Paolo had no objection to the photography of his penis as long as it were done by a woman, he said, and as one of Letitia's friends in town was a famous fashion editor with experience in these affairs, she was press-ganged into working on the project. Paolo was given marks on the floor of the studio and the camera was positioned exactly and screwed down, so that the distance and focus of all the shots would be the same.

Letitia inspected his organ minutely on the day of the shoot as she wanted no trace of tumescence in the first picture. Paolo stood bravely opposite the lens which was trained on his genital area. A quick flash and it was over.

'Now for the up version,' Letitia smiled, applying some effective squeezes to the limp article. The erotic possibilities of the American girl's presence at the scene and the physical attentions he was receiving quickly led to the desired erection, which was duly recorded. After these test shots had been developed the production team met at the hired apartment. Huge enlargements of the two pictures had been prepared, roughly the size of the format Letitia envisaged. They were laid side by side on the floor.

'Not bad, eh?' Paolo smirked, for the enlargement made his tool seem to be of gigantic proportions.

'Stunning,' agreed Betsy, the photographer.

'Very marketable,' Maurice said, with a wink at Paolo.

'You were my inspiration, darling,' Letitia said, then a little later, 'I realise that each model's penis must be measured, both limp and erect, so that we can print their vital statistics on each entry in the book.'

'Great idea, kid,' Betsy opined. 'Do I get the job?'

Paolo was commissioned to find fifty other models. Letitia wanted a catholic selection: young, old, fat, thin—a broad spectrum of the male sex, whose organs would, naturally, come in all shapes and sizes. Paolo insisted that no-one would be interested unless there was a fee. 'No Italian will show his prick without money,' he claimed.

'Oh, yeah? So why do I get the flashers on every street corner?' asked Betsy, with much feeling.

Eventually a price was fixed. None of the others were to guess that Paolo, waving bundles of lire in a variety of low dives and bars, offered only half the fee and pocketed the rest.

It happened by chance that Hemingway was in town, with Dorothy Parker in tow. Then Josephine Baker, cabaret star of Paris, arrived with several of the legendary Sitwells, Noel

Coward, and a string of minor glitterati and hangers-on. They all met up with Letitia in a fashionable bar and exchanged news. They enquired, naturally, about Fanshawe, the drunken novelist husband she had deserted. Dismissing this with an airy wave of her hand, she excitedly outlined her plan.

'Great idea, order me a copy,' Baker growled.

'Count me in too, honey,' Parker said. 'A collection of guys who can *all* get a hard on will be unusual, to say the least.' Noel lit another cigarette and posed magnificently, a silk scarf tucked into his immaculate Turnbull and Asher shirt, sporting the whitest of flannels, lizard skin two-tone shoes, and a handsome navy blue blazer. The effect was chic and fashionable.

'Letitia, dahling,' he intoned, in his inimitable plummy voice, 'I would volunteer for your brochure myself, but I'm afraid to say that my parts would be far too instantly recognisable to far too many people.' Everyone laughed uproariously, and Dorothy felt obliged to record the *bon mot* in her pocket book.

The evening ended at the Cipriani—where else? and Josephine Baker and Noel entertained with a few songs. Edith, the giantess of English literature wrote a few poems on the back of the menu, and Hemingway got drunk and fell in the pool. Betsy went home with one of the hangers-on, but was unwilling to give him the beating he wanted.

Letitia and Paolo returned to the apartment for another night of brief, intermittent bursts of physical ardour. She was overwhelmed. Each short episode, diamond sharp, and titillating, made her think of things like shooting stars and rifle fire.

Fireworks proper lit the sky, as Florence was *en fete*. Letitia had never been so happy as she was now, hop scotch-

142

ing from one ecstacy to another with her infinitely capable boy lover, feeding him chocolates and champagne between bouts, and dreaming of the art masterpiece she would eventually give to the world. Over the next few days every one of the hired models showed up. Letitia was impressed with not only their punctuality, but with their honesty, for they had been paid, if only half of the fee Paolo had insisted on, in advance.

'I recognise this guy,' Betsy whispered one day as a portly man posed with a massive erection she had helped to induce and measure for the records.

'Recognise his equipment, eh?' Letitia asked. 'No, it's the ring he's wearing,' Betsy whispered. 'Oh I guess it will come to me,' and then forgot about it as she pressed on with her work. It was all very pleasant and stimulating.

Ingrid Lindstrom Soderstrom, the eminent Swedish sexologist whose recent books had provoked a storm of revolutionary thinking among behaviourists, and whose pioneering work in Nordic health and strength movements had advanced the cause of naturism, had been sent for from Stockholm to prepare a masterly thesis on the male organ.

The basis of it was, she explained, that while the average Caucasian penis was of some fifteen centimetres in length, this meant that some were way below this, and of course, there were some that ranged to twice as much or more. Also the ratio from limp to erect was not consistent. Therefore a man with a minute penis could swell to enormous size, and a man with an extremely large piece might find it only thickening, rather than lengthening. All these theories were borne out in the preparation for the book. Some of the models, more reticent or shy, had difficulty in providing the second of the two poses that were required. Letitia had a lovely time assisting them to present themselves to their best advantage.

In all, she was enjoying the visit to Florence immensely. Paolo satisfied her every sensual need, and the gay company of the production team at dinner when work was over was a delight. However, a cloud loomed on the horizon as the book neared completion.

Someone had ratted to the press. Nasty articles began to appear in the newspapers, with insinuations of immodest behaviour, corruption, etc. Letitia was interviewed incessantly. The press hounded her to the point that an announcement was made that a certain office of the Vatican would ban the book. Letitia was horrified. 'All this work for nothing,' she cried. 'I can't bear it.'

'What a ridiculous suppression of vital information,' Ingrid, the sexologist stormed. 'Science should be unfettered. What an interference with a book that will become a standard work of reference, studied by sex clinics all over the world! This would never happen in Sweden, I tell you,' she raged.

Maurice said nothing, for he had realised that the book would make a tremendous impact in that shadowy world in which a certain kind of man takes solace from someone of his own sex, and began plans to publish a pirate version in Paris, perhaps on the presses of the notorious firm who were responsible for introducing the work of Henry Miller and other shocking writers.

Despondent, Betsy entered the Duomo, one day a little later, and listened to the Mass. The music was sublime and brought her some relief. Suddenly, watching a portly cleric at his duties, a strange sensation came over her. *I know that face*, she thought, and later, as he approached her at the communion rail, she was horrified to see the vast ruby ring she had noticed him wearing in the photographic studio. She rushed out of the holy place and ran back to the palazzo in which Letitia's apartment was situated.

'Hold everything,' she yelled. 'We're saved. Thank God for perverts and hypocrites. Gee, am I going to fix 'em. Letitia, come look here.' She rustled in the pile of photographs and found the one she was looking for. 'Here it is, the dirty old ram. Man of the cloth, eh? This guy has got the biggest dick in the book, and boy, do I mean biggest, and the big boss in Rome is making life tough for us. A bit of blackmail will do us no harm. Letitia, send a wire, baby, it goes like this, "Publishers delighted to have had co-operation of prelate in Milano STOP His full-frontal picture appreciated STOP Most impressive organ in book STOP Occupation of model raises tone of publication STOP Our discretion assured STOP Complimentary copy winging its way STOP *Ars gratia artis* STOP"'

When the telegram had been despatched, Letitia took Paolo to lunch in a little restaurant overlooking the River Arno, a romantic location where he had often stared into her eyes with the simulation of devotion over a dish of *osso-bucco* and a couple of bottles of Frascati.

'Goodbye, darling,' she wept. 'I must return to the Riviera. We shall meet again, maybe in London or Paris when the book comes out.'

Paolo also wept. Tears welled into his dark melancholy eyes, adding to the Renaissance style allure that he knew affected her so deeply. She passed him a very large bundle of lira under the table. He took it from her fragile hand, mouthing, with his incomparable fleshy lips, a kiss that signified his perpetual love for her, and wrapped her fingers around his appendage which he had conveniently removed from his trousers. 'Bless you, *carisima*!' he murmured, as the waiter brought the coffee.

Chapter Eight

'Ah, at last,' Sophie said peevishly when Bernadette returned home, for she had been alone for most of the day, feeling neglected as she whiled the time away in the secret garden room. 'Where have you been, for heaven's sake?'

'A little shopping, a little cocktail, a little visit to the couture. . . .' Bernadette's voice trailed.

'A little love, *sans doute*,' Sophie sniffed.

'Envy is not an emotion in which you should indulge, *chère cousine*,' the vicomtesse retorted imperiously, wagging a finger which was liberally decorated by gems from the House of Cartier. Sophie looked at her cousin intently. In spite of her nagging resentment she could not help admire the ravishing and utterly modish effect of the ensemble and accessories Bernadette wore so stylishly.

Perfect for modern daytime wear, her suit of aubergine gabardine wool, finely textured, was cut pencil slim over her hips and reached to exactly half-way across her knee-caps. The jacket sported a saucy peplum in the manner of Chanel, decorated with a fine strand of astrakhan, and the jaunty cloche hat, in a brave shade of cerise, was finished off with an osprey feather. The *glacé* kid shoes and clutch bag were in the same colour, all perfectly in tune with the darker tones of the rubies on the brooch and rings which added the final lustre.

Sophie, on the other hand, remained in her négligé, a see-through creation in lavender silk and Brussels lace, perilously low at the bosom, and revealing a great part of her creamy mounds. Her hair remained undressed and fell in a sweep over her bare shoulders. She spoke with some passion.

'It's hardly an enticing occupation, being left alone all day, playing solitaire, a boring game at the best of times, whose tedium is relieved only when one has an attractive man at one's side to help put the little balls in place. But I forgive you because you look so absolutely charming. I imagine you turned every head on the Croisette, *cherie*.'

'I knew your spirits would not remain crushed for long,' Bernadette laughed, 'and now I shall show you what I have brought you. *Voilà*, open it.' She threw a small package on her cousin's lap. Sophie tore off the ribbons and expensive wrappings, gurgling with pleasure. 'Oh thank you,' she breathed, 'what lingerie! Darling, you're too kind. These things must have cost a fortune.'

'They did,' Bernadette said, rather sardonically, for indeed she had parted with a large number of francs at the specialist boutique. 'But you deserve only the best. Try them on, my treasure.'

Sophie slipped out of her négligé. Bernadette noted with approval the firm texture of her cousin's body and the soft well-cared-for condition of her pale skin; the slope of her shoulders; well lifted and neatly rounded breasts; her long shapely thighs and the properly trimmed cover of her private parts. 'Your body is your greatest asset, *cheri*,' she said, running a polished nail down the length of Sophie's back and over the curve of her buttocks. 'How tight your little bottom is,' she murmured, gently squeezing the milky flesh with both hands, 'and how firm and flat your stomach,' as she ran her finger tips lightly around, fluttering and gently kneading.

147

Pressed closely to Sophie's rear she then explored upwards, massaging with slow outer circles on the breasts, rubbing daintily on the nipples with her thumbs. Sophie stretched voluptuously at these attentions, arching her back in a surprisingly athletic way, causing her rump to protrude and her head to fall backwards, releasing the long tresses of her hair downwards in a shining swathe.

'You are so lucky to have such hair,' Bernadette said. 'It is glowing with health, as is your entire frame. Let me see. Yes, you are magnificent.' Holding Sophie's finger tips she extended her arms wide, placing her cousin's to the side like a dancer's at ballet class. Then she stepped back to continue the inspection. 'Turn, slowly, *cheri*,' she commanded. Sophie obeyed, smiling with pleasure as Bernadette clapped her hands in approval. 'Heavens, if I were a man, I would be uncontrollable, I think, in the presence of such a Venus.'

'You're not so bad yourself, darling,' Sophie laughed, revolving on the discarded négligé which lay crumpled under her manicured feet.

'These strong thighs, *mon Dieu*, I imagine you use them to powerful effect, in your love play,' the vicomtesse questioned, as she ran her fingers down them, lingering to circle over the knees.

Sophie's nipples had by now begun to reveal, by their almost imperceptible swelling, the automatic arousal that another's contact with the erogenous zones will produce. She placed her palms over her bosoms, sighing lightly, in a half-hearted attempt at concealment. 'Yes I have been told I have strong action,' she giggled. 'Once I refused to release a lover from my grasp. My ankles were crossed so firmly across his back he could not make the graceful exit he wished. You know what some men are like. The moment they are finished they're off to the whisky bottle, or lighting up a cigarette. But no, this one I held on to with such determination and squeezed so hard with the prison walls, I kept him in confinement long after he went slack. It was adorable.'

'Mmmm,' Bernadette said, 'I must try it, the very next time; what a sense of power, it would be almost like draining a man of his brute strength, draining the last dregs of nectar from his exhausted body.'

'What a metaphor,' Sophie exclaimed, passing a hand briefly over the small mound between the tops of her thighs, for the reminiscence had moved her in a curious way. Her throat felt parched. 'Why don't we have a drink?'

'Why not? The sun is way past the yard arm, or whatever the ridiculous English say when they are dying for a drink,' Bernadette agreed.

'The English are not so ridiculous when it comes to making love, non?' Sophie pouted, making a little *moue*.

The vicomtesse laughed gaily, remembering the episode in the bathing complex. 'No, they are a very sporting race, darling. It must come from all that football, rugby and cricket they indulge in.'

'No, no, it comes because of the cold showers,' Sophie laughed uproariously in reply as they poured large drinks at the cabinet.

They sipped appreciatively, seated together on the divan, and suddenly remembered the items of lingerie that still lay on the small side table.

'Please try them on,' Bernadette urged. She lay back, resting her head in the brocaded cushions as Sophie began.

'But what is this?' she cried as she picked up the smallest flimsiest scrap of crimson silk. It was a triangle of no more than a few centimetres and had a narrow elasticated waistband.

'A G-string of course,' Bernadette answered. 'Chorus girls wear them in the cabaret, *non?*'

Sophie slipped into it and posed before the mirror. 'I adore the little rosebuds,' she squealed lightly, gazing at her reflection.

'It suits you to perfection,' her cousin said approvingly, 'but you must make a small adjustment here,' she added, rising and crossing to touch lightly at the crotch area of her cousin. 'Although I noticed that your pubic dimension is well groomed, a little further trimming is required. There are several slightly too long hairs which are not contained within the pouch. *Attends.*' With this she moved to the bureau, and opening a drawer, took out a small pair of nail scissors. 'Drop it a moment, *cheri.* I will fix it for you.' Taking each offending curling strand delicately between two fingers, she trimmed them neatly. 'Just so,' she said, 'not too much, not too little, but just right, so that there remains enough to be a pleasure, but not a hindrance to a lover.'

'How wise you are,' Sophie agreed. 'Too much causes some unnecessary entanglements, and too little is a hazard.'

'Absolutely! A woman's delicate area needs some cushioning, although for men it is a sacred temple, and a lover of consideration treats it with respect.'

'Devotion, I would say,' interrupted Sophie.

'Agreed,' Bernadette breathed, for like her cousin, her private parts had been the object of such devotion on many occasions, 'but, nevertheless, although for many aesthetic reasons of style and grooming, some trimming is required. Enough must remain to ensure that the moment when the most sensitive part is revealed is shrouded with an aura of mystery.'

These important considerations occupied the minds of the two women as Bernadette completed her task to perfection. '*Voilà,*' she exclaimed.

Sophie inspected herself in the mirror. Bernadette's art

had truly transformed the area in question. The triangle of scarlet silk snuggled against her mound, contrasting effectively with her pale skin, completely hiding the now charmingly groomed bodily hair. Turning round she could see the enticing way the fine elastic ran from the crotch between the cheeks of her bottom to join the low waistband. She smoothed at the minute garment with her finger tips, tracing the patterns of the small embroidered hearts which stood out in relief like tiny tokens of love. 'I'm afraid this occupation is somewhat stirring,' she breathed, feeling the warmth of her fingers translated to her part.

'*Naturellement*,' Bernadette enjoined, as she also was suffering the slightest protestation of arousal from the close contact of the toiletry in which she had been engaged. 'Nature will take its course, do not be ashamed.'

'*Mais non*, you are the perfect instructress, cousin dear,' Sophie proffered, reaching for the next garment. 'This is the most perfect pair of camiknickers I have ever seen. Your taste is impeccable. What handiwork, such fine stitching and lace. Why, the poor creature who made this must have slaved.'

'The first man to see you wearing them will slave for you more, darling,' said Bernadette, assisting her cousin to draw them on.

The clinging silk had a life of its own, billowing delicately as the wide legs of the pants were hoisted up Sophie's thighs. The wide gusset, which was constructed of pale coffee coloured lace, was sheer enough to allow a glimpse of the scarlet G-string underneath, and inset panels of the same revealed glimpses of the ivory skin of the thighs when the garment was in place.

'Ravishing,' exclaimed Bernadette, sipping at her cocktail. She went on a tour of inspection, circling round

Sophie, occasionally smoothing at the silk, passing her hands enthusiastically over her bottom. Finally she gave each buttock a friendly slap and the recipient made mock little squeals of pain. 'Oh, I am so sorry, did that hurt?' Bernadette said in the kind of voice with which one addresses a child in playful banter. 'I will kiss it better.' She slipped the camiknickers down a little and implanted several kisses on each cheek, in the meantime tutting and fretting with many sincere sounding apologies.

The secret room in which the ladies were contained rang to their laughter, and seemed, in that happy moment, never to have been put to better use in the hedonistic sense for which it was designed by the late husband of the vicomtesse. Their girlish behaviour would have charmed him, or his ghost if it roamed the elegant quiet space of its confines.

The late afternoon sun filtered through the azure glass of the domed ceiling, casting a warm glow on Sophie's flesh, and sparkling on the fresh cocktails they now prepared.

'And now this slip of a petticoat,' urged Bernadette. 'The moment I saw it, I knew it was destined for you.'

She assisted Sophie who raised her arms and allowed the thin film of transparent silk to glide down her body. Figure hugging and completely smooth as only the most costly fabrics are, the garment fitted like a glove.

A row of minute pearls ran along the lace trimming at the top which nestled against the breasts a centimetre above Sophie's now erect pink nipples. When she ran a finger across its length the tiny pearls pressed in a most pleasurable way into the skin of her sensitive mounds. She sighed voluptuously. 'I shall die when a lover does this to me,' she quivered.

'Or this,' Bernadette said, smoothing her hands downwards over her cousin's bosom, then over her belly and lastly the pelvic bone and the soft flesh underneath it.

Although this erotic centre was now covered with three layers of lingerie, the gentle pressure of the fingers was transmitted vibrantly.

'It is only with clothing of this quality that full sensation is guaranteed,' said Bernadette wisely. 'See what happens now.'

She took hold of the hem at Sophies knees and gently hoisted the slip upwards to approximately the waist, then left hold of it. Both watched in the mirror as the silk slipped and glided back into place as if drawn by some unseen hand. A shiver ran through Sophie's body, closely followed by a tremor in that of her cousin. 'It is fatally erotic. I feel disembodied.' Sophie whispered. 'It is as though the figure in the glass is someone else. I am watching another person to whom the most divine sensations are happening. Yet here I am trembling with excitement, sensations which are transporting me. Look how flushed my cheeks are.'

'The lovely reflection of your own lovely body is indeed at this moment watching your own arousal, and moreover, I am watching you. The real you I am holding in my arms, and at the same time watching myself,' the vicomtesse said, urged by a strange psychedelic set of sensations and the vision in the mirror. 'I am observing your pleasure, and at the same time aroused by being in such intimate contact with you, the silks, the lace, ah, I am transported. . . .' The voice of the vicomtesse trailed away. She ran her fingers over her own body, watching Sophie do the same to hers. Then they lightly touched each other again, marvelling in the flowering of trembling ecstacies which overtook them.

Sophie advanced towards the full length glass and pressed her body closely to it. Bernadette followed behind and placed her hands on her cousin's bare shoulders. 'I am privileged to see you like this. I have the feeling that I am witnessing the erotic arousal that can take place when sensations between lovers are enhanced by the clever use of fine fabrics. The touch of raw silk, the softness of its texture . . . I understand how these things can arouse a man.' She placed a small kiss on the nape of Sophie's neck and lightly tugged at her pink ear lobes. Sophie took hold of her hair and bunched it up to the top of her head to reveal more of her neck, with the consequence that Bernadette rained several more kisses to that area, more passionately, and then the merest tiny bite to the side, a bite which lingered gently as her tongue roved.

'We must cease this delicious play, darling, I am rather wet below. I confess my parts are on fire,' Sophie implored, gazing into Bernadette's eyes through the glass.

'On the contrary, I want now to discover what a man feels when he undresses his lover,' Bernadette said firmly, her hands stealing down to the hem of the petticoat. 'A woman needs to know the subtleties of love making if she is truly to understand the libidinous effect of play, undressing and so on.'

'Oh,' Sophie groaned, 'this game is killing me,' and her fingers went by natural instinct to stroke at her part, her nipples, and then back to her most sensitive region. She took as Bernadette slowly lifted the slip upwards, centimetre by centimetre, gasping as the material slid over her flesh. She complied when her cousin required her to lift her arms and squirmed feverishly against the mirror at the delicious sensation of it being hoisted tantalisingly up them at snail's pace, breathing in sharply at the moment when the garment was pulled clear and thrown away on to the carpet. Bernadette then proceeded to release the elastic of the camiknickers from Sophie's waist, and with enormous patience inched it over her hips, down her thighs and past her knees, before dropping them around her ankles where the garment lay in a glossy little pile. Sophie now appeared completely nude, save for the thin elastic of the waist and crotch bands of the G-string.

Bernadette lingered her hands over the cheeks of her rear, parting them slightly in order to take hold of the strand there. Sophie could feel the muscles of her love passage tense and vibrate. She pressed her belly and her soft vaginal lips on to the cool glass, rotating her hips. The no longer hidden small bud rubbed there excitedly, thrilling and quivering, sending wild messages through every fibre of her body.

Bernadette forced her hands between the mirror and Sophie's lower abdomen, first stroking at the crimson pouch material, and then stealing through the sides to play gently at the bush of dainty hair she had recently trimmed to such a refined shape. 'I am sure this is how he would do it to you,' she breathed, blowing gently into Sophie's ear. 'By now you would be extremely aroused, *non*? You would be dying for him to take you.'

'Oh, yes,' Sophie thrilled back to her cousin as she took hold of one of Bernadette's fingers and pressed it into her moist canel.

'But he would have to remove the final vestige of clothing,' Bernadette uttered hoarsely as with one swift movement she fell to her knees, pulling the G-string away to join the cami-knickers on the floor. She took speedy hold of Sophie's ankles one by one, lifting them to free the garments which were then tossed aside.

When she looked up Sophie had turned so that her back was pressed to the mirror, her own hands now clasped over her parts in a frenzied hold, and Bernadette surmised, with one finger deeply inserted. She watched as her cousin, with her eyes closed, and breathing rapidly, tossed her head from side to side and bent and stretched her knees in those few passionate seconds before she gasped in her pleasure, sinking on to the carpet in a delirium of sensual fulfilment, surrounded by the shining flimsy items of lingerie which had precipitated the afternoon's delightful play and its orgasmic conclusion.

Chapter Nine

A few days later, at a *thé dansant* which was being held in a rather louche hotel a few kilometres along the corniche, the sort of place where faded and jaded lovers repair their romances, Sophie was found instructing Dhokouminsky in the art of the tango and the foxtrot. It was part of her ongoing efforts to civilise the wild Slav dancer. She had already taken him to several galleries and exhibitions, some grand restaurants and a succession of boring museums, but to little effect. The raffish dancer had broken wind, burped, and generally ashamed her with his loutish behaviour, but Sophie was so enamoured that she persevered in the difficult task she had set herself. Even here, beneath the Japanese paper lanterns and bunting, surrounded by decorous middle-aged couples, some of whom had arrived dressed as pierrots and columbines in the manner of the period, he was continuing to be a menace.

He flirted outrageously with the hat-check girl, who admittedly possessed a gamine charm, and with the elderly waitress who at intervals brought them their cocktails. While the other dancers were engaged in a sedate foxtrot he whirled Sophie round in a poor imitation of a movie routine, knocking aside other dancers without apology, and in a perverse version of the turkey trot, managed to floor completely an elderly lady whose wig flew off.

Between dances he pawed at Sophie, biting her neck and arms, delicious attentions that she would have adored in another situation but were inappropriate here.

She was wondering how to get him away from the place when the band struck up a tango. He threw himself immediately at her feet and kissed her shoe. At first she refused to rise but his engaging grin and clicking fingers encouraged her to come into his grip. The slow passionate music had the assembled dancers enthralled. The old lady at the piano swooped her fluttering hands around the keyboard and the nubile accordionist added suitable arpeggios, while the violinist swayed seductively to the insistent rhythm.

It was a tormented afternoon. Some of the crowd were new lovers, their feelings were intense, and others were trying to come to terms with the various infidelities they had inflicted on each other. Frederick Delius had anticipated the scene in his *Walk to the Paradise Garden* in which two lovers confronted a tragic destiny. A mirror ball revolved over the swaying dancers' heads and the light from the Japanese lanterns threw pools of colour on to the floor. The warmth and the intoxication blunted the senses of everyone to all but their own immediate sensations. With their bodies pressed closely together, or even bestowing deep kisses on their partners, the couples dreamily entered an Argentian fantasy to the steady insistent beat of the small orchestra and the accompanying drum.

Dhokouminsky had a sentimental nature, being of Slav origin, and the seductive swaying rhythm of the tango entered his soul. Holding his partner Sophie so tight that she could hardly breathe he steered her around the floor in a graceful swooping action. She could feel the rising strength of an erection through the soft folds of her dress and the gabardine of his trousers. When he stopped in his tracks to rock her to and fro, his body, squeezed up tightly against hers, transmitted his urgent signals and in spite of herself Sophie could not resist making some response. Her breasts, so close to his chest, heaved against him with some passion, and activated by the compelling music she nuzzled in his ear.

His hands were now clasped around her behind, pressing deeply into her flesh through the silk of her dress and the crêpe-de-chine of her underwear. He rotated his hands against her rump in the same way that he rotated his pelvis, with its stiffened member against her crotch, sucking at her neck with burning lips. They danced in this manner for many minutes, their love juices lubricating their private parts in a tantalising anticipatory manner, swooning against each other in the extremes of their mutual ardour until he led her into a section of the ballroom where the flashing reflections of the revolving silver-mirrored ball in the ceiling could not penetrate.

There were a few other couples in this shady intimate area who were more or less as advanced in their sexual throes as our hero and his companion. More inhibited than Dhokou-minsky, they were prepared to go along with the conventions of the *thé dansant*, albeit in much closer contact than etiquette really required.

Such aquiescence was not for the premier dancer. In the darkest corner, but still where his every action could have been observed by a keen eye, he slid a hand down Sophie's dress, lifted the hem and brought his fingers up to her warm crotch, massaging it lightly in time to the music.

The cocktails, the sultry heat and the vibrant emphasis of the beat of the music led Sophie into immediate acceptance of his stealthy manipulations. Still dancing, she pressed the warm lips of her part to his fingers, and pressed her tongue into his mouth. When he returned the compliment by exploring her mouth with his tongue he pushed a finger slowly into her private part with a finger from his other hand pressed towards the same region from behind.

Pausing a moment in his attentions to her vibrant centre, he opened his flies and, bringing her hand down, wrapped it around his throbbing machine. She felt the jissom flowing freely from the tip and eased some of the love juice over his stiff head. With the other hand she lifted the skirt which was the sole fragile obstacle between them and eased away the crotch of her camiknickers to one side. Bending his knees he managed to introduce his swollen member into her lubricated opening a few centimetres. She gasped involuntarily, but the sound passed unnoticed in the music.

They were almost still now, only rocking gently to and fro, but the shock waves of pleasure that coursed through their bodies carried them into a transport far beyond their surroundings. Unnoticed by the other couples, they streamed their hot liquids at each other in a quite remarkable series of orgasmic thrusts, and, as the dancer reminded himself afterwards, in absolute time with the music.

Blissfully they made their way back to Monte Carlo in a horse drawn carriage. The ancient driver was long used to the idiotic behaviour of lovers, and had also passed the age when their antics affected him in any sensual way. Under the blanket which was thoughtfully provided, Dhokouminsky continued his stimulations of Sophie's lower reaches.

It was dusky and romantic along the coast road, with the remains of what had been a spectacular sunset. Sophie closed her eyes and yielded to his ministrations and ardent whispered expressions of undying love. The Slav dancer's hard muscular body almost enveloped her slimmer form, as he plundered into it, causing her to groan with delight and make little inward hisses of breath through her clenched teeth. It was as if she were a musical instrument which he could play to perfection, drawing the sweetest sounds.

As the carriage approached the border of the Principality, Sophie came near to a shattering climax. The whole afternoon and evening at the tango dance had excited every one of her senses to a manic degree. She pushed the burly dancer to one side, pleading for patience. 'I want you in bed, darling,' she whispered urgently in his ear,' and then she shouted to the driver. 'Hurry up, can't you, *mon vieux*? I want you to drop us at the Hotel de Paris.' Sophie could not have lasted as far as Bernadette's mansion which was a long way down the corniche, so a bed in the hotel seemed in order.

As the horse broke into a canter, woken from his stupor by the driver's whip, she snuggled up closely to Dhokouminsky and sought his flagrantly throbbing member under the blanket. The dancer was pleased on two counts. Not only was Sophie rendering him a thrilling sensation, but like the magical way they had danced the tango, it came in a perfectly musical and rhythmic manner, this time to the clip clop clopping of the old animal's hooves.

Arriving at the forecourt, they hurriedly adjusted their dress and entered the hotel. There was an air of fever about them which the grinning desk clerk recognised as being the urgency which can consume aroused lovers. He sprinted with the key, and escorted them to the lift with as much alacrity as if he himself were the lucky one about to indulge in a night of rapture.

Sophie and Dhokouminsky shot into their allotted room. Fire burned in their loins and, of course, in those of the desk clerk who fell to his knees at the keyhole. The pair had only got their clothes off and ripped open the covers of the bed when an assistant manager came along and found the devotee enthralled at the scene. He naturally ordered the Peeping Tom away, and equally naturally took up the same position as soon as the minion turned the corner of the corridor.

The dancer and his beloved Sophie showed that young man a few things that were, to say the least, educative, and we can presume that his pretty little wife also stood to gain. Such are the benefits that love can bring to the world.

Downstairs in the gilded dining room, Arthur's dinner with Galina, the blonde soubrette from the ballet, proceeded apace.

The buxom dancer from St. Petersburg had a warm nature and laughed a great deal, often at her own expense, especially over how she dealt with the elaborate sets of cutlery, napery and finger bowls that were the norm in the grand establishment but, alas, foreign to her.

She managed to use everything in the wrong order and mistook the finger bowl for a glass of vodka. The taste not being what she expected she naturally spat the water into the nearby ice-bucket. Arthur roared with delight at her completely natural behaviour and rectified the situation by calling for a bottle of her favourite drink, icily chilled and flavoured with caraway seeds. They toasted themselves, the ballet season, her success in the career she had chosen, friends, the head waiter and all manner of things and people, tossing the vodka down their throats in true Russian style.

In her very broken English, and with much gesturing, she told him an extremely risqué story. The incident took place when, much younger, she was dancing in a Russian circus. The tour took them to all the major cities of the motherland and was an enormous success, with its bears, elephants, clowns, acrobats and so on. She fell mildly in love with a handsome Cossack, the leader of a troupe of wild horsemen who performed brilliant acrobatic tricks as the sleek and highly trained animals charged round the circus ring.

This Ivan doted on her, she explained, following her everywhere like a sad little spaniel, and performing little attentive services for her like polishing her boots and carrying her baggage. He was so good looking and so dashing in the ring her natural admiration, prompted by his constant attention, grew and eventually her pretty head was turned. After performances they would stroll in the park or along a river bank and find a secluded spot where he could serenade her with his balalaika.

The memory of those sad Russian folk tunes brought a tear to her enormous green eyes and, swaying in her chair with another glass of vodka in her hand, she sang a plaintive refrain in a deep contralto, causing other diners to put down their forks and stare in amazement at the unusual pair.

She had finally succumbed to his charms one night under an especially romantic canopy of stars, after such a song had been crooned in her ear, and began to live with him in his travelling caravan. Their passion for each other knew no bounds and his demands on her body were rapture to her. Even at rehearsals he would slip away and return to the caravan for a few moments of mutual gratification, and he even took her on the straw of the stables between grooming sessions.

Their joy in each other was complete. Apart from admiring his polished but reckless-seeming horsemanship, she adored his generosity and good humour. What fun it was to travel the length and breadth of the vast lonely country with such a companion, she recalled, and how he had loved her dancing, her long blonde tresses, and her cooking over the open fire by the wayside.

Their passion led them into some embarrassing scenes as he wished to possess her whenever the urge came upon him.

One such moment came when he had drawn her underneath a circus wagon which unfortunately was pulled away by the workhorses at the very moment their coupling came to a climax.

The worst incident, she told the spellbound Arthur, happened late at night when the audience had gone home and the circus folk had gone to bed. It was stiflingly hot and Ivan had suggested a stroll to the tent where his horses were kept overnight. He wanted to show her a new stallion he had bought from the Caucusus, an animal which, when trained, would be the star of his act.

He led the beast from its stall and stealthily they went into the big circus tent. With only a bridle to steer with, he took the beautiful horse for a trot around the ring to get the measure of its natural pace and then vaulting on to its bare back did a couple of circuits at speed. It was exhilarating to watch. Galina clapped and cheered and suddenly Ivan swept her up in his arms and threw her into the space between him and the horse's flowing mane. The energetic movement of the stallion and the close grip of her lover stimulated her to a daring action. She threw off her blouse and continued the canter barebreasted. Ivan likewise discarded his shirt and slung it away over his shoulder.

As the horse moved faster round the ring he felt her breasts, rubbing his hands over their ample proportions and squeezing her lovely nipples. She could feel his handsome erection behind her and moved a hand round past her bottom to stroke it through his cossack trousers.

The rider, accustomed all his life to the equestrian arts, and especially the dare devil antics of the Russian circus, found no difficulty in releasing his member and in hoisting up her skirts, or even in introducing his throbbing organ to her eager recess. Her weight was nothing as he hoisted her up and brought her down on his bouncing tip. As the horse careered about the ring he eased his magnificently aroused and swollen penis still further inside her until the moment when it was completely thrust to the hilt. With an abandoned gesture she pulled her skirt over her head and kicked off her boots so that now she was completely naked, bouncing up and down in thrilling pleasure on that part of him she most adored.

At their climax the reckless Cossack threw his torso backwards causing his head to fall over the stallion's tail and his legs high in the air.

During a last breathless circuit, they pumped their juices out in orgasmic splendour, she shrieking out her ecstatic delight and he a barbaric shrill call which must have originated in the far off Steppes.

As he drew the foaming stallion to a halt and they slid exhausted, but in a state of rapture, from his back, they heard a tumult of applause. In the dim light of the tent they saw, to their horror, the entire circus company. A stable hand had heard a sound in the tent and had gone to arouse the members of the troupe in case there were undesirables, possibly thieves, in their midst.

Tears rolled down Galina's cheeks as she described how the company had entered stealthily and hidden behind the bench seats when they discovered it was only her and Ivan up to some naughty prank. All laughed uproariously, she said, and the ringmaster said 'Bravo, bravo, what a wonderful new act. Shall we work it into the show tomorrow night?'

Chapter Ten

M. Rognon was keenly disappointed that the English aristocrat, Lady Letitia, had not kept her promise to attend his current exhibition.

When he made enquiries, friends told him of her flight to Italy on the midnight express. They scandalised a great deal about Letitia's husband, the feckless Frederick Fanshawe, and his drunken ways, mentioning the vast sums of money that were being squandered on his alcohol addiction. Rognon, being of a practical Gallic disposition, with an eye for the main chance in business matters, thought that here was a case where cash could be better spent. He therefore invited Fanshawe to the elegant gallery in Antibes where the much publicised show, *L'Art du Vingtième Siècle*, was installed.

Rognon's premises were situated in the old town, high in the ramparts of the ancient fortress which dominated the bay. Skilful architects had insinuated, into a cavernous opening in the castle walls that had probably contained the original gaol, the most sophisticated exhibition space imaginable. It was full of the clear light of the Mediterranean, being completely surrounded by glass and fitted with furniture and shelving in bright chrome.

The dealer's reputation had grown considerably in the last few years, as he showed the work of new important painters and sculptors, fashionable masters of Expressionism, Art Deco and Cubism. His gallery was covered by critics from the international press and prestigious magazines, and his clients now included the richest and most eclectic of assiduous collectors.

Fanshawe was not impressed. He failed to understand Rognon's excitement as the dealer showed him around, or indeed why he used such elaborate effeminate gestures. He knew that Rognon was, to say the least, a committed heterosexual, and in private, away from his work, behaved like a normal gruff sort of fellow. But here he was, waving his arms about and drooping his wrists like a drag dancer at Minskis, as he pointed out the felicities of this painting or that.

'See, my friend,' Rognon said, swooping towards a huge canvas which was covered in daubs of daring and aggressive colour, 'the forms, the shapes and delineation of the figure. Ah, isn't it wonderful. The light and the chiaroscuro, breathtaking, don't you think?'

'It's unusual, certainly,' Fanshawe agreed, 'but tell me, why are there two raw fish instead of breasts on the fat lady?'

Rognon chuckled and poked him in the ribs. 'I suppose the artist made a meal of her. What a delightful record of the relationship that existed between him and his model.'

'And why is this woman's private part shaped like the hole in a guitar and covered with a fret and strings?'

'My friend, I can only suggest that the painter had made music on it,' replied the resourceful dealer, an oily grin playing round his mouth.

'You mean they buy this shit,' Fanshawe said incredulously. He determined immediately to buy some paints and canvas and see if he couldn't do as well, especially after inspecting the next picture which showed a grotesquely formed harpy swinging on a crescent moon over a sea which

167

was populated by long-haired ravishing mermaids. It was exactly the sort of vision he had when he had consumed a bottle of Pernod.

Nearby was a collage composed of headlines torn from newspapers such as *Figaro* and *Le Monde*, old photographs and clippings from catalogues advertising household goods. Prominent, over the centre of the composition, was a suspended lavatory bowl, and hanging overhead a broken violin.

'The work has deep mystery,' Rognon breathed in Fanshawe's ear. 'It is the masterpiece of the year. The overtones of eroticism are undeniably profound, and it is already sold. The price is a record for the gallery.'

Fanshawe was truly amazed. His formative years had been spent in Paris, surrounded by a throng of other American pseudo-intellectuals who, like himself, played the role of penniless bohemians thirsty to absorb European culture.

He was supported in his artistic endeavours by a very adequate monthly income, supplied by his father who owned a canning operation in Texas. There were many times when he had praised the Lord for the public's addiction to corned beef.

These earnest writers and painters had virtually taken over Montparnasse and Monmartre and kept the local hoteliers and restauranteurs very happy. How they had revelled in Les Halles late into the early hours, drinking the bars dry and amazing the keepers of the brothels of those *quartiers*, not only with the amounts of money they had to spend, but also with their staying power.

On the whole, however, Parisian culture had left them cold. Fanshawe's painter friends had developed a nice line in the sort of landscape that sells well to the tourist market. Heavily influenced by Monet, Manet, Maurice Utrillo, Cezanne, Van Gogh and many other French masters, they had managed to mass produce thousands of typically charming and innocuous street scenes and interiors, destined to end up on the walls of suburban sitting rooms. The real thrusting world of modern art had evaded these painters as surely as if they were living on the moon, and the writers were so engrossed with trying to understand the mysteries of James Joyce, D. H. Lawrence and Henry James that they never found their own language. It was in this trivial pursuit of the 'American Novel' that Frederick had foundered. He was still basically an all-American provincial boy whose principal strength lay not in his brain but in his testicles.

'I need a drink,' he said abruptly. As Rognon was also in need of alcoholic refreshment, they repaired to a taxi and a pleasant little drive to Juan les Pins where Rognon had a favourite fish restaurant.

The Chablis was beautifully iced and served by a charming waitress who kept their glasses permanently full. The *soles veroniques*, with their glazed peeled grapes and mildly cheese-flavoured sauce were delicious, as were the *croquettes* of lobster meat served on a bed of *morilles*.

After lunch the pair took coffee and liqueurs in the shaded garden verandah at the rear of the premises, attended by the lovely rounded-breasted girl who had served them inside. Her swaying hips and long lashed glances served to arouse some sort of post-prandial languor in the two, and a slight stiffening of their respective organs.

'Sex is a curse,' opined the failed novelist. 'It is the constant rasping greed of my body that has so far prevented me from producing a masterpiece. Gee, when I sit down at a typewriter I really object to the way sex rears its ugly head and gets in between me and the paper. Or sometimes, when I think I'm really into a good idea, there I go, I fall in love, or at least I get the hots for some girl or other and I simply cannot concentrate.'

Rognon was not impressed by his friend's apologia. He would have been more inclined to lay the trouble at the door of the demon drink. 'The agonies of creative people are a minefield. I'm full of sympathy. But remember, my friend, out of torture comes Art. You must suffer in order to create. Tell me an example of the kind of thing that troubles you.'

Warmed by the cognac which they were now consuming in large quantities, Frederick, who anyway had no interesting, angst-filled artistic revelations to make, being really not much more than a pretentious tourist, wracked his brains for a dirty story, which was really, he knew, what Rognon wanted to hear.

'I was living in the rue Latouche at the time, high on La Butte, starving in a little garret,' he lied. 'My new book wasn't going well. It was high summer and anyone with any brains had come down here to the south for the sea breezes, anything to escape the fierce heat of Paris. But I was stuck in this tiny little attic wrestling with six characters in search of an author. The heat was getting me down, my friend, I couldn't concentrate and deliver the goods. I remember, God, it was stifling and I'd run out of beer. The bar downstairs was closed and most of my chums were out of town. I took a nap, with all my clothes off, it was so goddam hot, and then I found myself pacing up and down, still trying to come to grips with the massive undertaking I'd made. It was a book of huge proportions, complex and neurotic. Compulsive reading I'd say, if only I could get on with it.

'I suddenly was amazed to see a woman in a window over the way. You know how those Parisian skylines—tiled roofs, chimneys and balconies—all merge together into a wonderful landscape, well there she was, standing at a window opposite my little attic. She seemed, as far as I could see, to be nude herself. I could only see her breasts, but they were naked.'

'Was she pretty?' Rognon asked.

'As a picture,' Fanshawe replied. 'I recognised her as being a singer from a café I had been in once. Dark haired, dark eyed, a glamorous little number with big tits. I felt a bit odd. You know how it is—a hot afternoon, and there I was slouching around with a bit of a hard on, thinking about Emily, my new girl friend who just came in from New England.'

'I suppose she must have noticed your erection. Was her window close enough for her to have seen in detail?' Rognon breathed.

'Sure thing,' Fanshawe replied. 'The bitch rolled her tongue round her lips and then stroked her breasts with her eyes fixed on me all the time.

'By this time I must admit I was getting a bit excited. I went to my window and smiled at her. She smiled back and pressed her lips to the glass of her window in a sort of kiss. Then she pulled all the pins out of her hair and shook it loose. She put her hands behind her neck and ran her fingers through her hair upwards, fanning it out and letting it fall. I guess she must have done it a dozen times.

'Do you know what she had the gall to do next. She stuck a finger in her mouth and sucked it in the most provocative manner, in and out, deep up to the hilt, then sideways along its length. Her eyes were teasing me. She was saying, "How would you like this to be happening to you, mister?" My hand was round my root by this time and my juices had really got going. I tell you my balls were hard as baseballs and I thought I'd shoot my load on the curtains.

'Then the hussy climbed up on something so she was more exposed. Her belly was now in view and she circled it with both her hands, wriggling her hips round and round till I nearly bust my gut. Her tongue kept sliding in and out of her

171

mouth, bright pink, and she wriggled it from side to side. I tell you I was throbbing like crazy.

'Suddenly her hands went out of view and I knew she was playing with her pussy, leading me on some more. Her body was quite still but her head was thrown back. She probably came that way because she pressed her whole body against the window and squirmed around like she was having a real good time.'

'Not a word was spoken?' asked M. Rognon, his voice trembling.

'Not a single word,' the narrator affirmed. 'It was all in dumb show and I was feeling pretty dumb myself by now I can tell you. I didn't want to jerk myself off and lose it, buster, so you know what I did? I climbed on a goddam chair and waved my prick at her. She blew me kisses and rubbed her breasts and made like she would like to get her mouth round my tool, but big as I was that would have been hard at ten yards' distance.

'I rubbed my dick a bit but not too much. I didn't want to shoot right then and there. So I leaned on the glass and pretended it was her. With my dick vertical on the pane I pressed up and down like I was having her. She was going mad I tell you.'

M. Rognon was now in a state of great agitation and almost took a swipe at the rear of the adorable waitress's behind in his passion. But he placed a hand in his pocket and held tight to his most precious possession as he implored Frederick to continue.

'She held a hand up to her mouth making like having a drink and pointed downwards. I looked at the clock. The bar downstairs would have re-opened by now and I guessed she was telling me we should meet there. Anyway she disappeared from view so I got dressed, stuffing myself into my trousers the best I could and got down those goddam stairs as fast as I could.

'I waited there for half an hour. Boy, did she put me on the wrack. I wondered if she'd cooled off, but anyway she came in and sat down straightaway at my table and bent over and stuck her tongue down my throat as if we were lovers. She called for a drink and went to work on my knees under the tablecloth and all the way up to my groin, as far as she could decently reach. The proprietor didn't flinch a muscle. We were the only customers and he hid himself behind the evening newspaper.

'Do you know what she did next? She threw her handbag up in the air and it landed under the table. "*Mon Dieu*," she yelled, and got down on the floor to retrieve what had fallen out. But she didn't bother with that. She opened my flies and took a good hold of me with her mouth, sucking so darn hard I found it difficult to keep a straight face in case the bar-owner looked across.

'I had to push her lips away and do up my buttons as I was so sure I'd spill, and I couldn't guarantee that I'd be quiet doing that. She came back up, licking her lips and putting a few things back in her bag. Still not a word was said.

'She stood up and wandered around to my side of the table. She muzzed up my hair and kissed me all over my face and neck, biting in all the right places. She really knew what she was doing. Then she shoved a hand down my shirt and played with my nipples and chest hair. She found my belly button and with the other hand unclasped my belt so she could go on down further.

'She found my knob and rubbed the juices that were running from it all down the length of my stem and squeezed my balls in a wonderful way, with her mouth clasped over mine.'

The nubile wine waitress passed by again. The eyes of both the men fastened on her as if she was the central object of the erotic story the novelist was weaving. She was, naturally, delighted at having aroused their attention to such a degree and brought them an extra cognac on the house.

Fanshawe went on to describe the remainder of the wordless sexual encounter; the reckless way they behaved in the under populated bar; and their final deliverance from the sensual traumas of the afternoon.

The amazing lady, who was indeed a singer from a *boite* in Montmartre, then sat opposite the tired novelist and extended a pink tongue down into a small glass of wine. She rubbed her tongue around her lips while she senuously applied loving pressure to her loins. She found the small bud which was at the seat of her pleasure, and by sliding a finger under the leg of her knickers, managed to bring herself to the point of complete ecstasy.

Frederick, being a man of the world, knew what she was doing. The knowledge of this aroused in him the barbaric instincts of primitive man. Watching her, he was inspired to let a hand stray down and undo his flies. His extended member was, by now, bursting with his activated juices and threatened to explode at the slightest touch. The merest caress of his member brought on the most enthralling muscular spasms and a tremor like an electric shock that travelled from his frenum down the stem of his distended organ and through his testicles to return up his spine.

When his orgasmic explosion occurred her riveting eyes were focused on his. She lifted her glass of cognac and drained the last few dregs, wiping her tongue around the interior, for all the world as if she was savouring his ejaculating fluid.

Then she ran her tongue around her carmine painted

mouth and said, voluptuously, curving her sensual lips, 'Monsieur, the hors d'oeuvre was delicious, may we now proceed to the main course.' And with that she picked up her handbag and wrapped her small feather boa around her shoulders, slightly quivering her tightly covered backside.

She left the café humming a little song which she had made famous in the *boite* where she performed, looking over her shoulder to where the novelist was essaying to tidy up the area of his crotch. 'Would monsieur like his meat *seignant* or *bien cuit*?' she asked.

'You naturally followed?' asked the breathless Rognon.

'You bet your sweet life. I belted up those stairs like there was no tomorrow,' replied Fanshawe, drawling the more now as he was near to complete drunkenness. 'I used her character like crazy in my novel. She opened up a whole new area for me that was original unexplored territory. I was so grateful to her, and boy, did I give it to her for a long period, we were perfect lovers.'

'Ah,' the art dealer sighed, 'it sounds blissful. And the novel? I presume it became a success. It was published?'

'God no,' the author replied. 'The bastards said I was good at narrative and short on dialogue. What do you have to do to impress those sharks?'

After such a revelation Rognon owed Fanshawe a story by return. He was unsure that he could dredge up anything as interesting as the arresting vision the novelist had conjured.

Men are always unsure of their own sexual exploits. They imagine that their friends are having much more fun, or worse still – on account of that dreadful affliction of the male species which is called penis-envy—that other men's girlfriends are having a better time than their own.

In spite of his modest reservations he managed to entertain Frederick on their walk back home to Antibes.

It was late in the afternoon by now and the early autumn sun was beginning its slow descent into the deep blue sea which they caught glimpses of as they rounded bends in the road on the way back. There was a heavy scent from the oleanders and pines in the gardens of the exclusive villas which were ranged along the road, the homes of rich foreigners and minor aristocrats who had chosen to put roots down in this very special enclave.

Aston Martins, Bentleys, Bugattis, Mercedes, Lancias and Alfa Romeos swished up the surrounding drives, depositing their well-dressed passengers at the evening's cocktail parties, and loud hot-jazz music came from the doorway of every villa they passed.

Lovers promenaded in the sultry evening air, their arms wound round one another, their mouths in each others ears, with the promise of pleasures to come.

In such a romantic setting M. Rognon was unsure about revealing the episode that Fanshawe insisted on him extracting from his memory bank. In these circumstances the story he was about to dredge up seemed rather louche, but as they were both well oiled it didn't matter that much in the end. 'Auto-eroticism has always interested me,' he began.

'What is auto-eroticism?' Fanshawe asked, not being too well acquainted with the latest psychological jargon.

'It is, or rather it suggests, or, it could be,' mumbled his friend who was playing for time because he did not really understand completely the subject he had so bravely embraced, 'a state of mind, or rather body, where a certain amount of sexual stimulation occurs without an outside influence, that is, where a man, alone in a room, is in a state of sensual excitement without any provocation what-soever from a member of the other sex.'

'Cut the lecture, chum,' his friend implored. 'We all know what it is to have a hard-on for no good reason.'

'Your story reminded me of something that happened years ago when I had a particular lover, an English girl who always managed to surprise me with her sexual fantasies. You have heard the English are supposed to be very austere and inhibited in their ways, regarding the affairs of the heart?'

'You mean the body,' interrupted his American friend.

'Quite,' Rognon continued. 'This particular girl forced me into playing a ridiculous game. It was charming, delightful sometimes, but my goodness, one was required to be as effective as a player at the *Comédie Française* to do it well. I will explain.

'We were in London at the time. I met Clarice in the reading room of the British Museum. We were both students of art and we continued to meet at the Victoria and Albert Museum, the Tate Gallery, the National Gallery and so on. Ah, those balmy evenings strolling around Bloomsbury. She was a charming girl, the daughter of a suffragette and a follower of the teachings of Beatrice Webb.' Fanshawe wished he would get to the point.

'She admired the Pre-Raphaelites enormously. We argued endlessly about the merits of those painters whom I considered to be pedants, narcissistic nature worshippers and sentimental old women.' He looked across at Fanshawe and realised that his thesis was lost on the ill-educated American.

'Anyway, to cut a long story short, she wore long skirts and she had waist long hair, Titian coloured, and she wore the most extraordinary clothes, bangles, beads, headbands and so on. It was all done to cover up the steaming passion which consumed her mind and body twenty-four hours a day.

'At night when all the extraneous garments were shed she was like any other ordinary mortal, but through the day she

177

was like a gipsy, a *gitane*, roaming the streets looking like a vamp in search of a conquest.

'We often met in the evening at a public house in Covent Garden, which was the haunt of fruit salesmen and market porters who drank into the early hours rather like they do in Les Halles.

'She came in one evening and sat beside me but pretended not to know me. She asked me my name and I said, "Nonsense, you know who I am or have you been drinking already?"

'She said she was a princess of a Polynesian tribe in Tahiti and her name was Khalua, so in return I told her that I was a Hungarian revolutionary with a mission to shoot the Prime Minister. I fell into her hands, you see, into the trap of playing the game. The Game. It is a British institution.'

Fanshawe raised his eyebrows. 'I hope there's a point to this British story,' he said wearily. 'In my experience the English are a frosty lot.'

'Not this Clarice, I assure you. At that time, though, in the Edwardian era, she was a rare bird. Girls were still in corsets and bloomers, but this delightful girl had radically thrown away such constricting garments. She was in a delirium, walking down the streets of London, thinking how shocked its stalwart citizens would be if they knew she had no underwear on, nor bust bodice, just her curvaceous body as nature intended. She was indeed an early feminist, a precursor of the heroines and tragic victims of D. H. Lawrence.' He went on to describe how their fantasies led them into many escapades, as on this occasion.

'Anyway,' Rognon continued, 'she suddenly said, "You are not a Hungarian anarchist, that is too far-fetched. I won't play," I said she was no more a Tahitian princess. "Go out of that door immediately," Clarice commanded, "and come back as somebody reasonably believeable or I shall go home forthwith."

'I went out, turned round three times, came back in, ordered a drink and wandered across to the table where Clarice sat drinking her beer. I said "Excuse me, do you mind if I sit here? It's so crowded in this bar."

'She was so modest, refined, and sat with her head lowered, the perfect picture of an English lady. When pressed, she told me that she was a governess, recently departed from her position in Worthing, a south coast resort, and I told her that I was an apprentice in the Inns of Court, articled to a famous lawyer.

'She cried a little. Although I knew, of course, that she was acting out a role, I felt obliged to ask her why she was so distressed. The fictitious story was remarkable.

'The minx made out that the husband of the household where she was employed had overstepped the mark in his dealings with her. One night he entered her room. She was reading by candlelight, absorbed in her book, a novel by Ouida. He was savage in his demands and pressed his hand over her mouth, asking her for sexual favours such as she had never heard of. She cried and resisted, but she was so afraid of the children in her charge, who were asleep in the next bedroom, hearing this brouhaha that she gave in to the monster's vile requests.

'The next morning the mistress of the house questioned her in a most intimidating and insolent manner. She insinuated that she knew a great deal about what had gone on in the poorly furnished bedroom with the gas turned down low. Perhaps the husband had boasted somewhat.

'"Monstrous," I cried, "and I supposed they dismissed you from their service?"

'"Alas," she wept, "I am alone in London without

179

employment, and with no savings. I do not know where to go or to whom I can turn."'

Rognon told the story so well that the novelist had to hold back an involuntary tear.

He continued with the gripping narrative. He offered to buy the unfortunate girl a little supper in a nearby Dining Room. Fortunately, due to the late hour, they were able to sit in a dark corner and go on with this thespian exercise. Of course, by now, the two participants were so engrossed in the titillating fiction they stayed in character superbly.

'"Poor child," Rognon sympathised. "I shall ask my superior whether a case could be brought against that blackguard."

'"Oh no," she implored. "I just want to retire to the country to a little cottage owned by my distant great-aunt and forget my shame."

'The small café was warm and lit by hissing gas lamps. Outside in the swirling London fog the newspaper boys were yelling the headlines. The police were seeking the latest mass murderer and there were reports of several brutal attacks of a sexual nature. But, inside, the simple food was warm and delicious, served in plain china bowls. We ate jellied eels and mashed potatoes, and the waiter went out to the public house for more ale. It was a glorious experience. Both Clarice and I thought we were back in the time of Charles Dickens.

'Over steaming cups of hot chocolate, the poor ex-governess asked me to escort her to Charing Cross station as she was so afraid of the dark, and anyway did not have enough money for a cab fare as well as her railway ticket.

'Thoroughly wound up in the story we wended our way through Covent Garden and along the Strand. I held Clarice close and tried to make her promise to write to me when she was settled. It was so affecting. I turned her towards me under the glare of a street lamp. Tears were streaming down her face. I was so involved in my acting that I failed to notice a small curious crowd gathering around us.

'We strolled on, getting nearer the famous terminal. Clarice suddenly ran away down a side street. I was panic-stricken. I raced after her and found her in the doorway of a seedy looking hotel situated in Villiers St., the notorious haunt of the prostitutes of the day.

'She had a cigarette in her mouth, and stood with a hand on her hip in a louche inviting gesture. She threw her arms around my neck and planted a wet kiss on my cheek. "Ello mister," she said "are yer lookin' for a good time?" Her free hand flew down to my crotch and she caressed me in the most suggestive way.

'I said, "You're cheating. This is not the way a governess from Worthing would behave,"

'"What on earth gave you that idea, dearie?" she said. "I'm a girl on the make." She slid her hand into my flies, which she had deftly opened.

'I was alarmed. People were passing by in the street and I thought they would notice us. But I must confess, what she was doing to my nether regions was so pleasurable that I turned my back to the street and pushed her further into the dark doorway so that she could proceed undetected.' Rognon sighed at the memory and proceeded to describe how her hand roved around his scrotum and through his pubic hair while she chewed at the lobe of his ear.

His thickening stem responded magnificently to her attentions and a pulse throughout its length brought her great satisfaction. After only a few seconds of this delicious, titillating massage she felt a small globule of his love juices appear at this tip end, and by gently peeling back his thick foreskin, she could spread this viscous liquid around his swollen glans.

'Then she said to me, "You must play the game. This is Act Two and I have changed character. You must do likewise."

"Alright, love," I said. "How much?"

"Five shillings to you, cos you're a gent, and you'll treat me nice I know," Clarice said. "Come on in, it's bleedin' cold out 'ere dearie."

'Without more ado,' Rognon told Frederick, 'she pushed open the door and led me inside.

'At a desk in the shabby hallway a tousled harridan sat reading the evening newspaper. Her black hair was piled in coils on her head and fixed with combs like a Spanish dancer might wear. Heavy gold earrings and chains and a fringed shawl helped to complete her picaresque appearance, as did the vermillion lipstick which had been lavishly applied to her full mouth. "Ere you are, darling," she said, handing Clarice a bedroom key and waving carelessly in the direction of the stairs. It was as if Clarice was well known to the establishment.'

'You don't say,' said Fanshawe. 'Do you reckon she was really on the streets?'

'I can say categorically that she was not,' replied Rognon with some disdain.' I expect that she had visited the place earlier in the day and made an arrangement with the madame in order to make her little charade the more convincing to me.'

'What a gal,' the novelist whistled, and he began to think that the scenario was good material for one of his salacious novels.

Rognon agreed and continued with his story. 'We bounded up the stairs and Clarice led me directly to a small room on the second floor. There was a single naked light bulb and flimsy curtains which could hardly keep out the light from the street lamps outside.

'Clarice lay languidly on the brass bedstead and pulled up her skirts, exposing her naked private parts which she lazily rubbed with both her hands.

'"Don't take all night, love," she crooned. "After all, I've got other business to attend to. You gents are all the same. You think for a few bob you've got me for the duration, but listen, love, after you, I've got to get me a dozen more blokes if I'm goin' to pay the rent this week."

'She lit a cigarette and let it dangle from the side of her mouth and then resumed her attentions to the area of her groin. I leaned over the foot of the bed and watched as she writhed her hips around with her knees splayed well out to the side. Her fingers teased her Titian pubic hair, parting the fronds from her pink lips, and ran up her soft white belly and down the insides of her thighs.

'She wet a finger with her spittle and circled it around the small bud she revealed and, with the fingers of her other hand, opened her outer lips to disclose the paler shining skin of the inner ones that were now glistening in the dim light of the overhead bulb.

'She slid a middle finger into her moist interior and continued the play on her clitoris with her thumb, gazing across at me under her lowered eyelids.

I was enthralled by this new aspect of Clarice. She had always been an enthusiastic, if not greedy, lover, but our encounters had taken place in her tastefully decorated flat in Bloomsbury. I had always been required to take the initiative in our lovemaking, and, so far, masturbation was not one of the variations we had used.

'Her finger slid in and out of her cleft and she heaved her hips in counterpoint to its action, groaning through her pouting lips which still sucked on the smouldering cigarette.' Rognon smiled and described how by this time, his penis was as hard as iron in his serge trousers and pressed against the metal of the bedstead. It was not an unpleasant sensation. As he began to move his pelvis, increasing the pressure he was applying, the bed creaked to his rhythm.

Clarice snapped her thighs together, drawing her knees up so that she was curled into a ball shape. Her finger was entrapped deep in her interior. On her side like this she rammed her part furiously against it, jerking her head into the pillow. Rognon moved to the side of the bed and withdrew the cigarette from her mouth. She gasped in her passion and flung her other hand around over her buttocks to insert another finger in her cleft from the rear.

His member was now in the clutch of both his hands, rigid and bursting with the fiercest throbbing he had ever known. Her half-closed eyes focused on its swollen tip and she ran her tongue round her lips, almost choking in her self-induced delirium. Squirming towards him across the bed she stretched her tongue towards his tortured penis. He pushed forward, offering the scarlet glans to her open mouth. It brushed against her lips as she rolled over away from him. Now she lay spread-eagled on her belly, with her well-fleshed buttocks pumping wildly against her hands which both clawed at her fiery part.

Rognon kicked off his boots and tore off his trousers. He leapt towards her intending to enter her from the rear, but she anticipated his move and rolled over, causing him to land clumsily and somewhat painfully on the crumpled coverlet.

She ran over to the marble wash stand which stood in the corner and hitched her bottom up so that she could sit on its edge. With her knees wide apart, flashing him insolent and provocative glances, she continued the manipulation of her vagina which she knew was driving him to distraction. She inserted two fingers and squirmed them around inside herself, her head thrown back against the wall.

Her groans became louder as she increased the pace. Rognon raced towards her. He grabbed her hair with one hand and pushed his member which threatened to explode towards her part, but she took hold of his wrist and implanted a sharp little bite which made him release her tresses. She also snapped her thighs together, refusing him entrance. His organ slapped against her belly, denied the satisfaction it sought, and his tongue which tried to enter her mouth was pushed aside.

Gleefully she ran to the bed again, tearing off her skirt and blouse. He lunged at her but she raised a foot to his chest and thrust him away reeling. She pulled off her stockings swiftly and, laying back on the pillows, dangled them over her breasts, arousing her nipples to a darker roseate and swollen appearance. Then she commanded him to join her but to promise to do exactly what she told him. Otherwise she would leave. She might even scream and accuse him of rape or attempted murder. Rognon had become her slave. His organ directed his brain. He stumbled towards the bed and lay with his legs apart as she directed him. She tied his wrists to the brass bedhead with her stockings after removing his remaining clothing.

Stark naked and feeling utterly helpless, he watched as she crossed over to the wash stand and brought back a pitcher of water and a sponge. She told him she was going to cool him off, but of course, the drops of water that she squeezed from the sponge and allowed to trickle on to his throbbing glans and down the length of his protuberance were torture of the most exquisite kind. It was another agony for her to leave this monstrously afflicted member alone and to run the cold sponge down his thighs and over his testicles, over his chest, his toes, his eyes. Then she stood astride him waving her fringed shawl delicately along the length of his body, avoiding only his member in the most cruel fashion.

She squatted over him, her Titian pubic hair lightly brushing his bursting tip, and lowering herself stealthily, parted her lips over it. By raising and dropping her launches she allowed his member a few brief and tantalising touches. He wanted to scream in his frustration, but she pressed a hand over his mouth and commanded him to be silent, to take his punishment like a man.

She took the very base of his member between two fingers and twitched it to and fro in an action like that of a metronome, crooning a silly little song. He was desperate for action of a more vibrant kind and took to heaving his pelvis, thrusting it upwards in a violent manner, the more so when she reached across to the side table and got one of her hair ribbons and which she tied in a neat bow around his raging flagpole.

She told him lovingly what a magnificent instrument it was. She cooed over it fondly and, pouting her lips, made little kisses not on it, but towards it, then made as if she was about to grab it but only ran the tips of her fingers lightly through the bush of his pubic hair.

He thought he would die if this torture continued. His head tossed from side to side on the pillow and his tongue ran feverishly around his lips. She listened to his breath coming in short choking bursts and watched intently the muscular spasms which were coursing through his body, twitching his belly and convulsing his maddened organ. She kissed his imploring eyes and gave him one of her fingers to suck. Then, passing behind the bedstead, she took hold one of his hands which were still tied to the posts by her silk stockings. She stroked his fingers and then pressed her soft parts on

186

them. He was aching to climax as she inserted his thumb inside her and then wriggled herself about it. She asked how much he would pay her and he replied he would give her anything she asked.

Lying on the bed he gurgled and yelled to his heart's content. The sounds he made were not unusual in that house. No-one would have raised an eyebrow, Clarice knew, so she prolonged his torture still further by sliding off his thumb and going round to the base of the bed to apply a similar therapy to a big toe. While she did that she dragged her fingernails from his knees to his ankles and then back again.

Her last act of torture, if that is what it was, for Rognon, in a delirium of agony and anguish was screaming for it to come to an end, was to squat over the poor man with a nipple pressed into the dilated oozing hole of his flailing quiver.

She said she didn't want his money but that she wanted to know that he loved her. Rognon yelled that he did as she stood up astride his body. As he made his fervent declaration Rognon's penis burst open from its beribboned bondage and shot his long awaited offering upwards in great pulsating waves towards his beloved, annointing her body with a wash of stupendous impulse and intensity. Simultaneously, Clarice thrilled to an overwhelming outpouring downwards to her enraptured slave in a series of shocking orgasmic bursts that seemed to rend her senseless as her body riveted into ecstacy.

Their juices ran and mingled with each other in abundance as she fell on him smothering him with kisses. They rolled around the creaking bed in a state of total bliss, and the ghosts of the hotel, if there were any in that house of wantoness and shame, must have rejoiced that, for once, true love had been celebrated within its portals, and in addition, not a penny had changed hands.

Chapter Eleven

Bernadette's luncheon party a week earlier had caused quite a few stirrings in the on-going *commedia divina* that constituted the Season that year on the Riviera.

Charles, having been deposed by the slim corps de ballet dancer Vladimir in his affections for Angelique, was feeling particularly mournful. Not only had he lost the doe-eyed chocolate seller, but he had been obliged to ditch the exhausting Edith in the direction of Brady, the muscular football player who, in his estimation, could better match her in sexual greed and staying power.

He mooned about the harbour in those moments when he was free from his business duties promoting the yacht-hire firm, casting about for a suitable replacement in his erotic life. He was peeved as well because his friend Arthur seemed to be having such a good time. After a bad start to the season, due to his infatuation for the adorable Annabelle, his officer friend, he noticed, had considerably cheered up.

He no longer stayed in bed late bemoaning his fate and composing stupid love letters. On the contrary, Arthur bounded out of bed in the guest wing of Bernadette's villa, tumescent or not, and positively rushed out of the house with such an enthusiasm that he must have been propelled by the scent of adventures of an amorous or sensuous kind, Charles thought with some envy.

He had plied his friend with leading questions and playful innuendoes but the staunch, upright officer had refused him any satisfaction. Arthur, whatever had been his indiscretions with Galina, the soloist from the Ballet Russes, or with his hostess and her cousin Sophie in the swimming pool in the garden of the villa, was not at all prepared to tease or titillate his friend by disclosure. Suffice it to say that after having been subjected to a barrage of boastful stories and inventions from Charles, Arthur was more than content to bask in the success he was now enjoying. When the officer lay in his bed snoring, completely exhausted, but completely satisfied from his encounters with Galina or her even more demanding superior, the ballerina Lidova, Charles wondered why his own summer was turning sour.

He had sometimes seen the slit-eyed Mongolian boy disporting himself from the rocks with Angelique. Their slim bodies looked so attractive curving through the water as they dived and raced happily through a free afternoon, he felt a gnawing envy over the chit of a girl to whom, as he freely admitted to himself, he had been less than generous. Curse the handsome thin boy, he thought, looking down at his growing paunch and thickening waist. But Angelique looked, he had to admit, much more beautiful than before. Her skin was now lightly tanned and glowing, and she had an air of ease and contentment that was never present when he had been her selfish lover.

Charles would have been envious to the point of distraction if he had known about Arthur's success with Bernadette and Sophie. Of course it would never occur to an English gentleman to compromise his hostess, therefore Arthur had not revealed the *histoire* of the morning in the swimming pool and the changing cabin. Charles would, though, have been gratified to know that Bernadette had plans in store for him. The lady, even in spite of her continuing flirtation with Marcel the couturier, and the double dalliance with Arthur, had been so impressed by her voyeuristic knowledge of the young man that she had determined to secure, both for herself and her cousin Sophie, at least one amorous encounter.

Marcel had been very busy. The season was demanding of his time and energy. In spite of this he still needed some relaxation after business hours and he had plied bountiful attentions on Vera Lidova, sending her flowers, gifts, and little loving notes. She, however, had been fairly occupied in keeping Vossoudossoulos happy enough in bed to ensure his continuing generosity and also with her new amour, the *ravissant* Arturo, as she called our friend from England.

Once she found Arthur backstage in a clinch with Galina behind a stack of scenery. They were rolling about on a wicker basket full of costumes. Vera was so incensed that the man who had pleasured her so magnificently the night before now had his tongue down the *corp de ballet* girl's throat, that she vowed forthwith to get her demoted to the back row of the chorus. Borzdoff would see to it, she was sure, otherwise she would leave and go to America. There they always needed talent like hers, and anyway the movies in California sounded promising.

She slapped Arthur hard on the backside and pinched Galina's arm. The poor girl could not cry out because a performance was in progress, but she thought she would get her revenge one night soon by putting powdered glass in the great ballerina's pointe shoes. Not only would her toes bleed, but Galina, being the understudy, would get the chance to go on in the role of *Giselle*. Arthur, however, was suitably repentant and made up for his misdemeanour by taking Lidova to Aix en Provence for a wonderful lunch and an al fresco coupling in an orchard the following weekend.

Vossoudossoulos was beginning to count the cost of his liaison with the ballerina. Not only did he have to pay her bills at the Hotel de Paris, but also horrifying bills for food which Vera supplied on such a lavish scale to the dancers of the company at his expense.

Dhokouminsky brought along his cronies and Sophie as well. The caviar and vodka flowed nightly in Lidova's suite. As the Greek was often out, sometimes paying a visit to the strange establishment run by Carlotta Bombieri, the Neapolitan dwarf in Marseilles, the bills ran up in an alarming way. The company even issued orders for picnic baskets to take to the beach for swimming parties by moonlight. The waiters were astonished to find a nudist colony a few metres from the public boulevard and were delighted when the crazy Russians bade them take their clothes off and join in the fun. But for a couple of weeks, at least, the millionaire was so absorbed with the bizarre life in the dwarf's bordello that the outrageous spending had gone unnoticed.

He had even invited Borzdoff, the impressario, and Frederick Fanshawe to go along with him for a day's fun because he had been so inspired by Carlotta's girls. Explaining to Lidova that he had shipping business to which he had to attend in Marseilles, the Greek had slipped off in his limousine and picked up the others. They had an uproarious lunch at a famous restaurant in Villefranche before setting out for the long drive to the port. Vossoudossoulos had instructed the driver to see there was an adequate supply of champagne and ice in the car, so they bowled along merrily afterwards, full of *bonhomie* and alcohol.

Bordzoff, surprisingly, had never been to a brothel. Perhaps that was not so odd since there was always a handful of young hopefuls on whom he could press his attentions with the promise of future stardom. Fanshawe, however, was an expert in the genre. Brought up as a wanton in Memphis, he had become acquaited with every whore house in Dallas, Chicago, San Fransisco, Maine, New York and New Orleans, to mention just a few of the places where he had dissipated himself.

He recalled a party in Denver where a naked negress had leaped out of a gigantic chocolate cake at a convention of gangsters to dance the 'Black Bottom', and another gastronomic feast which turned into an orgy of a kind when, in Acapulco, an ice-cream confection, life-sized in the shape of a voluptuous woman, was wheeled out from an ice-shed. In the fierce desert heat the ice-cream immediately began to melt and the male members of the party were required to lick it off the body of the harlot who was concealed underneath. He made a mental note to include the incident in his next salacious novel.

The threesome were ill-disposed for sport on their arrival in Marseilles. Carlotta viewed them with some apprehension, or rather distaste, on their arrival. She wondered if it would be good form to get their money in advance or to wait until later. After all, they were already so drunk that they might go without paying. On the other hand, the enticements that she had to offer might run them up a very large bill. It was one of the problems of the profession, *hélas*.

She first produced a Moroccan girl who shimmied voluptuously to the sound of finger cymbals. Her long performance was impressive, but unfortunately she had extremely bad teeth and an advanced state of halitosis. The next offering was a Spanish gitane who clicked her castanets so loudly the three begged for mercy, even though she was alluring in an Andalusian way. Two identical Japanese twins then appeared, with their tiny feet bound and constricted. They shuffled around playing oriental lutes, occasionally striking a pose which suggested that, like Siamese twins, they were available as a pair. But the three men found their mask-like white painted faces unappealing, and the kimonos they wore completely hid the possible mystery of their bodies.

Fanshawe, Borzdoff and the Greek lolled in their armchairs with wan expressions, overcome by the effects of alcohol and boredom. Carlotta began to get rather nervous. She did not have that much more to offer. In her experience, men who came inflamed with lust to her establishment chose an early offering. Then there was the possibility of further business. Was this to become one of those nights when her guests left unsatisfied?

In fast succession the remainder of her girls were dismissed. None of the men fancied a large Swedish blonde of uncertain age who was in the guise of Brunnhilde, complete with shield and spear, or a perspiring red-head from Liverpool, clad in floor length sables, who cracked a whip as if she were Anna Karenina driving a *troika*. Bombieri spread her bejewelled hands apologetically, calling for more refreshments, imploring the gentlemen's indulgence. It was so hard these days, she explained, to get the right girls, and when one did, they were so expensive and so untrustworthy, *mon Dieu*.

The resourceful brothel keeper was not to be outdone however. She went over to the gramophone and selected a record. It was a Neapolitan tarantella, bright and brittle. The

193

music came roaring out of the curved horn cracked and out of key, but the small fat lady did her best. She produced a tambourine and went whirling about the room, pausing occasionally to shake the instrument in an ear of one or another of her clients.

As her wild dance proceeded she began shedding her garments down to the tight little corset which held in her vast abdomen. Off came her rings and hair pins, her stockings, garters and knickers. Soon Carlotta was prancing absolutely naked. One of the girls restarted the record when it came to an end. Recommencing, Bombieri beat her breasts and buttocks with the tambourine and then fell to her knees with her head flung back to the floor, flailing at her mound of Venus with the diabolical instrument.

'It is the dance of St Vitus,' Fanshawe yawned.

'Sometimes it is induced by the bite of the tarantula,' said Vossoudossoulos knowledgeably.

'It is monstrous,' cried Borzdoff. 'I come here to get away from the ballet, gentlemen. There it is dance, dance, dance all the day. And what here do we have? A cripple, a dwarf, trying to audition for me. I am going, goodbye.'

'Wait for us,' the others cried, dashing from the gaudy room full tilt towards the car and the surer pleasures of Monte Carlo.

On the way back Fanshawe was startled to see his wife, Lady Letitia, strolling on the promenade with a handsome young man. He did not wave or command the car to stop, but instead grinned to himself, happy that she seemed to be engaged in a good time, perhaps an affair of the heart that would give him time off to enjoy himself in his own way.

Poor old Letitia, he thought, not a bad looker still; an elegant clothes horse, party giver and part-time drunk.

Typical of her English leisured class: a bit dim, unbearably bossy, used to the idea of hordes of servants, maids, butlers, the lot; not an ounce of brain, but perfectly capable of chatting twenty-four hours at a stretch, an exhausting woman he should have lost years ago.

How little he knew her, and how much he underestimated her. While she gave him the impression of being feckless and incapable, in fact she had gone on throughout their marriage having the most satisfying private life with a succession of interesting young men who adored her, or pretended to, such as the elegant Paolo in Florence. If Frederick was absorbed in one of his hopeless books, or if he had his head in the gin bottle, Letitia simply packed a valise and trundled off to Venice, Florence, Deauville or St. Moritz, anywhere where the bright young things of the day were holed up.

Away from the boring American she was amusing and charming. The boys adored her raffish talk, liberally spiced with the language of stable lads, her outlandish affected pronunciation and the tortured vowels so typical of the British upper crust. She cultivated those aspects of hers which were successful to such an extent that she became a quite lovable caricature of her former self; a whizz, a hoot, a shocker, they used to say of her. The Charleston era suited her although she was a fair deal older than its razor-sharp luminaries. The gilded youth of the day called her a sport. She was always the first to arrive at a party and the last to leave, and held everyone in fits with her eccentric mannerisms and shocking stories. She was idolised for her escapades in the niteries of London, the clubs of Mayfair and the great hotels like the Savoy and the Ritz, famous for being the first to wear the daring new short dresses baring her knees, and notorious for the daring vivacity she showed in the new dances. A band leader had fallen in love with her, as did a

High Court judge and a fashionable photographer who enjoyed the privilege of being the Royal favourite. She sent them on their way after breaking their hearts mildly, and now she was esconced in the Riviera captivating a new crowd. The young man was Charles, newly delivered from Edith, the muscular lady from Chicago.

The two had met in the yacht harbour of Antibes when Charles had appeared with the captain and crew of a vessel he had just leased to a newly arrived party.

An old flame of Letitia's had invited her aboard to discuss the possibility of her joining them for a trip to Corsica. While she was deliberating this delicious proposal she had gradually fallen for the tall, handsome ships' broker.

They were delighted that they had mutual acquaintances. Indeed it was only a few days ago that she had been to lunch with the vicomtesse at the mansion where he lodged with Arthur, who, incidentally, happened to be the son of an old school chum of hers.

So it was perfectly natural that they should go off hand in hand to lunch at a shaded bistro in the old part of the town. They drank pastis, icy cold, and a couple of bottles of Vouvray, charmed in each other's company. How handsome she thought he looked in his white drill trousers, cream silk shirt and knotted kerchief as he sat there perfectly relaxed ordering the simple food of the café. They ate abundantly of *salade nicoise*, decorated with black olives and anchovies, *carré d'agneau aux herbes de Provence* and *tarte aux cérises*, and afterwards sat at a table by the side of the bustling market drinking their Benedictines.

'Darling, you can tell me everything,' she said roguishly. 'A boy as handsome and virile looking as you can't be in the South of France for long without getting up to some mischief, and pretty fast too, if I've got your measure.' She wheedled everything out of him without much difficulty, because Charles was not exactly a reticent chap when it came to describing his sexual exploits, even to a lady. He told her the story of his affair with Angelique, and how it had now come to grief on account of the dreadful slant-eyed boy from the Ballets Russes. 'You don't seem too miffed,' she laughed, egging him on to reveal his next exploits with Edith.

Charles was more guarded here and measured his words carefully. It was one thing to describe the hot afternoons with the compliant shop-girl, another to admit the defeat and exhaustion he suffered on and under the body of the American nymphomaniac who had caused such pain in his groin and such discomfort to his scrotum. Such a confession, he thought, would not recommend him so well to this lady who was obviously used to the ways of the world and who eyed him so lasciviously over the rim of her liqueur glass.

To use a few white lies is forgivable in such a situation. He realised by instinct that Letitia was not only amused but titillated by his anecdotes, and made rather more of the tiring affair with Edith than he should have done. But after all, they were in a discreet corner, underneath an umbrella, of a bustling location where no-one was interested in their talk; it was hot, they were mildly intoxicated, well fed, and absolutely sure in their own minds that the afternoon would not end before they consummated their sensuous longings to enjoy each other's company to the full in a convenient bed.

As Frederick had gone to Marseilles for the day, and possibly, she thought, the night, they drove to her hotel at Cap Ferrat. Letitia had been extremely stimulated by the cheeky boy's talk. When she threw him the keys of her car, she climbed in the tourer and snuggled close up to him.

It was an exciting drive. The car sped along with the top open and they were buffeted in an exhilarating way by a

197

strong wind that threatened to turn into the Mistral of that coast. The air smelled strongly of sea and pine trees and the wonderful wild scents of the *maquis* above the corniche.

Letitia was divinely happy. Charles was such an open boy, she thought, an honest physical type who would enjoy an amorous encounter just for what it was, and not make the mistake of falling into the trap of that stupid thing called love.

He was thinking something along the same lines about her, when to his satisfaction, he felt a hand lightly fall on his lap. He shifted a little in his seat to adjust her hand to a more stimulating position, but of course without taking his eyes, for one second, off the dangerous bending road.

Her head was leaning on his shoulder and he could feel her warm breath on his neck, then her soft lips as she eased away his silk scarf to get to his bronzed skin. He could feel the hairs on the back of his neck bristle and a stirring in his private parts. Trying hard to concentrate on the narrow twisting road, he barely noticed that one by one she was opening his fly buttons. The stealth of her operation was born of long practice on similar drives across the Yorkshire moors near her ancestral home, perhaps travelling to a hunt-ball or on the way home with a paramour from a grouse shoot.

Her finger tips touched the still-loose skin of his penis after they had wound their way through the dense matt of his bush. When she took hold of the organ she was impressed with its weight and thickness, but perhaps a little disappointed that her attentions had not already led to the stiffening that she expected.

Letitia, snugly wrapped around her beau's neck, was unaware of the concentration he had to put into his driving. A larger number of his brain cells were sending signals to many other parts of his body and nature's course would inevitably be a slower one than if he were, say, lying on a divan.

In due time she felt the thickening that she wished for begin, first with a slow stirring and then with a noticeable small throb. As his organ lengthened and swelled she revelled in its growing hardness. As the first major contraction of the main muscles in his penis signalled to her the power of this organ, he grinned across at her in a wolfish way, bending his head to kiss her lightly on the cheek, then settled back to enjoy the drive as pleased with himself as any pasha in a harem whose every whim is taken care of.

She explored further down to his scrotum and beyond that to the hard muscle which ran between his legs to his backside, then slowly began to massage the now-rigid stem. It was most enjoyable, he thought. The part of his mind that had to stay with driving the car denied the one hundred percent sensation that would have happened otherwise. Starved of total attention, his vital organs were slowed down in a most delicious and effective way. He wondered if he would be able to last the whole way to the Italian border at Vintimiglia if necessary, without coming to the climax that such a wonderful manipulation would normally engender.

The stimulation she was applying affected Letitia in a powerful way. Her own parts were burning fiercely without even being touched and her small breasts were suffused with warmth and longing. She wondered whether to ask him to stop the car and consummate this ardour in a roadside gully or up a bank in the bushes that overhung the road. Or would it be better to go on showing him her affection in this special way until they reached the hotel?

Charles now seriously began to wonder if he could last that long. He put a hand over hers and withdrew it from his crotch. 'Sorry, darling,' he said, 'you're driving me mad. I don't want to come in my trousers. I want to save it for you.'

She kissed his hand and then allowed it to go back to the steering wheel. 'I don't want to rush you sweetheart,' she said. 'How much farther is it?'

'Not much longer,' he said in a gruff voice.

'You can take a bit more then, I should think,' Letitia murmured in his ear. She lowered her mouth over his still-throbbing vital part and caressed its tip with her tongue, her face buried deep in his lap.

He stirred his crotch and pushed the swollen tip further into her mouth until no more of his length could enter. Then he settled back to concentrate on the hazardous road and sent a stern warning to his penis to stop jerking and throbbing. They continued in this way for several more kilometres, both blissfully absorbed in the sensations they were giving each other.

Soon they came to a long tunnel cut into the rock. At its end he could see the bright scintillating azure of the sea focused like a view from a telescope. There were no other cars, either oncoming or going in his direction. He blared the klaxon and shouted in his glee. Letitia sucked hard at his most precious possession, grateful to have found a nice new friend with such charming manners, good stories to tell, and an organ that would soon be giving her riveting pleasure. To hell with it, she thought, I can't wait, and sucked with even more dedication.

Charles shot his precious liquid into her mouth as the car roared out of the tunnel into the brilliant sunlight whose intensity in no way eclipsed the dramatic potency of his overdue but amazing orgasm.

Chapter Twelve

Bernadette's preparations for the party to celebrate the end of the Season in honour of the Ballets Russes were proceeding apace. But several things nagged her and Sophie when they sat in conference about it.

'It's all very well having the *beau monde* trampling through my house, and those barbaric Russians,' the vicomtesse complained, 'but what about us? I think we've been very slack in getting the attention of those two English boys, and who else will escort us?'

'I quite agree,' her cousin sighed. 'Marcel is all right for you, but although that wretched Dhokouminsky has sufficed for a while, I really begin to tire of his primitive ways.'

'Marcel will not do at all. He's lost his head to Vera Lidova,' Bernadette replied, 'and, as the hostess, I cannot possibly pair up with a man who is going to fasten himself on to another woman for the whole evening.'

'Quite,' said Sophie.

Bernadette remembered the promise she had made to her cousin that one day she should have the pleasure of seeing the young English gentlemen at their *toilette*. 'You remember the delicate affair we witnessed through the peep-hole and the two way mirror? Arthur declaring himself to Annabelle, the plump little debutante?' she enquired.

201

'I do indeed. It was literally breathtaking,' Sophie answered.

'I think it was extremely decent of us to steal away and leave the lovebirds to their cooing,' Bernadette said with a smile, 'but surely there would be no harm in having another tiny peep when the two boys are alone? Then we might be able to decide, in a civilised way, which one we each intend to pair up with.'

'A capital idea,' her cousin enthused. 'When shall we do it?'

'Right now! They are back home at the moment. I saw them come down the drive together a few minutes ago. Come on, darling, there's no time like the present.'

They were soon reclining comfortably in the salon which contained the elaborate spying devices which had been installed by the considerate vicomte. Bernadette had the foresight to bring along a large pitcher of White Lady, an explosive cocktail whose composition she had learned from the many English naval officers of her acquaintance, it being the most favoured drink on offer when ladies were present at any British Fleet's visit to the coast.

Both the men were sprawled on their beds, naked as the day. Sophie and Bernadette took it in turns to peep through the spyhole in the latticed silver and jade screen; but as the pair were relaxed in conversation, just as any two men might be in a similar situation, and there being no erotic connotation, the two ladies were content to lie back on their divans and merely enjoy listening to the masculine talk. It was revealing, to say the least.

'Come on old bean, that just won't do. I know you've been very busy the last few weeks. I saw you myself with that skinny ballerina, Vera Lidova. Don't deny it,' Charles began. 'Here, did I tell you about Letitia, the other day? My, what a woman, a greedly little gobbler!' He rose to pour them a drink at the chiffonier.

Arthur was, in fact, a great deal more relaxed than he had been earlier in his *sojourn* on the Riviera. Alas, he thought, it will soon all be over, duty calls once more. But his transformation into a skilled lover much in demand by the ladies had so thrilled him and robbed him of inhibition that he was proud to tell Charles some of his latest exploits.

Bernadette waited with baited breath, fearing that he might touch on the incident involving herself and Sophie in her swimming pool, but thankfully it was excluded from his catalogue.

Firstly he revealed to Charles every erotic detail concerning his lost love Annabelle who had returned to England, and then went on to a graphic account of his liaison with Galina, the *corps de ballet* girl, speaking fondly of her ample breasts and the wonderful oral techniques that she had learned from her Cossack lover. Then he spoke with some rapture about the vivid lovemaking of Vera Lidova, especially in the orchard in the country near Aix en Provence when they had startled a young goatherd by the ferocity of their orgasmic screams.

The grand ballerina's extreme agility had provoked some extraordinary variations of coupling. One scenerio had involved her throwing her feet backwards over her head and planting her legs wide in the splits so that they were at right angles to her torso. In that position she had implored him to place his organ in her mouth and kiss her private parts the while. Another amazing attitude was struck when she took her right ankle and pulled it high above her head, with her back against a knarled old olive tree. He had taken her thus, with her leg pointing skywards to the hot sun that poured down into the ancient grove, ramming his member deep into the widened opening of her innermost recesses. How she had laughed, he recalled, locked in his arms, with his engorged organ thrust as far as was humanly possible into her lubricated secret garden of delight. They had rolled slowly down a bank of sweet-smelling thyme, pausing occasionally to throb their enflamed muscles simultaneously, into a stream of icy mountain water where they had thrashed their bodies into a delirium of tortured, but exquisite, release.

The women lay in a state of suspended animation on their divans. Neither had imagined that men reveal their sensual secrets in such a way. It was the beginning of a new understanding of the male psycho-sexual process.

Now it was Charles's turn to bring his friend up to date concerning his adventures. He skated over Angelique, since he still smarted from having been surpassed by the slim and wiry bodied Mongolian, but he dwelt at some length on Edith and her rampant desires.

Without admitting how her libidinous and aggressive sexuality had exhausted him, he gave a fascinating account of some of their activities. Sophie and Bernadette found their hands straying involuntarily to their already moistened parts as Charles elaborated.

Edith's long flanks were used to great advantage, he explained. Her bronze thighs, clasped around his back, imprisoned his palpitating organ in most of the basic positions of their coition, but for variation she was fond of lying on her back on top of him, with her knees drawn up, and her two feet clamped vice-like around his stem. She also favoured sitting on his chest with her rear pressed against his face while she nibbled his delicate parts.

There was always a sense of imprisonment, Charles explained, the feeling that once they started to couple she was so entranced she would not release him from her iron grip. The muscles of the walls of her vagina were so strong that, by squeezing, she could keep him in a permanent state of erection, and if she released him for a second and his limpening organ slipped away from her, she devised a new and thrilling experience that would suffuse his flagging membranes.

Sometimes she found that secret place between his buttocks that many women are afraid to touch and with a moistened finger traced circles around the dark circle and then inserted a probing thumb, pushing and stirring it with the same intense rhythm as she used on the length of his stamen.

After he had pleasured her in a fairly normal, average way she would apply oil to her body and slither over him, entrapping his penis between her swollen breasts, and by massaging it with her protuberances urge his detumescing fulcrum back into splendiferous size.

Sophie groaned and rubbed her own breasts in sympathy and Bernadette could not resist sliding a finger into her orifice, imagining that Charles's mushroom-shaped glans was pressing into her and causing the drenching juices that were flowing from between her intensely aroused labia.

Sophia pressed a finger to her lips and bade Bernadette come and take another look through the spyhole. It was clear that both men were, by now, in a slightly tumescent condition.

Arthur's hands had been inspired to roam down to his mildly stimulated and bulky appendage. Casually scratching at the hair that grew in profusion over the mound of his groin, his fingers crept down to tease at the skin of his scrotum.

Charles, walking about the room as he told his story, was in no less of an aggravated condition. As he paced the room his heavy penis swung with each stride, fascinating the onlookers. The ladies gasped and gazed into each other's eyes, signalling their yearnings to one another.

'I should tell you one more thing about this absolutely remarkable girl,' Charles continued, grinning. A shiver passed through Bernadette's body as he fondled himself gently in an abstracted sort of way as he continued his reminiscences. 'Have you ever done it the Greek way?' he asked his friend.

'I don't know? What is it?' Arthur asked, and then remembered a story that Vera Lidova had told him concerning Vossoudossoulos. He wondered if it had any relevance.

'This American amazon wanted everything,' said Charles. 'She had to put her tongue in every orifice I possess. I mean every one.'

There was a short silence, and in the small adjoining salon, the two women held their breath.

'Not every one, surely,' said Arthur, agog.

'Every one,' Charles affirmed. 'And in return she wanted me to do the same. She went through my ears, my belly button, my mouth, the lot, and I did the same for her, but there was one bit I couldn't manage.'

'I know what you mean,' said Arthur.

'Dick was alright there. I didn't mind that, so I gave it to her, with two fingers up the other hole and a thumb on her clitoris. I suppose that's the way they like it in Chicago.'

'My God, you've been around,' Arthur said, with some admiration in his voice. 'Is there anything left for you to do?'

'Yes, there is,' Charles replied. 'I want to get into the vicomtesse's knickers before the Season's over, or else that gorgeous fat little cousin of hers.'

'Strange you should say that,' Arthur mused, carefully remembering to keep mum about his previous encounter with the pair. 'That's something I've been thinking about myself. Either one will do. How about we toss for it?' He produced a coin and threw it in the air. 'Heads you get the lady of the house, tails the cousin.' They both fell to their knees to retrieve the coin.

'OK, that's it. Happy?' asked Charles.

'You bet,' his friend replied.

The ladies crept from the room with staring eyes and open mouths, astonished at this turn of events, and ignorant of the outcome of the throw. Outside the door, when she had recovered her composure, Bernadette said to her companion, 'They have sealed a bargain. Do we let them keep it?'

'*N'importe quoi*,' replied Sophie. 'An Englishman's word is his bond.'

Chapter Thirteen

It was a balmy day in Menton. Soft white clouds were propelled across a silver blue sky by the warm winds from Africa, and the perfumes of the Jardin Botanique wafted over the Promenade, intoxicating the senses of the lovers who strolled there. In the hotels the more elderly visitors, many of them English, for this was their favourite resort, were content to read and play bridge but the young folk indulged in headier sports.

All the way along the beach there were games of volley-ball and shuttlecock and battledore, and the snazzily dressed bathers splashed in the foaming water like sea sprites. The striped one-piece costumes of the boys in bright primary colours of red, blue and yellow made a vibrant counterpoint to the purple and magenta bloomers and mopcaps that were fashionable among the girls that year. Yachts of all sizes were to be seen dipping and bobbing in the waves, their multi-coloured sails dyed in kaleidoscopic shades, and the fishermen made an attractive local diversion landing their catches and drying their nets on the rocks.

It was a picturesque and intensely stimulating scene. Couples sported in the swell or lay canoodling on the hot sands, applying aromatic oils to their tanned bodies, sensually turning on their backs to soak up the warmth of the ever-present sun. The energy involved in these activities was considerable and had to be constantly replaced. No wonder the traders were doing such frantic business in ice-cream, baguettes, fruit squash, peanuts and, of course, an endless variety of cocktails at the numerous beach-side brasseries.

It was here the bright young things quenched their thirst and enjoyed the gossip of the day. As strolling accordionists and violinists serenaded the customers, Millie could hear who was now dating Mabel, and Humphrey could relate to William the latest about Doris's abandoned behaviour. Scandal was the required ingredient to make the mixture fizz, but none of it was malicious or spiteful. The new age insisted on lightheartedness and frivolity. It was not to question the morality of one's aquaintances' behaviour, rather to be absorbed in the one central issue—that is, whether everyone one knew was having a jolly good time.

Angelique and Vladimir were certainly in the best of spirits. It was Sunday, therefore they could both avail themselves of a blissful day off work.

Her long hours in the shop, followed by the skinny boy's amorous attentions through a great deal of the hot nights in her stifling attic, had enervated her to a degree, but she was happy with the Mongolian looking youth. He was kind and laughed a lot, brought her silly little presents, the most he could afford on the pittance he received from the grasping Borzdoff, and even now was carrying her on his back, galloping along the beach as if he were a donkey.

Angelique hooted with glee. She had no envy of the idle rich who surrounded them. The climate was wonderful, the pleasures of the sea and sand were free, and she was sure the slit-eyed boy loved her with all his heart. Of course he did, and he would miss her when the company left Monte Carlo for an extended tour of South America, but that was a parting neither of them cared to contemplate at the moment.

His body ached from the rigours of classes, rehearsals and performances that was a dancer's lot. Every morning he dragged himself out of bed and massaged his over-stretched muscles. The entire company was expected to be at the *barre* by ten o'clock, dressed and warmed up for the ritual of the daily drumming by the ballet master. Bends, stretches, contractions and extensions of every possible kind doubled up the dancers' already anguished bodies, and then on the main floor of the studio they had to go through the most punishing series of balancing tricks, turns, leaps and travelling steps for another whole hour and a half. This daily morning session was but merely a preparation for the rest of the day's work, which could be rehearsals of the classic works in the repertoire or the even more demanding athletics required by the new choreographers. The jazz age manifested itself in the avant-garde productions which were now the rage. The principal contributors included Picasso, Stravinsky, Nijinsky, Bakst, Debussy, Benois and a host of other prolific composers and designers.

The cultural and philosophic aspects of the ferociously modern works that these luminaries produced evaded young Vladimir. He merely tried to get the steps right and hang on the beat in the discordant and complex music, but he had been noticed lately for his striking looks and the way his tautly controlled body managed the flow and impulse of the new choreography, and was in sure line for promotion to junior soloist.

All these considerations went unheeded as the pair gambolled and frolicked on their free day in Menton. Angelique had brought a picnic basket filled with an array of cheap but delicious food which she had bought in the market:

210

sausages, cheese, bread, grapes, olives and a flagon of white wine which she placed to cool in a shaded rock pool.

When the *jeunesse dorée* rose as one at twelve and made off for the expensive restaurants for lunch, the pair had the beach to themselves and revelled in their privacy. They spread out their towels in a quiet spot on the far side of a landing jetty, in the lee of a derelict old fishing boat, hidden completely from the view of the few folk who might still be promenading along the sea front in the intense glare of the noon day sun. It was quiet and peaceful now the other bathers had departed so they lay still and dozed, refreshing themselves in the golden sunlight, with their toes lapped by the almost still water's edge.

Angelique nestled her head on Vladimir's chest, listening to his deep contented breathing and contemplating her good fortune, before she too drifted off into a light slumber.

The only sounds that could have disturbed them were the slight creaking of the old boat moored on the shingle and the occasional slap of a small wave against the deserted jetty. A few seagulls squawked overhead, and in the distance the hum of traffic and passers by diminished as the lunch hour got into full sway, bringing an atmosphere of quiet calm to their private location.

Vladimir woke to find his girlfriend draped over his body with her hand resting lightly on his groin. This, together with that sensation that often happens to men asleep and dreaming, accounted for the small swelling that had occurred in his member. He lay still for a while, revelling in the sweet smell of her seawashed hair and her sun-kissed complexion, enjoying the frissons of the musculatory tensions that started in his scrotum and then passed up the length of his stem to finish with an extra spurt of energy in his slowly thickening glans. It was a luxurious, lazy occupation,

211

thus engaged, with closed eyes, to concentrate on the very central pursuits of his young body.

As the force within his penis increased he noticed that his involuntary throbbing was strong enough to lift Angelique's hand each time his stem rose away from his abdomen. Although she was soundly asleep her fingers closed more firmly around his now thoroughly awakening penis. He smiled to himself, pleased that even in this slumbering state she seemed to worship that part of him which had given her so much pleasure over the last few weeks.

The tension in his sexual parts had now increased to the point when he was no longer so relaxed under her provoking arm and grasping fingers. By clenching the muscles of his buttocks he began to raise his pelvis from the towels on which they both lay, stirring his stiffened and pulsating organ against her hand in a more purposeful way. His breathing became louder and faster, causing her to stir in her dreams.

He flicked a tongue in her ear and sucked gently at it and nibbled lightly on the lobe. A deep sigh escaped from her parted lips, and slowly awakening to his arousing attentions, she started to rove the hand that enclosed his rigid manhood, passing it firmly down over his testicles which squirmed in his wet bathing drawers, and along his thin hairy thighs.

His hands, which had until now been placed contentedly behind his head, then came around to cradle her and caress her small but firm breasts. Then he ran a finger over her lips and pressed the tip of it, into her mouth. With the other hand he traced patterns down her back and into the crack between the cheeks of her behind, causing her to writhe against his movement and press her mound of Venus against his hip bone.

She slid a hand under the leg of his costume and slowly explored inside the damp garment, delicately stroking and

212

picking at the skin of his scrotum and tweaking the hard part of his flesh that ran through the sac. The tip of his bulb thrust with some force then against his trunks making a very perceptible bulge. He raised himself on his elbows to watch Angelique's fingers add to this shape as she investigated further, gently massaging the length of his considerable and now almost bursting apparatus. Her fingers closed tightly around the ramrod-like palpitating penis and squeezed fondly, the tip of her forefinger lightly playing over the opening and the first drops of fluid that began to appear. Then she pulled her body further across his prostrate form and, sliding off the shoulder straps of his bathing costume, fervently kissed his hard nipples, running her tongue round them in fast exciting circles which were matched by the circles she made around the exposed head of his glans and also the withdrawn foreskin.

He pulled her completely over his body but her hand still clutched possessively around his stem, and her crotch pressed firmly against it. Writhing her hips in a rotary fashion she began to work faster at his massively aroused member and she wriggled her free hand underneath his neck, which she attacked in a flurry of long hard passionate kisses.

Vladimir was more or less impassive to all of this, enjoying the rapacious attack on his frame, but sometimes when the blood flow erupted too strongly he arched his back in an impulsive way, lifting Angelique with him and then collapsing, squeezing her harder into his embrace. It was inevitable that this arousal should lead him into a storm of passion. He tore off the costume, pushing her to one side for a moment, and threw it away on the sands. Then he rolled over on top of her and straddled her in a powerful lunging movement, thrusting her thighs up so high that her knees almost touched her shoulders. At first his organ pressed only into her belly,

213

but he moved his hips skilfully so that, trapped between their bodies, and lubricated by his flowing jissom, it enjoyed a minor but exquisite version of the exercise it would have undergone had it penetrated between the lips of her well oiled part.

His tongue explored her mouth, thrusting greedily, and he ran it over her eyelids, murmuring incomprehensible endearments in his particular dialect, hoarse but tender pronouncements of his devotion. He paused to draw her costume down her body and then pulled it away from her ankles and made gradually for her naked centre by biting up the insides of her calves and thighs, giving each leg in turn the same compulsive attention. These alternative and almost frenzied bites brought exquisite pleasure to Angelique who lifted her crotch from the ground in anticipation of the kisses he would rain on it when the upwards journey was completed. But he held her marvellously in suspense by burying his face in her breasts instead, trying to suck each one completely into his mouth, and running his tongue rapidly around her stiffened, outstanding nipples. He then worked his way down between the small lovely mounds, and gnawed at her belly with his hands behind her, manipulating her buttocks. His tongue became buried in her navel and his lips enclosed the surrounding flesh while his hands came round to her front in order for him to be able to play on the hard button of her clitoris with his thumbs.

One by one his finger tips explored the outer region of her enflamed part, through the hair of her pubis and over the outer lips of her opening and then the softer pale pink inner lips that were in desperate need of penetration. But Vladimir placed himself on his knees between her thighs, and parting her lips with thumb and finger placed the head of his member against the soft vibrating flesh, only to rub it gently in the

214

flowing moisture that she was copiously generating.

She groaned and rolled her head on the towels, begging for him to enter, pulling at his hips in a desperate, urgent fashion. Then, by pushing his hands away from his member, taking hold of it herself and raising her hips, managed to introduce just the very tip. He held her under the small of her back and pulled her up and down towards his penis, but his hips remained perfectly still. Each small movement enclosed her lubricated passage around this engorged object, but only for a few centimetres, gently but tantalisingly enfolding the mere tip.

Angelique implored him for more, but he grinned and released his grasp. Sitting back on his heels opposite her, he placed his hands under her armpits and drew her torso forward and down so that her mouth could gain contact with the stem he had just withdrawn from her. She held the main part of it with two hands, her fingers intertwined, and kissed its head lovingly, teasing little pecks and bites that wandered around its rear side and the taut fibre of his frenum, causing shock waves of sensation to course through his body, and successive bursts of his lubricant to pour out which she lapped at in wonder.

His hands spread down her back and he found again the soft, moistened entrance that had suffused his every wakening thought these last few weeks. First with one finger, and then with two, he brought her to the nadir of her climax and she drenched his hand with her juices, still with her mouth on his stem.

She threw herself on to her back and opened her legs wide, opening the lips of her part with the fingers of each hand. His spasming organ slid into her innermost region in one sliding ecstatic movement and then rested inside while he throbbed the muscles in its length against her tightened walls. The two

215

lovers were pressed so close together there was no more of his shaft to take up and with a hand underneath her he could feel the bag of his testicles squashed against her opening. Without any further movement of his pelvis, he was so aroused he spent inside her, his tongue twisting and turning in her mouth, matching the waves of dynamic energy that sent his hot seminal fluid roaring into her passage in a constant stream of throbbing impulses.

The tide had turned and was creeping up the deserted beach, lapping around their ankles and then their knees as they lay motionless in a state of stupefied fulfilment. As the water reached their joined crotches, as if by some pre-arranged but now unspoken signal they started to move their pelvises, at first slowly, in long curving arches that took the tip of his organ to the very outer portals of her sanctum where it rested briefly before beginning a majestic progress inwards again, at an indolent pace that suggested they had the whole afternoon on the beach in which to indulge themselves. In fact the waiters were gathering up bills and banknotes, and bringing back small saucers of change to the tables of the diners only a couple of hundred yards away. The crowd would be re-appearing soon. With each slow stroke, Vladimir, holding on to Angelique's shoulders from underneath for better leverage, brought their parts together in a vice-like clamp, each time throbbing his member with one long engorging pulse.

The tempo underwent a gradual acceleration until a new staccato rhythm was induced. Their bellies and crotches slapped together at this furious pace and their moistened parts sucked a noisy urgency at each other.

Satyriasis in such a one as this lithe boy is hard to assuage. Like the effect of food and drink on other mortals, indulgence in love breeds a craving for more in those that

216

suffer the syndrome. The man of average sexual capacity can sustain himself through a certain amount of sensuous activity, obviously in different degrees according to health, temperament and arousal, but where he will eventually detumesce and snore in deep sleep, the real satyr will be propelled on yet another wild course of sensuous action, abandoning his mind and body in frenzied copulation.

Vladimir could see the first of the returning bathers. At first just the top of a head, and then a lady's parasol. He could hear chatter and laughter, and then he saw full length figures treading down the steps to the beach to the point where the ensuing crowds would fan out and find their own nooks and crannies to while away the afternoon. With his eyes on the leader of the pack, a stern-looking, military kind of man, accompanied by a pompous overblown wife, he pumped into Angelique at the speed of lightning. She had no idea, of course, that their idyll was obliged to come to a speedy end from such public necessity, she only thought that the increasing speed and ardour of Vladimir's thrusting attack was prompted by his lust for her. She responded with vigour, throwing her hips tempestuously and locking her legs around his back in a grip that forced him even deeper inside her. Passing seagulls slightly masked the sounds of her orgasmic cries as Vladimir brought them both to a swift conclusion in a fantastic crescendo of pumping thrusts that tore the juices from their very souls and flooded them into near unconsciousness.

For a few seconds, but it seemed like an hour, the threatening advance of the colonel and his wife brought them nearer to the joyful lovers. It was only the scrunch of their feet on the pebbles that brought the Russian satyr enough to his senses to dash for the discarded bathing costumes. His own haste prompted a speedy response in Angelique. They pulled their

217

drawers on in a trice and ran for the cover of the sparkling Mediterranean like a pair of gleeful fauns from ancient Arcady.

Menton was the choice of venue also for Edith, Charles's recently deposed amour, and hunky football player Brady, the hero of Detroit.

The brawny boy had to leave that afternoon. He was sorry to be leaving the delights of the Riviera behind him; the parties, the dancing, the beach games, the sailing and so on. However, he was suffering the same kind of neurosthenia that Charles had experienced as a result of the Charleston dancer's sexual enthusiasms. Virile and muscular as he was, he had shrunk nevertheless to a shadow of his former self. He was going to need a lot of Texan steak and ice-cream to build himself up for the Dodgers's next season, he thought, and was grateful that the cultural peregrination through Europe, which his pretentious father had planned for him, would give him some relief from Edith's rampaging attacks on his person.

The hefty girl, however, had promised to turn up in the fall to see the kick-off to the season. He would have to find her another playmate if he was going to keep his place in the team, he reasoned to himself, as he pitted his large frame against her in a gruelling tennis match. They were playing in the grounds of the celebrated Palace d'Hiver, that monument to Art Nouveau which stands imposingly on the hill behind old Menton.

For two hours at the hottest part of the day when the sun beat down mercilessly, Edith had reduced him to a rag. Expert at serving, and with a punishing line in back-handed smashes, she had beaten him to a frazzle. They now sat on the terrace sipping *citrons pressés*, with her heavy thighs weighing mightily over his as she sprawled triumphantly in her chair. 'Shame you gotta go, honey,' she leered. 'Tell me again, what time's your train?'

Brady made a tactical mistake here. He should have brought the time forward a couple of hours. After all, a white lie does no harm, and in his exhausted state he would have been better off allowing himself time for a bath and a couple of hours sleep before setting out on the train ride that would take him along to Genoa and thence to Florence, Turin, Venice and Rome on his culture seeking expedition. 'I gotta be at the station at seven o'clock,' the stupid boy replied.

'Ain't that jerst dandy, honey. You jerst wait here and ah'll be back in a minute,' Edith drawled.

The clerk at the reception desk looked up attentively. *'Oui, madame, puis-je vous aider?'*

'You certainly can. Give me a double room with a *grand lit*, OK?'

The clerk gazed at the perspiring girl, her dishevelled hair, and her soaking tennis outfit. *'Vos baggages, madame?'*

'Oh, I ain't stayin'. Ah just want to get washed up, and my husband's gotta rest before he takes the train into Italy,' she gurgled.

The clerk handed her a key. *'La salle numero soixante-neuf, madame, mes compliments,'* he instructed, with the meerest suggestion of a libidinous leer across his oily face.

'Gee thanks,' Edith said over her shoulder on her way to fetch the lamb to the slaughter. 'Hi, come on honey,' she yelled to Brady. 'You ain't getting away from me yet,' and she hauled him to his feet and led him through the highly decorative lobby past the bellboys and waiters who all knew that room number sixty-nine was reserved by the greasy clerk

219

for lovers of a particular kind as it was situated directly over the chandelier of the *grand salon*. For many years it had been the custom of the staff to place bets on whether these hot blooded clients who booked in for the afternoon would gain the accolade of having caused the immense ornamented light fitting to tinkle in sympathy.

Alas, no-one made any money that day. Most of the staff, eyeing up the frame of the six foot six sportsman and the over-developed muscles of the Amazonian marathon dancer from Chicago, decided they were a good bet for a resounding tinkle. Keeping a furtive look out as they served afternoon tea in the *grand salon* they were, in the end, grossly disappointed that there was not even a single quiver of a crystal pendant.

Brady threw himself, exhausted, on to the vast bed. His masculine pride would not let him complain when Edith tore off his shirt and his shorts as butch men find it anathema to admit defeat in the wars of love. She tasted his limp penis. It was a little salty from the perspiration caused by the energetic game, but she found the healthy male scent and flavour stimulating.

Burrowing deeply into the soggy folds and creases of his vital organ she wondered why her attentions were producing no hardening effect. 'Aw, come on, baby, don't play hard to get,' she implored, stroking his hairy scrotum and tweaking his unresponsive penis. 'I just gotta have you one more time. Can't you get this little old pecker interested just enough for a quickie?'

Brady knew that in Edith's sensuous repertoire a 'quickie' simply did not exist. Once started into copulation her desire knew no bounds. Like the Flying Dutchman on his relentless voyage, the Crusaders searching for the Holy Grail, or the ancient alchemists seeking the elixir of life, Edith, embarked on a sexual voyage, was unstoppable. Her quest for sensation and her unquenchable thirst for orgasmic climax were endless and painful for her partners, as Charles had, to his discomfort, already discovered. She had left behind her on her grand tour a phalanx of disordered men and boys suffering from sore foreskins, swollen testicles, embarrassing love-bites and aching glands.

Brady had already gone through those symptoms, and though he was almost recovered, not having seen her for a few days, he did not feel prepared to undergo another onslaught. He had the instinctive intuition of an athlete in this respect. His body was the instrument of his success and his place in life. How he had nurtured it, pumping iron in the gym, wielding Indian clubs, weightlifting, rowing and skipping. The beautify symmetry of his muscles, his wide deep chest and powerful biceps were a tribute to his dedication in the search for the pinnacle of physical perfection that he desired. How else was he to induce the rapturous worship of the fans of football in Detroit?

The mirror in his bedroom back home had been his best friend in this self regarding exercise. He loved to sleek his body with oil and pose in his sportsman's pouch in front of it, admiring his burgeoning frame. Sometimes if his love of himself caused a little arousal in the area of his crotch, he dealt with the problem swiftly and surely, also in front of the mirror, marvelling, in a similarly onanistic way, at the strength of the muscles of his genital equipment and their lavish distribution of his seminal fluids. Not that Brady was vain. On the contrary, his search for perfection led him to criticise many of his personal physical flaws, he was so absorbed in his development as an object of veneration. Though he was proud he was not a narcissist. How could he be when, having had no more than a smattering of education, and certainly with no knowledge of the classical world, he thought that Echo was something that came back when you yelled out in the Grand Canyon?

Edith tried another tack when she realised she was on a fruitless path. 'God, you're so beautiful,' she sighed, lying over him. 'You get me so excited. I just love your body, it's so big and strong. I feel you could just sweep me up into your arms and carry me away, and brother, would I go along with you.' Her fingers explored the hardness of his abdomen and the taut muscles of his chest, and then the length of his fine thighs and calves. 'Just like Tarzan,' she murmured, 'or actually, those pictures I've seen of Greek sculptures. You know honey, you're just like one of those Apollos. My what a body.'

She applied a finger to her clitoris, rubbing at the protruding appendage with some enthusiasm. 'See what you do to me,' she said, 'I admire you so, I can't imagine a better formed man.'

'You really think so?' Brady asked huskily. He was touched by this reference to his beauty. Perhaps, he thought, all that hard work in the gymnasium had been worth it if the results precipitated such admiration.

'Oh, sure,' Edith readily agreed, noticing the slightest thickening of the organ which had been, until now, disappointingly limp. 'Any girl will tell you, what we like is a fine shaped guy with lots of tough muscles, not coarse and ugly, but handsome like you, darling, artistic, if you know what I mean.'

'I sure do, sweetheart,' Brady said, turning over so that Edith could massage his back.

She ran her firm hands over his shoulders and down his spine into the cleft between his buttocks, lingering to feel the twitch of his muscles when she touched the area between his legs. Then she felt underneath him and satisfied herself that the increase in his genital size was continuing. 'My, my,' she purred, the most attractive man on the Riviera, and I have him all to myself. What more could a girl ask for?'

'You think I'm a good looker, huh?' Brady asked, wanting even more assurance.

Edith wished her litany of praise could come to an end. She wanted action not words, but she felt that she could not lose out after her next tribute. 'Honey, if I were a painter I would want to spend my life trying to get your wonderful body on canvas. Every one of these hard ridges and fine bones. Your handsome face and those burning eyes which tear me apart, honey. God you're so adorable.'

She ambled on in this vein while the footballer stretched extravagantly underneath her, flexing every fibre in his body in thanks for her adoration, and for the fine erection that resulted. He threw her on her back and said 'You're not so bad yourself, sweetheart,' and poised on his knees between her opened thighs, took hold of his now firmly hardened instrument in his two hands.

'Oh, let me do that for you,' she implored, wishing that once she had hold of the object she might be able cunningly to introduce it to her own throbbing part and gain the satisfaction she craved.

'When a guy's tired, and boy did you wreck me on the tennis court, it's better this way,' she said, pressing her proffered hands over her own centrepiece.

With his eyes closed, in wonderment at the adoration he aroused, his hands flew up and down his instrument at great speed.

Edith gripped his testicles with one hand and with the other paid scrupulous and intensive attention to her nether regions. 'Gorgeous,' she squealed, 'my God, you're gorgeous,' and she watched as he brought himself to a massive climax without once lessening the furious speed of his attack on the brutally swollen member.

Her own efforts had brought her also a merciful release, she shuddered and groaned as his sperm showered over her body and simultaneously her owns fluids cascaded her into rapture.

When she opened her eyes Brady was no longer between her thighs. He stood in a shaft of sunlight which filtered through the venetian blind of the window, in the classic pose of the body builder, fists clenched, biceps taut, buttocks and pelvis thrust forward.

'Gee thanks honey,' he said, 'I begin to see what you mean.'

Later, around the time Angelique and Vladimir were packing up the remains of their picnic and their wet bathing togs, Brady having made off for his luggage and the train to Vintimilia, Edith drove back along the coast road.

She came by chance upon the small hotel at Roquebrune which held tea dances. The reader will remember that it was here that Dhokouminsky ravished Bernadette's cousin Sophie during an impassioned tango some weeks earlier.

Business was slack, but the few customers seemed to be having a good time in the *salon de danse*. By coincidence Dhokouminsky was again in attendance, though this time he was accompanied by a male friend, the famous Russian baritone, Boris Oblomov.

Stalwart friends of old, when they had been graduates of the Academy of Arts in St. Petersburg, the two had fallen into each others arms in a great bear hug on the steps of the casino in Monte Carlo a few days back when the singer arrived to start rehearsals for the opera season which was to commence at the end of the ballet's sojourn in the theatre. They had similar temperaments, both gruff and uncompromisingly masculine in their approach to life and to women, of whom they were both inordinately fond.

The pair had already consumed a large number of cocktails and had commandeered a table by the raised band-stand in order to be able to peep up the skirts of the lady saxophonist and violinist. Thus engaged they were telling each other a series of scabrous jokes and filling in on their recent amorous exploits.

The aforementioned tango had been the inspiration of the visit. Dhokouminsky and Oblomov were seriously considering whether it might be possible in this hot-house climate, with the swaying seductive rhythms and romantic melodies of the tea dance, to conjugate with a complete stranger in a similar manner if a frustrated enough female could be found.

Oblomov thought, when Edith entered, that he was looking at such a lady. Flushed and perspiring from her car ride in the hot early evening sun, the athletic American was seated on a small gilt chair that was really too small for her highly developed posterior. Her legs were splayed wide in a manner that an earlier generation would not have dared to affect, and a cigarette in a holder helped to convey a louche appearance that appealed to the Russians. She nodded her head and tapped her foot in time to the music. It was tame stuff by her standards, used as she was to the crazy rhythms emanating from the deep south of her native country and the hot jazz which had followed the enticing tunes of Scott Joplin.

A waitress approached the men's table, knowing they would be good for another order. Oblomov called for champagne and three glasses and then lurched over to Edith and asked her to dance. The band were fortunately playing a stately waltz at the time, a dance he could just manage in his inebriated state. He was charming and smiled profusely, held Edith at a correct distance and complimented her on the short beaded dress she had changed into after Brady departed.

Soon the three were cosily grouped together chatting like old friends. The champagne flowed and they nibbled at little plates of hors d'oeuvres; it was amusing and gay, the conversation full of suggestive remarks and sly innuendoes. Edith loved it, it was much better than sitting by herself, and the two handsome Russians appealed to her not only for their witty conversation but for their dashing good looks. Each man danced in turn with her. She was naturally impressed with Dhokouminsky's ability on the floor and went so far as to tell him he should turn professional. He roared with laughter at the idea, especially as she told him she could get him work as a gigolo in the States.

Oblomov was very amused by this notion. 'Not bad situation for ageing principal dancer of Ballets Russe,' he grinned. 'You know every doorman in New York is a cousin of deposed Czar?'

'Quick, please take me back to the table. There's someone I don't want to see,' Edith said urgently to Dhokouminsky later as he was leading her in a foxtrot.

Charles had entered with the Lady Letitia draped on his arm. They looked blissfully happy. Fanshawe had obliged by going on a drunken binge with a couple of cronies that would last several days and Letitia had telephoned her new beau to meet her at the hideaway hotel. Charles was dressed in an immaculate dinner jacket and she wore a flowing dress and cloak of midnight blue velvet. They were, to Edith's chagrin, an undeniably handsome pair, even though it was obvious that Charles was young enough to be her son.

When they took the floor many a female eye roved over the good looking Englishman, and all the men approved of his taste in women. Letitia was certainly in stunning form. The new dalliance with Charles had brought fresh colour to her cheeks, and she had been inspired by the romantic liaison to buy new clothes and perm her hair in the latest style.

Inevitably Charles noticed Edith in the company of the two Russians. He paused for a moment in the dance and bowed slightly in her direction. She lifted a hand in a laconic fashion and immediately turned her attention back to the conversation.

'My God. I know that woman with your friend there,' Oblomov said. 'Tell me who that young man is,' he added in a teasing voice.

'Oh, he's just a guy I know, just one of the gang. He runs the yachts at the marina. I met him a few times,' she answered vaguely.

Oblomov roared with laughter, slapping his thigh with glee, and called for more champagne. The sight of Letitia had stirred the memory of a scandalous happening some years earlier, an event which rocked the world of the opera and which was recounted whenever singers got together for drinks, which we all know is a very frequent happening.

Oblomov was engaged to sing Iago in *Otello* by Verdi at the Royal Opera House in Covent Garden, London, with his colleague Alfredo Agnelotti performing the title role. Alfredo, Oblomov explained, was a brilliant and celebrated international performer of great distinction, but like many Italian singers, had a reputation for being temperamental and explosive in his dealings with producers and management. 'You know, darling,' he said, 'tenors always very naughty, not like baritones, like me, very good boy, very nice. I sing good, I take the money and run.'

227

In his fractured English he told how Alfredo always insisted on a particular condition in his contract under the heading 'special arrangements'. Tenors, Oblomov revealed, on the whole refrained from sex for a few days before an important performance, rather as boxers and athletes tend to save themselves. Baritones on the other hand, he grinned, indulged themselves right up to the last minute. It helped to get the low notes, he added with a wink, when you were really tired. But Agnelotti was different. However hard he tried he simply could not hit the high notes unless he had made love immediately before a performance and so he obliged management to provide him with female company in his dressing room an hour before the curtain rise, and the special stipulation was that the contract was null and void without this provision, for sound medical reasons and the condition of his voice. This arrangement clearly cost the theatres quite an extra amount on top of his fee, but it was worth it; Agnolotti's performances were invariably sold out completely and the reviews in the newspapers ecstatic.

The Opera House manager in London had some luck arranging this business for that particular production. It so happened, Oblomov related, that an English lady of some substance, Seraphina Ormesby-Gore, a dilettante and amateur singer of small talent was so enamoured of the Italian tenor that she willingly agreed to take on the delicate responsibility of ensuring that the star singer would be kept happy and in good voice. Frustration, she realised, would result in cracked notes and a wobbly vocal line. The lady took her work seriously and presented herself promptly at the stage door every evening *Otello* was to be performed. She was led ceremoniously by the stage manager to Agnolotti's dressing room where champagne and a brocade covered *chaise longue* awaited her.

The great singer's performances entranced London's music lovers. There was such a wild enthusiasm black marketeers openly sold tickets on the streets at vastly increased prices and the cheap gallery tickets were queued for all night by the poor music students who were avid for this once-in-a-lifetime opportunity to hear the maestro sing.

A gala performance was scheduled for a particular evening, to be attended by the Queen and her entourage. Florists went to work on the foyer, the grand staircase, and the lobbies with mountains of flowers, and silk draperies were hung from the royal box. It was magnificent and costly, a superb setting for the great lady and her party, when they stepped out of their horse drawn carriages and entered to the applause of the respectful audience.

Backstage, however, was in total chaos. Seraphina had sent a note round to the stage door begging to be excused from her duties on account of the bout of influenza which had taken her. She was not only laid low, but of course she did not want her idol to become infected with the hideous germ.

Agnoletti raged at the management, they had broken his contract. It was null and void, he would not sing, he could not sing, without the agreed preamble on the divan. He was not going to ruin his reputation so lightly, and they could go to hell.

The conductor was obliged to begin the overture again. The stage manager knew from his score exactly how many minutes after the curtain rise the star made his first entrance. He dashed to the female chorus room to see if anyone would oblige, but there were no takers. Downstairs the managers beat on the star's dressing room door, imploring him to make an exception to the rule on account of the royal nature of the occasion. The other principal singers gathered in the corridor, enthralled by the scandal the tenor was creating. The chairman of the governors hovered trembling outside the Royal Box. Eventually he summoned up the courage to give a light tap on the door. It was opened by the Lady Letitia, who in her capacity as Lady-in-Waiting was present in the box with Her Majesty.

The chairman spluttered and mumbled his apologies for the late rise of the curtain and Letitia conveyed his message to the Queen. She slipped out into the vestibule and enquired if the problems were of a technical nature or was there any way in which she could assist.

When the poor wretch told her that the Italian refused to perform, that the disgraceful man would never be engaged at that house again, and that the evening would have to be cancelled, the gravest insult to Her Majesty, Letitia strode towards the pass door which led to the stage and beyond to the dressing rooms. Pushing aside the assembled company and stage hands, she burst into Agnolotti's room.

Her loyalty to King and Country and to her beloved mistress was such that by the time the overture had been played twice and the opening scenes completed, Alfredo Agnolotti made a triumphant entrance and sang superbly throughout the evening.

Letitia returned to the Royal Box smiling. Yes, she thought, the show must go on.

It was late when Oblomov, Dhokouminsky and Edith left Roquebrune for Monte Carlo. The short journey by taxi was pleasant, all three squashed up in the back like old chums, with the bear-like paws of the two men placed intimately on her knees.

On leaving the hotel Edith had confronted Letitia. 'I hope

you're getting enough, honey,' she said. 'These English guys sure are stingy when it comes to the hard stuff, and I don't mean money.'

Charles had coughed and blushed but Letitia simply looked perplexed. Her lover, after all, was a great improvement on the drunken novelist who had lain limp and snoring in her bed for the last ten years; and even at that moment she had her hand in his trouser pocket, hidden by the tablecloth, and in possession of his cherished centrepiece.

'What a coarse girl,' she said. 'Do we know her? And who are those blackguards with her?'

'Never seen her, darling, not a clue,' Charles answered. 'I expect she's a tart and they're going off for a threesome. Care to dance?'

He was right in his deduction, but in fact the event was to take place the next day. The two Russians were canny enough to know that they had consumed far too much drink that day to be in good form as lovers, therefore they arranged to pick Edith up the following morning at twelve.

The agenda was a leisurely drive to Eze en Haut, a charming rustic village in the foothills where it was proposed to eat a wonderful lunch.

The hamlet was primitive, almost in ruins. One could hardly tell where human habitations started or finished, it was such a ramshackle collection of cottages, barns, sheds and lean-tos, all jumbled together on the hillside. Pigs and geese ran together in the main street and in the numerous small alleys, donkeys were tethered on every corner, and a flock of sheep lay in the road outside the one and only, but celebrated, restaurant.

The genial patron brought pastis and vermouths to the table with a large basket of *crudités*, olives and wholesome bread from the village bakery. The three ate while an elderly singer performed idiosyncratic folk songs, accompanying himself on the guitar. Then they ate the food of the mountains: roast kid, flavoured with herbs, wild boar cooked on a spit and a stew of hare in red wine and juniper berries. Several hours later they were offered fresh ripe figs and a platter of goats cheese and grapes, followed by coffee and liqueurs. It was a gastronomic feast both in proportions and in excellence and the three diners lay back in their chairs smiling in great contentment at its conclusion. Dhokouminsky decided they should take a stroll to aid the digestion of this mammoth meal and after purchasing another bottle of brandy they set off.

A path leads from the village to Eze Sur Mer, hundreds of feet below. It was used by the smugglers in the old days to bring contraband goods up the hill from ships in the small harbour. The path follows a precipitous route, over boulders and the entwined roots of tall trees, through numerous small gushing streams and a series of steps cut into the rock, many of which have been worn away by the tread of feet and the erosions of time.

They began the descent, laughing and giggling, sometimes sliding on their backsides when they came to a wet patch and tripping over hidden obstacles. The men were courteous to Edith, stopping her from falling. With each little assistance their hands grew braver, digging more deeply into her breasts and her thighs as they lifted her down from a rock or helped her pass under an overhanging branch. On one particularly steep slope Dhokouminsky threw Edith over his shoulder and carried her in a fireman's lift, slapping her bottom as he did so, and at another difficult junction all three slid down a grassy slope and finished in a heap together at the foot of a knarled olive tree.

Oblomov produced the brandy from his coat pocket and they all took copious swigs. Edith lit a cigarette and lay back on the velvety grass in an abandoned attitude, telling the two men what a gorgeous day she was having. They agreed, and offered her some more brandy. Never one to stint herself, she took another copious draught of the potent liquid and soon lay half asleep with her head in Oblomov's lap and her legs carelessly thrown over Dhokouminsky's chest.

She loved it when, in this drowsy state, she felt hands stroking her hair and other hands removing her shoes. The second pair then stroked her ankles and the undersides of her feet. It was refreshing after such an arduous walk.

The hands at her neck began expertly to trace cunning little patterns at her throat and when she smiled in compliance at this attention, Oblomov's mouth came down over hers and delivered a tender but firm kiss. She could feel the hardness in his trousers through her neck and, by parting her thighs and exploring with her toes over Dhokouminsky's torso and belly, she found a similar swelling at his crotch.

'We did not have a pudding, after all. Only boring cheese and fruit,' Oblomov said as the two men then each took an ankle and parted her legs wide. It was delicious for Edith to have the pair bite their way up the insides of her legs in this splayed position and for each to find one of the outer lips of her part. They rested there chewing on her now-swollen labia and tasting at the inner lips in turn, delicately probing with insistent tongues.

Their hands squeezed her breasts and tweaked her large nipples. She groaned appreciatively and reached for their respective organs. Edith was not a girl to stand on ceremony, she had them both out, weighing them up in a trice, and decided that two birds in the bush were better than one. Her mouth closed on Oblomov's pride, sucking tenderly, and then on his friend's, so that he should not feel left out. The two men equally took turns to pleasure her in the most intimate ways and with increasing ardour as their swollen members became more aroused. If one took to kissing her nipples, the other took the damp area between her thighs and the moist recesses which now throbbed with the most delightful sensations, and then they switched over to give each other a chance to enjoy her body to the full.

Soon the trio were completely naked in the shaded dell in which they lay. It began to be difficult to know who was doing what to whom, as the saying goes. They writhed in the grass in an endless permutation of groupings, all three seeking maximum stimulation, but of course Edith was the one most in the thrall of ecstasy since she had two men intent on body worship, and this had never happened in her life before. She felt like a goddess with two supernatural attendants as Oblomov and Dkokouminsky brougher her to the edge of hysteria with their probings, kisses, and manipulations.

One lay on his back and drew her over him manfully while the second lay over her pressing his penis into the cleft between her buttocks. They they all rolled over and one attacked her mouth with his organ, teasing her lips and then introducing it slowly between them while the other played with the tip of his glans at her shuddering opening, moistening it with his jissom, and pressing just the tip in, causing her to call out for more. But the pair were experienced in these erotic moments. Lifelong practice had given them great expertise in foreplay. There was no possibility of them spending themselves too soon or of climaxing the girl until she was well and truly at the point of satyric excitement. She began to bay like a she-wolf, anguishing for the deep inward thrust of one of the organs that had been tormenting her and this they gave her, but at first in small measure.

Oblomov held her hands out to her side and covered her

234

mouth with a long deep kiss while his friend parted her thighs and slid his bursting penis in her up to the hilt, only to lie still while she writhed her hips wildly from side to side, trying to encourage a more active response from him. All he gave her was the constant throb from the veins and muscles of his member, but without the pelvic action she craved. He slowly withdrew and his partner took his place, repeating the same action. They turned her over and repeated something of the same kind from the rear, but always stealthily and without the pressure she wanted, in the most outrageously teasing way, winking at each other, and confidently aware of their own and each other's sexual prowess.

Oblomov lay back and prised her parts over his organ, with her crotch straddled across his loins, while Dhokouminsky plied his penis to her mouth, and then they reversed the roles after a few seconds, barely letting her enjoy the one sensation before the other began. Her lathered outpourings were now considerable and she felt that without orgasm she would scream in frustration. She attacked her parts with her own fingers when they temporarily released her from a particular grip, but they quickly removed her hands to their own parts and clamped them there firmly, pushing through her tightened fingers in a mocking simulation of the release she desired. Edith implored and begged for one of them to finish her. The two men thought that would be far too simple a resolution to the orgiastic afternoon.

In an extremely deft and expert manner, one from the front and one from the rear, they both managed to insert their pulsating organs into Edith's quivering body, and, working in clever counterpoint against each other with their pelvic thrusts, brought her and themselves to the most magnificent and synchronised orgasmic climax.

Edith, for once, was deeply satisfied.

Chapter Fourteen

'How would you describe Camille?' M. Rognon said to his crony Laffite, grinning broadly in a lascivious manner, wishing to impress and maybe arouse his other friend Duclos in a sensual manner.

'Leonine,' Laffite replied. 'The one word describes her. She is a lioness.'

'Of the mattress?' questioned Duclos.

'*Mais naturellement*, in what other way do we consider female acquaintances.'

'Well, there are the considerations of the kitchen, the laundry, *mon cher ami*,' intoned the fat, perspiring Duclos between burps and drags at his Gauloise.

'Of course,' Rognon intervened, 'but with a girl like Camille, who would want her to spend time cooking or washing when she is much better employed in her natural profession.'

'And what is that, I pray?' asked Duclos, who so far was not privy to the pleasures Camille bestowed on those fortunate men to whom she took a passing fancy.

'She is an angel of the *boudoir*, *mon brave*. There is no finer on the whole of the Riviera.'

'Why have I not been introduced to this paragon?' Duclos asked, aggrievedly—his own marriage having broken down, and his recent lover having deserted him for a rich broker from Algiers, his erotic life had come to a shuddering halt.

'You shall meet her ere long, my friend. She is just what you need,' Rognon growled in a voice that spoke chapter and verse of his predilections and his long greedy enjoyment of the libidinous pleasures of the bed chamber.

'And how would *you* describe Camille, then,' asked Laffite of Rognon, winking and stroking his beard in that affected old-fashioned way which he thought showed him off as a dandy.

'Auto-erotic,' Rognon answered. 'She is like the engine of a motor car which, by some extraordinary invention, needs no sparking plug. Or one of those perpetual machines which turn only from the effect of sunlight.'

'Her loins are self-arousing,' explained Laffite for the benefit of the bemused Duclos.

'Her juices flow like Niagara Falls. She needs no physical contact to generate arousal,' added Rognon.

'She is a nymphomaniac, *alors*?' Duclos asked in a hoarse whisper. 'Goes with anybody?' At last he thought, a sexual athlete who would not tire of his gross appearance and sloppy manners.

'On the contrary. She is very choosy. Because her self-induced pleasures are so freely available, she is aloof with men, very picky indeed. Is that not so, Laffite?' Rognon asked.

'It's a lucky man who stirs Camille.' Laffite breathed in Duclos' ear.

'What kind of bloke stirs this Amazon, then? Does she go for the young ones, the pretty boys who have no staying power, or,' he leered, 'does she fancy a guy like me who's been around, knows the ropes and can give her a good time?' Duclos wished to know.

237

'Who can tell?' Rognon mused, calling for another round of pastis.

They had sat many hours in this particular café, and had drunk more than a few cognacs with their coffees, then devoured a large plate of Toulouse sausage, several bowls of *pommes frites*, a large *tarte aux poires* with cream, three jugs of local wine, and now gone back to their favourite aperitif in readiness for the approaching dinner hour.

The air was thick with the aroma of Gitanes and Gauloise, blue wreaths of smoke billowing up to the whirling fan set in the ceiling. It was the kind of raffish estaminet which tries to cultivate a certain kind of Bohemian atmosphere, with candles tuck in empty wine bottles and imitation wax fruits and vegetables strung along the beams, and also a never ending detritus of sugar wrappers, toothpicks, match boxes and so on which the clients were encouraged to throw on the sawdusted floor. The perfect place to arrange a bet, read a free newspaper, get drunk, or indulge one's fantasies in lewd chat about girls.

When the drinks arrived, Rognon drew his wicker chair closer to the table in conspiratorial fashion. The others followed suit, puffing deep on their cigarettes and sipping at the cloudy glasses of pastis. An hour passed by in agreeable comradeship, marked at intervals by calls for further rounds of drinks and fresh packets of Gauloise.

Rognon explained the mystique of Camille and her peculiar affliction. It transpired, at great length, and with much invention, piling fiction on fact, that the said Camille, niece of an acquaintance of Rognon, had been expelled from her convent school in mysterious circumstances. The child had been sent to a variety of other establishments, but none had kept her for long. The parents were given no satisfactory explanation for this series of damaging dismissals, and eventually she had been brought before a child psychologist, at the age of just sixteen, and referred to an expert who had studied deeply at the founts of Jung and Freud and now ran a fashionable clinic in Zurich.

The clinician had fallen deeply in love with his client and been obliged to leave in disgrace for the United States and a fresh career. The parents were agog with worry that everywhere the child went she caused havoc. A Harley Street physician was brought from London. He pronounced the first true diagnosis of poor Camille. He explained that women also can be the victims of that terrible affliction which on the whole upsets male members of the human race, satyriasis—a condition which can best be described as the permanent engorgement with blood of the genital parts, leading to lascivious behaviour in males, pain, dizziness, fainting, exhaustion, and sometimes madness, let alone the adverse effect on their long-suffering partners.

'But that describes me exactly!' yelled Duclos at this point in the narrative.

'Stop boasting,' Laffite ordered. 'Your trouble, I'm told is that, on the contrary, you can't usually get it up.'

'Oh, no, I suffer, look at this bulge right here,' Duclos moaned, pointing at the protuberance which seemed fit to burst through his fly buttons.

'You're just a dirty old man. You've got excited by the story. Shut up,' Rognon said testily. 'You don't want it any more than either of us, and when you get it, I don't suppose you're very good.' So Rognon unfolded the story, interrupted at times by lewd comments from Laffite and Duclos.

At first Camille had no idea that she was so unnaturally orientated, sexually speaking. She imagined that all girls had the constant thrilling excitements down in their knickers that she enjoyed, and spoke joyfully about her transports with

239

everyone, this perhaps explaining some of the embarrassments of the original convent and the other educational establishments. Eventually it was explained to her by the kind English doctor who specialised in psycho-sexology that, on the whole, girls reach orgasmic climax only after physical contact with the male of the species, and in some cases, even then rarely. He said that she was like a living volcano, continuously on the boil and liable to erupt, whereas most females' sexual parts could be compared to a dead volcano unless scrupulous attentions were paid by an obliging lover.

Even as the great physician spoke, Camille suffered, or rather, enjoyed, the most delightful orgasm which brought a rosy glow to her cheeks and alerted the medic, who promptly suggested a vaginal inspection. The particular cut of his suit, his lavender scented cologne, and the hair on the back of his hands had done their worst to her, poor girl, as even in the case of the *curé* at the clinic who had ravished her senses with the musty odour of books and incense that he emanated in a spiritually uplifting masculine way when he administered communion to her.

Duclos was by now beside himself with libidinous thoughts. 'What does she look like?' he demanded gruffly, his thick voice signifying to all the extent of his arousal.

'Tawny, long-legged, wolverine,' urged Laffite, with a vivid memory of her appearance.

'Nineteen years old, the rage of Paris on the cat walk. The couturiers fight amongst themselves to have her model their collections, and she poses for all the top artists. Picasso drools over her,' Rognon added, his greedy voice betraying his lust.

'When shall I see her,' Duclos begged, 'this self-generating power-house? My God, would I like to get her in bed and show her what a man can do.'

At that moment a tall, incredibly beautiful girl advanced

towards them. Duclos caught his breath so hard he almost choked to death. Her skin was coppery and shining, straight from the beach where she had been sun-bathing and causing erections in literally hundreds of pairs of swimming trunks. Her hair, which hung down to her waist, was vivid auburn, streaked by sunshine with flecks of bright gold. Her manner of walking was voluptuous to an extraordinary degree, involving a spell-binding swaying of the hips, with her mound of Venus pushed aggressively forward with that tilt of the pelvis which is the mark of the professional mannequin.

Duclos, whose underpants were already damp from the frisson he found in the story, felt his member spring to full erection, as did Laffite. Rognon had already jumped to his feet before that particular condition could strike him, so the fall of his well tailored suit was in no way impaired. 'Come, darling Camille, how lovely to see you. Come and join us at our table.'

The amazing girl, who possessed that quality or assemblage of qualities which gives the eye or other senses intense pleasure, in other words a timeless beauty, was truly a breathtaking example of the kind of female who becomes an icon in the canon of a great painter, viz Raphael, Tintoretto or Leonardo da Vinci. Other comparisons could be made with the unnerving attractions of those beauties who inspired immortal symphonic creations, desperate novels of undying passionate love, or drove men to drink and insanity in tragic circumstances.

Her brooding leonine presence was sharpened aciduously, as a cocktail is by lime juice, by the brilliance of her flashing amber eyes. They could admire, mock, worship, torment, or cauterise at will, with a repertoire of expressive looks, burning in such intensity that any man on whom they fell could be reduced in a second to a gibbering slave, drooling idiotically, with the faculties of his brain running amok in an explosion of the libido.

She swayed, as if impelled by some unheard music, towards the table, bestowing brief glances on men at other tables nearby; piercing and heart-breaking looks that the recipients would swear afterwards had lasted for whole minutes at a time.

Rognon, Laffite and Duclos watched this benificent progress across the floor in a dazed condition. The amount of alcohol which they had consumed no doubt contributed to the miasma of emotions which now engulfed them, but collectively they registered that kind of idiocy which the bourgeois display at the screening of a new film when the starring vamp arrives in an impressive Cadillac; or the mindless sycophantic stupefactions the hoi-polloi and the under-privileged show if, for some reason, they come within more than a kilometre of anyone of royal descent.

Camille was possessed of charismatic qualities which the greater majority of cinema actresses would murder for, and the underlying truth of the situation was that she used them unknowingly. As she sashayed through the café, she had absolutely no idea of the disturbance she was creating. The all-male customers of the estaminet naturally supposed that her heated glances were for their benefit, each imagining that her fire was reserved for them. On the contrary, she, in the manner of the mythical huntress Diana, sought her own prey. Between the door and the rear of the café she had already experienced two sets of convulsive passion.

The first was aroused by a workman in greasy overalls whose massive fist was poised with a forkful of *boeuf bourgignon*, and the second by a gangling pimpled youth in pebble glasses who lounged at the bar with a *café au lait*, sucking on a cube of sugar with an air of such youthful innocence that

Camille's heart went out to him, in quick succession of the labourer, causing a second quivering in her loins and a further dampness in her crotch.

Still flushed from these two sensual moments, she paused and extended a hand to Rognon who, licking his lips lasciviously, felt as if the entire blood flow of his body had, in an instant, coursed towards his genitals. The congregation, for that is what the worshipping clientele had become in Camille's presence, watched with bated breath as Rognon pulled up a chair.

Clad simply in a tight skirt of tangerine jersey cloth which clung provocatively to her perfectly shaped bottom and a brief bandana of silk which was bound tightly around her bosom in the fashion of the day, flattening her breast tomboyishly, she presented a perfect picture of modern woman, emanicipated and lovely.

Her beauty far outstripped that of even the most compelling fantasies of any of these men. In their wildest erotic dreams, tortured in their crumpled beds, with their hands clutching at their genitals, not one had encountered such a woman.

The breathless moment had a similar precursor when Aeneas alighted on the shore of Carthage and discovered Queen Dido, and another when the crazed Heathcliffe encountered Catherine in an English novel much admired by the sensuous French, the work of one Emily Brontë, the poetess of the dark moors of the north.

'Hi chaps,' this paragon uttered, 'anyone got a fag?'

Ten men, at least, rushed forward thrusting packets in her direction. Lighting up, she fixed the cigarette she chose in a chic little black holder and puffed with pursed lips.

She stood still for a moment, swaying on her heels, savouring as if she were hooked on some miracle or other like hashish or opium. Pouting her lips which were glossy with bright lipstick, she lazily blew smoke into a ring and watched with a quizzical expression as it turned upwards and floated towards the fan. Every man in the saloon was intensely moved by this insouciant gesture. Her mouth, curved into a lovely circle, became an object of desire, a sculpture to be venerated. Fantasies rang in every head. Here was a mouth to be cherished with a million kisses and then to be applied to that pounding agonised fulcrum of the sexual urge, the very tip of which, of each individual customer, was poised and willing in fantasy to be the conquerer of this radiant beauty.

'Thought I'd just pop in and say hello,' she said brightly, brushing a hand through her marcelled waves. 'Anyone going to buy me a drink?' Rognon, startled into action, called for a grenadine, a syrup he knew she enjoyed. 'So, what are you boys up to?' she asked of the trio who were old enough to be her father.

'Waiting for you, sunshine,' Lafitte leered. 'You'd light up any day.'

'These pigs are so rude not to introduce me to such a divine young lady,' Duclos smarmed, reaching for her hand and placing a greasy kiss on it. 'I am Duclos, Albert Duclos. *Enchanté*. At your service. How adorable, I have never seen a more beautiful woman,' he burbled, with a lot more of the same kind, lingering and pawing at her small hand.

Rognon pushed him away and took his place. 'You said you would dine with me,' he said feverishly.

'Don't go out with that randy old goat,' Laffite pleaded. 'I know a wonderful restaurant in the mountains. My car is outside.'

'Dinner is prepared at home, mademoiselle, and waiting,' Duclos interrupted. 'Will you not accompany me?'

Throughout this conversation the trio's hands roved,

touching when they could in order to press a point, whispering into her ear, and fixing her with smiles which they supposed to be charming and inviting but which in fact only betrayed the state of drunken lust that drove them on. Camille sat impassively.

A mirror on the back wall showed all of the remaining clientelle leaning forward in an attempt to overhear the conversation. The door of the establishment was also reflected. Camille's eyes settled on the figure of a tall handsome *gendarme* who entered and sauntered to the bar. He ordered a *cappuccino*.

The trio began to tell dirty stories, a mode often employed by intending seducers who imagine that salacious tales will arouse the female sexual drive. Camille listened attentively, for she was a good sport and thoroughly modern. She laughed in all the right places, sipped her drink gaily, and seemed to be enjoying herself immensely. This emboldened her admirers whose stories grew more daring, with sly little innuendoes and chuckles. Several other men laughed and joined in the fun, drawing up their chairs closer to Camille's table, ostensibly with a sense of jovial camaraderie, but in reality to peer at her nipples which showed through the bandana which covered her breasts, and the garter which became visible when she crossed one slim long leg over the other.

Another reality was that Camille's attention was focused on the *gendarme* in the way that a chameleon is fascinated by a basking fly. Not a soul in the café realised it, but as he raised his frothy cup of coffee to his heavily moustachioed lip, another of the peverse symptoms which afflicted Camille so often, wracked her body, causing her to clench her thighs together tightly. Another occurred a few seconds later when she observed the *gendarme* run his tongue over the moustache in order to remove the froth which had adhered. A third was occasioned when the young officer replaced his uniform cap, tilting the peak to a jaunty angle, with an approving squint in the mirror. The fine figure of a man would have been flattered out of his mind if he knew that such a small masculine gesture, handsome and arrogant as it was, could have aroused such passion.

So would all the others, who fondly imagined they were working their way into Camille's heart. But such is the vanity of men! They see a creature such as the young woman who was lionised that day and wish that their lust is reciprocated. When it is not, frantic with unfulfilled desires, they drink themselves to distraction, or visit houses of ill repute and fantasise the love they buy into an imaginary encounter with the object of their sensual instinct. In severe cases, even previously well adjusted mature men resort to those onanistic youthful practices of frustrated adolescence. The writer is sadly obliged to assure the reader that certain members of the crowd present at that evening in the Café Flore may have taken the latter of the options mentioned above.

Camille thanked her hosts, rising to her feet and smoothing her skirt gratefully over the middle area that had received such stimulating sensations. 'Thanks chaps,' she smiled in her most breathtaking fashion, 'you can't possibly know what a good time I've had. Goodnight.'

M. Rognon smiled and kissed her hand fervently. When she had left, her departure marked by a lot of chair scraping as men rose to make their farewells, he sat for a while with a blissful expression on his face. It will be remembered that it was he who tried to explain what he knew of Camille's strange medical condition. Although he often behaved like a buffoon in the company of his lecherous cronies, at heart he was a sort of minor intellectual. While the rest of them, blinded by the young lady's physical attributes had rushed headlong into flirtation and attempts at later seduction, he alone had pondered the clinical implications. His fevered imagination along these lines brought about the first auto-erotic self-induced emission he had suffered since he was a boy of twenty, an involuntary ejaculation of a magnitude and strength which amazed and delighted him. Not so powerful as the one he fondly remembered from all those years ago, but nevertheless a landmark of virility that was commendable for one of his age, shocking habits of diet, booze, cigarettes, and so on. 'Think I'll take a small brandy now,' he said, smiling like the cat which has had the cream.

As the party broke up, he remembered that he had an appointment with a rich client who was interested in the work of a dynamic sculptor he had recently discovered. He made his goodbyes to Duclos and Laffite and proceeded to the gallery. On the way he was almost knocked down by a silver Rolls Royce whose driver had to swerve in order to avoid his drunken, stumbling attempt to cross the boulevard.

Bernadette and Sophie were on their way back to the mansion after a highly successful shopping expedition to Nice. The limousine, driven by Jean-Paul, purred expensively along the corniche, with the two ladies comfortably ensconced in the back seat surrounded by numerous small parcels which were beautifully wrapped and ribboned.

The boot compartment was stuffed with the larger items, boxes containing dresses, coats, fur stoles and a large number of pairs of shoes, all purchased at the exclusive boutiques the pair favoured, and on the front seat by the driver was a crate containing a small fortune in objets d'art, porcelain and an antique tea service. It was blissful, they reflected, to be able to spend without thought for tomorrow.

Bernadette's fortune was so extensive that she had no firm idea of its gross amount. The monthly figures from the bank merely confirmed the success of her late husband's wise investments, which were spread throughout the world of commerce on a wide basis that ensured continuing prosperity. To her surprise she had recently discovered that she owned several flourishing hotels at fashionable resorts on the Riviera and a share in a Swiss ski centre. Steady profits continued to accrue from the family vineyards in Provence and the scent factory in Grasse, and quite large sums had now begun to come in from the investment in M. Rognon's art gallery in Antibes with the increasing demand for high quality paintings of the Cubist school.

Sophie, though not so profoundly rich as her cousin, was nevertheless well provided for. The generous Nabob had maintained many flourishing connections in the worlds of shipping and banking, as well as owning conglomerates in the Far East which dealt in the export of silks and semiprecious stones. This far flung empire had passed into Sophie's hands on his sad demise, apart from a few bequests to his various ex-wives, and Sophie employed a host of international brokers to deal with this inheritance, amazed by the large amounts that accrued in foreign banks all over the globe. If she turned up in Bangkok, Sydney, Istanbul, Rio de Janiero, or wherever, strange men rushed to greet her, pressing large envelopes of cash into her hands. It seemed such a casual way to deal with a large fortune. Bernadette warned her that this scattered wealth stood in need of clever organisation, that cheats were common in the business world. In other words that she needed a trusthworthy associate to help her draw the strands of the purse strings together. A husband perhaps, she queried.

'I suppose so,' Sophie said with a sigh. 'I'm having a wonderful time. I have you darling, and simply lovely friends, the occasional flirtation, or even lover, but I can't help thinking that a solid, reliable husband might be the er . . .,' she tailed off.

'I've been thinking the same, my dear, 'Bernadette said with more enthusiasm. 'This endless round of gaiety is all right; we have great fun; our security means we can go anywhere, do anything; but really, at the top of a mountain, when one is contemplating a divine sunset, one needs to share the experience with a soul-mate, don't you think, not a casual friend.'

'Agreed,' Sophie repied, 'but for heaven's sake, where are these wonderful men that one is going to share one's life with? Have you found one yet, I certainly haven't.'

Bernadette leaned forward to press the button which would cause the glass division to close, putting Jean-Paul out of earshot. 'What about your savage Russian, darling,' she teased, 'Dhokouminsky, the ballet star?'

'That buffoon? Come, come, now, what do you take me for? He's a charming rogue, and wonderful as a lover, possibly the most effective I've come across,' Sophie said appreciatively, 'but you don't expect me to make a permanent attachment to such a villain? For one thing his brain is in his prick. Apart from pirouettes, he can only think of sex, though I must say, he does do it rather well.'

'What about Arthur, the English officer? Now there's a gentleman if ever I saw one,' Bernadette proposed. 'Straight of back, precise and dignified, the Englishman at his best. And you can't deny his ability to charm a woman.'

Sophie blushed at the memory of her one encounter with

249

Arthur, the morning she and her cousin had ensnared him naked in the swimming pool and the following rapturous conjugation with the pair of them in the changing room. 'One can't make a relationship for life on the basis of having a good time in bed,' she chided.

'Perhaps not,' Bernadette replied, 'but it's a good beginning.'

The two practical women, being French to the core, and having realised that they should get their lives in order, made strenuous efforts over the next few days to come to some conclusion. They considered, being daughters of France, that they had responsibilities, not only to themselves and their future comfort, but to both of their respective late husbands. They had been neglectful of their business duties. Perhaps they would, if they went through a complete roster of their male acquaintances, come up with the right partners for life.

Rognon was dismissed as being too fat and too advanced into real middle age. Frederick Fanshawe was not considered at all, and anyway he was already married. Vossoudossoulos was thought to be short on charm, and his own fortune was so immense that he would have no time or interest in administering theirs. They were both interested in Marcel. Plenty of charm, good looks, an attentive and considerate lover, he had his own successful couture, was expanding into expensive beach wear, and about to open a branch in Paris. Ten out of ten! Young Charles, Arthur's friend, was briefly considered, being a handsome fellow and fairly rampant in his sexual life, but dismissed for having shown no interest in this department to either of the ladies.

'I know all about the little girl in the chocolate shop and the common American brat,' Bernadette pronounced, 'and I hear now he is in cahoots with poor Letitia.'

'Poor Letitia—what nonsense! She's having a wonderful

time. What a release from that dreadful Fanshawe,' Sophie exclaimed. 'I have never seen her looking so radiant.'

'That's not the point,' Bernadette countered. 'Apart from the odd smouldering look the man has certainly never made an approach to either of us.'

'Neither did Arthur. If you remember, we did the kidnapping,' her cousin giggled.

The debate continued over dinner that evening, one of the rare occasions when they were without guests, and they could talk in confidence. The problem, as always, was the shortage of unmarried men. Handsome widowers would have been acceptable, but these rare commodities were quickly snapped up. Travel abroad in search of the elusive partners was considered but rejected on the grounds that they needed a fair length of time to get to know their men before committing themselves; hasty marriages were not advisable, and who wanted to leave the blessed Riviera for such an extensive period? In the end Marcel and Arthur won the lottery.

Bernadette was enormously fond of her dressmaker, and she was sure that her affection could turn to love. Besides, he was a prudent and honest man. With the extra wealth from her he would be able to put the day-to-day running of the salon into efficient hands and concentrate more on pure design as well as involving himself in Bernadette's portfolio.

Sophie admitted to an overwhelming lust for Arthur. He was the man of her dreams, she declared, young enough to mould into a sauve and sophisticated lover, and he certainly had the equipment. In addition, when she had bought him out of the British Army, he could return to the Mediterranean life which he so obviously adored, and from there take off anywhere in the world with her in the pursuit of business and pleasure.

With these important considerations well and truly out of the way the ladies set about the preparations for a great party which would celebrate the Season; a glittering affair which would surpass anything the entire fabulous Riviera had ever experienced.

On the great day caterers' vans started to arrive at dawn and florists came with a lorry load of exotic blooms to decorate the mansion. Wine had been brought specially from Bernadette's own vineyard in Provence and crate after crate of champagne was rushed to the ice-house.

Jean-Louis, the household's chef had surpassed himself in the preparation of the principal items for the buffet luncheon which was to be provided for the two hundred or so guests that were invited, and Jean-Paul, the chauffeur, helped to carry out the vast amounts of china, cutlery, chairs, tablecloths and serving dishes of all kinds that were needed.

Dozens of extra maids and waiters had been hired. Among them, though Bernadette did not yet realise it, was Angelique. She was thrilled to have been offered the day's work since it meant that she could be there with her Vladimir, who, though invited, was not allowed to bring a guest since he was only a member of the *corps de ballet*. That privilege was reserved for the stars such as Vera Lidova.

The invitation, for two o'clock in the afternoon, stipulated informal clothes (Bernadette was aware that the hardworking and poorly paid body of the Ballets Russes could not afford grand clothes) and suggested that guests bring bathing costumes in order to be able to enjoy the pool.

A negro jazz band which had been playing in Deauville for the summer and had come down to Monte Carlo for the approaching autumn season had been engaged for the day, as had a Tzigane orchestra, complete with cimbalom, and a team of flamenco dancers and singers from Seville who were currently on tour in the area.

The gardeners had swept and garnished the grounds into an even greater perfection. The grand sweep of lawns, the terraces and grottoes, the herbaceous borders and rose arbours had never looked better. Into these enchanting vistas groups of tables and chairs were set, rugs were laid, and striped umbrellas were set up to provide shade.

Bernadette and Sophie masterminded the complicated arrangements, adding little touches like posies of flowers for centrepieces, place cards and boxes of cigarettes. By the time the guests began to arrive, the whole scene was perfect. An atmosphere of quiet luxury pervaded the terraces and gardens, a charming festive air that was a sincere tribute to the Ballet from the hostesses.

As usual the dance company fell on the food without ceremony, not caring a fig for the order in which they tried the many courses, piling their plates with an amazing variety of foodstuffs and gorging themselves greedily.

Vera Lidova was no exception even though she had the pretensions of being an international artiste of some repute. She fought with Dhokouminsky for the largest prawns and finished off a whole salmon by herself. Incongruously she was wearing long white silk gloves. Occasionally she dabbed at them with a napkin to clean up the stains of salad dressing and mayonnaise which ran down them, convinced she was behaving like a lady.

Dhokouminsky devoured half a turkey, a dish of *foie gras*, a wedge of camembert, an apple flan, a bowl of pineapple soaked in kirsch, a lobster, a couple of bottles of wine, stuffed mushrooms, caviar and chocolate gateau before collapsing in a deck chair for a snooze.

The large bizarre company all behaved in the same way. It was as if they had just been released from a labour camp in Siberia, never had food disappeared so fast. Jean-Louis wept

253

when he saw his confections, prepared with such loving care, demolished with such ruthlessness. Bernadette comforted him by telling him the dancers could not resist such exquisite dishes, but the poor chef could only dry his eyes on his apron and return to the kitchen to fix up some more food for the latecomers who would otherwise go hungry.

The sated ballet people lay on the lawns or sauntered around the grounds, marvelling at their rich surroundings, and the hostesses repaired to the corner of a shady terrace with some of their acquaintances for a more leisurely meal which had thoughtfully been set aside away from the ravaging hordes.

Arthur was nowhere to be seen. Bernadette presumed he was with either Galina, the young soloist, or her rival Lidova, but she promised Sophie that he would be found and brought to her forthwith.

Letitia and Charles sat close together, arm in arm, hoping that Frederick Fanshawe would not show up. Bernadette had not invited him but he was a well known gate-crasher who could smell free drink a mile away. Marcel sat with his arm around the vicomtesse, complimenting her on the wonderful party she was giving, and Bernadette responded with an encouraging squeeze of his hand.

M. Rognon had brought along a client of the gallery, a Parisian lady who controlled the buying and selling for a handful of rich art lovers and therefore was a welcome member of his growing circle. The lady, besides being a useful customer, and already proved herself to be quite stirred by Rognon and had graced his bed with considerable charm and a number of sexual variations which had been so far unknown to him.

Vossoudossoulos had already tired of Vera Lidova and was looking forward to the arrival of an old flame, a desirable

Lebanese woman of considerable personal fortune who had in her repertoire a number of Middle Eastern pelvic tricks learned in the *souk*. She was used to the domineering ways of Arabs and had none of the arrogance or wild ways of the eccentric ballerina. Borzdoff had managed to extricate a large number of francs from the millionaire after he had threatened to tell the world's press about his affair with Lidova. He had the cash to spare so it was better to pay up than risk offending the belly-rippling lady he was expecting any day from Damascus.

Vladimir whipped off Angelique's apron as soon as her principal duties were over and led her away from the terrace to join his comrades.

Charles, seated with Letitia, watched the lithe pair disappear with some regret, but Letitia regained his attention with a light pressure on his groin and a tender kiss on the lips.

Edith the Charleston dancer appeared, uninvited but claiming to have been brought along by Oblomov and Dhokouminsky. She glared at Charles and Letitia, wondering what he could possibly see in the slim, slightly wrinkled faded English rose, but Charles smiled politely and enquired in the sweetest manner if she was having a good day.

'Oh, yeah, it's real fun,' she glowered.

'Splendid, we must have a little chat sometime,' Charles replied.

Thus dismissed Edith went searching for the randy Russians who had entertained her so well the other day on the mountain path after lunch. She was not pleased to find Dhokouminsky at ease with a *corps de ballet* girl in a swinging hammock and Oblomov in the grip of an aristocratic opera fan who had recognised him from his last appearance at the Casino when he had such an enormous success singing the title role in the celebrated Tchaikovsky opera *Eugene Onegin*.

'Hi, boys,' she said gaily, passing by the foursome who were so completely absorbed in the pursuit of love that they did not even notice her. But soon she was swept up in the first swimming party of dancers who threw off every stitch of clothing as soon as their digestions allowed and dived into the limpid inviting waters of the pool.

Edith, a natural athlete, won their admiration for her breast stroke which involved an effective use of her well-shaped mammaries. She also impressed them with her swallow dive, back-flips and somersaults into the pool from the high diving board. She was beginning to consider which of these handsome muscled men would make an effective partner for her when she was picked up bodily by Dimitri Vaganov, one of the team, and swept off into a clump of bamboo where she surrendered to his Slavic ardour gratefully, and afterwards expressed her thanks by impressing on his detumescing organ many long protracted kisses.

Their coupling had been watched, of course, by a gaggle of naked boys from the *corps de ballet* who possessed just enough decorum to allow the affair to come to an end before signalling their intention of joining in the fun. One by one they rode her like wild stallions mount their mates in the tundra of their native country bringing the muscular American to a crescendo of breathless orgasm again and again.

'Boys, oh boys,' she cried, 'my God, what are you doing to me? I must be drunk or something.' The truth was that she was stone cold sober, and the nymphomaniac nature of her sexuality was not only reasonably satisfied, but she also thirsted for more. It was so flattering to have these lithe bodies pressed round her in such a crush.

In her intense rapture, with her eyes closed, enthralled with every new invasion, she neither knew or cared that Dhokouminsky and Oblomov had joined in the fray. They

256

sent away the already satisfied young boys and concentrated themselves again in a repetition of the scenario that had galvanised her so well the other day on the mountain.

'Gee,' she said, when she came to her senses after their promiscuous onslaught, 'you two guys are so good I should take you back to the States.' Of course all three of them knew that she was lying if she implied the two had been her only lovers that afternoon. 'Perhaps,' she added, winking, 'we could get together again later.'

Jean-Paul, Bernadette's chauffeur, was in a dilemma that afternoon. There were so many young people there at the party, loads of young girls who already had much worldly knowledge and were already serviced by attractive well-equipped males, that he felt ill-disposed to seek out adventure. The only woman that he could approach, it seemed, was the opera fan who had been infatuated with Oblomov. Well into her fifties, but an attractive lady of ample proportions, stylishly dressed, and giving off an aura of quiet cultivation, she seemed an ideal candidate for his particular attentions.

As it was officially his day off Jean-Paul was clad in casual clothes, the present of a rich lady who had been his recent *patronne*. She had adored his bathroom techniques; the lathering, the shampoos, the impulse showers, and the intimate spongings he had bestowed on her gross body, and had opened a Swiss bank account in his name in gratitude.

He wondered if Madame X was another suitable subject. He excused himself interfering in the conversation she was holding with Borzdoff and told her that he was the vicomtesse's chauffeur and that when she required, he was at her service to drive her home. His pretty speech was delivered in such silky tones and his sultry Provençale good looks impressed themselves so much on the lady that she felt impelled to leave straightaway.

'*A votre service*, Madame,' she murmured, gazing at her under his lowered eyelids with a certain burning enthusiasm she could not mistake for the servitude of an employee.

They made off for the Negresco Hotel immediately. She chose to sit in the front seat with Jean-Paul by her side and naturally allowed her thigh to brush against his, and then a hand to rest on his knee while she thanked him for his solicitude.

She admired the dark hair which just brushed his collar and the velvety eyes which he turned meltingly towards her at intervals. Catching her breath she wondered if the flirtatious conspiracy, for that is what any reasonably sophisticated person would by now have recognised was beginning, was suitable for a woman in her position, and with a servant too, to make it worse. Being a 'new thinker', she brushed aside such fears and, on arriving at the hotel, immediately ordered champagne to be brough to her suite and proceeded into the lift with the compliant Jean-Paul.

Their conversation was gay and irrelevant while she slipped into the dressing room and changed into a black *piegnoir*. He threw himself back on a divan and opened the champagne with practised ease. He poured two full glasses which they drank down thirstily, then another two, for they were both anxious to lose whatever inhibitions remained.

She told him how lucky her friend Bernadette was to have such a handsome driver and he returned the compliment by saying that she was the most charming lady that he had ever encountered at his employer's residence.

Jean-Paul began by spilling some of the wine down her *peignoir* when he refilled her glass. He had to dab at it then with a napkin and also at the damp skin underneath, which made her bosom heave in an unmistakable way. Madame X then admired his suit and ran an appreciative hand down the crease of his trousers as she asked him who his tailor was.

It was flippant and relaxed, but like the mating rituals of jungle animals, the encounter moved on irresistibly towards a conjugation. He found himself bestowing a light kiss on her shoulder and then on her willing mouth and she tried hard to find a burgeoning hardness in his trousers, but the reader will remember that Jean-Paul was not noted for the size of his organ, and she overlooked the small object.

On her instructions he rang down for more champagne and when it had been delivered he slyly drew her towards the bed and lay down beside her. The *peignoir* was now open, revealing her bosom. He poured a little of the wine over each of her nipples. The bubbles smarted and tickled her in an unexpected and delicious way, and her pleasure was compounded when he leaned over her and carefully licked off each drop. He repeated the same on her navel. The small hollow held the champagne without spilling for a while but eventually the tickling sensation made her laugh and she turned, spilling the liquid on to the sheets. He stroked her buttocks and ran a finger in the crack between them, rubbing his bristly chin up the length of her spine, making her shiver with delight.

The channel between her legs was now damp with her desires. He took up the champagne cork that he had just removed and played with it at the mouth of her part, passing it over her lubricated outer lips and then slowly and carefully introducing the rounded end in between the paler inner lips. She writhed in pleasure at this introduction of what she thought was his own love machine, and cried for him to take her there and then, but he only introduced a finger and then two fingers, roaming gently in her innnermost regions. Her deep breathing and occasional whimpers told him that she was approaching a climax. He found her outstanding bud and licked at it hungrily, flicking with his tongue, returning the champagne cork to its place just within her moistened walls, and with a free hand played a thrilling squeezing game on her outstanding nipples.

Then a great inspiration came to the chauffeur. He reached for a pillow and placed it under her bottom so that the area of her crotch was lifted up from the bed. Slowly and with great precision he poured champagne a drop at a time over her soft pubis. The sparkling liquid ran over the edge of her mound and down the lips of her entrance. He opened them with his fingers and let the bubbles cascade around her most private part and then leaned down to suck them away.

It was a delirious experience for Madame X who promised herself she would order a gold watch for Jean-Paul the very next morning, but as far as he was concerned, the orgasm he had suffered inside his trousers and the grateful cries of the lady were sufficient payment. He was also glad to have added to his repertoire.

By some strange alchemy, in the odd and bizarre twist of life's peculiar ways, the closest of Jean-Paul's few acquaintainces, Alphonse Duparc, also held a certain fascination for women on account of a particular predilection.

Alphonse, shy, reclusive, almost to the point of eccentricity, had little time for the normal intercourses of the social scene. In fact, Jean-Paul was his only male companion. Occasionally they sat together over a beer, hardly talking, but mutually satisfied in a gloomy sort of way with each other's presence, as sometimes men are if they do not engage themselves with permanent partners of the opposite sex.

Alphone had been employed for some years as the projectionist-in-chief of the principal cinema in Monaco and was much valued by the owner for his scrupulous and attentive devotion to his work.

Immensely tall, emaciatedly thin and stooping, he spent endless hours in the hot stuffy projection box to the detriment of his complexion which was deathly white. Locked away in this fashion, endlessly winding and re-winding reels of celluloid, lacing them into the machines, repairing and testing, he had become careless of his appearance, though he was scrupulous in every detail of his personal cleanliness. His long bony fingers were manicured to perfection, and his untrimmed grey hair fell almost to his shoulders, sparklingly shampooed, but without even a nod in the direction of fashion.

During his long working hours he had no time for refreshment, save for a large jug of *citron pressé*. The smoking of cigarettes was naturally banned as a fire hazard, conversation with his young assistant was rendered almost impossible on account of the incessant roaring whining machinery, and in truth all attention had to be fixed on the grainy images being projected and focused on the silver screen of the auditorium. It was an ascetic life, but a satisfying one. Alphonse and his apprentice felt privileged in being the first citizens of the Principality to view each new cinematic masterpiece. Through the small glass window they looked out into the darkness of the salon and took great satisfaction in the immense beam of light which carried forward such arresting representations. Alphonse, at the controls of the projectors, lived in a state of sublime happiness. The iconography of Hollywood passed before his eyes daily. Garbo, Gilbert, Chaplin, Pickford, Valentino and all the other luminous stars of the cinema firmament slipped through his fingers into the reels and sped across the dark space to be conjured up in awesome magnification.

Small wonder that Alphonse Duparc felt sublimely satisfied with his life. The fantasy of the cinema occupied every

261

single moment of his days, and his nights were filled with dreams of glamorous stars, intrigues and adventure. He never knew the torture most normal healthy men suffer, for instance, in a period of their lives when love is unrequited, or perhaps when circumstances create a situation when the degree of amorous or erotic arousal endured far outweighs the amount of physical release, in an ejaculatory sense, that is the male requirement. On the contrary, the projectionist was gratified to the full, content beyond all his expectations, save for, alas, just one small gnawing and obsessional factor. If Alphonse had not found his metier in the cinema, without doubt he would have become a professional taster.

He was blessed, sometimes he thought cursed, from birth with an outstanding set of taste buds and an advanced olfactory sense, both natural and God-given attributes which draw most recipients of such gifts into the commercial world of food and drink. As the reader understands, merchandise such as tea, coffee, wine, cheese and so on, is marketed on the advice of specialists who sniff, taste, gulp and spit, savouring and rolling around in the mouth in gourmandising manner, until the product is deemed fit for sale. Equally the perfume industry is controlled by expert sensualists. There is a degree of fanaticism and of course much secrecy in the creation of a new scent. Each and every new product is distilled from a profusion of ingredients, rare and costly items which only an expert nose can evaluate.

Alphonse would have been a natural in this trade. One can only say that if his talents in this direction had not been utilised, at least he had found contentment in his chosen skill. Moreover, when his work was done, the lights switched off and the doors of the cinema barred and bolted, he indulged his remarkable senses of taste and smell in a manner which, if not profitable of wages, benefited certain ladies of his acquaintance and provided thus yet another service to the community.

Close by in the *quartier*, and Monaco is truly an intimately grouped township, Alphonse had a variety of charming, welcoming ports of call. A little before midnight on most evenings he would present himself at one or the other, tap on the door and be admitted. In each case the welcoming hostess was a lady of style, warm and inviting, if just a few years past the first bloom of youth. His bath would be run and a glass of champagne set at the ready. While Alphonse slipped into the refreshing waters, the lady made the last touches to a delicious supper, usually served on a tray in the peaceful surroundings of a drawing room discreetly lit with low lamps or candles. The scenario of these intimate evenings never varied. There was a charm in this consistency, both for Alphonse and his lady friends, as total relaxation and comfort could be drawn from the pleasant familiarity of the scene. Perhaps it will suffice to describe, then, just one particular event.

'Good evening, *mon ami*,' said Renée as Alphonse slipped through the door of the apartment, stooping so as not to bang his head on the frame. 'It's rabbit stew tonight, *mon cher*, deeply aromatic with the herbs of Provence, the oils of citron fruits, virgin olive oil, garlic, spices and bay leaves.'

'You are kind, Renée,' he said, kissing her lightly on the forehead, 'I can't wait.' With that, he immersed himself in the marble bath and scrubbed every particle of his white flesh till it shone like alabaster. He shampooed his hair, cleaned his teeth, shaved, showered in cold water, towelled himself dry, and slipped into a fresh dressing gown of cool cotton. These ablutions made him feel refreshed, cleansed of the day's dirt and smells. His senses were alive and tingling, thrilled by the sharp rich odours emanating from the cuisine. The champagne bubbles raced round his mouth and down his throat, further stimulating and preparing his taste buds, so that when he attacked the dish of food he almost reeled with the sensations it provoked.

Renée, who had dined earlier, watched approvingly. 'Dear boy, I love to see you devour my food. It is a compliment to my cooking, the relish you show.'

Alphonse licked his thin ascetic lips. '*Quelle création*,' he murmured appreciatively.

'And now, a little sorbet, *cheri*, do you think, to clear the palate?' Renée suggested, as she knew of long practice that her friend would not take heavy dessert.

The ice was delicately flavoured with muscat grapes, barely enough to taste, but just enough to perform the cleansing action required of it.

'Wonderful,' he said. 'I am truly satisfied,'

'In that case, come, my darling,' Renée breathed, leading him by the elbow towards the great divan in her boudoir.

The room was lined with swags and ruches of pale blue silks and satins, pleated and draped in expert style by an expensive decorator, and the few tastefully arranged pieces of furniture were of the gilded Louis Quinze period. Everything spoke of wealth and self indulgence, especially the large Venetian mirrors which were placed at various angles to the bed to provide a complexity of views to anyone reclining on it. A single flame burned in an antique silver lantern, casting a soft glowing light over the couch.

Renée slipped out of her flowing négligé and stretched, with an expressive long sigh, before lying down. Her body was, if no longer finely tuned, still well designed. Interesting womanly curves and creases which would have delighted a painter such as Greuze formed a harmonious picture. The delicate shade of her skin tone was matched exactly to the colour of the satin sheets which she peeled back lazily, and her pale blonde hair, neatly coiffed into a chignon, was of the same pastel palette. The small V-shaped triangle of hair at her crotch was trimmed so short that in the dim light of the room it seemed to be non-existent, and she was also shaved in the armpits. In all, an impression of a comely, warm, and sanitised woman of perfection that would have aroused any man of natural instinct.

'Come,' she said, in a low voice, closing her beautiful grey eyes, gracefully beckoning with a hand which was decorated by a single large diamond. 'I am sure that you have endured a hard day. Relax. I am yours as you wish.'

Alphonse, still in the cotton robe, dropped to his knees at the foot of the bed. He parted her toes one by one, bestowing little kisses to each, noting the fine film of apricot coloured varnish she had carefully applied. Then he caressed the soles of her feet, kneading and massaging in a most comforting way. His long fingers stroked and lightly scratched at every centimetre of her insteps and around her ankles, causing the most charming sensations to run up Renée's legs. She clasped her thighs, moaning slightly.

'*Ravissant*,' she uttered, barely audibly.

'It was lily of the valley, *n'est ce pas*, the talcum powder you dabbed on your toes, eh?' Alphonse enquired. 'The *muguet des bois* which I adore.'

'Correct, *mon cher*,' came the reply.

Alphonse's fine nostrils sniffed their way up her shin bones and proceeded to investigate Renée's knees, while his hands explored the erogenous zones behind them, worming their way into the soft flesh he found.

'You have rouged your knees,' he said. 'The colour is indistinct as you applied it sparsely, but I detect a certain oil of roses which was used in its manufacture.'

Now his hands were roving over her thighs, pushing her own away from the grip in which they had been engaged, followed by his lips and tongue, burrowing and licking. Renée parted her legs wider, allowing him more access to the inner parts of her thighs. His strong thumbs pressed in unison upwards and downwards along the length of the main inside muscles, almost as far as where the thighs met, but tantalisingly avoiding the neat little bush and the swelling lips underneath it.

Renée gasped in her pleasure. She knew this ritual from long practice and was certain that her principal seat of pleasure would eventually be attended to, but the slow process was agonisingly drawn out. She licked her lips voraciously. 'I can't stand it. I die,' she moaned.

'Hush, I am concentrating, *cheri*,' Alphonse urged. 'Is this not the perfume of a new soap, one you have not used before? Wait a moment. Yes, I have it, verveine, green and woody, the smell of lush valleys after the rain. Ah, it is one of my favourites.'

Renée's cave of joy was hot and lubricating heavily, envious of the attentions being piled so cruelly close. Her hands wanted to travel down her body to apply some release, but Alphonse took her wrists and, opening her arms wide, pinned them into the pillow. His long limp organ dangled over the centre of her body as he straddled across her with his knees planted on either side of her hips. As he nosed carefully in her cleavage, it brushed at the little reddened button which had emerged protrusively from the sanctum between the aroused lips of her maddened genitals.

'There is but one drop of perfume here,' he said, 'between your breasts, and just one also underneath each of them, having passed his slim pointed tongue over her creamy flesh. 'What a cocktail of pleasures you have prepared for me, I adore it.' He tasted again before pronouncing. 'Aha, although it is suble, I know I can isolate the principal ingredients. Violet, civet, lime, a hit of musk, and something slightly peppery. A new one by Schiaparelli, *non?*'

Renée threw her legs in the air and, crossing her ankles around his buttocks, pulled hard, flattening his emaciated body to her own plump form. She could feel the length of his limp penis against her belly and squirmed underneath it, re-arranging her pelvis in an effort to make it come into contact with her more intimate parts.

But Alphonse was off again, like a hunting dog on the scent of his quarry. He threw himself to the side, sniffing at her neck, her hair, sucking behind her ears and at her mouth in search of the varied odours contained in these regions. Renée was transported by this hunting scene, and as Alphonse dipped his tongue deep into her mouth, came to full fruition, twisting and turning her body in a paroxysmal orgasm of rapture.

'Cachou,' he yelled triumphantly. 'You have been sucking cachous.'

Renée could barely nod her agreement. Her panting breath and fluttering eyelashes signified the extent of her transport. She gazed at him in gratitude, sighing deeply.

Alphonse's olfactory senses were now rampantly in full flow.

Renée's warmth and satisfaction caused her pale body to glow. He watched her neck and heaving breasts radiated a pink suffusion caused by the waves of sensation that had engulfed her. Now there was a light but healthy scent of perspiration which seeped into his nostrils, and a stimulating warm odour of a more animal nature such as is aroused by physical love.

Alphonse's member began to swell and gentle throbbing movements pulsated through its length. Renée took hold of it tenderly. A small drop of liquid appeared at the purple tip.

'Let me taste it,' she pleaded. 'Why should you have all the fun?'

'Well, just for a moment,' he said gruffly as he knew he was soon to come himself to his own inevitable climax.

He allowed her to pass her full lips briefly over the glistening tip, watching her with great affection as she did so, but soon tore his engorged member from her grip and dived headlong down the bed, reversing positions to place his mouth over her ravished but still thrilling part. He smelled deeply at her fount, rubbing his lips and tongue over every small crease and crevice, lingering lovingly at the small enflamed button which for all its diminutive size was the focus of her libido.

'Aaaaah,' she cried as his tongue entered her, penetrating with the most exquisite probings. 'I die,' she gasped, as the ultimate olfactory sensation for Alphonse brought him with savage urgency to the point of no return and his life force crashed into action, alerting his pent-up love juices.

As the hunter drank deep at the well he climaxed profusely, satiated in every pore and in every fibre of his senses, pouring his grateful thanks over Renée's ample bosom, causing her once more to flood with the overwhelming sensations that a refined and diligent partner can bring to the love of his life.

Chapter Fifteen

The season on the Riviera was drawing to a regrettable close. Holidaymakers packed their suitcases and left for home, looking bronzed and fit, well exercised from the beach games, swimming and tennis.

The café and hotel owners were exhausted by now, looking forward to the day the awnings and blinds would come down for the last time, and the pavement chairs and tables could be put into store.

There were tearful scenes at the railway stations along the coast. Beach boys and gigolos, maiden aunts, retired colonels, de-frocked clergy and folk of all types had come to the end of all kinds of holiday romances, and of course hundreds of bright young things who had been stimulated by the free and heady atmosphere of the Riviera into their first taste of the carnal delights of love, vowed to their partners that they would return next season.

For the lucky ones still remaining there was one final social occasion to grace the scene, a last heady celebration of the joys and splendours of the jazz age at the Côte d'Azur, where fashion and attitudes had contrived to make the Twenties such a memorable decade.

At Bernadette's mansion, on the night of the reception to mark the final performance of the Ballets Russes, the pace was furious. Those fortunate enough to be invited to this, a most prestigious affair, vied with each other in the sumptuousness and outlandishness of their costume.

The theme of *Commedia del Arté* was well taken up with many representations of the voguish Harlequin and Columbine. Some went so far as to impersonate Charles Chaplin, the clown of the cinema, and there were at least half a dozen gorillas and accompanying Fay Wrays. A well known sadist took the opportunity to dress in tropical gear and brandish a whip in the manner of Eric von Stroheim, the movie director. There were also several muscular beach boys, clad in nothing but a piece of leopard skin, representing Tarzan. Lady Letitia, just returned from Florence, fell in love with two of these promptly.

The entire company of the Ballets Russes tore off their improvised costumes and disported themselves, again naked, in the swimming pool, save for Lidova who was making one last impassioned attempt to regain the affections of Vossoudosoulos. She wanted him to accompany her on the tour of South America that the company was about to undertake, if only to pay her hotel bill, but the millionaire was adamantly committed to the Lebanese woman who was much cheaper to keep.

Galina bade a fond farewell to Arthur in the turbulent pool. How she had enjoyed his over-sized organ, she told him, but their affair was over, the harsh world of the theatre was splitting them apart.

The same sentiments were being expressed by Dhokouminsky who was trying, without much success, to detach himself from Edith, Oblomov having hidden himself with a *corps de ballet* girl in the quiet of the changing rooms.

The gypsy band played furiously and the dancers took up their tempting rhythms, clad only in the briefest of towels, and as the evening got darker, wearing nothing at all.

Couples took turns providing an impromptu cabaret. One pair threw themselves with abandon into an Apache routine. Their faked slaps and punches were so realistic that M. Rogon waded in and tried to rescue the girl but he got kicked in the behind for his trouble and the pair crashed on to a brilliant finale where the boy threw his partner into the pool from over his head in an amazing fish dive.

Bernadette and Marcel strolled through these antics with detached amused smiles on the faces.

'They are like children released from school,' he said.

'More like prisoners let out from gaol, I think,' she rejoined.

In the twilight of the evening a bonfire in a pit was lighted to roast the carcasses of several lambs. Needless to say that the fiery Russians felt themselves obliged to leap over the flames, barefoot and naked, in a simulation of their Polovstvian Dances which had been an outstanding success of the Season.

As the night fell, the haunting sounds of the blues came stealing through the gardens as the negro jazz band struck up with a Dixie lament. Close couples danced cheek to cheek in the shadows and then sometimes stole off for closer, more loving contact in the bushes.

Sophie found Arthur alone by the bridge over the island. He held her tight and they danced slowly together, his lips on the nape of her neck. She wondered if his dalliances with Lidova and Galina were over, but anyway the company would soon be in another continent, she reassured herself.

As the fires died down and the hungry folk gathered round in the night to watch the meat cook on the spit, Arthur led Sophie back towards the house, followed by Bernadette and Marcel. They passed a sobbing Angelique lying prostrate over her darling Vladimir, the slant-eyed boy, who must leave her tomorrow.

The first fireworks roared into the night sky, and the crowd yelled in delight.

Later, as the display burst into an extravagant finale, rockets and flares in myriad colours exploding into the blackness with a thunderous crashing roar, Bernadette and Sophie, in their respective rooms, gave themselves up at the end of the whirlwind Season to the men of their choice. Arthur and Marcel, being not only gentlemen in their prime, but both possessed of the most exquisite manners, individually ensured that the attentions they paid to their hostesses resulted in both these adorable ladies arriving simultaneously at a fruition of passionate love, whose intensity matched the explosive brilliance of the pyrotechnic display which entranced the intoxicated revellers who danced on into the night.

Summer was over. Smoke hung over the bonfire and the first leaves of autumn fell on the garden outside.

IRIDIAGNOSIS

Every organ and part of the body is represented in the iris, and this book reveals how every disturbance or change can be recognized and the correct diagnosis made.

GW00715399

IRIDIAGNOSIS

Diagnosis from the Eyes

by

VICTOR S. DAVIDSON
N.D., D.O., D.C., D.A.

NATURE'S WAY

THORSONS PUBLISHERS LIMITED
Wellingborough, Northamptonshire

First published in this series 1979
Fourth Impression 1983

ISBN 0 7225 0478 0

Printed and bound in Great Britain by
Richard Clay (The Chaucer Press)
Bungay, Suffolk

CONTENTS

INTRODUCTION

During the years 1840 to 1850, Dr Von Peckzely, of Budapest, Hungary, made his great discovery of nature's records in the eyes.

When he was a boy of ten years, he was playing in the garden and caught an owl. While he was struggling with the bird, he broke one of its limbs, and, on looking into the owl's large eyes, he noticed in the iris of the bird – at the moment when the bone snapped, the appearance of a black spot. He later verified the area where the black spot formed to correspond with that of the leg.

Even in those early days, Von Peckzely was interested in the study of nature and healing. He prepared a splint and put it on the limb, and kept the bird for a pet.

During the healing process of the leg, he noticed that the black spot in the eye became overdrawn with a white film and surrounded with a white border, denoting the formation of scar tissues in the broken bone, as he learned later.

This coincidence impressed the boy a great deal and he remembered these facts after becoming a doctor.

For some revolutionary activity during student days, Von Peckzely was imprisoned in 1848. He found time and leisure during his stay in prison to pursue his favourite theory, and he became more and more convinced of the importance of his discovery about the owl. In time he was released from prison and eventually, after continuing his studies, became an internee in the surgical wards of the college hospital.

Here he had ample opportunity to observe the eyes of patients before and after accidents and operations, and later prepared a chart of the eye.

Many well-known scientists have devoted their lives to diagnosis from the eyes.

In America great leaders have added to the science by their discoveries, among the great physicians being Drs Lindlahr, Kritzer, Lahn and other well-known practitioners.

Lindlahr said that the eye is not only as the ancients said, 'the mirror of the soul', but it also reveals changing conditions of every part and organ of the body. The iris of the eye contains an immense number of minute nerve filaments, which receive impressions from every nerve trunk in the body.

Every organ and part of the body is represented in the iris in a well-defined area, and the nerve filaments muscle fibres and minute blood vessels in these areas portray by certain signs and colour pigments the changing conditions in the corresponding part or organ.

By means of various marks, signs and discolorations in the iris, nature reveals inherited disease taints, such as sycosis, scrofula, psora, etc. Nature also reveals by such signs, marks and discolorations, acute and chronic catarrhal inflammatory conditions, local lesions, destruction of tissues, all kinds of drug poisonings, as well as the results of accidental injury and of surgical operations.

By means of this art we are able, from the eye alone, to tell the patient his inherited and acquired tendencies towards health and disease, his condition in general, and the state of every organ in particular. Thus, reading the record in the eye, we can predict the different healing crises through which the patient will have to pass on his road to health.

The eye reveals to us changes in vital organs from their inception, and thus enables the patient to overcome by natural living and natural means of cure the threatening disease.

Diagnosis from the eyes confirms Hahnemann's teaching, that all acute diseases have a constitutional background of hereditary, or acquired taints, and, finally, it reveals the gradual purification of the system from morbid matter and the readjustment to normal conditions, under the regenerating influences of natural living and treatment.

In this book I have inserted a chart which clearly outlines in the iris of the eye the corresponding areas of every vital part and organ in the body.

V.S.D.

CHAPTER ONE

ANATOMY OF THE EYE

The organ of vision (*organon visus*) consists of the eye (*oculus*) and of the appendages of the eye (*organa oculi accessoria*).

The eye consists of the optic nerve (*nervus opticus*) and the eyeball (*bulbus oculi*). The accessory organs of the eye include the eye muscles (*musculi oculi*), the fascia of the orbital cavity (*fasciæ orbitales*), the eyelids (*palpebræ*), the conjunctive and the tear apparatus (*apparatus lacrimalis*).

BONES OF THE ORBIT

The eye is situated in a depression of the anterior portion of the skull. This depression is pyramidal and is called the orbit. The base is forward and outward, and consists of the roof, floor, and two sides, the external and internal. The apex is backward and inward. There are four angles to the orbit and seven bones compose its walls.

They are named:

1. Sphenoid: wedge.
2. Ethmoid: sieve.
3. Frontal: forehead.
4. Malar: cheekbone.
5. Palate: floor of orbit.
6. Superior Maxillary: upper jawbone.
7. Lachrymal: thin scale at inner angle of orbit.

In the orbit are nine openings, large and small, to admit the different nerves, arteries and veins. They are as follows:

1. Optic foramen, through which pass the optic nerve and central artery.

2.   Sphenoidal fissure, through which pass the third and fourth nerves and the ophthalmic vein.

3.   Spheno-maxillary fissure, through which pass the ascending branches of the spheno-palatin ganglion to supply the periosteum (fibrous sheath of bone).

4.   Anterior ethmoidal foramen, through which pass the olfactory nerve and ethmoidal artery.

5.   Posterior ethmoidal foramen, through which pass the posterior ethmoidal artery.

6.   Supra-orbital notch and foramen, transmits the supra-orbital artery, vein and nerve.

7.   Infra-orbital, transmits the infra-orbital nerve and artery.

8.   Malar foramen or foramina, through which pass branches of the tempora-malar nerve.

9.   Nasal duct, conducts the tears to the nose.

The eye is well protected by a cushion of fat in which it is set, and is held in place by six recti muscles, which also move the eye in different directions.

MUSCLES AND NERVE SUPPLY

The principal functions of the muscles are as follows:

Superior rectus turns the eye up.

Inferior rectus turns the eye down.

Internal rectus turns the eye in.

External rectus turns the eye out.

Superior oblique or pulley muscle moves the eye down and out.

Inferior oblique turns the eye out and up.

No movement of the eye is performed by any one muscle alone, but by several muscles working together. The first four muscles (recti or straight muscles) have their origin at the apex of the orbit and are attached to the sides of the eyeball. These muscles would pull the eye back into the orbit but for the adjustment of the oblique muscles. The superior has its origin at the apex of the orbit, but passes through a pulley at the front of the orbit, then back to the equator of the eye, and is attached under the superior rectus muscle.

The inferior oblique has its origin at the front of the orbit. It passes backward and is attached back of the equator of the eye under the inferior rectus. The last two pull the eye forward, while the other four pull the eye backward. By this method the eye is held in perfect poise.

The third nerve supplies all the muscles except the superior oblique, which is supplied by the fourth nerve, and the external rectus is supplied by the sixth nerve. These are named the extrinsic muscles, as they are outside of the eyeball.

The intrinsic muscles are the sphincter and dilator of the iris, and the ciliary muscles. They are supplied by the third, sympathetic, and fifth nerves. The iris is the curtain of the eye, and regulates the amount of light entering in. The ciliary muscles control the focus of the crystalline lens or the accommodation of the eye for different distances.

The muscles of the eyelids are the *orbicularis palpebrarum* supplied by the seventh nerve. They close the lids. The Levator Palpebrarum, supplied by the third nerve, raises the lids.

SOLIDS AND FLUIDS

The eye is composed of fluids and solids. The fluids are the aqueous humour, crystalline lens, and vitreous humour. These are all clear, transparent fluids, and are known as the refracting media.

The solids are the sclerotic coat. A hard, dense, fibrous membrane which, with the cornea, forms the external coat of the eye. It preserves the shape of the eye, and is well fitted for the attachment of the external muscles.

The choroid is immediately beneath the sclerotic coat, and is richly supplied with blood vessels and nerves. It includes the ciliary muscle, ligament and processes, also the iris.

THE OPTIC NERVE (From Spalteholz, *Atlas of Anatomy*)

The optic nerve is variably curved in the orbital cavity; in the vertical direction it is curved so as to be slightly bayonet-shaped, in the horizontal direction slightly 'S'-shaped, behind lateralward, in front medianward convex, and enters into the posterior surface of the eyeball about 4mm medial from, and somewhat below, the posterior end of the optic axis. It is enclosed in its three sheaths – the dural, arachnoidal, and pials sheaths, known collectively as the *viginæ n. optici*, which are continuations of the brain membranes, and at the eyeball go over into the sclera.

The outer thickest dural sheath, consisting of tough connective tissue, is derived from the dura mater and forms the periosteum lining, the *foramen opticum*. Following upon this is the delicate arachnoidal sheath, a continuation of the arachnoidea, and upon this a continuation of the *pia mater*, the pial sheath, which is connected by five strands with the arachnoidal sheath and sends septa in between the bundles of nerve fibres. The sheaths are separated from one another by the *spatia intervaginalia*, and between the dural and arachnoid sheaths in a continuation of *cavum subdurale*; between the arachnoidal and pial sheaths a continuation of the *cavum subarachnoideale*; both of these extend forward as far as the sclera, but do not communicate with one another there.

THE EYEBALL

The eyeball lies surrounded by fat, fascia and muscle

in the orbital cavity, and presents, roughly speaking, the form of a sphere. It is formed of the contents or nucleus of the eyeball in the interior, and of the coats of the eye ensheathing these externally. The former from before, backwards, are:

1.   The *humour aqueous*.
2.   The *lens crystallina*.
3.   The *corpus vitreum* or glass body. The coats of the eyes are concentrically laminated and consist, from the outside, in, of:
     a.   The *tunica fibrosa oculi*.
     b.   The *tunica vasculosa oculi*.
     c.   The *retina*.

The eyeball resembles a section of a sphere, fairly complete only in its posterior half. The anterior half possesses a frontal, shallow circular indentation (*sulcus sclerea*), from which the most anterior part projects as a small segment of a sphere with smaller radius of curvature. This projection belongs to the cornea, the other part of the surface to the sclera, so that the sclerea indicate at the same time the external junction between the cornea and the sclera.

The *tunica fibrosa oculi* is a tough, thick membrane, completely enclosing the eyeball, and conditioning its form. About five-sixths of it consists of the non-transparent sclera and the remaining one-sixth of the transparent cornea which surrounds the anterior pole.

The Sclera, white or hard coat of the eye, is a tough connective tissue membrane, usually of a pure white colour. It is thickest at the entrance of the optic nerve, the sheaths of which go over directly into it, and, passing forward, it becomes gradually thinner as far as the attachments of the straight eye muscles, the tendon bundles of which interweave with it and strengthen it in its most anterior part. It is loosely covered in its anterior part by the *conjunctiva bulbii*, and is thus far also visible in the lid slit as the white of the eye. In front the non-transparent bundles of the sclera go directly over into the transparent ones of the cornea. This transition occurs outside and inside somewhat further forward than intermediately, so that the sclera in a way forms a groove, known as the *rima cornealis*, for the reception of the margin of the cornea.

Just behind this transition, in a furrow of the sclera, runs a circular blood vessel called the *sinus venosus sclerae*, which is bounded internally by the *ligamentum pectinatum iridis*. The sclera is perforated behind by the *n. opticus*; bundles of connective tissue arranged in the form of a network separate the individual bundles of nerve fibres from one another and form a perforated plate called the *lamina cirbrosa sclerae*, for the passage of the latter. In addition, the sclera possesses openings for the passage of the arteries, veins and nerves ciliaries.

On its outer surface it is united by a delicate network with the surrounding *fascia bulbi*, which, however, does not inhibit the movability of the eyeball. Its innermost layer lies in direct contact with the *tunica vasculosa*, is coloured brownish by various pigment cells, and is accordingly called the *lamina fusca sclerae*.

The cornea is a colourless, transparent, non-vascular connective tissue membrane, and has the shape of a flat, round bowl, curved so as to be convex in front and concave behind. At the margin (*limbus corneal*) the sclera above and below reaches somewhat further forward than medial and lateral, hence the circumference of the cornea viewed from in front looks like an ellipse with its longest diameter placed transversely; viewed from behind it is circular.

The anterior surface of the cornea resembles

approximately an ellipsoid of revolution only in the zone of the pole; it is thereby a little more markedly curved in the vertical direction than in the transversal. Its thickness is greater than that of the neighbouring sclera, but diminishes gradually from the margin onwards, and is least at the point of greatest convexity (*vertex corneal*). The convex anterior surface (*facies anterior*) lies free to view in the lid-slit and is covered by the *epithelium corneal*, a direct continuation of the *conjunctiva bulbii*, which is attached for the most part loosely on the anterior surface of the sclera, and is connected with it firmly only in a narrow, often ridge-like strip (*annulus conjunctivæ*) immediately surrounding the cornea.

The *epithelium cornea* rests upon the narrow, very transparent *lamina elastica anterior*, and this goes over behind into the laminated *substantia propria* which forms the main mass; then follows the *lamina elastica posterior*, which resembles the anterior, but is thinner, and finally the *endothelium cameræ anterioris*; this covers the *facies posterior* of the cornea, forms the anterior boundary of the anterior chamber of the eye filled with aqueous humour, and is sometimes lateralward upon the *angulus iridis* and the anterior surface of the iris.

The tunica vasculosa oculi, with its main mass, lies directly on the inner surface of the sclera; only its most anterior portion, the iris, projects inward free into the bulbus from the region of the *rima cornealis*, approximately transversely to the optic axis. The part lying against the sclera is divisible into a larger posterior smooth portion (the *choroidea*), and a narrow anterior ridged portion (the *corpus ciliare*); it is firmly fused with the sclera behind only at the entrance of the optic nerve and in front at the *rima cornealis*, but otherwise is separated from it by a slit-like lymph space (*spatium perichoroideale*), lined by endothelial cells and studded with numerous fine, pigment-holding *lamellæ*, which is bounded externally by the *lamina fusca sclerea*, and internally by the most superficial layer of the *choroidea* (*lamina suprachoroidea*), and is perforated by some vessels and nerves. All portions of it are very delicate and contain an extraordinarily large number of blood vessels, and numerous nerves and ganglia. The *corpus ciliare* and the iris contain muscles in addition.

The choroidea is very thin and includes approximately the posterior two-thirds of the eyeball, and is sometimes lighter, sometimes darker, according to the amount of pigment it contains. It possesses behind a round opening for the passage of the optic nerve. In it five layers are distinguishable. Upon the *lamina suprachoroidea* follows the pigmented *lamina vasculosa* with the coarser vessels, namely, the roots of the *v. v. vorticosæ* and nerves, then the layer of medium-sized vessels, then the non-pigmented *lamina choroid capillaris* with the blood capillaries, and upon this the *laminæ basalis*, the two latter being recognisable only microscopically. In contact with the latter is the *stratum pigmenti* of the retina, which remains attached to it even after separation of the retina.

The iris is a round disc with a round opening, the pupilla, which does not lie exactly concentrically, but deviates from it somewhat downwards and nasalward. At its lateral margin (*margo ciliaris*) it proceeds from the ciliary body, and by its medial, free margin (*margo pupillaris*) it rests on the anterior surface of the lens. Its medial margin lies in front of the plane of the lateral margin, so that the whole disc has the form of a very flat funnel. On widening of the pupil it becomes narrower and thicker. Its greatest thickness lies near the *margo pupillaris*, and corresponds to the junction between the *annuli iridis*; from there on it diminishes toward the thin *margo ciliaris*; less so towards the *margo pupillaris*. The

anterior surface is visible through the cornea as far
as the marginal part and is of variable colour
according to the pigment it contains. About 1mm
from the *margo pupillaris* runs a jagged line, which
separates a narrow inner zone, *annulus iridis minor*,
from a broader outer, *annulus iridis major*. In the
former, small anastomosing ridges run to the *margo
pupillaris*, which itself is formed by a fine notched,
dark brown edge belonging to the *stratum pigmenti
iridis*. In the outer zone run several usually
incomplete circular contraction grooves (*plicæ
iridis*), concentric to the *margo pupillaris*; in addition,
when there is little pigment in it, the vessels are
visible as radiating tortuous whitish lines. The
posterior surface of the iris is covered by the *stratum
pigmenti iridis*, is uniformly black, and is studded
with very fine radiating folds. The nerve supply to
the iris is motor, sensory, and sympathetic.

The retina is the inner nervous tunic of the eyeball.
It is formed by the expansion of the optic nerve
within the eye, and is the perceptive structure of the
eye. There are eleven distinct layers of the retina.
Naming them from within, out, they are:

1. Internal limiting membrane.
2. Optic nerve fibre layer.
3. Vesicular or layer of ganglion cells.
4. Internal molecular or plexiform; a granular
   layer.
5. Internal nuclear layer.
6. External molecular or plexiform; a granular
   layer.
7. External nuclear layer.
8. External limiting membrane.
9. Layer of rods and cones.
10. Pigmentary layer.
11. Fibres of muller.

It is here, upon that portion called the Macula
Lutea, or yellow spot, that the photograph of what

we look at is made. The cones are abundant and distinguish between colours.

The optic disc is situated a little to the nasal side of the macula and is the blind spot of the eye. The optic nerves pass backward and inward until they meet. This point of union is called the optic chiasm or decussation. From the chiasm to the brain it is called the optic tract. The function of the optic nerve is to convey the picture to the brain, giving us the sense of sight.

The ciliary body is composed of ligaments, muscles and processes. The ligament is a narrow ring of circular fibres, about one-fortieth of an inch thick, and whitish in colour. The ciliary muscle is the chief agent in accommodation, that is, in adjusting the eye for far and near objects.

The hyaloid membrane is a delicate, transparent membrane surrounding the vitreous humour.

The crystalline lens is a double convex lens, having its greatest convexity on the posterior side. It is perfectly transparent and consists of several concentric layers. It is contained in a capsule and receives its nourishment from transparent, polygonal, nucleated cells covering the inner surface of the capsule. It is held in place by the suspensory ligament, sometimes called the 'zone of zinn'. It has about ten dioptres of refractive power.

The capsule of tenon is a membrane of two layers, one of which is attached to the eyeball, the other to the cushion of fat. They play one on the other as the eye moves in different directions. In enucleating the eye great care is taken to leave one membrane on the fat, the other on the eyeball.

The conjunctiva is the delicate mucous membrane lining the eyelids and covering the external portion of the eyeball. It is very firmly attached to the eyelids, and that part is called the *palpebral conjunctiva*. It is loosely attached to the eyeball, and

that part is called the *ocular conjunctivea*. It is
continuous from the margin of the lids to the
margin of the cornea, where it ends. This
membrane is involved in many diseases of the eye.

The lachrymal gland is located under the arch of the
eye. It is about the size of an almond and its
function is to flush the eye. It is not used to moisten
the eye, as the conjunctiva furnishes its own
lubricant. Tears pass across the eye to the inner
corner till they reach the *puncta lachrymalia*, whence
they are carried through the *canuliculi* into the
lachrymal sac, then through the nasal duct into the
nose.

The eyelids are two thin, movable folds placed in
front of the eye, protecting it from injury by their
closure. The upper lid is the largest and more
movable, and is furnished with a separate elevator
muscle. When the eyelids are open, an elliptical
space is left between their margins, called the *fissura
palpebrarum*, the angle of which corresponds to the
junction of the upper and lower lids and are called
canthi.

The outer canthus is more acute than the inner,
and the lids here lie in close contact with the globe;
but the inner canthus is prolonged for a short
distance inwards towards the nose, and the two lids
are separated by a triangular space, called the *lacus
lachrymalis*. On the margin of each lid is a small
conical elevation, the *lachrymal papilla* or *tubercle*, and
apex of which is pierced by a small orifice, the
punctum lachrymali, the commencement of the
lachrymal canal.

The meibomian glands are situated upon the inner
surface of the eyeballs, between the tarsal cartilages
and conjunctiva, and may be distinctly seen
through the mucous membrane on everting the lids,
presenting the appearance of parallel rows of
pearls. There are about thirty or forty in the upper

lids, and somewhat fewer in the lower. The use of their secretions is to prevent adhesion of the lids. Occasionally one or more of these glands becomes infected, constituting the so-called *meibomian cyst*.

CHAPTER TWO

THE BODY PICTURED IN THE IRIS

It is through the sympathetic and cerebro-spinal nervous systems and their branches and their intimate connection between the various parts of the body and the iris. Thus we have the scientific explanation of the system of diagnosis.

Any irritation of any part of the body is transmitted through afferent nerves to the autonomic brain centres which send, in response to stimulation, a rush of blood to the affected part through efferent nerves, causing swelling and congestion. This in turn is transmitted through reflex nerve stimulation to the corresponding area in the iris. Kritzer says that this causes vascular projecting ridges which run radially from the ciliary to the pupillary borders; this in turn raises the normal white fibres of the top layer of the iris, making them plainly visible to the unaided eye. He says further that this phenomenon does not in any way affect the vision, but it explains why every acute process shows white in the iris.

A decrease takes place with lessened congestion and eventually it fades away altogether. Through suppression or neglect the acute processes naturally become gradually chronic, causing a passive congestion .— a venous stasis. A similar stasis (Kritzer states further) occurs in the vascular layer of the iris, causing a darkening of the corresponding part, due to the accumulation of dark venous blood.

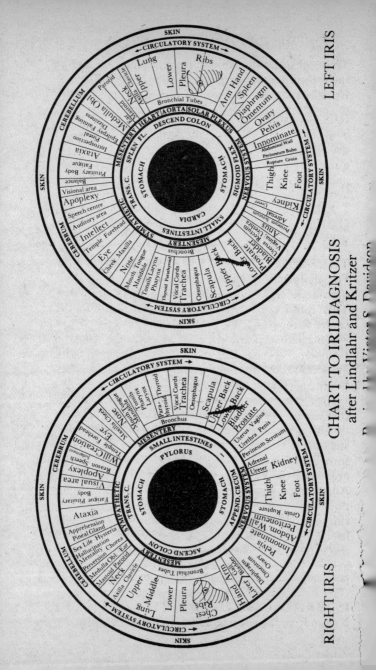

CHART TO IRIDIAGNOSIS
after Lindlahr and Kritzer

LEFT IRIS

RIGHT IRIS

Tissue destruction through injury, etc., shows black spots through the severance of the nerve connection with the corresponding area in the iris.

DRUG COLOURS

The different colours corresponding to certain drugs, such as red for iodine, greenish yellow for quinine, etc., found in the iris are created by colour pigments carried into and deposited in the surface layers of the iris through the capillary circulation.

In order to guide the student and others to a good grasp of iridiagnosis, the following guiding points will be of benefit.

THE STOMACH

For diagnostic purposes let us call the navel or umbilicus, as it is called, the centre of the body. This could correspond to the black pupil in the centre of the chart.

On looking at the chart it will be seen that the stomach shows as the first circle. Wherever there are found dark lines or spots in this region we may be sure there is some gastric disturbance.

Now one of the easiest drug poisons to locate in this area is bismuth – mostly taken for digestive disturbances, and showing in the stomach area as a steel-grey irregular circle. Of course, lead workers sometimes have this colour showing in the stomach area, but the circle is perfect instead of irregular. All medicines which reveal themselves in the iris are poisons. Is not medicine-taking perfectly ridiculous? Now you can enlighten your patient or friend by telling him what he is suffering from, and the medicine he has been taking without having to ask him. This is one of the greatest provers of the facts of iridiagnosis.

INTESTINAL TRACT

Next we come to the intestinal tract. The areas are

marked on the chart. We do not expect to find this area as clear as other parts of the iris because most ailments commence in the stomach and intestinal area. Then again, we know that this is the area where there are often accumulated waste materials – so we can expect to find a darkening or discoloration of the intestinal area in diseased conditions.

How can the blood be kept clean if this area (which may be about 26 feet long) has its tubes or walls all clogged with poisonous materials and, maybe, further poisoned with medicines? Seeing that this area supplies nutrition through its walls, we can see how easily poisons get into the bloodstream. In children we may find dark spots in this area, and it may indicate worms. Under Nature Cure treatment, of course, the iris changes its colour to a more normal blue or brown due to the internal house cleaning. It may be worth while to mention that oil of garlic is useful for the elimination of worms, and assisting in cleansing the intestinal tract as a beginning treatment.

Now the pancreas can be observed. If diabetes is present we will find a discoloration in that area. The same with the appendix area – if a white triangle is present, and there is pain in the right lower abdomen, then it is likely that appendicitis is the diagnosis. A white line may indicate only congestion.

SYMPATHETIC NERVOUS SYSTEM
The zig-zag circle of the sympathetic nervous system is the next consideration. This is always present in health and disease. Any irregularity, and the area it juts outward to, means irritation in that organ. In this chart I have left the S.N.S. as a plain circle for convenience. Remember this wreath, as it is called, is zig-zag in the iris.

GENITO-URINARY ORGANS

The genito-urinary organs and the reproductive organs cover the kidneys, adrenals, prostate gland, uterus, urethra, and bladder. Minute black spots in the bladder or kidney area indicate stones. Dense spots in the uterine area indicates fibroid tumour. If other conditions are present we will find dark lines in that area. Congestion and irritation will reveal itself in the following areas by various spots (such as red spots surrounded by white when iodine has been used), and white lines showing acute processes or dark lines showing chronic irritation, etc.

OTHER AREAS

Trachea, back, oesophagus, scapula, spinal column, thyroid, tonsils (minute black spots show removal), bronchus (dark spots showing bronchitis), mouth, tongue, nose, mandible, maxilla, cheek, eye, ataxia area – noted in venereal cases, etc. Wherever white clouds are showing, as, for instance, in the liver area, this may indicate enlargement, whereas dark clouds may indicate hardening processes going on. The same with other organs. The spinal column is indicated in the chart by a thin line running downward through the seventh cervical, twelfth dorsal vertebræ, fifth lumbar, sacrum, and coccyx. A white line may indicate spinal disease.

CARE WITH DIAGNOSIS

With regard to the eye area, care should be taken in diagnosis. I have noticed recently six cases where there were no lesions in the eye area, yet the patients had some defect in vision. I found the visual area (sight centre in the brain) showing a definite lesion, and quinine with its greenish-yellow colouring in the upper part of the iris. In each case the eyesight has improved under natural treatment and especially under Lindlahr's system of neurotherapy.

Experimenting and tabulating with cases of pituitary, para-thyroid, and disturbance of balance, I was able to locate and add to the science of iridiagnosis these areas in the iris.

Lesions found in other areas will explain themselves to students who have good powers of deduction. For instance, if heavy greenish-yellow discolorations are showing indicating quinine poisoning, then there may be symptoms of dizziness, colour blindness, enlargement of the spleen, as I found in a recent case, etc.

Enough has now been said to help the student, and also anyone else interested in the study of iridiagnosis. A mastery of this subject leads to efficiency in naturopathy. I hope this book will help many to the realization of the dangers of drugs and medicines; that they will disseminate its teachings and so help to bring about, in the course of time, a much-needed revolution in healing methods. It is pitiful to see the sodium rings, the iodine spots, the bismuth signs, the aspirin taker's eyes, the quinine eyes of passers-by – knowing full well that they are slowly poisoning themselves.

DEFINITION OF IRIDIAGNOSIS

A science revealing pathological and functional disturbances in the human body by means of abnormal markings and changes of colour in the iris of the eye.

This great discovery by Dr Ignatz Von Peckzely, of over a century ago, is based upon the fundamental truth that the iris of the normal man, woman or child is of a uniform texture, without lines or spots, and of clear colour, being either blue or brown. Whereas the almost universally found spots in the iris denote abnormal changes taking place in any part or organ of the body, thus exposing any deviation from the normal bodily structure or function.

In the development of chronic diseases we distinguish the following four distinct stages of encumbrance (as shown by Lindlahr):

1. Hereditary and congenital stage (accumulative).
2. Acute or subacute inflammatory stage (primary reactive).
3. Chronic stage (secondary reactive).
4. Destructive or chronic destructive stage accompanied by loss of tissue (stage of failure).

Chronic disease never develops suddenly in the human body, as Nature always endeavours to prevent its gradual development by acute and subacute healing efforts, revealing white grey lines in iris. This is in accord with the fundamental Law of Cure. If, however, these healing efforts of healing crises are checked, or suppressed by any means whatever, then they are followed by chronic after-effects, revealing dark lines or marks in the iris.

STAGES

First Stage

Inherited (hereditary and congenital) tendencies are recorded in the iris of the eye in three ways – by colour, density, and hereditary lesions.

1. The colour of the iris indicates whether the vital fluids and tissues are pure and normal, or whether they are affected by disease taints and foreign substances.
2. The density, that is the woof or grain of structures composing the iris, gives us information about the firmness, vitality and general tone of the tissues of the body.
3. Hereditary and congenital lesions in the form of shady grey, usually ovoid or spindle-shaped lesions in the irides of the offspring, indicate

weakness or disease in corresponding organs, or parts of the bodies of the parents.

Second Stage (Acute or Subacute Stage)
The acute stage of any disease shows only by a white line, or cloud, which may appear long before there are any manifestations of disease. For example, pulmonary tuberculosis may be diagnosed from the iris oft-times long before the tubercle bacillus can be demonstrated in the sputum, although in this connection it is claimed that the earliest possible diagnosis can be established with the use of the X-ray.

The subacute stage borders between the acute and chronic stage, and shows in the iris as a greyish or light grey discoloration. This sign appears in cases where nature's healing and cleansing efforts have been checked or suppressed by various means, such as exposure to wet and cold, lowered vitality, or by ice-packs, drugs or surgical treatment. The pathological changes from the acute to the subacute stages are accompanied by atrophy of structures in the corresponding organs or tissues.

Third Stage (Chronic Stage)
Retention of toxic materials, lowered vitality, and the inroads of pathogenic micro-organisms into the system, gradually cause decay and destruction of tissues. Simultaneous with the changes in the organs or tissues, similar changes take place in the corresponding areas of the iris. In these fields of the iris the tissues lose their vitality, dry, shrivel, and turn dark. As a result of this, the white signs of acute inflammatory lesions become intermingled with dark shades and streaks. When examined with a strong glass, it will be noticed that these dark areas are more or less depressed.

Fourth Stage (Destructive Stage)

In the advanced stages of destruction of tissues there appear in corresponding areas of the iris the dark areas or holes, which extend sometimes right down into the black pigment layer of the iris.

NATURAL COLOURS OF THE IRIS

The colour of the iris in the new-born of the white race is blue, and is caused through the absence of pigmentation. Pigment only develops after birth.

There is a great deal of conflicting data available on the iris colours as a result of exhaustive investigation by so many scientists engaged in the study of the human race. However, the best authorities claim that there are only two normal colours of the iris.

1.   Light azure blue.
2.   Light hazel brown.

Other colours are known as mixed colours, and are either due to racial characteristics or to the deposition within the system of various crude drugs, which make for the yellow, green, and steel grey shades, and, of course, these are subject to change through various hereditary and acquired influences. As a result of this, irides are oft-times spoken of as being of these particular colours.

DENSITY

The colour changes that are often spoken of and observed in the iris are, in themselves, indicative of the conditions of the health of their owner. The lighter the colour – either blue or brown – the better the individual's health and recuperative powers. The discolorations in the iris have a still further significance, however, as they disclose a truth which is destined to bring about a radical revision, both in the theory as well as in the practice, or the administration of drugs in physiological doses. The colour, spots and discolorations in the iris positively denote the accumulation of drugs in the system, taken in what are now called physiological doses, either internally or externally. Thus iridiagnosis conclusively proves two facts:

1. That drugs are not always eliminated entirely from the system.

2. That because of their retention in the system and because of their constant irritation, drugs often are causative factors in chronic and malignant diseases.

While the colour of the iris is indicative of hereditary taints and of the degree of purity of blood and tissues, so does density indicate the degree of vitality, the power of resistance, and re-cuperative power of the individual. Homoeopathic medicines do not show in the iris and are therefore non-poisonous.

NORMAL DENSITY

Lindlahr states that: 'In an iris of normal density the structures comprising the stroma and surface layer of the iris are normally developed, and arranged in an orderly manner, so that they lie in smooth, even layers, like the fibres of a piece of good linen.' When the layer of endothelial cells (coming from the embryonic endodermic layer) covering the stroma is perfectly intact, then the iris is of normal density, and presents a surface of crystalline clearness with a beautiful glossy appearance. Such an iris is the rule among wild animals which live in the open, but it is very rare in the human kingdom.

DEFECTIVE DENSITY

In an iris of defective density, the nerve and muscle fibres in the surface layer and stroma are unevenly developed and arranged. Some are swollen and some shrunken. Some are entirely obliterated. In all cases of defective density, however, the fibres are disarranged and crooked, and are not in any definite order whatever.

An iris of defective density presents an abnormal discoloration as well as an abnormal grain or texture, and it will be obvious, therefore, why defective density also indicates lowered vitality and weakened resistance.

FOUR DEGREES OF DENSITY
Density No. 1 or Good
In irides of this density the colour is normal, and there are no abnormal signs except, perhaps, a few straight white lines. Such irides are the rule in the animal kingdom, but are very rare in the human kingdom.

Density No. 2 or Common
The white lines are increased and more tangled. There are a few hereditary lesions and some dark lines indicating subacute catarrhal conditions; also some nerve rings.

Density No. 3 or Poor
In these irides white lines are more prominent and tangled. They contain several nerve rings. Signs of subacute and chronic conditions are numerous, and there are several closed defects.

Density No. 4 or Very Poor
In these irides signs of chronic and destructive conditions predominate. The nerve rings are partially dark and there are numerous closed lesions. Prognosis in these cases is not good.

SYMPATHETIC WREATH
Immediately around the intestinal area on the iris chart we have what is called the sympathetic wreath, which corresponds to the sympathetic nervous system. As every cell and part of the body

depends for life on the sympathetic nervous system, which acts as a storage of energy, we are not surprised to find that from this wreath every organ and part of the body radiates.

The sympathetic wreath is seen near and around the pupil as a zigzag circle, being white in the blue as well as in the brown iris, although it may be discoloured in some cases by drugs and morbid encumbrances. The area of the sympathetic wreath is the only exception which is seen in the iris in health as well as in disease. In the chart in this book I have drawn the wreath as a perfect circle for convenience. The student should remember, however, that it stands for the zigzag circle.

The distinction between the normal and abnormal conditions of the sympathetic nervous system is indicated by an irregular condition of the sympathetic wreath in disease, and the normal or regular condition of the wreath in health.

Any deviation from the normal regularity of the circle denotes a corresponding irregularity in the functions of the organ towards which it points. For example, a general widening and branching condition of the sympathetic wreath corresponds to a flabby, flaccid, dilated condition of the intestines. Such a relaxed condition is causative of flaccid constipation by virtue of the fact that the musculature of the intestines is too weak to contract, and thus propel the food residue.

This condition is known as colonic stasis, and is caused through the lack of tone and deficient peristalsis, or of muscular movements of the intestines. From this it is plain that in such condition enemas are particularly contra-indicated, because the habitual injection of warm water still further dilates the already weakened intestinal walls. The correct treatment for such a condition would be to give a large amount of bulk in the diet by increasing the amount of the green leafy vegetables and fruits, all of which are rich in cellulose and fibrous material, and also to treat the reflex centre in the spine which contracts the intestines. A mild application of sinusoidal current applied to the abdomen is also very efficacious.

On the other hand, a small narrowed sympathetic wreath signifies a correspondingly spastic or rigid condition of the intenstines. This is causative of spastic constipation. This is also a factor in the cause of haemorrhoids, because of there being a likelihood of straining at the stool, with the resulting stasis and protrusion of rectal blood vessels. The indicated spinal treatment in this condition would be to give stimulative treatment on the eleventh dorsal vertebrae, and thus dilate the intestinal musculature. Progressive dilation of the rectum will also do much to relieve this condition.

DIAGNOSTIC ILLUSTRATIONS

When the sympathetic wreath is pointing or jutting towards the peritoneum and lower abdomen, it indicates an impaired function of the gastro-intestinal tract, with the resulting stasis and distention of the colon, especially of the descending colon and sigmoid flexure. This sign is also very often seen in cases of splanchnoptosis.

When pointing towards the generative organs (right iris) it indicates a lack of functional activity of these organs, such as impotency.

When pointing towards the *cæcum* (right iris) it indicates a distention of the *cæcum*, and first part of the ascending colon. This condition is often noticed in patients who have had an appendectomy performed upon them, and in consequence of which there is a lack of natural lubricant for the ascending colon, up which food residue must be forced against gravity. Contrary to general medical opinion, we know that the appendix is a useful organ, and is used as a lubricator, because of its secretions.

When the sympathetic wreath is distended towards the rectum, the patient will complain of tenesmus (rectal pain with spasmodic contraction of the sphincter ani). A symptom of this condition is a false desire to defecate or evacuate the bowels.

When pointing towards the nose, and if a white line is visible in the area of the nose, it denotes an exaggerated sense of olfaction. If a dark line is found in the nose area it denotes an impairment or complete loss of the sense of smell, due to a degeneration of the Schneiderian membrane, the mucous membrane which lines the nasal fossæ.

When the wreath is distended in the heart region (left iris) it often denotes an hypertrophied heart or myocarditis.

In fact, whenever the sympathetic wreath points to the area of any organ, it indicates an abnormal, or subnormal, condition of that particular organ.

NERVE RINGS
Nerve rings and curved thread-like circular lines, which appear half-way between the pupillary and ciliary border of the iris, and are formed by the contraction furrows of the iris.

In the blue or brown eye they are either white, grey, dark, or black, and are brought about by:
1. An over-irritated condition of the motor nervous system. This may show as a complete circle.
2. Emotional states of the patient.
3. Pain or congestion in any special organ.
4. A subacute condition of the nervous system.
5. A chronic condition of the nervous system.
6. Actual destruction of nerve tissue.

These etiologic factors explain why nerve rings appear and disappear in the iris corresponding with the ebb and flow of the emotions and disease processes.

White nerve rings indicate an irritated, over-stimulated condition of the central nervous system, or of certain parts of it. If the nerve rings form a complete circle they indicate a high nervous tension, such as that which a student, or some professional men, are constantly under.

If the rings are white, and are restricted to a particular area, they denote local acute inflammatory processes causing congestion and pain.

Examples of this may be found when white nerve rings show in the region of the bronchi, pleura, and lungs, indicating acute bronchitis, pleurisy, or even pneumonia, or when they are found in the brain region, indicating headaches, or an inclination to dizziness and faintness. One may find other marks or discolorations in the dizziness or fainting areas in the iris.

When in the lower part of the iris, and particularly in the area of the genito-urinary organs, they indicate in females dysmenorrhea. In the male, when in the region of the cerebellum, they indicate spasms, convulsions, and fits of anger.

These white nerve rings are also occasionally observed before, or during, a healing crisis, and in this way the physician is able to tell in which organ an increased activity is going on.

GREY OR DARK NERVE RINGS

When the nerve rings appear grey or dark, they mean that the corresponding portions of the nervous system have passed from the acute, over-irritated state to the subacute or chronic state.

Dark nerve rings in children denote hereditary weaknesses. Under natural treatment it is particularly interesting to note the gradual change of the dark nerve rings into grey and then into white, and in time the entire disappearance of even the white nerve rings. Convergent white lines originating from the centre may indicate nervous collapse.

BLACK NERVE RINGS

Nerve rings which are absolutely black indicate an atrophy, or an actual destruction of nerve tissue, such as would be found in tabes dorsalis or the various forms of paralysis.

LYMPHATIC SYSTEM

The Lymphatic System, which is part of the Circulatory System, comprises the lymph vessels, the lymph capillaries, and the lymph glands. They are the first tissues to offer resistance to the invasion of bacteria or any foreign matter.

The sign of the lymphatics in the iris is often spoken of as the lymphatic rosary, because the sign appears in the form of white flakes in the outer rim or circulatory system of the iris, resembling the beads of a rosary. Wherever these white beads or flakes appear, they indicate inflammation and an engorged condition of the lymph nodes in the corresponding parts of the lymphatic system. In the later stages they indicate an atrophic condition of the lymph glands. Occasionally we find the flakes discoloured with the characteristic pigments of drug signs.

A distinction must be made between the lymphatic rosary and the sign of arsenic, because, owing to the fact that arsenic has an affinity for the spleen and lymph glands, and shows up in the form of white flakes, it is often mistaken for the lymphatic rosary. However, the lymphatic rosary only appears in the outermost rim of the iris, just inside the scurf rims (skin area), in an orderly manner like the beads of a rosary, but the flakes of arsenic may appear singly or in irregular groups anywhere in the outer half of the iris.

When the lymph nodes and lymph vessels of the internal organs are affected, the lymphatic rosary shows in the iris in the areas of those organs.

SCURF RIM
The Skin

Of the many functions of the skin, perhaps the following are of most importance:

1. Protective.
2. Cosmetic.
3. Sensory (touch, pain, heat, cold).
4. Excretory.
5. Absorptive.
6. Thermotatic (regulator of body heat).

The amount of carbonic acid given off by the skin in ratio to that which passes through the lungs is about 1-150 or 1-200. The amount of sweat excreted per day is from 500-2,000 cubic centimetres, or from 1 to 4 pints. This, of course, may be either visible (sensible) or invisible (insensible) sweat. The amount of skin on an average human body is about 20 square feet, and this contains approximately from 2,500,000 to 3,000,000 sweat glands, each of about $\frac{1}{4}$ inch long. These glands are found in the under layer of fats, and constitute a drainage of from $2\frac{1}{2}$ to 3 miles.

The outer rim of the iris, where the iris joins the white of the eyeball, or the sclera, as it is called, corresponds in the body to the cutaneous surface or skin. If the skin is normal, healthy, or active, the rim of the iris shows no abnormal discoloration. If, however, the skin is weak, enervated, atonic, or in an anæmic and atrophic condition, there appears in the skin area of the iris a dark discoloration, which is called a scurf rim (from the Greek term 'scorbutus', meaning scurvy). This scurf rim is found usually in cases of hereditary encumbrances, or where there is a history of hot bathing, or the use of too warm or heavy clothing. It also appears after the suppression of skin diseases and eczematous eruptions on the heads and bodies of infants and children. Sometimes this dark ring is complete all around the iris, but occasionally it appears in certain portions or segments of it.

When the scurf rim is especially heavy in the brain region it denotes a brain encumbrance, and the patient will have one or more of the following symptoms:

1. Inability to concentrate.
2. Dullness.
3. Headache.
4. Dandruff.
5. Pediculosis capitus (head lice). These parasites are nature's scavengers. A comb and cold water should only be used. They disappear when the body becomes internally purified.

An elevation of the scurf rim in the liver and spleen regions indicates the suppression of eczematous diseases. A dark spot on the scurf rim in the foot region indicates an encumbrance in the foot, such as could be brought on through the suppression of an excessive foot perspiration. In these cases you will nearly always find an associated kidney lesion. A dark spot on the scurf rim in the area of the rectal or genital organs indicates the suppression of catarrhal discharges from these organs.

Nature sometimes causes a recurrence during a cleansing crisis period. Often the balance centre shows a discoloration indicative of head treatment upsetting mental equilibrium and causing tiredness.

PSORA OR ITCH SPOTS

In civilized countries, especially those where the suppression of scabies and other itchy skin eruptions is extensively practised, about 65 per cent of all eyes show in the iris sharply defined dark or muddy brown superficial spots ranging in size from that of a pinhead to that of a buckshot. These spots iridologists designate as itch or psora spots, because they appear after the suppression of itchy eruptions and of psoric parasites. The presence of these spots in the iris is also indicative of a tubercular or malignant diathesis (tendency).

It has been observed in many instances that suppression of psoric eruptions resulted in the formation or enlargement of the scurf rim, as well as in the appearance of the itch or psora spots. This is probably due to the weakening of the skin by suppressive agents, such as mercurial, sulphur, or other poisonous salves and ointments.

The word 'Psora' was adopted by Hahnemann, the father of homoeopathy, from a Greek word signifying itching, and he applied the name to certain skin diseases which are characterised by intolerable itching. These morbid encumbrances have no special affinity for any organ or part of the body, and psora spots are therefore found anywhere in the iris, for as with other poisonous substances, psora also develops in any organ or part of weakened resistance or lowered vitality.

Psoric spots are often found in patients who give a history of *pediculosis capitus* (head lice). These patients will tell you of having developed headaches shortly after the little scavengers have been disposed of by repeated coal-tar product shampoos. Quite a few cases of petit mal, and even grand mal (epilepsy) have been traced directly to just such successful suppression of pediculosis, which is in reality only a form of vicarious elimination. These parasites live and multiply only on filth accumulated in the body through faulty elimination and neglected hygiene. Retention of such putrid tissue in any organ sets up a chronic irritation, and may in time lead to the development of malignancy, especially in cancerous soil.

Psora is generally eliminated through scrofulous skin eruptions, boils and carbuncles, and is nature's effort to assist the body toward a cure.

CLOSED, OPEN AND HEREDITARY LESIONS
Closed Lesion
Kritzer describes closed lesions as any spot in the iris indicating a toxic condition of any organ formed by an inflammatory exudate which surrounds the affected part, thus inhibiting its spreading into adjacent structures. This condition is accurately reproduced in the iris by a white border encapsulating, or surrounding, a dark spot or sign, and this white border is usually ovoid, or spindle-shaped. The same sign can be observed in cases of healed injuries, and in cases where diseases in their chronic or destructive stages have been arrested and cured by Nature Cure methods.

Open Lesion
In an open lesion the spot or sign is only partially surrounded by white, or sometimes it is not surrounded at all. The total absence of the white circle is usually seen in patients of low vitality, where the disease or lesion is progressive.

Closed lesions are therefore less harmful than open lesions, but, nevertheless, they denote a latent encumbrance which may become active at any time, particularly so when the vitality is very low.

Hereditary Lesion
An hereditary or congenital lesion is any spot, sign,

or other abnormal discoloration in the eyes of the new-born. This lesion may be entirely surrounded by a border of white, and when so, it is spoken of being a closed hereditary lesion, or it may be only partially surrounded by a white border, or even not surrounded at all, and is thus spoken of as an open hereditary lesion. A closed hereditary lesion denotes latent morbid encumbrances, and the organs in which they are found should receive special attention, especially during healing crises, for during these periods these latent encumbrances may develop into open hereditary lesions, and may be kindled into activity by Nature in her endeavour to rid the organism of impurities.

CHAPTER THREE

THE USE OF MEDICINES

Medical men have long attempted to segregate the various chemical processes of the body, and to find accelerators or retardants for the individual chemical processes performed by the major organs and glandular structures. Partly scientifically, but largely empirically, many medicinal or chemical agents have been worked out which are thought to more or less perfectly serve these purposes when applied to one or other of the many chemical processes involved.

Up until the days of modern medicine all manner of queer concoctions were prescribed, on the supposition that they would, by some miraculous but certainly unknown method, perform the hoped-for cure. Modern medicine has been built upon the supposed specific action of the particular ingredient in the acceleration or retardation of a particular chemical process to influence the faulty chemical action, and thus restore the body to normal.

A large and varying amount of useful information has come from this widely popular method of treating disease, but yet, even today, medical results are still very much a matter of speculation.

Unfortunately, most medical effort has been devoted to an attempt to correct a faulty chemical process that was in itself caused by some more distant, and less understood, cause. The great strides made in modern therapeutics have been in the direction of getting behind these heretofore hidden causes by a fuller realisation of the basic elements of which life and health are the expression. In the words of the world-famous Dr Henry Lindlahr, of Chicago: 'We are now pulling disease out by its roots.'

Even today, however, drugs used to correct the chemistry of individual processes in the body occupy a large place in the practice of medicine, although it is now almost universally agreed that whatever is put into the system with the exception of wholesome food, regardless of its beneficial effects upon a given process, taxes the bodily activities out of proportion to the good it renders, and almost invariably adds a destructive burden to the work of the eliminative organs.

DRUGS

The most important, and the more common, sources from which we acquire foreign substances, which accumulate in the fluids and tissues of the body, are de-natured foods, cosmetics, chemicals handled in the arts and industries, patent medicines, and drugs. The drug signs, which show in the iris, indicate the amounts or quantities of the drugs which the system has failed to eliminate, and not always the quantities of the drugs used.

Only after sufficient time has elapsed for the drug

to accumulate in some part of the body does the sign appear in the corresponding part of the iris. The signs of iron, quinine, and coal-tar products have been noticed two months after their administration, but the metallic poisons, such as mercury and lead, usually take a year or more before they can be demonstrated in the iris.

MERCURY OR HYDRARGYRUM – DEPURATUM QUICKSILVER (Hg)

A white, heavy liquid metal. In the blue eye mercury or quicksilver shows as a whitish, or silvery, grey circular line of a metallic lustre in the circulatory area of the brain region. In the brown eye it shows slightly more bluish, or even greenish. When mercury is taken with potassium iodide (KI) it may show in the entire circulatory area much like a sodium ring.

This latter sign should not be confused with the 'Arcus Senilis', which is really an opacity of the periphery of the cornea found in the irides of the aged.

MEDICAL USES

1. *Locally* as an astringent.
2. *Externally* for pediculosis, and as mercurial inunction against ringworm and other parasitic skin diseases.

ACCIDENTAL ABSORPTION

Amalgam tooth fillings may cause chronic mercurial poisoning by virtue of the fact that the mercury comes in contact with the salt contained in the food, thus forming bichloride of mercury ($HgCl_2$).

SYMPTOMS OF MERCURIAL POISONING

1. Mercurial stomatitis.
2. Profuse and sticky saliva of a distinct metallic taste.

3. Foul breath.
4. Ulcerated and sore gums, swollen tongue.
5. Hutchinson's teeth – peg-shaped incisor teeth notched on the cutting edge, found also in cases of congenital syphilis).
6. Progressively, the patient may have necrosis of the jaw.
7. Dyspepsia.
8. Diarrhœa, alternating with stubborn constipation.
9. Stool may contain sulphate of mercury ($HgSO_4$).
10. Mercurial eczema.
11. Ulceration of mucous membranes and skin.
12. Softening and pains in the bones.
13. Peripheral neuritis or anæsthetic patches.
14. Impaired reflexes, followed by various forms of paralysis, such as locomotor ataxia, paralysis agitans, or paresis. Usually after several years. (Lesion in ataxia area.)
15. Anæmia caused by the destruction of erythrocytes.
16. Itching of the anus and rectum.

Eliminated under natural treatment by skin eruptions, such as carbuncles, furuncles, ulcers, abscesses, open sores, and hæmorrhoidal discharges, and as nose bleeds. Also by excessive salivation. Hence one of our sayings: 'A person may become physically and mentally disturbed before becoming well.'

IODINE (I_2)

Iodine is a poisonous, non-metallic element with a metallic lustre, found mainly in ashes of seaweeds and has for years been widely employed as a first-aid prophylactic and a general antiseptic, despite the fact that it irritates, burns, and frequently causes serious injury to body tissues. It, however,

has the advantageous features that its stain shows
just how effectively it is applied, and also prevents
its being washed away, or rather fixes it in the field
to be sterilised or made aseptic. It is also presumed
that the stain provides for more than a superficial
penetration into body tissues. No other poisonous
drug shows more plainly in the iris, but the signs
differ according to the mode of absorption.

Internally
Shows as bright red, reddish brown, or even orange
coloured spots or blotches. Sometimes these spots
are surrounded by white borders, indicating that
the poison is causing irritation and inflammation,
or that it is in process of elimination.

Externally
The drug shows as an orange or pinkish hue, and
appears in the form of streaks or sometimes as
pinkish or reddish clouds.

The signs of iodine are a brighter red, and are
more diffuse than itch or psora spots. Usually the
history of the patient will be sufficient to enable the
physician to differentiate the signs. Iodine does not
appear to have any special affinity for any
particular part of the body as other drugs have, and
we find the drug showing up in all parts of the iris,
but more frequently in the areas of the liver,
kidneys, gastro-intestinal tract, lungs, pancreas,
and brain.

ALLOPATHIC USE
Antiseptic dressing for wounds.

SYMPTOMS OF IODISM
1. Inflamed gums, palates, and fauces. In fact,
   the entire throat, from the mouth to the
   pharynx.

2. Coryza, with bursting pain over the frontal sinuses.
3. Cough, and frothy expectoration.
4. Abdominal pain, nausea, diarrhœa.
5. Glandular atrophy, especially tests, ovaries, and mammæ.
6. Anæmia, emaciation, and general debility.
7. Neuralgia, disturbed intellection with ophthalmia, salivation, vomiting, polyuria, and cutaneous eruptions.

SIGNS OF ELIMINATION OF IODINE

1. Catarrhal discharges from the nose and throat.
2. Intense headaches.
3. Swelling and redness of gums and hard and soft palates.
4. Foulness of tongue.
5. Excessive salivation.
6. Palulæ.
7. Acneform, vesicular and pustular skin eruptions.
8. Open sores and hæmorrhoidal discharges. Lindlahr gives details of a case of multiple neuritis and chronic severe headache, caused by drinking iodine accidentally.

QUININE ($C_{20}H_{24}N_2O_2\,3H_2O$)

Quinine is the most important of the alkaloids derived from cinchona, and occurs as a white, flaky, odourless, bitter powder which is very slightly soluble in water. The uncombined alkaloid is seldom employed, its more soluble salts being used instead.

Sign
Shows as a yellowish, cloudy discoloration, sometimes greenish, and sometimes approaching a

hue of reddish brown, according to the chemical combinations which it has entered into. Small quantities produce a yellowish discoloration of the sympathetic wreath only.

Affinity
Quinine has a peculiar affinity for the brain, eyes, ears, stomach, and bowels, and in old malarial cases it shows also in the regions of the liver and spleen. It is this drug which gives the blue-eyed individual the characteristic green eye, making it resemble a cat's eye.

ALLOPATHIC USES
1. Appetizer and bitter tonic during convalescence and in cases of general debility while taking depressing remedies like mercury, lead, etc.
2. Used as an antipyretic against all febrile diseases, especially malaria, and all conditions resulting from the same.

ACCIDENTAL POISONING
Hair tonics, patent remedies, cold cures, such as Bromo-quinine, etc.

SYMPTOMS
Digestion is impaired, and the patient has a gastric catarrh when the drug is taken in small doses. When taken in large doses, quinine irritates the mucous membrane and causes vomiting and diarrhœa, followed by chronic constipation. It may also cause renal irritation, which is oft-times accompanied by hæmoglobinuria.

Nutrition
This is stimulated, and the excretion of waste products increased, by small doses. Large doses,

however, diminish the amount of urea, uric, and phosphoric acids in the urine, thus interfering with elimination.

In the Blood
Quinine interferes with the oxygen carrying function of the red blood cells, and diminishes their number.

Circulation
Quinine taken in small doses will increase the cardiac functions, but when taken in large doses it will inhibit the cardiac motor ganglia of nerves and depress the heart, sometimes causing it to intermit, and finally arrest it in diastole, thus causing death.

Temperature
In fevers a rapid decline of temperature takes place, due to the depressive action of the drug on the heart, and general circulation.

Nervous System
Small doses of quinine will stimulate the cerebral functions. Large doses will cause chronic quinine poisoning or *cinchonism*, symptoms of which are giddiness, tinnitus aurum (ringing noises in the ears), with impairment of hearing and vision. Sometimes these patients also suffer from daltonism, which means colour-blindness.

A case that came under the observation of the author showed this symptom very plainly. The patient, who was an elderly lady, had taken large quantities of quinine when she was a child, as she was then living in a malarial district. Upon being questioned as to her ability to distinguish colours, she told the author how, only a few days before consulting him, she had bought what was apparently a brown coat for her daughter, and on taking it home, she was quite surprised when her daughter told her it was a green coat.

Coma

Quinine taken in toxic doses causes coma, weak pulse, and sometimes convulsions. It has caused, in some cases I have observed and had under treatment, insanity, loss of memory, and morbid depression.

Skin

Quinine taken in large doses causes cutaneous eruptions, such as erythema, urticaria, or herpes.

Eliminated

Quinine is eliminated through the skin, causing itchy eruptions resembling scarlatina or measles. Also through the kidneys as an amorphous alkaloid, and through acute catarrhal purging and hæmorrhoidal discharges. Frequently the taste of quinine comes back during its elimination.

BROMINE (Br$_2$)

Bromine is a non-metallic, reddish, volatile, liquid element which unites with many metals to form bromides. Bromides are therefore compounds formed by the replacement of the hydrogen in hydrobromic acid by a metal, or an organic radical. The bromides, official in the United States Pharmacopœia, are of ammonium, calcium, hyoscine, potassium, quinine, sodium and zinc.

Bromides show in the iris as a whitish or yellowish white crescent in the upper regions, indicating that the drug exhibits a special affinity for the brain and sympathetic nervous system. Anæmia must be differentiated, which shows up as a bluish crescent.

The most common salts of bromide are *potassium*

bromide (KBr), *ammonium bromide* (NH₄Br), and
sodium bromide (NaBr), all of which act as
depressants and narcotics, particularly to the brain
and nervous system. They are also powerful
depressants on the heart, and sex organs. The salts of
bromine, in addition to serving as pain killers and
sleep producers, are specifics for epilepsy.

SYMPTOMS OF BROMISM

Bromides cause catarrhal conditions of the upper
respiratory tract, increased salivation, headache,
dizziness, melancholia, impotence, bromacne,
neuro-muscular weakness, premature senility,
paralysis, insanity, cardiac depression, foul breath,
and anæmia.

Bromides are eliminated mainly by the kidneys
in the form of increased urination and by skin
eruptions. They may also cause mucoid
accumulations in the mouth and acute catarrhal
elimination from various mucous membranes. The
patient may also complain of diarrhœa, nose
bleeds, and abnormal perspiration.

ARSENIC (As)

The element arsenic is a steel-grey metal which
forms a number of poisonous compounds.

In the early stages arsenic shows as greyish-
white, veil-like specks over the region of the gastro-
intestinal canal or respiratory tract, according to
the portal of entrance. Later, arsenic shows in the
outer half of the iris as greyish-white flakes,
resembling snowflakes. These flakes may appear
singly or they may appear in irregular groups in the
circulatory area.

ACCIDENTAL POISONING

Paris Green, Naphthaline, and other insect and
vermin exterminators.

The drug may be absorbed from sprays used against parasites and insects on vegetables and trees.

SYMPTOMS OF ARSENICAL POISONING
(*Arseniasis*)

1. Progressive muscular atrophy.
2. Neuralgia.
3. Peripheral neuritis.
4. Catarrhal discharges from all mucous surfaces.
5. Numbness and tingling in the extremities.
6. Waxy complexion.
7. Loose brittle hairs and nails.
8. Arsenical eczema.
9. Photophobia.
10. Lachrymation.
11. Cold tingling sensation in back.

ELIMINATION

Arsenic is eliminated during healing crisis by excessive activity of the kidneys, bowels and liver. It may also cause catarrhal discharges from all mucous surfaces. The patient may shed the hair, and there may be various skin eruptions, such as boils, carbuncles, running sores, and even dandruff may be present.

SODIUM (Na)

Sodium is a silvery white lustrous alkali metal, the salts of which are extensively employed in medicine as well as in the arts. The metal itself is official in the British Pharmacopoeia, but only its salts in the United States Pharmacopoeia.

The sodium ring is found in the irides of persons who use sodium and other inorganic salts in large amounts. These deposit round the walls of the blood vessels and form in the iris a broad whitish ring, the so-called sodium ring of a slightly metallic lustre in the area of the circulatory system or lymphatic system. Often it is greyish white in colour, seen in the brown eye.

This ring may entirely surround the iris, or it may be found only in parts, depending upon:

1. The quantities of the inorganic salts not eliminated.
2. The powers of elimination of the person concerned.
3. The part of the circulatory system that is considered the weakest.

When a sodium ring is seen in the iris it may indicate any of the following:

1. That the patient has had rheumatism and has been treated with sodium salicylates. Sodium helps to cause valvular lesions. The salicylates often produce symptoms similar to quinine.
2. That the patient may have been suffering from an acidity of the stomach for which bicarbonate of soda has been taken.
3. That the patient may have consumed large quantities of baking soda in the food taken, such as would be found in soda crackers, cakes, and bread, or he may have used common table salt heavily.
4. That he may have been subject to the habitual use of saline cathartics or mercurial salts.

Salt is a marked dehydrant, and because of this fact it withdraws the juices from muscle fibres and hardens them.

The over-seasoning of food with common table salt may temporarily stimulate the perverted taste-buds. The proportions of salt, however, and other condiments have to be gradually increased because of their deteriorating effect upon the taste-buds provided by Nature as a protection against consuming unwholesome food.

The elimination of salts from the body is

comparatively easy, and depends upon:

1. The absolute elimination of all salts from the diet or for medicinal purposes.

2. The increased consumption of the green, leafy vegetables and fresh fruits which are rich in the acid-neutralising and organic mineral elements.

3. Stimulation of all the eliminative functions by natural drugless treatment.

SULPHUR (S)

Brimstone is an element which occurs in a native state in volcanic countries, and is of a bright yellow colour. It occurs as a crystalline solid or as an amorphous powder, and combines with oxygen to form sulphur and sulphuric acids, and with many of the metals and non-metallic elements to form sulphides.

When taken in the inorganic form, this drug shows in the iris in the area of the stomach and intestines as a yellow or dark brown, sulphur-like colour. Its first effect is to stimulate these organs, but this is soon followed by a sluggish, atrophic condition. Whenever the sulphur sign is seen in the iris, the sympathetic wreath will also usually be seen in a distended, irregular condition which also indicates a sluggish condition of the intestinal tract. At times, when the iris is discoloured with both quinine and sulphur, it may be difficult to distinguish one drug from the other; in such cases the dark brown sulphur shade neutralises the yellowish-green shade of quinine.

ALLOPATHIC OR MEDICINAL USES

Sulphur is used in various skin diseases, and is also a common home remedy in the form of sulphur and molasses. In most of the lumber camps of Canada, sulphur ointment is used for treating scabies, which is very prevalent among the lumbermen. The fumes of burning sulphur were formally used extensively in the disinfection of rooms after being occupied by a patient with a contagious disease. It is used in sulphur baths and the curing of some fruits.

It is interesting to note that in homoeopathic practice the trituration of sublimed sulphur with sugar of milk, which is employed as an anti-psoric remedy, does not show in the iris because of the fact that the highly potentised sulphur is so refined that it is no longer inorganic, but is really in the organic state.

ELIMINATION

Under strictly natural treatment, sulphur may be eliminated in the form of severe diarrhœa, the fæces have the characteristic sulphur-like odour. It may also be eliminated through the skin, and in the form of dandruff.

STRYCHNINE ($C_{21}H_{22}N_2O_2$)

Strychnine is an alkaloid from *Nux vomica*, and occurs as colourless crystals of a white crystalline powder, which is odourless, but of an intensely bitter taste.

Strychnine shows as a white wheel-like circle of filiform or perfect proportion around the pupil in the region of the stomach, indicating that the drug has a special affinity for this organ. On close inspection, lines or spokes are seen radiating from the pupil.

The drug is used as a cardiac and general tonic; a nervine and as a stomachic in the form of *Nux vomica*.

SYMPTOMS OF ACUTE STRYCHNINE POISONING

There may be cardiac weakness with low blood pressure. The stomach may be in an atonic or atrophic condition, with a spastic concentration in the pit. The patient may suffer from hypo-acidity, indigestion, and fermentation, with the resulting gas formation. Like all powerful stimulants, the first tonic effects of the drug on the digestive organs and the heart are followed gradually by weakness and progressive atrophy and paralysis. There may also be a false desire for food, malassimilation, constipation, anæmia, and emaciation. Strychnine may also do great injury in sex debility by irritating and exhausting the already irritated erection and ejaculation centres, these centres being located in the lumbar spine.

ELIMINATION
Strychnine is eliminated and accompanied by pains in the back, cold perspiration on the forehead and chest, and the vomiting of blood and sour bitter mucus.

COAL-TAR PRODUCTS
Acetanilid, creosote, aspirin, phenacetin, saccharin, hair remedies and greases, etc.

These drugs show in the upper part of the iris as a greyish veil, but not as a perfect crescent, like bromides.

Phenacetin produces a pigmentation ranging in colour from grey to light yellow, and this discoloration proceeds from the sympathetic wreath outwards.

Coal-tar products must be differentiated from bromides which show up as a whitish or yellowish-white crescent in the brain area. Coal-tar products cause headaches and nervous conditions.

OPIUM
The inspissated juice from the unripe capsules of a species of poppy.

Opium shows in the iris as pure white straight lines radiating in the form of a star from the pupil or the sympathetic wreath outward, especially to the upper part of the iris. These lines of opium are not in any way superficial, always seeming to be deeply seated. They gradually become darker if not eliminated.

ALLOPATHIC USES

Opium acts first as a stimulant, and later as a sedative. It is occasionally used as an anodyne hypnotic, analgesic, and diaphoretic. The poison has a special affinity for the stomach, bowels, and sympathetic nervous system.

MORPHINE

Morphine, from Latin *Morpheus*, the God of dreams or of sleep.

Morphine is the principal alkaloid of opium, and its action is similar to that of the mother drug. Its sign, however, differs from that of opium in that it appears in the iris as fine white lines which are very superficial and radiate from the pupil outwards, especially to the brain areas, later becoming dark if not eliminated.

COCAINE

Cocaine is an alkaloid derived from coca, which occurs in large colourless crystals very slightly soluble in water.

The sign of cocaine is very similar to that of morphine. The only way to differentiate it is by studying the objective and subjective symptoms of the patient. Cocaine is used to produce local anaesthesia and anaemia by paralysing the sensory nerves and contracting the blood vessels. It is also used as an anodyne and sedative. All of these agents reduce pain and produce sleep because they are poisonous paralysers. They do not contribute in the least way to removing the cause of the pains and insomnia. They merely benumb and paralyse the brain and spinal centres of perception and sensation.

SALICYLIC ACID

Derived from salicin; a glucoside obtained from the bark of several species of willow and poplar. It occurs as a white crystalline powder of bitter taste, soluble in twenty-one parts of water.

Salicylic acid in the iris shows as a whitish grey cloud or veil spreading unevenly over the outer margin of the iris, but being more pronounced in the upper part. It resembles very closely a whitewash, and if abundant, tends to efface the peripheral border of the iris. It is frequently associated with the sodium ring. The drug has a special affinity for the gastro-intestinal tract, which it leaves in an atrophic condition, resulting in malassimilation, malnutrition, and defective elimination. These conditions show in the iris by a browning and gradual darkening of the areas of the stomach and intestines.

ALLOPATHIC USES

1. Antiseptic in surgical dressings, ointments.
2. For excessive perspiration and night sweats.
3. As an antipyretic.
4. Chronic cystitis when associated with foul urine and phosphatic deposits.
5. Specific against acute inflammatory rheumatism in the form of sodium salicylate, but lately administered hypodermically so as to avoid gastro-intestinal irritation.

SYMPTOMS

In addition to the symptoms produced by other

coal-tar products, salicylic acid also gives rise to:
1. Dullness of hearing and dimness of vision, ringing noises in the ears, pressure on top of head.
2. Nausea.
3. Diarrhoea alternating with stubborn constipation.

ELIMINATION

Salicylic acid is eliminated during crisis by:
1. Severe indigestion with cramps in stomach and bowels.
2. Nausea and vomiting.
3. Acne-form and pustular skin eruptions.
4. Acute catarrhal elimination and inflammation of the mucous membranes, especially of the nose and throat.

VACCINE VIRUS

Vaccine virus shows as a black or muddy brown spot, which is distinctly superficial, like a speck of dirt. This spot is always surrounded by white, indicating that the virus, wherever it is in the body, is causing irritation and has an inflammatory area round it. Vaccine virus has also a tendency to darken the entire iris, and it may cause white lines to appear in the areas of the liver, spleen, and bladder, showing that these organs are endeavouring to throw off the morbid encumbrance.

The vaccine virus spot must be differentiated from the itch or psora spot, which is not surrounded by white.

RADII PUPILLARIS MINORES OR RADII SOLARIS

These signs are straight brown or black lines, tapering to a fine point, and radiating in the form of a star from the sympathetic wreath, or pupillary zone, to the other margin of the iris. They are found most frequently in brown eyes.

The exact significance of these signs is as yet not well understood, although some authorities are of the opinion that they are caused through gastro-intestinal disturbances. However, they are of doubtful diagnostic importance, and must not be mistaken for lesions, although they may be associated with mental and emotional strain in elderly people.

HEMIPLEGIA

The sign of hemiplegia (a one-sided paralysis) is always seen in the opposite iris, contrary to all other records which show in the corresponding iris of the affected side. The lesion is always demonstrable in the corresponding brain centre, because the controlling centre of the eye reflexes is not involved in a hemiplegia.

NICOTINE

Nicotine has a similar effect upon the colour of the iris as has vaccine virus, in so far as it causes the iris to assume a dark, smoky appearance. In examining the irides of heavy smokers there is also usually found a number of nerve rings, owing to the irritation of the motor nervous system, and some abnormality of the sympathetic wreath in the heart region corresponding to the functional heart disturbance of the tobacco smoker. With heavy smokers Kritzer says that there is profuse perspiration.

BISMUTH (B₁)

A dark steel-grey irregular circle in the digestive tract of the iris shows that bismuth has been taken. Ulcers show up in this area as minute black spots, whereas tubercular areas show up the same except that they are smaller spots. The pancreas area, which is next to the duodenum in the chart, may also reveal these spots in disease. When bismuth has been taken, these spots may appear as dark blue.

Bismuth is used in different preparations for indigestion and painful conditions of the stomach or bowels. It has a sedative action in cases of vomiting or diarrhœa.

The carbonate and oxychloride are used as an aid to X-ray diagnosis.

Bismuth preparations are used externally as dusting powders or as cosmetics. It affects the nerves of the upper region of the spinal cord, and we find it often associated with neuritis and kidney complaints. It is eliminated in a similar way to lead.

CHAPTER FOUR

DIAGNOSIS TECHNIQUES

It has long been realised that the human body is in reality an exceedingly complex chemical laboratory. With the scientific developments in modern chemistry it has become evident that the chemical functions performed in this great laboratory are marvellously intricate and varied in nature.

The food we eat, plus the water and oxygen we consume, are the chemical agents utilised as raw materials by this laboratory. These agents are converted with the various gross and specialised tissues as needed. Complex chemical reactions take place constantly day and night. Therefore it is obvious that what we eat has a vital bearing upon what we are.

The chemical functions of the body, however, are performed not alone in the stomach, intestines, and other organs of the alimentary system, as the endocrines or ductless glands play also a very important part. The building of a new cell, or the destruction of an old one, is a complex chemical process called metabolism. This process of building up and breaking down proceeds constantly from conception until death; and if uninterrupted would predicate the eternal life of the cell were not the process subject to degenerative influences, until finally the curtain is drawn in the cataclasm called death.

FAULTY METABOLISM OR ACIDOSIS

In individuals whose metabolism is markedly disturbed, and as a result of which there is excessive accumulation of acids in their systems, there will usually be seen in the irides a superficial milky-white or chalk-like deposit which sometimes causes the colour to be mistaken for azure blue. This discoloration usually covers the entire surface of the iris in cases of extreme hyperacidity, while in milder cases there are whitish spots covering the parts of the iris, which correspond to the organs where the accumulation of acid is localised. The ability to thoroughly understand and recognise this acidosis sign is very essential, as the inexperienced may mistake it for an azure blue eye. Acidosis is a very common ailment, and the examination for this sign should be a routine procedure. The brown iris shows, on examination, an amber colour, and cloudy when acidosis is present.

EXAMINATION TECHNIQUES

In examining the irides of a patient it is well to observe some definite sequence in the procedure. First of all, the patient should be seated in a comfortable chair which is fitted with some form of head-rest. The chair should be fairly high, so as to avoid necessitating the doctor stooping down unnecessarily over the patient; and, of course, the patient should face a window where there will be a plentiful supply of daylight. In examining the eye under any very intense light, it is well to remember that the pupil will normally be contracted somewhat, and this often causes the condition of the sympathetic wreath to be wrongly interpreted.

The sequence of signs which should be looked for are as follows:

1. Colour.
2. Acidosis.
3. Scurf Rim.
4. Nerve Rings.
5. Psora.
6. Drug Signs.
7. Acute Signs.
8. Subacute Signs.
9. Chronic Signs.
10. Destructive Signs.
11. Closed Defects.
12. Density.
13. Sympathetic Wreath.
14. Circulation.
15. Arcus Senilis.

In addition, it is, of course, wise to notice carefully any local sign of a constitutional disease, such as the condition of the conjunctiva in biliary disturbances, the condition of the lens in diabetics, etc.

The student or practitioner should make a very careful study of this subject. Continual practice is necessary to become expert in this work. Progressive physicians and students will find this work a great aid in their work on Natural Healing. It is one of the greatest and most accurate methods of diagnosis in existence at the present time; at the same time, it is hardly known.

CASE ILLUSTRATIONS

1. Symptoms of neurasthenia in man aged 40. Served with the army in the tropics. Recent mental disturbances. Iris showed greenish-yellow discoloration over entire iris. Took large doses of quinine for past three years. Committed suicide.

2. Engineer. Blue eye. Sulphur signs from drinking from a well containing sulphur water. Boils periodically due to elimination of sulphur.

3. Blue eye. Man aged 48. Served with navy. Symptoms of sclerosis of spinal cord. Iris showed record of mercury and arsenic having been previously administered. These caused the disease to develop in my opinion.

4. Man aged 40. Nephritis, psoriasis, gastro-intestinal toxaemia, high blood pressure. Iris showed bismuth, quinine, arsenic, and acidosis. The retained bismuth is helping to cause blood pressure because of its clogging effect in the kidneys. Nature is attempting to get rid of the acidosis by producing psoriasis.

5. Young woman aged 26. Whitish blue iris. Sodium ring present. Treated for rheumatism for some years with sodium sal. Heart lesion present. Iris cleared considerably under natural treatment. Now fairly healthy.

6. Lady aged 40. Well-defined iodine spot in left ovary. Left ovary removed surgically.

7. Man aged 39. Tremor left arm with wrist-drop. Iris shows steel grey, perfect circle around pupil. Probably absorbed lead through working with red lead, paints, etc.

8. Woman aged 37. Constant stomach irritability despite previous dieting. Mercury ring of a metallic lustre showing. Mouth filled with

amalgam fillings, eighteen of them. Alkaline diet
helped her. Metallic taste in mouth from eating
fruit. (Fruit not indicated.)

CONCLUSION

Truth is a true statement, an agreement with
reality, and in the fine arts, a faithful adherence to
nature. Those who read this book, no matter
whether they are laymen or professional men and
women, will find this book full of truths, for the
facts are continually being demonstrated by
naturopaths the world over. The naturopath has a
different way of treatment to all other practitioners,
because in the first place he works along lines
corresponding to the law of cure. If he treats you by
spinal manipulation (mechanical treatment) then
he is aiming to increase the power and activity of
the various organs, and stimulate the various
centres in the spine, as, for example, the epigastric
centre in the upper part of the spine, genital centre
in the lumbar spine, etc. In other words, he aims to
remove the cause of the disease, because he knows
that behind symptoms there is always a cause.
Whether the cause is through dietetic errors, drink,
or drug poisons, emotional states or the
accumulation of acids, results are more certain
because he is working along natural lines toward a
cure.

An attempt has been made in this book to help
you on your evolutional path, and to show you a
saner way towards health and its maintenance. It
may help you to avoid the pitfalls on your road and
save you endless trouble.